ON A WING
AND
A PRAYER

BLUE FEATHER BOOKS, LTD.

This book is for Marni, a beautiful woman who provided inspiration and love throughout the writing of this novel; for my sons Heath and Dane, two wonderfully accepting and diverse young men who love their mom—no matter what; for my daughter-in-law Kacie, who makes my son happy and who I believe is thoroughly amused by her whacko mother-in-law; for my Mom, who is the best friend and Mom a writer could have; for my loving family, whose unwavering support and acceptance made the expression of my inner self possible, and for the love of my life: my grandson Kyren, who brings immeasurable joy to our family. Finally, to my sister, Penny: I love you and I am proud of you, Sissy. Hang in there and continue to believe in yourself.

ON A WING

AND

A PRAYER

A BLUE FEATHER BOOK

by

Karen D. Badger

This is a work of fiction. All characters, locales and events are either products of the author's imagination or are used fictitiously.

ON A WING AND A PRAYER

Cover design by pinfeather and Anne M. Clarkson
Cover photo credits: KCC (Jungle) and D. M. Schnuth (Plane in Flight)

A Blue Feather Book
Published by Blue Feather Books, Ltd.
P.O. Box 5867
Atlanta, GA 31107-5967

www.bluefeatherbooks.com

ISBN: 0-9770318-1-0

First edition: September, 2005

Printed in the United States of America and in the United Kingdom.

Acknowledgements

Many thanks to all of my friends, who believed in my talents and encouraged me to forge ahead, even when the going was rough, and a special thank you to Ili and Kev for providing the forum through which my work reached its first readers. A loving thank you to Sheri for her technical wisdom and guidance, and for not squishing me like a bug when I wrote her into the story! Finally, many thanks to Day and to Blue Feather Books for the exhaustive editing and formatting work.

Chapter 1

"Let's see, *Alien Insurrection, Planet of Lost Souls, Galaxy Ten*... Hey, what's this?" Cass removed the volume in question from the shelf and read the title. "*Stargazer II*. Hmm, interesting title. Sounds like the name of a space ship."

Oblivious to the other bookstore patrons browsing the shelves around her, Cass opened the book and looked at the inside sleeve of the dust jacket. "Let's see what the cover says. 'Part II of a tale of bittersweet love... human meets alien... falls in love...' Yadda, yadda, yadda. 'Struggle to fit into each other's world... For more information on the author, see the back sleeve and cover.'"

She flipped to the back inside cover of the book. 'Roxanne Ward... native New Englander... lives on the seacoast of Maine... author of several best selling science fiction novels, including *Starflight* and *Stargazer*. Ms. Ward brings her own brand of romance to the science fiction arena... must-read novels... romance interlaced with mystery and intrigue.'

Cass closed the book and looked at the cover again. It was black with stars shooting outward from the center. *Stargazer II* was printed in bold silver letters across the top of the page.

Sounds interesting, Cass thought. *But not much good without Part I.* Holding the book in her hand, she searched the shelf for *Stargazer*. After ten minutes of looking, she had come up empty.

"Damn," she said under her breath. "Oh, well. I'll look in a bookstore in San Jose tomorrow."

As she was replacing the book on the shelf, the back cover caught her eye. Retrieving the book, she turned it over in her hands for a closer look. Staring up at her were the most magnificent emerald green eyes she had ever seen. Cass felt her heart lurch. The nearly translucent eyes were set in a wholesome face framed by pixie cut red-gold hair. The eyes smiled up at her as she took in the slightly upturned nose, full lips bent into a crooked smile, rosy cheeks, and bright sparkle emanating from the depths of green.

1

"Wow!" Cass was oblivious to the odd looks she received from those around her and the flush that colored her face. "Be still, my beating heart."

She stood there for several long moments, staring at the picture until she was shaken from her enchantment by a firm hand on her arm.

"Hey, lady, if you aren't buying that, then hand it over. I've been looking for that sequel for some time now," a voice said.

Cass looked at the man. "Ah… yes, I'm buying it. Sorry." She forced her feet to move in the direction of the register.

Cassidy Marie Conway, what good is this book without Part I? Acting on impulse again, aren't you, girl? You know that leads to nothing but trouble. Her inner voice scolded her as she handed $23.95 to the clerk and accepted her bagged purchase. Cass walked through the mall, having an internal conversation, her free hand gesturing as though she had a visible companion in front of her.

Look, I know it seems like impulse, but the book looked too good to pass up. I'll find Part I in San Jose tomorrow.

Like hell it looked too good. What looked too good was the picture of the author. Always a sucker for a pretty face, huh, Cass? Enforcer taunted.

Cass's inner voice, affectionately nicknamed the Enforcer (or "E" for short), had made its first appearance when she was just a child. E was Cass's constant companion—especially during the recent trouble with Patti. The voice was a protector of sorts, always looking out for her, most often in matters of the heart. Sometimes she listened, but today she shook it off as she made her way to her rental car and drove to the Dallas airport.

After landing in San Jose, Cass went directly to where she had left her car in the employees' parking lot. She opened the door, threw her bags onto the front seat, and climbed in after them.

It was sweltering hot again; temperatures were in the low 100s, and her car felt like a kiln. It had been locked up in the heat for the past two days, and the temperature build-up in the car was making it smell as if it were about to ignite. It certainly felt that way to Cass as she started the car and turned the air conditioner on high.

"Okay, time for dinner," she told herself as she pulled out of the parking lot.

Cassidy Conway seldom ate at home. In fact, she never ate anything she had to cook, since she was afraid she would poison herself and die alone from her own cooking. Therefore, she was a familiar sight in a particular diner that was located a couple of miles from her condo.

"Hey, Cass," Angela said as Cassidy entered Angel's Diner and went directly to her usual table.

"Hi, Angie," Cass replied, a comfortable camaraderie having long since been established between herself and the proprietor.

Looking at her favorite customer, the older woman recalled the first time she had laid eyes on the tall, dark-haired woman. Cass had been with her girlfriend, Patti. Cass seemed to be preoccupied with the attractive blonde, and was obviously very much in love. Not long after their first encounter, though, Angie had noticed a change in Patti's behavior and immediately suspected trouble. For the next several months, there was no sign of either Cass or Patti, until one day Cass came in alone. She looked drawn and tired. Her forlorn state went straight to Angie's heart and she immediately took Cass under her wing, where she had remained ever since. Angie shook her thoughts away as she brought the usual cup of coffee to Cass's table and placed it in front of her. "Tough flight, huh? You look beat."

"I love you too, Ang." Cass reached up to touch the side of the other woman's face. "You sure know how to make a girl feel good, my friend."

Angie chuckled. "What's not to feel good about? Who wouldn't want to look like you—with that long black hair and those brilliant blue eyes?" She shook her head. "Not to mention those legs that go for miles."

Cass laughed. "Bet you wouldn't want to be six feet tall."

Angie nodded as she assessed her friend's figure. "Nice bone structure, nice shape, nice..." She nodded at the shapely breasts. "If I were packaged the way you are, being six feet tall would be the least of my worries."

Cass was easily embarrassed, and she blushed under her friend's scrutiny, pretending to focus on the menu.

"So, what can I bring you tonight, hon?" Angie asked, holding up her order pad.

"Oh, I don't know, Ang. Why don't you bring me the clam chowder and a chef's salad with light Italian?" She closed the menu and handed it back to the waitress.

"Okay, sugar. It'll be right up." Angie left to place Cass's order.

Cass sat waiting for her meal, drumming her fingers on the table and looking around with bored indifference. Finally, her mind drifted to the novel she had purchased earlier that day in Dallas.

"Hey, Angie." When the waitress turned to look at her, she called, "Be right back," and went to her car to retrieve the book. Returning to the table, she laid the book off to the side of her place setting with the back cover facing upward and the emerald green eyes staring right at her.

"She's a pretty one," Angie said, startling Cass.

"Huh?" Cass asked, embarrassed at having been caught daydreaming.

"I said she's a pretty one. Good writer, too. Can I see the book?"

Cass reluctantly handed the book to the waitress, watching nervously as Angie looked over the cover.

"*Stargazer II*. Hey, I just finished the first book in this series. Roxanne Ward is a very good writer. You'll have to lend this to me when you're finished."

"You just finished Part I?" Cass asked, suddenly alert.

"Yeah. I assume you've read it, since this is Part II." Angie said.

"Well, actually, no. I was going to try to find it in town tomorrow. Would you consider lending it to me?" Cass asked.

"Sure. I'll give it to you when you come in for breakfast tomorrow morning, okay?" Angie offered.

"Uh, is there any way I can get it tonight? I have a couple of days off and I'd kind of like to get started reading."

Angie looked closely at her customer and friend. "What is it about this book that makes you in such a hurry to read it, Cass?" she asked, handing the book back to her.

"Noth... Nothing in particular," Cass stammered, her attention focused on the back of the dust jacket.

Angie followed Cass's gaze. A knowing smile crossed her lips. "Oh, I see."

"What?" Cass asked innocently, blushing again.

"Like I said, she's a pretty one. You've got good taste, Cass." Angie's observation made Cass blush even more.

Cass returned to the diner that evening at closing time and followed Angie to her home. After two cups of coffee and more conversation than Cass really wanted, she left for her condo with *Stargazer* tucked securely under her arm.

She went into her bathroom, turned on the faucets, and filled the tub with comfortably hot water. While it was filling, Cass sprinkled in some fragrant bath oils, intending to spend the next hour relaxing and reading. She tied her hair into a knot on top of her head and slipped into the warm water. After her long frame slipped below the surface of the water, Cass rested her head on the built-in foam pillow. She reached over to the stool she had pulled up beside the tub, grabbed *Stargazer* and started to read.

Several hours later, in the wee hours of the morning, still sitting in a tub of now-cool water, she snapped the book closed. *Finished.* Cass leaned her head back against the pillow and winced at the stiffness in her spine. She'd been sitting in one position far too long. Her buttocks and legs had lost all sensation, and her toes had the shriveled appearance of prunes. Tears were flowing down her cheeks in reaction to the dilemma faced by the star-crossed lovers in the novel: one human, one alien, subject to the prejudices of both their worlds; destined to live in each other's hearts and minds, but impossibly separated by space and time.

Cass placed the novel on the stool and wiped the tears from her cheeks. Very carefully, she maneuvered herself into a sitting position, then a standing one, knowing she would soon be dancing around like a fool from the intense prickling that would signal the return of feeling to her lower body. She grabbed the towel and methodically dried herself before stepping out of the tub. Sensation returned as expected, bringing with it an excruciating tingling that lasted for several minutes. Cass clung to the towel rack in discomfort until it subsided and she could walk around normally. Then, still naked, she picked up the book and headed to her bedroom. She put *Stargazer* on the dresser and pulled on a t-shirt before climbing between the cool sheets.

Sleep was a long time coming. Cass lay staring at the ceiling, thinking about the lovers and the woman who had created them. "Roxanne... Roxie... Rox." She sounded the name out on her lips, liking the resonance of it. "Roxanne Ward, native New Englander... seacoast of Maine," she mumbled, just before she finally drifted off to sleep.

Ah, Saturday morning. Cass stretched herself awake. *I love weekends.* As part of her contract with the airline, she didn't fly on weekends. This meant that she was seldom booked for a flight that kept her away from home for more than two days. Cass was fluent in

Spanish, so she usually flew into Mexico and Central and South America. She'd fly domestic routes occasionally, such as the flight to Dallas the day before. The airline had needed coverage and it just so happened that she was available. So, for a change of pace, Cass had accepted the flight. Lying in bed, she thanked her lucky stars that she had. Otherwise, she might not have found *Stargazer II*.

Cass placed her feet on the floor and stood. Reaching her arms high above her head, she pressed her palms toward the ceiling, clasped her hands together and canted her torso from side to side, stretching her abs and shoulders.

"God, that feels good." She lowered her arms and shook them out, slipped into a pair of boxer shorts, then moved into the kitchen to set up the coffeepot with "Raspberries and Cream." While the coffee brewed, Cass stepped out into the hallway of her condo and ran down the stairs to retrieve the morning paper from her mailbox. Making her way back to her apartment, she unrolled it and scanned the front page. She found nothing of real interest, so she threw the paper onto the kitchen table and poured herself a cup of coffee.

"Nothing like a good cup of coffee to start the morning." Cass savored the raspberry flavor as she carried her morning cup of caffeine into the living room and sank into an overstuffed chair. Retrieving the remote, she clicked on the TV and went directly to the Weather Channel, just in time to catch the local forecast. "Damn. Rain today. In this heat, it'll be so humid that the air conditioner won't touch it," she complained aloud. Then she stopped for a moment.

"Great. Now I'm talking to myself. Cassidy, you've got to get a life," she said, feeling very alone. Cass clicked off the TV, reached for her coffee and sat back in the chair, her mind wandering to a time three years earlier when she hadn't been so alone, but had wished that she was. She'd been a battered woman, physically and emotionally, and she just couldn't take the abuse any longer.

Cass and Patti seemed to be made for each other. Both six feet tall, they complemented each other in every way. Cass was dark, Patti was blonde. Cass's creamy skin covered intricately toned muscles; Patti was tanned, and muscular from spending many hours in the gym lifting heavy weights. Cass was friendly and outgoing; Patti was distant and stoic, except around Cass, with whom she was outwardly affectionate and loving. Both women were strong-willed, determined, and independent. They were rarely apart, and the love they had for each other shone on their faces.

After two wonderful years full of love, adventure and travel, things suddenly went sour. Patti started coming home late from the gym and turning the stoicism she showed to the world on Cass. The silence was deafening for the dark-haired, blue-eyed woman. Cass considered herself a communicator, and always verbally reinforced her love for Patti. She cherished the long talks she and her lover had shared, especially the ones they had while lying in each other's arms after making love. During a few horribly destructive months, all that had changed.

Patti became confrontational instead of loving. When she spoke to Cass at all, she snapped out short, sarcastic comments that made Cass feel ignorant and small.

Most of the time, Cass's attempts at communication were met with the silent treatment, and she never really understood what she had done to warrant such abuse. She was starving for loving feedback, but received cold, silent, hateful looks instead.

Patti grew obsessed with working out, growing meaner and meaner with each fiber of muscle she developed. One night, Cass questioned her late arrival home, and the inevitable finally happened. Patti struck her, sending Cass flying into the coffee table, where she gashed her head on the edge. The drive to the emergency room was tense, filled with apologies and promises that it would never happen again. That was the first of many trips.

After several months of broken promises, Cass packed her bags and left. Two days later, Patti was found in her car, parked outside the gym. She had overdosed on a combination of narcotics and steroids. Cass never forgave herself for her lover's death, and believed that her actions had driven Patti to suicide.

For the next three years, Cass ran away from personal commitment. She merely enjoyed brief encounters with women she met on her flights. None of them offered any promise of permanency, which was perfectly acceptable to the pilot. She was content with her solitude, but she was getting lonely.

Taking a deep breath, Cass rose from her seat and refreshed her coffee. Standing at the kitchen counter with her backside leaning against the cupboard, she stared straight ahead, eyes unblinking. As she sipped the brew, she tried desperately to chase away the memories of those nightmarish months.

Never again, Cass. Do not give your heart freely, girl. You will only be hurt and disillusioned. Protect yourself. Build those walls— they will keep you safe, Enforcer repeated, and Cass renewed her resolve to stay uncommitted and uninvolved in any serious relationship.

The decision felt good. Cass topped off her coffee cup and then reached for the package she had brought home with her the night before. Reaching inside, she pulled out *Stargazer II* and carried it into the living room, where she settled into the overstuffed chair with her long legs curled under her. She turned on the light next to the chair, took one more look at the picture on the back cover, opened the book and began to read.

Cass was captivated. Never before had she read a science fiction novel that had such an emotional impact on her. As far as she was concerned, science fiction came in two flavors: filled with details about the operation of space ships and battles with futuristic weapons; or filled with blood and gore, focusing on the horrifying aspects of monstrous aliens. This was why Cass loved science fiction. She could escape into fantasy worlds where she didn't have to deal with the emotional side of life.

Stargazer had been different. It had left her emotionally tender and crying in a tub of cold water the night before. *Stargazer II* took her already raw emotions and stretched them nearly to the breaking point. She could not put the book down, even going so far as to carry it with her into the kitchen as she retrieved a container of yogurt from the refrigerator. Cass then returned to the living room and spent the next several hours curled up in her chair. A rainstorm raged outside, and flashes of lightning periodically illuminated the room while an emotional storm raged within her heart.

At the end of the story, the two lovers lay in each other's arms, their last breaths mingling as they professed love and devotion beyond the realms of physical existence. Cass felt such an intense ache in her heart as they died that she was unable to stop sobbing.

She closed the book and placed it on the end table as she wiped the tears from her face. The catharsis had turned her into an emotional wreck. It had been a long time since she had felt that vulnerable, and all at once Cass needed to feel protected. She retreated to her bedroom, where she ensconced herself securely under the covers. She pulled her knees tightly against her chest and allowed the pain from her time with Patti to flow through her.

As abusive as Patti had been, Cass had still loved her. Their separation was devastating; Patti's death had nearly killed Cass. That same sense of loss washed over her as she thought again of the dying lovers at the end of *Stargazer II*. New waves of pain engulfed her tortured soul and tears spilled over her cheeks again. Finally, physically and emotionally exhausted, she fell into a fitful sleep.

Cass rolled over and looked at the digital clock on the nightstand. "7:16" illuminated the face in bright red numbers. She sat up and rubbed her hands over her face and through her hair. *Wow. I must have been really tired to oversleep like that. I'm normally up by six a.m.* After climbing out of bed, she shuffled into the kitchen and found a half-filled pot of coffee still on the hotplate. Stopping short, she stared at the coffeepot with a look of confusion on her face.

You're slipping, girl. Good thing there was still coffee in the pot. You could have burned down the whole condo, leaving it on all night like that, Enforcer scolded as Cass reached over and clicked the heater off.

Her stomach growled loudly, protesting that the container of yogurt she had eaten while she was reading was not enough to sustain it for such a long period of time. "All right, all right, I'll feed you. Just settle down, okay?" The answer was another rumble rolling up from her stomach.

Cass was such a terrible cook that when she ate at home, she depended on prepackaged foods. She grabbed a package of crackers from the sparsely stocked pantry and took a brick of cheese from the refrigerator. She checked it for moldy spots, then sliced off several pieces to eat with the crackers. With her meal piled onto a paper plate, she went into the living room and sat down again in her favorite chair. As she reached over to place the plate on the end table, she saw *Stargazer II*. It caused yet another wave of emotional pain, and she took a deep breath. *Damn it, get a grip. It's just a story.*

She grabbed the remote and turned on the TV, which was still tuned to the Weather Channel. "The storm that hit the area earlier today caused extensive damage in outlying regions, with downed tree limbs causing power failures." The forecaster's voice droned on, and Cass was about to change the channel when his words sank in. *Today? Did he say* today?

Clicking furiously through the channels, Cass found the preview channel and looked immediately at the bottom left corner of the screen. There, faithfully displayed, was the time. It was 7:42 p.m.

"Holy shit, it's still Saturday! I must have slept the whole afternoon away." She shook her head in disbelief. "Cassidy, you are in big trouble here, girl. Talking to yourself, crying yourself senseless over some story... You need to get a grip before you really lose it."

She pushed the plate of half-eaten food aside, picked up *Stargazer II,* and looked at the author's picture again. "I'll bet you don't have this problem," she said to the photo. "You probably live a simple, happy little life in your picturesque New England town, surrounded by friends and family—probably a husband and a couple of kids—sitting in your little hammock on the beach, laptop in hand, writing away while the kiddies build sand castles around you and the hubby is off earning a living."

Sometimes, Cass longed for that kind of life. She knew it would never happen, though. She would not let herself fall in love again, exposing herself to the loss and devastation that came with it.

Cass ran a finger over the face on the dust jacket. "You certainly are a beauty," she said. "And very talented, too." Melancholy feelings of longing for lost love filled her heart. "I wish I could tell you how much this story has touched me." She opened the book to the inside back cover and re-read the short author's bio. A sentence at the end caught Cass's eye. *Visit Ms. Ward's website at www.roxie_sf.com, or send her an e-mail at Rox@Starship.com.*

Butterflies suddenly fluttered in Cass's stomach. *God, do I dare?* She stared at the e-mail address. *What would it hurt?* she asked herself. *Just a brief note telling her how much I enjoyed the book, that's all. She probably won't answer. Writers are a busy lot, after all.*

Resolving to follow through before she lost her nerve, Cass went to the spare room she used as an office and powered up her computer. She sat fidgeting in her chair, nervously going over what she wanted to say while she waited for the machine to boot. Finally, it was ready. After logging on to the Internet, she went to her mailbox and selected "New Message." She composed her message and read it over several times before she was comfortable enough to send it.

Dear Ms. Ward,

Just a brief note to tell you how much I enjoyed the Stargazer *series. They touched a part of my heart I have kept closed and guarded for several years. You are a very talented writer, and I hope to read more of your work soon. By the way, you are also a very beautiful woman. I hope you have someone who appreciates you.*

Sincerely,
C.C.

Taking a deep breath, knowing that the action would be irreversible, Cass pressed the "Send" button. She immediately regretted the boldness she'd exhibited by adding the last two sentences. She shrugged. "Oh, well. She'll probably just file it in the recycle bin."

As she powered down the computer, her stomach once again made its demands known. She glanced at the clock on the desk and noted that it was 10:03 p.m.

Wow! I can't believe it took you two hours to write three lines. Cassidy, I'm starting to worry about you, big-time, said Enforcer. *Jesus, girl, get a grip. Pull your life together. You need to get laid. Yeah, that's it! You have all this sexual tension just building up, making you crazy. Go on out, find yourself some willing chick and do the nasty all night long. You'll feel better in the morning."*

Cass shook her head, clearing her mind of such thoughts. *I should go to bed. Tomorrow's another day.*

With that, she turned off the desk lamp, took a quick shower and crawled into the bed, which she had left unmade. Within moments she was asleep, dreaming of red-gold hair, emerald green eyes, and alien lovers.

Chapter 2

Rox opened one eye and glanced at the nightstand. "6:00 a.m." was illuminated in bright red numbers. *Damn! Why do I always wake up before the alarm?* She rolled stiffly out of bed and planted her feet securely on the floor, then slowly eased herself into a standing position, grunting and groaning along the way. *God, I hurt this morning,* she thought, shuffling slowly to the bathroom.

Rox had a general idea of how she looked—her red-gold hair sticking up at all angles and her face all puffy—so she didn't bother looking into the bathroom mirror. There wasn't much she could do about her looks, anyway. Only time would help. Bathroom chores finished, she pulled on a robe over her nightshirt and made her way into the kitchen to start a pot of coffee, then slipped her feet into sandals to go outside and retrieve the morning paper.

She shuffled back into the house, sat down at the table, and scanned the paper. Nothing of real interest caught her eye, but it was a good way to pass the time while she waited for the coffee to finish brewing. When it was finally done, Rox struggled to her feet and walked to the cupboard for a clean coffee cup. She filled it, then painfully made her way outside and sat in the glider on the deck.

Rox loved this house. It was a beautiful three-story Victorian that sat directly on the beach. She had purchased it two years earlier, using royalties from *Starflight*. Immediately after her purchase, she'd had a deck added to the back of the house, which was the ocean side. The deck had become her favorite place to sit and think, or to contemplate life, love, happiness and sorrow—just as she was now. The smell of the ocean and the sound of the seagulls in the early mornings filled Rox with feelings of hope and renewal, while the sunsets that lit the sky with brilliant shades of red gave her peace and serenity after long days of writing.

A loner, Rox had few acquaintances and only one close friend. This was Nikki, who was the only one who really knew her heart and accepted her unconditionally. She loved Nikki very much, and they had been best friends since college. It was to Nikki that Rox had turned for validation when she'd decided to be a writer. When things became too rough to bear, it was Nikki she ran to, and Nikki who came to her at any hour of the night when Rox needed to be held and comforted. Nikki was understanding, accepting and a wonderful friend.

She was also very protective of Rox, and so was Jerri, her partner. She had offered on several occasions to take care of Rox's problems for her, but Rox couldn't allow that. Her life was already out of control, and letting Jerri take over for her wouldn't help. Only Chris could help, and he had no interest in doing so.

He had been the foreman of the crew that had built her deck and remodeled her office space. Rox had been immediately attracted to his unkempt blond hair and deep brown eyes, and before long they started dating. Just an occasional dinner or movie, or just a quiet walk, hand in hand, along the beach. She had been quite smitten. Unfortunately, the feeling hadn't lasted.

A seagull squawking nearby distracted her from her thoughts. *Probably hoping to be fed.* Smiling at the bird, she threw her hands out to the side and said, "Sorry, bud, no breakfast here," and watched it fly away.

Tilting the bottom of her cup skyward, Rox finished her last sip of coffee and then struggled to her feet to get a refill. Instead of returning to the deck this time, she slowly climbed the two flights of stairs to her office in the attic.

Like most of the old houses that sat near the ocean, Rox's house had a lookout and a widow's walk on its top floor, from which sea captains' wives had once watched for their husbands' ships. The side of the room that faced the ocean was enclosed by floor-to-ceiling windows, and French doors opened onto the walk.

Whenever a storm came, Rox loved to stand in front of those windows and watch the ocean rage. It filled her with excitement and made her catch her breath with such wonder and awe at the power of nature that it often brought tears to her eyes.

Many long hours had gone into redecorating her large, airy office space. She had commissioned the same company that built her deck to install a floor-to-ceiling stained-glass window in the west wall of her office, so the afternoon sun would shine through in brilliant colors. That end of the room contained an arrangement of chairs, couches, end tables and scatter rugs. The couch facing the windows was actually a hide-a-bed that she used when she wrote far into the night and didn't want to disturb Chris by coming to bed so late. The other end was set up with her desk, and bookcases that held her reference library. She'd even had a small kitchenette installed, to limit interruptions in her writing due to such basic necessities as eating.

Rox had planned an early start to her writing day. She'd lost valuable time the night before... time consumed by heart-wrenching events, events that seemed to happen with increasing frequency and regularity, of late. Taking a deep breath and thinking that she really had to get her life back under control, she turned on her computer.

"Roxanne! God damn it, I want an answer when I talk to you," a voice boomed from the doorway.

Rox was so absorbed in her writing that she had shut out the rest of the world. At the sound of the angry voice, she looked over her shoulder toward her office door. "I'm sorry, Chris. What was it you said?"

Chris appeared in the doorway, hands braced against the doorframe, anger darkening his features. "I asked you where my blue work shirt is. Find it for me, *now*."

"Chris, I'm in the middle of a chapter. It's in the dryer. Please go... arrgh!"

Chris crossed the room in three steps and grabbed Rox by the throat. Pulling her face close to his, he spat, "I told *you* to get it. I won't put up with your shit, Rox. If you know what's good for you, you won't push me. Now, get my shirt!"

Rox nearly fell to the floor as she was released. "All right, all right," she said, fighting back the tears. "I'll get it."

Feeling that it was not safe to leave a file open on the screen with Chris around, Roxanne turned back and saved her story, then turned the computer off. She didn't trust him when it came to her computer, and was afraid that she'd come back and find all her work erased from the hard drive.

Chris noted the time Roxanne was taking to secure her work. "You know, Roxanne, I'm beginning to think you care more about your computer and your writing than you do about me."

Rox tried to avoid the imminent confrontation, though in her heart she knew he was right. "Chris, sweetheart, don't be foolish." *It pays the bills, Chris. That's more than I can say for you.*

"Then move your ass and get my shirt. Oh, and I need some money. The guys talked about maybe meeting after work for a few drinks. If I'm not home for supper, I'll be home late. Don't wait up for me."

Rox didn't want to give any money to Chris, who now worked only when it was convenient. The only benefit to complying with his demand was that it meant he would be gone for several hours, which would give her some peace and quiet. She took forty dollars from her purse and handed it to Chris, who shoved it into his front pocket without so much as thanking her.

Taking a deep breath, Rox rose from her chair and painfully made her way down the three flights to the cellar, where she retrieved Chris's shirt from the laundry room. *Why am I so stiff and achy this morning? What makes last night different from all the other times he's knocked me around? Maybe it was falling over the coffee table? Yeah, that must be it.*

"Okay, baby, fire up," she said as the computer booted. Rox drummed her fingers impatiently as she waited for her Star Trek wallpaper to appear. It was only eight a.m., and with Chris out of the house for the whole day and most of the night, she was looking forward to really putting a dent in her new book.

Finally, the system was ready. Before settling in to write, Rox logged onto the Internet to check out the writers' chat group in which she was currently engaged. Surprised at finding no one else on-line, she belatedly remembered it was Sunday and the chat group normally took that day off.

At least someone gets Sundays off, unlike Chris.

Three weeks earlier, he had suddenly begun working weekends on a big construction job the company had won. That's what he'd told her, but she suspected he was having an affair. Her eyes were drawn to a small envelope icon flashing at the bottom right corner of her screen. *Humph… e-mail. I wonder who's calling?* She double-clicked on the envelope and opened her mail.

She had three pieces of mail: one from the science fiction mailing list she subscribed to, one from her mother, and one from CConway@Flyboy.com. *Probably fan mail.*

Rox decided to leave the unknown writer for last, and read the other two e-mails. The one from the mailing list was a poll to rate the popularity of recent sci-fi movies. *I'll answer that one later.* The note from her mother was a reminder that she and Chris were invited to dinner the next weekend. *I hope the bruises have faded by then. Hell, I've got to figure out how to avoid new ones between now and then.*

The last note was indeed fan mail. It read:

Dear Ms. Ward,
Just a brief note to tell you how much I enjoyed the **Stargazer** *series. They touched a part of my heart I have kept closed and guarded for several years. You are a very talented writer, and I hope to read more of your work soon. By the way, you are also a very beautiful woman. I hope you have someone who appreciates you.*
Sincerely,
C.C.

A very beautiful woman? Rox thought. *You should see me right now. I look great in black and blue.* She smiled wryly as she sat back and read the note again, trying to get a feel for what the writer was like.

Okay, let's see... flyboy.com... probably a military pilot. I'd say... fortyish... single and heartbroken, judging by the "guarded heart" comment. He's obviously a sucker for a pretty face. I really need to put a different picture on my jacket covers; the one on **Stargazer II** *is drawing way too many letters from wackos. I'd be hard pressed to produce a better picture today, though. It'd take some pretty tricky camera angles or creative touch-ups to hide the bruises. Two years ago, when this picture was taken... before Chris, I didn't have to worry about any of that.*

If only I hadn't hired him to supervise the building of my deck. If only I hadn't fallen for him before I really knew him. Chris was of average height, muscular and very good looking. "A real charmer," as Rox's mother loved to say. *If you only knew, Mama.*

Her parents absolutely loved Chris, and he spent a great deal of time intentionally charming her parents, which kept any suspicions at bay. At least she wasn't foolish enough to have married him. There was no lack of nudging on her mother's part, but Rox's busy writing schedule hadn't left her the time necessary to organize a ceremony. Every day, Rox thanked God for that good fortune.

She sat back and sighed. Here she was, two years later, nearly 27 years old and living with a batterer. *God, how did I get myself into this mess? Better yet—how do I get out?* She stared at the computer screen, which had blurred beyond reading. Blinking several times to bring things back into focus, she realized that she hadn't answered the fan mail still on the screen on front of her.

"Okay, Roxanne, get a grip."

She grabbed the mouse and selected "Reply" at the top of the screen, then poised her hands over the keys. *Shit! What do I say to this guy? Do I tell him the truth and say, "No, I don't have someone who appreciates me. I live with this bully who beats me on a regular basis; come rescue me," or do I lie and say life is wonderful? God, I hate to lie.*

After several minutes of staring at the screen, she settled for something in between.

> *Hi, C.C.,*
>
> *Thank you so much for taking the time to write. I really appreciate hearing from readers who enjoy my work.*
>
> *Thank you also for the compliment on my appearance. It's been a while since I've been told that I am beautiful. It was like salve for my soul at a time when I sorely needed it.*
>
> *I'm glad you enjoyed the Stargazer series. I'm currently working on my next novel, which I hope to publish later in the fall.*
>
> *Thank you again for writing,*
> *Rox Ward*
>
> *P.S. I can guess by your user ID that the second C in C.C. means Conway, but what does the first C stand for?*

Taking a deep breath, knowing that the action was irreversible, Rox pressed the "Send" button. She immediately regretted the unwritten plea for sympathy she had added to the note. She shrugged. "Oh, well. He'll probably just file it in the recycle bin."

Chapter 3

At seven a.m. on Sunday morning, the sun shone through the slotted blinds and fell across the bed in stripes. Feeling the heat from the sun's rays, Cass rolled onto her side and pulled the sheet over her head.

"Go away."

The sunbeams persisted, raising the temperature beneath the sheet.

Damn it, Cass, you should have closed the blinds last night, her inner voice shouted.

"Okay, okay, I'm awake," Cass mumbled, throwing off the covers and propping herself up on her right elbow. Her eyes were closed, her head lolled over toward her right shoulder, and her long hair hung across one side of her face. Cass stayed like that for several moments, until her head rolled backward and caused her to jerk awake.

"Damn." She forced herself into a seated position and pulled her knees in to sit cross-legged. She propped her elbows on her knees, rubbed her hands over her face and scrubbed the sleep out of her eyes, then sat up straight to stretch her neck from side to side. "Wake up, Cass."

Finally awake, Cass threw off the sheet and climbed out of bed, then padded over to her dresser to retrieve her spandex running shorts and bra. Moments later, she was dressed and heading out the door for her Sunday run, a utility belt strapped around her waist to hold her money and water bottle.

Before starting her run, she stopped at her mailbox to stretch, then reached in for the newspaper. She unrolled it and scanned the headline: "Colombian Drug Dealer Eludes Authorities." Cass glanced briefly at the article.

Colombian drug lord Carlos Santonio eluded police Saturday as guerrillas opened fire and provided him with

18

ground cover, killing one policeman and injuring two others. Santonio is wanted in the United States and several Central American countries on charges of drug trafficking and smuggling.

"Frickin' drug dealers," Cass mumbled. "They all need to be strung up by their balls." She re-rolled the paper and shoved it back into her mailbox. *I'll read that after my run.*

Cass ran her usual five-mile route, which led her to Angie's diner for breakfast. Stopping outside the door, she took a few minutes to cool down and stretch again before entering and heading directly to the ladies' room to splash cool water on her face.

Angie saw her en route and greeted her with a good-morning smile. "I'll have a cup of coffee waiting for you when you're finished washing up." True to her word, she put a cup of strong black coffee at Cass's usual table, along with a breakfast menu. Moments later, she returned to take Cass's order.

"What'll it be this morning, gorgeous?" she asked, smiling.

Indicating the coffee that had been waiting for her at the table, Cass said, "Ang, if you weren't already married, I'd kiss you."

"Well, sweetness, if I wasn't already married, I'd let you." Angie's pert reply made Cass chuckle. "What can I tempt you with this morning?"

"Let's see... I'll take the vegetarian omelet, wheat toast, and a side of home fries."

"Hungry this morning, huh?" Angie commented as she wrote down the order.

"A container of yogurt and a few crackers yesterday just didn't cut it."

"You know, Cass, you need to settle down with someone who can cook. It would save you a lot of time and money."

"No, thanks. I kind of like being footloose and fancy free."

"And lonely?"

Cass looked at her friend through narrowed eyes.

"Oh-oh, kind of overstepped my bounds there, huh? Okay, I know when to make a strategic retreat. I'll be back in a few minutes with your order." Angie turned and walked quickly toward the kitchen.

Cass sat looking at her hands, clasped together on the table.

She's right, you know. You are lonely. You really do need to find someone to share your life with, Enforcer said. *Just do it cautiously... be careful who you choose. You don't need another Patti.*

I won't expose myself to that again.

You also can't go through the rest of your life alone and miserable. Get a life, Cass. Not everyone you meet will be like Patti. Those one-night-stands are only good for one thing and you know it. You need someone to have a meaningful relationship with, Enforcer chided.

"I can't!" exclaimed Cass aloud, eliciting stares from the other patrons. She looked around nervously then slid down in her chair, trying to make herself invisible.

Damn it, get a grip.

At that point, Angie appeared with breakfast. "Okay, one veggie omelet and a side of home fries. Like a refill on that coffee?" Angie asked as she put a plate down in front of Cass.

"Only if you join me," Cass said, her voice plaintive.

Angie saw the quiet desperation in her friend's eyes. "Sure, sugar." She smiled and grabbed Cass's coffee cup. "I'll be right back."

Moments later, Angie was back with two cups of coffee. She slid into the seat opposite Cass and began the conversation with a question. "So, did you get a chance to start the book?"

"Started it and finished it," Cass said. "All in one night, and sitting in a tub of cold water."

Angie smiled. "It *was* a good book. Couldn't put it down, could you?"

Cass shook her head as she chewed a mouthful of food.

"When are you going to start Part II?"

Cass looked at Angie with a pathetic smile, then caught her bottom lip between her teeth.

Angie looked at her incredulously. "You're kidding, right? Don't tell me you've already read that one, too!"

Cass nodded her head.

"Cassidy Conway, is reading all you've done since you got home on Friday?" Angie asked in surprise.

"Ang, I couldn't help myself. The books were so good."

Angie reached out to place a hand on Cass's arm. "Cass, I'm worried about you. Here you are, a beautiful young woman, and you spend your entire weekend holed up in your condo reading.

Sweetheart, you've got to get out and meet people. How are you ever going to meet Ms. Right if you aren't out there looking?"

Cass put down her fork and wiped her mouth with her napkin. Placing it in her lap, she leaned back in her chair and looked at her friend. "Angie, I'm afraid. After Patti…"

"Patti wasn't your fault, Cass. Near the end, even *I* could tell she was using. Whenever the two of you came in for dinner, it was obvious that she was high on something. And besides, that was three years ago. It's time to put all that behind you and move on. You need someone to share your life with. Life is too short, sweetie. Don't waste it."

Cass nodded solemnly, and downed the rest of her coffee. She put the cup back on the table, set some money down to cover her tab, then stood up and kissed Angie on the cheek. "Thanks, Ang. It feels good to know someone cares."

"That I do, Cass. You know I'm here for you, right?"

Cass squeezed the waitress's shoulder. "Thanks," she said. "I'll see you around dinnertime, okay?"

"Your favorite is on the menu tonight—Italian meatloaf."

Cass left the restaurant smiling and walked back to her condo at a leisurely pace. She got the newspaper from her mailbox and climbed the steps to her apartment. Throwing the paper on the coffee table as she walked by, she headed directly to the bathroom, where she stripped off her running clothes and jumped into the shower. Afterward, since she wasn't expecting any visitors, she donned a pair of high-cut black bikini briefs and a short black tank top that reached to just above her navel.

Lounging on the couch, she reached for the paper and started scanning the various articles. She flew quite regularly into Bogotá, so she read the whole article on the Colombian drug lord. Aside from that, not much held her interest. She fished the crossword puzzle out of the classified section and discarded the rest.

Cass spent the next hour absorbed in the crossword. When she had completed it, she put the section aside and looked around for something else to do. She saw the TV's remote control, grabbed it, and clicked to the TV preview channel. As she read through the listings, she saw something that piqued her interest. *Fried Green Tomatoes*, Sunday, noon. Looking at her watch and realizing she had a two-hour wait, she cursed. *Damn! I really* do *need to get a life. It's only 10:15 a.m., and I've already run out of things to do. This really sucks.*

Cass got up and started to pace. *Come on, think.*

Shopping? Nah, I hate to shop. Movies? Nah, too early in the day. Reading? Nah, I've read everything... wait.

Cass stopped dead in her tracks and looked toward her office, then headed for its door.

Until that moment, Cass had never given much thought to booting up her computer. Thus, she had never before realized just how long it took to complete the boot-up and login cycle.

"Come on, you piece of sh... ah, finally." She clicked on "New Messages" and waited while the system queried the server.

"God-damned system." As the list of new mail was produced, she muttered, "It's about time," and looked eagerly at the two items. "Let's see, spam, and... yes! Rox@Starship.com! She replied to my note, I can't believe it!" Cass hurriedly clicked the mail icon next to the address.

> *Hi, C.C.*
>
> *Thank you so much for taking the time to write. I really appreciate hearing from readers who enjoy my work.*
>
> *Thank you also for the compliment on my appearance. It's been a while since I've been told that I am beautiful. It was like salve for my soul at a time when I sorely needed it.*
>
> *I am glad you enjoyed the* Stargazer *series. I am currently working on my next novel, which I hope to publish later in the fall.*
>
> *Thank you again for writing,*
> *Rox Ward*
>
> *P.S. I can guess by your user ID that the second C in C.C. means Conway, but what does the first C stand for?*

Cass read the response three times. *Something doesn't feel right about this. This part right here.* She touched a line of text on the monitor with her fingertip. "...like salve for my soul at a time when I sorely needed it." *I wonder what she meant by that?*

Whoa... take it easy, there, Cass. Don't go jumping in without testing the water. This chick could mean trouble. Remember Patti? Remember—take it easy... take it slow, Enforcer reminded her.

Look, E., Cass said to her alter ego, *you said just this morning at Angie's that I needed someone, now you're changing your tune. Make up my mind, will you?*

I know what I said, Cass. Just take it slow, okay? I don't want us to get hurt again.

Cass sat back in her chair and read the note again. The words *"Remember Patti"* flashed through her mind, bringing with them a wave of fear so intense that Cass pushed herself away from the computer and stared at the screen. Her heart in her throat, she reached for the mouse and moved the cursor to the upper right-hand corner of the screen, closed the window and proceeded to shut down the computer.

She got up from her chair and paced back and forth in front of the computer, arms wrapped around her middle. *Why am I feeling so paranoid about someone I don't even know? It's just a piece of e-mail. She lives on the other side of the continent, for Christ's sake.*

Cass stopped pacing and took a deep breath. *Okay, I can do this. This is not Patti, it's Rox. I don't even know her; she can't hurt me.* She punched the power button and once again went through the tortuous routine of booting up the computer and accessing her inbox.

She sounds harmless enough, Cass thought, reading the note again. *Okay, I'm going to do it.* She clicked on "Reply."

Hi, Rox,

Thank you for taking the time to respond. I really didn't think you would. I know writers are very busy.

I can't imagine why it's been a while since anyone complimented you on your looks. The photo on your book cover is absolutely beautiful. Initially, I bought the book more for the picture than the contents, but I was captivated by both once I started reading. You are a truly talented writer. I'm looking forward to your next book this fall.

I will understand if you are too busy to reply to this second note, but I had to reiterate what I thought of your beauty and your work. Both are truly stunning.
Thanks again for replying,
C.C.

P.S. The first C is for Cassidy.

Without hesitating, Cass hit the "Send" button, then sat back and sighed. *There. I wonder if she'll respond to this one. I hope she doesn't take the remark about her beauty as an idle comment, because it sounds like she really needs to hear it right now. I wonder why?*

Cass glanced at her watch. *11:45 a.m.* "Why does it take me so long to respond to e-mail? This one took more than an hour! Oh, well, at least it killed some time. My show's coming on in fifteen minutes, so there's just enough left to nuke a bag of popcorn and settle in."

Chapter 4

Rox was very pleased with herself. She glanced at the digital clock on her desk. "2:44 p.m." was illuminated on the LCD. In six hours of writing, she had produced two chapters. Now it was time to take a break. She hadn't eaten all day, and she needed to start dinner in case Chris came home early. She had learned to be prompt with the evening meal, since all hell would break loose if dinner wasn't ready on time. If Chris chose to stay out late, she'd heat it up for him when he finally decided to come home. Rox hoped he'd be so late that she could be in bed by the time he got in. That way, she stood a better chance of escaping another confrontation.

She closed her word processing program and shut down the system, then went in search of a snack. After making her way down the stairs and into the kitchen, Rox took bologna, pickles, cheese, lettuce, a tomato and mayonnaise from the refrigerator. She threw all the ingredients together into a sandwich, leaned back against the counter and took a big bite, closing her eyes and savoring the unique combination of flavors.

Rox recalled the first time Chris had seen her eat one of those sandwiches. He had accused her of being pregnant, which in his mind equated with her being unfaithful, since he detested children and was extremely careful not to impregnate her. He had beaten her and forced her to take a home pregnancy test, which had, predictably, turned out negative. Rox had never received an apology for the beating. She also never ate that sandwich again in Chris's presence. She saved that particular delicacy for times when he wasn't home.

Her snack finished, Rox cleaned away the evidence and put the remaining foodstuffs back into the refrigerator, then took a roast out of the freezer and placed it in the microwave to defrost. Planning to put it in the oven in about an hour, she grabbed a diet soda from the refrigerator and limped back up two flights of stairs to her office to continue working on her book.

She decided to check her e-mail before she resumed her work, and found two new messages. The first was from her publisher, asking for the weekly status report on her new book.

"So he wants an update, huh? Okay, then, here goes." Rox clicked the "Reply" icon at the top of her screen and began to type.

In response to your inquiry on the status of my book, I am pleased to inform you that I have made significant progress over the past few weeks. I estimate completion within the next month, barring unexpected setbacks. As is customary, I will send the entire manuscript to you as soon as my beta readers have completed their first review. Until that time, I will continue to send periodic status reports upon request. Please let me know if you have further questions.
Sincerely,
Roxanne Ward

Rox was uncomfortable about building contingencies into her delivery schedule, but with her father's illness and Chris's erratic behavior, she was loath to commit to a firm delivery date. Satisfied with her response, she clicked the "Send" button and sent the note on its way before moving on to the second piece of new mail.

The second e-mail was from CConway@Flyboy.com. *Ah, C.C.* She double-clicked on the mail icon.

Hi, Rox,
Thank you for taking the time to respond. I really didn't think you would. I know writers are very busy.
I can't imagine why it's been a while since anyone complimented you on your looks. The photo on your book cover is absolutely beautiful. Initially, I bought the book more for the picture than the contents, but I was captivated by both once I started reading. You are a truly talented writer. I'm looking forward to your next book this fall.
I will understand if you are too busy to reply to this second note, but I had to reiterate what I thought of your beauty and your work. Both are truly stunning.
Thanks again for replying,
C.C.

P.S. The first C is for Cassidy.

Rox smiled. "Thanks, Cassidy, I really needed that. Cassidy, that's a very cool name." *He thinks I'm stunning, does he?* she thought. *Well, I guess I used to be. Before Chris, that is. These days, I seem to have this permanent bluish tint to my face. Well, we're supposed to go to Mom and Dad's next weekend, so that means no more beatings this week.*

Rox read Cass's note again. *So you bought my book based on the picture alone, huh? My publisher was right—sex sells. I wonder how many other guys bought the book for the same reason? Oh, well. I'm glad you liked the story, at least.*

Rox hesitated before answering the message. "From the sound of it, this guy doesn't really expect a response, Gerald, but what the hell. What can it hurt?"

She had addressed the stuffed giraffe sitting on the desk next to the computer. Gerald had been a gift from a fan who had read her first book, two years earlier, and he had been a constant writing companion ever since. Rox clicked on the "Reply" button and responded.

Hi again, Cassidy.

First, let me say that I really like your name. It's quite unusual, and I believe unique names encourage their owners to be just as unique.

I'm never too busy to respond to an appreciative fan. Thank you for your kind words -- you are far too generous in your appraisal.

Hasn't anyone ever told you not to judge a book by its cover? Buying my book solely on the basis of the picture on the back cover was risky. The book could have turned out to be crap. Still, I'm glad you did, and even more glad that you enjoyed the story.

By the way, I noticed that your user ID is Flyboy.com. I assume you're a pilot? Just curious.

Later,
Rox

Rox hit the "Send" button and watched as the note went irrevocably on its way.

Sighing deeply, she exited e-mail and entered her writers' chat room, where she spent the next two hours trading information and advice with fellow authors. As a relatively new author, Rox gained great benefit from the chat room. It allowed her to communicate and seek the counsel of veteran writers, most of whom had written best sellers at one point or another in their literary careers.

At five p.m., Rox finally logged off the Net and opened Word. For the next five hours, she threw herself into her story, totally absorbed in her latest tale of alien love and intrigue. At ten p.m., thoroughly exhausted but elated with her progress, she went to bed.

Rox was dreaming. She was in a field of flowers, wearing a diaphanous gown of cream-colored crepe that billowed in the breeze. Walking slowly through the field, she stopped to pick flowers, smelling each one before adding it to the growing bouquet in her arms. Every now and then, she glanced up at the sky and smiled into the sun, basking in its warmth on her skin.

Suddenly, she saw a form approaching from across the field. It didn't appear menacing. The closer it got, the more Rox was convinced it was a woman—one taller than herself, with long dark hair. She wore a gown identical to the one Rox had on, and Rox thought it was odd that they were dressed alike. The woman was not picking flowers, but was walking slowing toward Rox, her fingertips gently brushing the tips of the blossoms as she passed by.

Rox felt no fear as the stranger continued her slow approach. Soon, the woman was close enough for Rox to see that she was quite beautiful—tall and slender, with long dark hair and piercing blue eyes. She walked with self-assured confidence, and Rox wondered who she was.

The woman stopped directly in front of Rox, looked down into her eyes and smiled.

"Who are you?" Rox asked, as she gazed into azure depths.

"I am the other half of your soul."

Rox frowned in puzzlement, and laid her palm flat against her heart. "My soul?" she asked. "I didn't realize it was missing."

"I have always possessed it, through countless generations of time. I have known and cherished it through many lifetimes. Each flower in this field represents one of our lives together. Those you hold in your arms are ones already past; those not yet picked are yet to be lived. We are soulmates: past, present, and future."

The woman reached forward to cradle Rox's face between gentle hands. Unable and unwilling to look away, Rox was captivated by the sea of blue into which she was staring. The pounding of her pulse increased sharply, just from the woman's touch.

The woman slowly lowered her head. As soft lips descended slowly to within a hair's breadth of her own, Rox became certain that a kiss would surely cause her to lose consciousness.

"Roxanne! Roxanne, you bitch! Where are you?"

Rox jolted awake and sat upright in bed. Totally disoriented, she reached to touch her lips. Her eyes darted around in the dark as she tried to determine where she was. Finally, she realized that she was at home and in bed. It was 3:08 a.m. At that moment, she also realized that the voice she had heard belonged to Chris, and he was on a rampage.

"Oh, my God, no," Rox whispered as Chris burst into the room. She suddenly felt sick to her stomach.

"You filthy bitch!" Chris roared. "You filthy, good-for-nothing goddamned bitch!"

Rox couldn't see well in the darkness. "Chris, what is it?" she asked in a tiny, fearful voice.

"What is it? What *is* it? I'll show you what, bitch!" Chris said. He grabbed a handful of Rox's hair and dragged her out of bed, down a flight of stairs, and into the kitchen. Once there, he threw her up against the counter, where she crumpled to the floor.

"There, that's what!" Chris said, pointing to the microwave.

Rox struggled to her feet, looking confused, until all of a sudden she remembered the roast she had put in there to defrost, earlier that afternoon. The look on her face was one of sheer terror. *God, no!*

Chris grabbed her and slapped her across the face, sending her flying across the room and into the refrigerator.

The next thing Rox knew, Chris's belt was in his hand and her back was on fire.

Chapter 5

It was two p.m. when Cass's movie finished. Even though she had seen *Fried Green Tomatoes* several times, it always left her crying. "Poor Idgie," she sobbed. "To lose the love of her life like that. Thank God she still had Ruth's son."

The movie reminded Cass too clearly of the relationship she'd had with Patti before things went terribly wrong. Patti was so much like Idgie—devil-may-care, flaunting authority—and she herself was so much like Ruth, down to earth and solid. The major differences were that, in real life, it was her Idgie who had died, and there was no child left behind for her to love. Cass was alone with her memories and her pain.

She pointed the remote control at the TV and switched the set off. Still holding the remote, she curled up on the couch and wiped her eyes with the back of her hand. Cass then rested her head against the arm of the couch, stared straight ahead, and let her mind wander back to better days.

They carried a picnic basket packed with sandwiches, fresh fruit, wine, cheese and crackers as they made their way to the river's edge. There, they spread a blanket and sat cross-legged, facing one another. They talked and ate for the next several hours, feeding each other bits of food, tongues raking across fingertips as morsels were slipped into mouths. They shared sips of wine from long-stemmed glasses, and occasional kisses. By the time the meal was over, the aura of sensuality was palpable and the atmosphere was charged with sexual energy.

Reaching forward, Patti pulled Cass into her lap so that her long legs straddled Patti's waist. Chest to chest, they faced each other, eyes locked in sexual combat as their hands roamed up and down each other's torso. Placing a hand on the small of Cass's back, Patti gently lowered her to the blanket. She covered Cass's mouth with her own, lying directly between the legs of her dark-haired lover. Patti's

right leg was stretched out, and her left knee was bent to support her
weight as she pressed her abdomen into Cass's core.

"I love you, Cass," she whispered hoarsely as she devoured
Cass's mouth. For hours, until both were sated and weak with sexual
fulfillment, the two caressed and loved each other.

The ringing of the telephone snapped Cass from her reverie, and
she wiped moisture from her cheeks before she reached over to lift the
receiver.

"Hello?"

"Hi, Cass, this is Angie. I'm just calling to see if you'd mind
bringing *Stargazer II* with you when you come to the diner tonight.
I'd like to read it."

"Uh… sure, Ang." Cass sniffed back another tear. "Sure."

"Cass, are you all right?" Angie voice was filled with concern.

"I'm fine, Angie, really." Cass was unconvincing, even to
herself.

"Cass, I'm off early tonight. You're coming home to spend the
evening with Roger and me, okay? It sounds like you could use the
company."

"No, really, Angie. I'm fine."

"I won't take no for an answer," the older woman said firmly.
When only silence answered her, Angie said, "Cass?"

"Okay, okay. For a couple of hours," Cass agreed. "And Ang,
thanks. I'll see you at the diner around five."

A couple of hours somehow turned into four, and Cass unlocked
her condo door at precisely 10:09 p.m. She always enjoyed spending
time with Angie and Roger. Roger was quite a character, and Cass felt
sure that he could make even a statue smile. After relocking the condo
door and throwing her keys on the coffee table, Cass went straight to
the bedroom, stripping off her t-shirt along the way. Stopping beside
her bed, she unbuttoned and unzipped her shorts, allowed them to fall
to her ankles, then kicked them off. Moments later, she crawled into
bed, pulled the covers up to her chin, and fell into a deep sleep.

Cass opened her eyes and found herself lying in a field of
wildflowers. The sun was shining; it warmed her skin with its touch.
She blinked several times and rubbed the sleep from her eyes, then sat
up. She was wearing a diaphanous gown of cream-colored crepe. Cass
rose to her feet and turned in a circle, looking all around at the
apparently endless field of flowers. A feeling of euphoria filled her
heart, and she began to stroll through the field. As she walked, visions

came to her—visions of what she knew were past, present and future lives, and visions of a beautiful golden-haired woman.

Suddenly, everything was clear. She had a purpose, a goal, a mission. She had to find the woman who was invading her mind. As Cass continued to walk, she eventually noticed a figure in the distance. She drew nearer, and realized it was a woman—small in stature, with short, red-gold hair—who was picking flowers and inhaling the scent of each one before adding it to the growing pile in the crook of her arm. Could this be the woman in her visions?

Cass approached the woman and stopped in front of her, looking down into beautiful emerald green eyes. The woman did not seem to fear Cass; however, Cass's own heart was beating wildly.

The woman looked directly into Cass's eyes. "Who are you?"

"I am the other half of your soul," Cass heard herself answer.

The woman raised her hand to her heart. "My soul?" she asked. "I didn't realize it was missing."

"I have always possessed it, through countless generations of time. I have known and cherished it through many lifetimes. Each flower in this field represents one of our lives together. Those you hold in your arms are ones already past; those not yet picked are yet to be lived. We are soulmates: past, present and future." Cass explained.

Cass then found herself reaching forward to cup the small woman's face, her heart pounding with excitement at the intensity of emotion coursing through her.

The woman seemed unable or unwilling to resist Cass's advances. She stood there, apparently captivated by the moment, tilting up her face eagerly to accept the lips that were descending toward her.

Suddenly, Cass bolted awake and sat up, looking around herself in a disoriented fashion. It took a moment for her to realize she was in her bed. She looked at the clock. *Midnight.* Cass eased her legs over the side of the bed and rested her elbows on her knees. Her head in her hands, she sat there for long moments, trying to remember the dream. The details were sketchy, at best. The only clear memory she had was the face of the young woman. Lifting her head and staring blankly straight ahead, she whispered, "Rox."

Cass had a sick feeling in the pit of her stomach. Something was wrong. She stood at the foot of the bed for a moment, then paced restlessly back and forth, trying to make sense of the dream. *I wish I could remember more of it*, she mused. *Something about soulmates… past, present and future lives. I wonder what it means?*

It means you're losing your marbles, girl, Enforcer piped up. *Get a grip, Cassidy. Soulmates? Past, present and future lives? Give me a break. Don't tell me you're falling for that spiritual mumbo-jumbo? Sheesh. You need help, and you need it bad. Do something before you lose it completely.*

Cass couldn't get the image of Rox out of her mind. *Why would I dream about Rox? It must be because Angie and I spent so much time talking about* Stargazer *this evening. I have Rox on the brain. Yeah, that's it.*

Cass went to the window and looked out into the dark, starless night. *Why is my gut twisted in a knot? What's wrong?* "Damn," she whispered.

Wide awake, Cass continued to pace, trying to get the petite woman out of her mind. Finally, she acknowledged that it was a waste of time and effort, and decided to take the opposite approach. She would check her e-mail and see if the author had responded to her last note.

Cass went to her office, switched on her computer, then turned and left the room to get a glass of cool water. She knew she would put her foot through the monitor if she had to stand there and wait for the machine to boot up. Moments later, she returned and logged on to the Internet.

"Okay, Rox, talk to me," she said as she selected "New Messages." There it was. One new message, from Rox@Starship.com. Cass's heart flip-flopped with excitement. Opening the mail, she read:

Hi again, Cassidy.

First, let me say that I really like your name. It's quite unusual, and I believe unique names encourage their owners to be just as unique.

I'm never too busy to respond to an appreciative fan. Thank you for your kind words -- you are far too generous in your appraisal.

Hasn't anyone ever told you not to judge a book by its cover? Buying my book solely on the basis of the picture on the back cover was risky. The book could have turned out to be crap. Still, I'm glad you did, and even more glad that you enjoyed the story.

By the way, I noticed that your user ID is Flyboy.com.
I assume you're a pilot? Just curious.
Later,
Rox

Cass smiled. *She's curious about me,* she thought. *Cool.* For some reason, that small spark of interest from a person she didn't even know filled her heart with giddiness. She couldn't explain it.

"All right. You asked, I deliver." Cass selected "Reply" at the top of the screen.

Hey, Rox.
Thanks for replying. I really appreciate it.
Cassidy was my mom's idea, so I'm glad you like it. The guys at work tease me about it sometimes. They ask me how the Sundance Kid is doing these days. Real jokers, those guys... but heck, I've learned to grow a thick skin over the past several years. BTW, I usually go by Cass.
You're right, I am a pilot. I work for Southern Lights Airline, out of San Jose. I fly mostly into Central and South America. Every now and then I take a domestic flight, like when I found your book in Dallas.
As far as the book turning out to be crap, there's not a chance. How could someone so beautiful produce anything less than perfection? I was captivated by both the book and the picture.
The author's bio says that you live on the seacoast of Maine. If you don't mind sharing, what town do you live in? Are you directly on the ocean? I love the ocean, especially at night, and most especially during a storm.
Anyway, thanks again for replying. I really do appreciate it, and I hope to hear from you soon.
Cass

Cass pressed the "Send" button, sat back and smiled, then frowned. *Why are you constantly in my thoughts, Roxanne Ward?*

Sighing deeply, she reached over and initiated the computer's shutdown routine, and watched as it slowly went to sleep. *That's exactly what I need to do. I have an early flight tomorrow,* Cass thought, and dragged herself off to bed.

Chapter 6

Rox opened her eyes and peered into the darkness. Her cheek was resting against something hard and cool, and total silence enveloped her. As she slowly lifted her head, she felt the skin on the back of her neck crinkle into painful folds and send bolts of fire down her back. She froze into statue-like stillness as she allowed the wave of pain to pass. *Rox, you have to get up. You can't spend the night on the floor. Come on, you can do it.*

She forced her body into motion and slowly climbed to her feet. The skin on her back felt like it was torn, shredded like a linen sheet stretched too far. Grasping the edge of the kitchen table, she stood still for several long moments, praying that the fire would diminish. She was weak-kneed and nauseated, her white knuckles gripping the edge of the smooth wood surface as tears streamed down her face. Several moments later, her stomach settled and she slowly righted herself and moved carefully into the living room. There was no sign of Chris, and she assumed that her abuser had gone to bed.

Making her way to the downstairs bathroom, Rox turned on the light and immediately winced, a reflex that was extremely painful due to the bruises and cuts she saw reflected in the mirror.

My God, how can I possibly explain this to my parents? There's no way I can let them find out about this, not when Dad has so little time left.

She couldn't disappoint them with the truth, not given the way they felt about Chris. Rox refused to send her father to his grave with the knowledge that his little girl was living in an abusive situation. No, she would live with it. She would make her excuses and get out of the dinner invitation this weekend, and then make it up to them somehow.

There was no way Rox could navigate the stairs, so she moved slowly across the living room carpet and sat gingerly on the edge of the couch. Very carefully, she lowered herself and lay on her side, placing her bruised face on the throw pillow. She pulled the quilt off the back of the couch, and then arranged it haphazardly over her lower body. Rox forced herself to relax, and released the tension from one body part at a time. The pain slowly eased, and she consigned herself to sleep.

The next morning, Rox was startled awake by the ringing of the telephone. She jumped up at the sound, but quickly crumpled back into a painful heap on the couch, trying hard to catch her breath and answer the phone before the caller hung up. Fighting tears and gasping for air, she picked up the receiver.

"He... hello?" Rox rasped into the phone.

"Hey, Rox. Are we still on for shopping today?"

"Nik...." Rox cleared her throat, "Nikki?"

Several long moments of silence followed.

"Nikki?" Rox asked again, in a weak voice.

"Oh God, Rox, not again! I'll be there in five minutes. Don't move, okay?" Nikki's voice was desperate.

A dial tone came from the phone before Rox could summon enough breath to answer. Fighting back tearful memories of the night before, she placed the receiver shakily back in its cradle. Then she noticed the note by the phone.

"I'll be out of town on a job for the next few days. C." That was all it said. No apology, no explanation. Rox was surprised that Chris had left a note at all. It was unlike him to show even that much consideration.

She took a deep, painful breath and closed her eyes. Minutes later, the front door burst open to admit a five-foot two-inch fireball.

"Goddamned son-of-a-bitchin' bastard!" Nikki cursed, seeing her friend's condition. "Chris, you motherfucker, where the hell are you!" she yelled into the house.

Rox looked up from her position on the couch, tears clouding her vision. "He's gone."

Nikki went immediately to Rox's side and sat next to her on the couch. She took Rox into her arms and held her tenderly as the injured woman cried out her sorrow.

"It's okay, baby. Cry it out, love." Nikki placed light kisses on Rox's forehead, and tears streamed down her own face as she rocked her friend back and forth. Several moments later, Rox's breathing stilled as she fell into a light sleep against Nikki's shoulder.

Nikki was shaking with anger as she silently examined her friend. She brushed Rox's golden bangs off her forehead and noted the multiple cuts and bruises on her face and neck. "Sweetheart, why do you stay in this relationship?" she whispered.

Nikki closed her eyes and rested her head on the back of the couch, remembering the time six years ago when she had first met Rox. Rox had been eager, bright, assertive, independent and dedicated—very different from the way she was now.

As an advocate of women's rights, journalism major and a reporter for the campus newspaper, Rox made a point of giving women's issues a lot of press. That didn't always sit well with certain groups on campus. One group in particular, The Gentleman's Club, took offense to what they considered her "anti-male" campaign. One evening, while crossing campus at dusk, Rox was accosted by a member of the club. He cornered her in a secluded alcove of the Fine Arts building, and was proceeding to teach her a lesson by showing her what a good man could do. Before he had the chance to do anything, however, he found himself the recipient of a hefty blow to the back.

Rolling off of the still-struggling Rox, he had looked up and exclaimed, "What the fuck?"

"I'll what-the-fuck you, you filthy son of a bitch!" shouted the short blonde, as the sturdy chunk of wood she grasped slammed against the assailant's chest.

Rox rolled to her feet and straightened her clothing as she watched the petite wild woman demolish the would-be rapist with a tree branch.

The perpetrator finally managed to roll away from the branch-wielding Fury and scramble to his feet, then hurriedly limp away. The rescuer threw the weapon down and looked at Rox. "Are you all right?"

"I am now, thanks to you." Rox extended her hand. "Roxanne Ward."

"Nicole Davenport. Nikki." The blonde broke into a big smile and reached out to shake Rox's hand. "I don't think he'll be bothering anyone else tonight," she added, watching the man limp across campus.

Rox followed the direction of Nikki's gaze. "No, I don't think he will," she agreed, looking back at her rescuer.

"We need to report him to campus security right away. Come on, I'll walk you over there."

Rox nodded. "Okay, but only if you let me buy you a cup of coffee afterward. It's the least I can do to show my appreciation."

Nikki smiled. "Make it a beer and you've got yourself a date,"
she said, as she walked along with Rox.

"Rox, when Jerri finds out about this, Chris is toast. You know
that, don't you?" Nikki reached up and wiped tears off her own face
with the back of her fist.

Nikki's partner, Jerri, was her emotional opposite, being
possessed of a mild-mannered disposition—except when the people
she loved were in danger. She would not take kindly to this latest
episode.

For the next couple of hours, Nikki sat and held her friend. She
hummed lullabies, lightly rubbed her hand up and down Rox's arm,
and plotted vengeance against Chris.

"Mom... Mom, I'm sorry. I know you and Dad were looking
forward to dinner this weekend, but we just can't make it. Chris is out
of town on a job, and it'll be the perfect opportunity for me to get a
lot of writing done. My publisher is sending me e-mails daily, asking
for status reports," Rox explained. "Yes, I know it's only Monday,
and I suppose things could change before the weekend, but please
don't plan on it. I know we promised, Mom, but it can't be helped.
Maybe next weekend, okay? I'm sorry. Kiss Daddy for me, okay? All
right, Mom, I'll talk to you later. Bye." Rox slowly placed the
receiver back in the cradle and stared at it for long moments before
looking up at Nikki, who had been pacing back and forth beside her.

Nikki stood still and opened her arms to her friend, who
willingly went into them. As she wrapped her arms tightly around her
injured friend, Nikki felt Rox stiffen. She pushed Rox away from her
and held her at arm's length. Narrowing her eyes, Nikki reached up
and unbuttoned Rox's nightshirt. Rox was too tired to fight her, and
let her do it.

After a moment, Nikki had the baseball jersey unbuttoned and
pushed off Rox's shoulders, never breaking eye contact with her
friend during the unveiling. Finally, Nikki turned Rox around and
looked at her back. "Oh, my God!" Nikki exclaimed, and ran into the
bathroom.

While her friend was emptying her stomach, Rox slowly and
silently pulled the jersey back up and buttoned it, keeping her eyes
downcast. Moments later, an ashen-faced Nikki was once again
standing in front of her, lifting her chin with two fingers and looking
into her face with such sympathy and love that Rox fell once more
into her arms and just stood there, allowing her friend to hold her.

A long while later, Nikki kissed Rox's cheek and led her to a chair at the kitchen table, then went through the refrigerator looking for omelet ingredients.

"Nikki, I'm really not hungry," Rox protested as she watched her friend prepare the meal.

The little blonde turned to face her friend and put her hands on her hips. "Rox, you've got to eat. Look at you. When's the last time you ate a decent meal? For Christ's sake, girlfriend, you're killing yourself. Between your job, your starvation diet, and that thug you're living with, you look like a Third World refugee!"

Rox cringed. "I love you too, Nik," she said, trying to lighten the mood.

Nikki placed the bowl of eggs on the counter and went to wrap her arms around her friend's neck.

Rox's hands came up to grasp Nikki's arms affectionately, as she leaned her head against her friend's.

"Rox, sweetheart, I am so worried about you. I half expect to see your name in the obituaries some morning," Nikki said, in a raspy voice. "Please walk away from this, please."

"I can't, Nik," she whispered back. "I won't break Daddy's heart like that." She was more broken-hearted at the prospect of losing her father to cancer than at the abusive situation in which she was living. "You know that he's dying, Nik. The doctors give him less than six months, and he thinks Chris and I are happy. I can't shatter that illusion."

"*You* will die before your father does if something doesn't change soon," Nikki warned, drawing a startled look from her friend. "I'm sorry to put it so bluntly, Rox, but it's true. It's only a matter of time before Chris kills you."

When Rox just stared at her hands, clasped in front of her on the table, Nikki sighed and went back to cooking breakfast.

It was nearly dinnertime before Rox could convince Nikki to go home, assuring her that she had recovered enough mobility to take care of herself. Rox appreciated Nikki's help and concern, but she really wanted to get back to her writing. She actually *was* receiving e-mails from her literary agent asking for status reports, just not as often as she'd told her mother.

Nikki kissed her soundly. "I'll go, but only if you promise to call if you need anything."

"I will, I promise. And thanks, Nik."

After a gentle hug and another kiss, Nikki went home, trying to think of the best way to share the news of this latest abuse with Jerri.

Finally alone, Rox made her way up to her office, sat down in front of the computer, and rested her bruised forehead against the monitor screen. While she waited patiently for the system to boot up, the phone rang.

"Hello?" she said.

"Rox, this is Jerri. Rox, I'm gonna kill that… that… "

"Jerri, you'll do no such thing, do you understand?" Rox said. *Damn it, Nik, did you have to get her all riled up too?*

"Chris cannot continue to get away with this. It won't stop, you know, not until it's too late," Jerri warned.

"Jerri, please," Rox interrupted.

"No, Rox, you can't sacrifice yourself like this—not even for your father," Jerri said angrily.

"Jerri, I think that's *my* decision to make, all right? Now, I love you dearly for worrying about me, truly I do, but it *is* my decision."

Only silence met her rebuttal.

"Jerri?"

There was still only silence on the line.

"Damn it, Jerri, answer me. I don't need shit from you, too."

There was another moment's pause before Jerri answered. "I'm sorry, Rox. It's just that… well, it's killing Nikki and me to see this happening to you. You don't deserve it."

"No one ever does, my friend, no one ever does. I'm okay, Jerri. I'll be fine in a few days. Chris won't be back before Wednesday or Thursday. That will give me plenty of time to recover, *and* to figure out how to prevent this from happening again."

"The only way to prevent it, Rox, is to get rid of that good-for-nothing creep!"

Rox smiled. Nikki was so much more colorful in her expletives than her partner was. "In time, Jerri, in time." She sighed. "Good night, my friend. Kiss Nikki for me, okay?"

"All right, Rox. Take care of yourself. We'll check up on you tomorrow. Bye."

Rox waited until she heard Jerri disconnect, then replaced the receiver. She sat back, and decided to read her e-mail before beginning to write. She clicked "Get Messages," and five new posts scrolled in. Third on the list was CConway@Flyboy.com. Rox decided to save that one for last, and quickly read and replied to the remaining four. Most of them were short blurbs from her friends in the writers' chat room. That task out of the way, she clicked on the remaining e-mail, then gingerly rested her sore back against the chair to take her time reading the message.

> *Hey, Rox.*
>
> *Thanks for replying. I really appreciate it.*
>
> *Cassidy was my mom's idea, so I'm glad you like it. The guys at work tease me about it sometimes. They ask me how the Sundance Kid is doing these days. Real jokers, those guys... but heck, I've learned to grow a thick skin over the past several years. BTW, I usually go by Cass.*
>
> *You're right, I am a pilot. I work for Southern Lights Airline, out of San Jose. I fly mostly into Central and South America. Every now and then I take a domestic flight, like when I found your book in Dallas.*
>
> *As far as the book turning out to be crap, there's not a chance. How could someone so beautiful produce anything less than perfection?*

Rox lifted her hand to her mouth to stifle a sob.

> *I was captivated by both by the book and the picture.*
>
> *The author's bio says that you live on the seacoast of Maine. If you don't mind sharing, what town do you live in? Are you directly on the ocean? I love the ocean, especially at night, and most especially during a storm.*
>
> *Anyway, thanks again for replying. I really do appreciate it, and I hope to hear from you soon.*
>
> *Cass*

Rox's eyes were filled with tears. She exited e-mail, then sat back in her chair and stared at the screen. She was no longer in the mood to write. Fighting the urge to shut down her computer and just go to bed, she maneuvered the pointer to the Word icon. Within moments, her imagination transported her into the world of aliens, and she had effectively escaped the nightmare that was her life.

Chapter 7

Monday morning. Cass wondered where the weekend had gone as she rolled over and turned off the alarm. *Damn, I've got a flight into Veracruz today.* Situated on the Mexican Gulf Coast, Veracruz was a popular tourist attraction, but it was a long flight and usually entailed a layover of at least one day, sometimes two. Cass sighed, wishing she had never volunteered for specialized flights. At least commercial flights were on regular schedules. At the time, just after Patti had died, the specialized flight schedule kept her busy and kept her mind off Patti.

Cass grumbled as she climbed out of bed and got into her running clothes and shoes. She stepped onto the treadmill and programmed the machine to a speed of 4.5 miles per hour for her fifteen-minute warm-up. Soon, she had the belt moving at 8 miles per hour and had inclined the bed ten degrees. Cass ran for the next half hour, until she was drenched with sweat and her quads were twitching with the strain. After another fifteen minutes of cool-down and some stretching, she was ready for the shower.

Standing under the spray, Cass placed her hands against the wall and allowed the water to cascade over her head, savoring the feeling of tiny, needle-like jets bombarding her skin. Eyes closed, she remembered times she had stood in that very spot, in that very position, with strict instructions to keep her hands firmly against the shower wall. Strong, callused hands had moved over her skin, up and down her body and across her breasts and abdomen, only to slide down between her legs. Words of love had been whispered into her ear from behind.

She threw her head back and pressed her body into her invisible lover, and a moan escaped her lips. All at once, Cass realized that she was alone. She straightened and dropped her chin to her chest, an insatiable tightness coiling in her gut.

She sighed, reached for the soap and face cloth, and then proceeded to cleanse her body and mind of the physical and emotional workout she had just given them.

As she toweled herself dry, Cass couldn't keep her mind off her loneliness. She craved the feeling of someone wrapped in her arms, of coming home to someone who loved her; shared moments feeding each other morsels of food in front of the fireplace, shared kisses that turned into wild nights of passion, tender looks and caresses while watching a movie together on the couch. *Angie was right—I am lonely.*

Better to be lonely than heartbroken, Cassidy. Remember that, Enforcer reminded her. *You'd better think long and hard before committing yourself again. You need a safe relationship, one that can't hurt you. How about that e-mail chick you've been corresponding with? She's a whole continent away. How much safer can you get than that?*

Cass blinked several times before her surroundings swam into focus. *E-mail.* She hung the towel on the rack and pulled on her robe. *Rox. I wonder if she's answered my last message?* She hurried into her office to boot up the computer.

While she was waiting for the system to come on line, she went back to the bedroom, dressed in her uniform, and combed out her long, dark tresses. Back at the computer, she logged onto the Internet and opened her inbox. It was empty. Disappointed, she shut down the computer.

She's got a life of her own. She isn't sitting around waiting for your notes, you know.

Cass finished preparing for work with a heavy heart. It was going to be a long two days in Mexico. She decided that if she hadn't heard from Rox by the time she returned, it was probably a lost cause. Sighing deeply, Cass closed the condo door behind her and headed to her car.

Cass watched as the crew loaded the last of the medical supplies onto the plane. They were bound for the severely drought-stricken areas outside of the port city of Veracruz. The outlying areas were impoverished, so the goodwill mission would alleviate a severe shortage of critically needed medical supplies.

It took most of the morning to load the cargo, and it was nearly three p.m. before Cass's plane left the runway. They had a stopover in

Juarez, so the flight would take approximately six hours. She would land at the Veracruz airport around nine p.m. that evening.

Twenty minutes into the flight, they were at cruising altitude. Cass leveled the plane and engaged the autopilot, then released her safety belt and pressed the illuminated button to notify the passengers that they were free to move around the cabin. Settling back, she rested her head against the back of the seat and closed her eyes for a moment.

"Are you okay, Captain?" a flight attendant asked, placing her hand on Cass's shoulder and squeezing affectionately.

Cass opened her eyes and looked up at the woman. Ginny was a tall, shapely woman who had a wild mane of blonde hair, blue eyes, and a beautiful smile that showed off deep dimples. She had been part of Cass's flight crew for the past six months, and made no secret of the fact that she found the dark-haired pilot attractive.

Cass smiled. "I'm fine, Ginny. Just a little tired, that's all. Thanks for asking." *That's certainly the truth*, she told herself. *I did lose sleep in the middle of the night.*

Ginny slid her fingers over Cass's shoulder. "Can I get you anything, Captain? Coffee, or a soft drink?"

"Coffee sounds good. Black, please." Cass smiled again.

Hey, Cass, here's your chance; she certainly seems willing, Enforcer urged. *You've got a layover in Juarez. All you need to do is get her alone in the cockpit. Hee, hee, hee. Funny how they call it a cockpit, huh? Must be a reason for it, don't ya think? I'm telling you, girl—you need to get laid. It'll do us both some good. What do you think?*

Cass shook off the enticing thought as she accepted the coffee Ginny handed to her. *There's not exactly enough room, or privacy, in here for that.* She glanced at Brian, her co-pilot. *Maybe when we land in Veracruz.* Cass let her hand linger a little longer than necessary on the one handing her the coffee cup.

Ginny looked down into blue eyes that nearly mirrored her own, and read the promise in them. She smiled nervously, her heart fluttering at the prospect of a sexual encounter with the beautiful Cass Conway. "I, ah... I'd better get back to the passengers." Ginny murmured, and turned to leave the cockpit.

"Thanks, Ginny."

You've still got it, Conway, Enforcer bragged, as Cass watched Ginny's hips sway down the narrow aisle.

Cass sipped her coffee and sighed with deep satisfaction at its rich, full-bodied flavor. *Ah, Ginny, I hope you make love as well as you make coffee.* She took another sip of the flavorful brew.

To her dismay, Cass was caught up in security checks during the layover in Juarez, both on the plane and in the administrator's office at the airport. She had no time to set up a date with Ginny for the night in Veracruz. *I'll have to ask her on the flight to Veracruz,* she thought, as she taxied the plane down the runway for takeoff. The wheels rose gracefully from the runway and the plane made its ascent into the clouds.

Once the plane was at cruising altitude and locked into autopilot, Cass turned the controls over to Brian and went in search of Ginny. She had no success.

"Karen," Cass said as she approached one of the other flight attendants. "Do you know where I might find Ginny?"

"I'm sorry, Cass, I thought the dispatcher told you." At Cass's quirked eyebrow, she continued. "She received an emergency call from her family and had to return to San Jose."

"Thanks. I hope it wasn't anything too serious." Cass's forehead creased in concern for Ginny, and in disappointment for a lost opportunity to share a night of sexual fulfillment.

Damn. I was looking forward to feeling alive again. I hope Ginny's family is okay. She returned to the cockpit.

The flight landed on schedule in Veracruz. After filing her flight log and checking the schedule for unloading her cargo, Cass arranged for lodging. Then, she went in search of something to eat. She was back in her room an hour later, lying across the bed thinking about what might have been. Some time later, worn out by lack of sleep the night before, she drifted off.

* * *

Rox was still in bed early Tuesday morning when Nikki let herself into the house.

"Rox? Rox, where are you?" she called. She had seen her friend's car in the driveway, so she knew Rox was home. "Rox?" Nikki checked the back deck, living room and kitchen before she headed up the stairs. She went directly to Rox's room, which was on the second floor.

"This house is way too big for you, Roxie," Nikki muttered. She turned the handle of the bedroom door, and slowly pushed it open.

She was half hoping that Chris had come home the night before. *I have a fight to pick with that son of a bitch.*

Nikki peered into the quiet room and saw Rox spread out on the bed, alone. She was lying on her stomach, with no shirt on, and the covers were thrown off of her upper body. Her hair masked half of her face and her arms were tucked under the pillow. Nikki tiptoed over to the bed and stood there, looking down at the welts that crisscrossed Rox's back.

"God, that must have been so painful," she whispered, sitting on the edge of the bed next to her friend. A tear of sympathy escaped as she opened the bag she had brought and emptied its contents onto the comforter. From them, Nikki chose a tube of soothing ointment and squeezed a generous amount into her hand. Rubbing her hands together, she climbed onto the bed and straddled Rox's butt, being careful not to touch any of the welts.

Rox began to stir, and Nikki bent over and whispered in her ear. "Shh. It's okay, Roxie. It's just me, Nikki. It's okay, sweetheart."

Rox immediately relaxed as Nikki smoothed the salve over her injured back and gently rubbed it in, moving her hands slowly up and down over the marked expanse. Rox moaned as the salve cooled the heated welts, wincing as Nikki's hands moved over the tender skin.

"Rox, honey, you've got to leave Chris. If you could see your back… God, girl, it rips my heart out to think of how this must have hurt," her friend whispered as she bent low to reach Rox's shoulders.

Rox felt her eyes burn as Nikki's words touched her heart, and tears welled up and spilled over.

When Nikki had covered Rox's entire back, she helped her slip a t-shirt over her shoulders, then lay down next to her on the bed. Gathering the injured woman in her arms, Nikki gently kissed Rox on the temple. "Rox, come home with me. Jerri and I don't want you to be here when Chris comes back."

Rox closed her eyes tightly, which allowed more tears to escape. "Nik, I can't. This is my home, and I won't leave it. I can't," she said in a small voice, burrowing her head deeper into Nikki's shoulder and tightening the arm she had thrown over her friend's midsection.

Nikki nodded. She'd known that would be the response. "We are so afraid for you. Please think about it, love. Okay?" Her concern was evident in her voice. Rox nodded.

"Go back to sleep." Nikki kissed Rox's temple again, then reached down to pull the comforter over both of them.

* * *

Cass awoke in the middle of the forest, an intense feeling of foreboding settling in the pit of her stomach. She sat up and looked around, confused by her surroundings. She drew her knees up and rested her elbows on them, then dropped her head into her hands. After rubbing the sleep out of her eyes, she looked around again. She appeared to be alone, with her only companion a still-smoldering camp fire.

She realized that she was no longer dressed in her flight uniform. Instead, she wore boots, leather trousers, and a muslin shirt with long, billowy sleeves. The shirt was held loosely closed with thin leather laces, and its sleeves came down to wide cuffs at the wrist. A leather vest completed her outfit, and with a wry grin Cass decided that she looked like Errol Flynn in his early pirate movies.

The air was cool, so she collected scraps of wood and branches from around the camp, and rebuilt the fire so she could sit comfortably and think about where she was and how she might have gotten there. As she basked in the warmth radiating from the flames, she heard a distant scream from the forest.

Cass jumped to her feet and ran toward the sound. Soon, she came across two figures struggling. As she neared the cloaked pair, she realized one was a woman, being beaten unmercifully by the larger person.

Jumping into the fray, Cass threw her body weight against the figure assaulting the woman, which knocked all three of them to the ground. The victim collapsed where she had been released, and lay there semiconscious as Cass struggled with her assailant. As they rolled around on the forest floor, Cass managed to land a few good punches on the attacker's chin before she was shoved off onto her back. She rolled out of the way as the man dove toward her, then scrambled to her feet. As the attacker attempted to rise, Cass kicked him full in the face with the side of her foot, sending him crashing to the forest floor in an unconscious heap.

Cass approached the man cautiously. She used her toe to poke him and assure herself that he was out cold. Still cautious, she knelt and rolled him onto his back to see who he was.

As far as she could make out, the man seemed to be relatively good looking, with a muscular build and wild, white-blond hair. He sported red leggings and dark suede boots that laced to his knees, a loose-fitting white shirt much like the one Cass wore, and a leather tunic that slipped over his head and was held together by a leather belt that sat low on his hips.

Cass's inspection of her foe was interrupted by the sound of whimpering. In the excitement of battle, she had forgotten the victim, who lay a few feet away. She used the assailant's own leather belt to tie his hands behind his back, and went to assist the fallen woman. She was lying on her stomach, her hair in wild disarray and her cloak falling in tatters around her shoulders, partially obscuring her face.

Cass reached out to touch the woman's shoulder. When she recoiled in pain, crying out in terror and begging to be left alone, Cass spoke in soothing tones as she carefully removed the cloak. The clothes beneath the cloak were also torn. At first, Cass wondered what could possibly have damaged two layers of cloth like that. Then she realized what had happened, and had to fight to hold the contents of her stomach down. The woman had been whipped.

After carefully removing the rest of the woman's clothing, Cass soaked some of the cloth in a nearby stream and washed the vicious wounds. Having done the best she could with what little she had, she returned to the assailant's still-unconscious form and removed his cloak. She carefully draped the cape over his victim's back, then gently rolled her over, pulling the woman into her arms in the process as carefully as she could. Cass eased the front of the cloak together, and brushed damp hair from the woman's bruised face. The eyes that opened then were the most magnificent emerald green. Cass frowned, then her brows shot skyward as she realized where she had seen those eyes before.

"Rox," she whispered.

A piercing sound pealed through the air.

"Son of a bitch!"

Cass bolted into a sitting position and looked around, realizing that the sound she was hearing was her travel alarm clock. She reached over and shut off the offensive device, then lay back down on the bed.

As she looked up at the ceiling, Cass realized she was soaked in sweat and that her breathing was ragged. She raised a shaky hand to her forehead to push back damp bangs, and tried to make sense of her dream. "Rox, why am I dreaming about you? The forest, the clothes, the time period—what do they mean?"

Closing her eyes, she tried hard to remember the dream. She remembered the forest, the blond attacker, and... "God, the whip marks!" Cass opened her eyes and stared at the ceiling. "Please tell me it was just a dream," she whispered into the air.

Several minutes later, she threw her long legs over the side of the mattress and sat up. Taking a deep breath, she realized that she had fallen asleep in her uniform the night before. "Damn." Standing, she shook off the effects of the nightmare as she removed her clothes and headed to the bathroom for a hot shower.

* * *

Rox felt gentle fingers brushing her hair back from her face. She was half lying, half sitting, in someone's lap, and her back hurt like hell. Her eyes opened, and she looked into a sea of blue. She had an intense feeling of *deja vu* as she looked up at creamy skin, high cheekbones and long, dark hair that framed beautiful features. Rox closed her eyes again, and tried to clear the cobwebs from her mind.

"Rox?" a voice asked.

Her eyes flew open to look straight into Nikki's green eyes.

"Nikki?" She painfully pulled herself into a seated position. Her eyes darted around the room looking for the blue-eyed beauty she had been staring at just moments before.

"Are you all right?" Nikki asked.

Rox looked at her friend. Confusion still clearly written across her features, she nodded her head. "Yeah, yeah, I'm okay. What time is it?"

Nikki glanced at the clock. "It's a little after ten in the morning. You must have been exhausted, to have slept so long." She brushed back Rox's hair. "Here, let's get this t-shirt off so I can rub some more salve into those welts."

Lying face down on the bed, Rox allowed her friend to minister to her wounds. Nikki noted the uncharacteristically taciturn compliance. "Want to talk about it?"

Roxanne shrugged her shoulders. "Not much to say, Nik."

"Why do I get the feeling that this is not about Chris?"

Rox lifted her head and looked back at Nikki. "Am I that transparent?"

"No, not really. It's just that you looked pretty confused when you opened your eyes a few moments ago. If you want to talk about it, I'm here to listen."

Roxanne allowed Nikki to finish rubbing the salve in before she sat up and put her t-shirt back on. Sitting cross-legged on the bed, she faced her friend and took a deep breath. "Nikki, do you believe in dreams?"

"You mean, do I think dreams have meaning?"

Rox nodded.

Nikki drew her knees to her chest and wrapped her arms around them. "Gee, I don't know. I've never had a dream that's come true, but that doesn't mean it can't happen. Why, Rox? What were you dreaming about?"

A little embarrassed, Rox looked down at the comforter then glanced back at her friend. "I've dreamed, twice now, about a beautiful, blue-eyed, dark-haired woman. Different dreams, but the same woman. I don't know what it means."

Concerned, Nikki placed a hand on Rox's arm. "I don't know either, but I hope to God you don't have that dream when Chris is around. This whipping will look like a slap on the hand in comparison. Rox, Jerri and I really do want you to come and stay with us for a while."

"I can't, Nikki. Please try to understand."

Nikki pulled her hand back. "No, Rox, I will never understand. Look, I know that you're doing this for your father's sake. You want him to believe you live an ideal, fairy-tale life, but you're killing yourself in the process. Can't you see that? Sweetheart, I don't want you to become a statistic. Please come home with me."

Rox remained mute, her eyes fixed on the comforter.

Nikki sighed. "All right," she said. "I can't force you." There was a slight pause, then: "At least promise me you'll call the moment things start turning sour. Don't let them get out of hand again, please. Jerri and I will be here before you have a chance to hang up the phone. Okay? Please, promise me that."

Rox was crying, tears falling into her lap as she nodded her agreement. Nikki leaned in and wrapped her arms around Rox's neck, rested her cheek on her friend's head, and held her as she cried.

Moments later, Rox broke the embrace and sat up straight, wiping her eyes. She took a deep breath. "Nikki, I really have to get to work. I have a deadline to meet for this next book. Why don't you go home and spend some time with that wonderful wife of yours before she has to go to work tonight? I'll be all right, I promise."

Nikki took Rox's bruised face in both her hands, and drew her in for a kiss. Touching her forehead to her friend's, she said, "Promise you'll call if you need me, Rox."

Rox kissed Nikki on the nose. "I promise," she whispered.

"Okay, then." Nikki released her friend and stood to go. They walked arm in arm into the hallway, then parted company at the stairs to the attic. "I'll let myself out, Rox. Remember your promise, okay?"

"I'll remember."

After one last hug, Nikki set off on her way home and Rox went up to her workroom and booted up her computer.

Chapter 8

"Okay, let's get the e-mail out of the way before we get to work, Gerald," Rox said to her giraffe friend as she clicked on the "Get Messages" icon. "Huh. Five messages—one old and four new. Damn, that's right; I never answered Cass's last note. I hope he doesn't think I'm rude," she muttered as she opened the message and re-read it.

Afterward, Rox sat staring at the screen and debating just how honest she should be with this person. *Should I bare all and confess to living a life of pure hell? Should I confess that my last two books were based on my fatalistic certainty that I'm destined to form impossibly doomed relationships?*

She decided to compromise.

Hi again, Cass.

Your job sounds very interesting. I hear Mexico and Central America are beautiful. Do you get a chance to do any sightseeing, or do you just fly in and out? Someday I would like to travel, to see the world and to experience the beauty the Earth has to offer. You are very fortunate to have that opportunity.

I live in the town of Rockland, Maine, and yes, my home sits directly on the ocean. I love the ocean, and like you, I especially love it during a storm.

Thank you for the compliments on my work and my appearance. I'm afraid that circumstances don't always allow me to look as attractive as that picture might suggest. Also, I'm glad you weren't disappointed by the story. It was written during a time of traumatic upheaval in my life, and quite frankly, I'm surprised it turned out as well as it did. I'm currently engaged in writing another science fiction story, which also has a romantic theme. I'm afraid this one will be equally difficult to write.

Sometimes my writing provides an escape from reality, into a world where truly loving and dedicated relationships exist, and where love is so intense and so real that it becomes tangible; a world where people never hurt the ones they profess to love. It's a pity that print doesn't always emulate life, Cass. If you ever meet the woman of your dreams, reach out and grab her, treat her like a queen, and don't ever let her go. She will love you forever for it.

Look at me, philosophizing. I'm certainly in no position to give advice on love, and writing love stories certainly doesn't make me an expert on relationships. Forgive me for overstepping my bounds.

Well, you are probably very busy, and I have a book to write, so I will say 'adios' for now.

Sincerely,

Rox

"There, that's one down and four to go." Rox sent the message and opened the next one. She finished with the rest of the e-mail, and settled in to write. As usual, she became totally absorbed in her latest alien adventure and wrote well into the day, stopping only for coffee and for calls of nature.

Day faded into twilight, and Rox decided to take a short break. Storm clouds had been brewing all day, and the sky outside her lookout was filled with dark, heavy clouds. Rox could feel the excitement of the pending storm building in her chest as she shut off the lights in her office and threw the French doors wide open, allowing the wind to sweep in and swirl around her.

She stepped out onto the balcony overlooking the ocean, walked up to the railing and threw her arms open wide. She closed her eyes, raised her face to the sky and smiled, inhaling the salty scent of the sea as the wind whipped her hair. Suddenly, a clap of thunder loud enough to shake the entire house ripped through the night. Rox gasped, and then let out a guttural scream from the recesses of her soul as lightning lit up everything in sight. Her skin tingled and her hair seemed to stand on end from the static charge. Torrential rains followed the thunder, drenching her to the skin as she stood, smiling broadly, her arms still spread to the elements. Her chest was filled with such exhilaration that she thought she'd burst.

The sensation of rain pounding against her tender skin, the claps of thunder vibrating through her very being, the electric crackle of lightning—all served to heighten the intensity of the experience. Rox's emotions reached such a fever pitch that she was gripped by an almost orgasmic climax, in which she released the pain and humiliation she had suffered the previous day at Chris's hands.

Rox knew that the intensity of emotion she had just gone through would enable her to write far into the night. Sometimes, the energy generated by a storm was enough to fuel her through several days of nonstop writing. She screamed again as thunder crashed and lightning danced across the sky. It would be a good night for writing.

* * *

"This is your captain speaking. We are currently entering a region of extreme turbulence, so please return to your seats and fasten your seatbelts securely. Remain in your seats with your seatbelts fastened until the seatbelt sign is turned off. Thank you." Cass recited the cautionary words over the intercom as she maneuvered the plane through the storm.

"I hate flying in storms," she complained to her co-pilot.

"I know what you mean," Brian replied. "Have you ever flown a plane that was hit by lightning?"

"Oh, yeah. The last time it happened, the static electricity made my hair stand on end. Fortunately, none of the plane's vital operating systems were affected. I wouldn't want to fly a crippled plane through a storm like this," Cass replied.

"I hear you."

Cass sighed. The storm was just the culmination of a day that had gone wrong since the beginning. After waking up from that strange dream, she'd arrived at the Veracruz airport to discover that the grounds crew had staged an impromptu strike, protesting long hours and low pay. The last thing Cass wanted was to be held over in Mexico because of a labor dispute. She was not very good at the waiting game, so she was chomping at the bit by the time airport officials arrived at a temporary settlement with the workers. As evening drew near, her plane was finally loaded and fueled for the long flight home. Then, to her increased annoyance, the weather forecast indicated storm conditions directly in her flight path.

The storm forced Cass to reduce speed, so the flight was nearly 90 minutes late. It was ten p.m. before she finally stepped through the front door of her condo and dropped into the nearest chair. Resting her head against the cushion, she sighed deeply, glad to be home. She kicked off her shoes, loosened her necktie, and released the top few buttons of her dress shirt.

Thank God I have tomorrow off, so I have the luxury of sleeping in. After being away from home for nearly two days, that will sure feel good.

Cass closed her eyes and thought again of the dream that had jolted her awake that morning. She felt slightly ill when she recalled the whip marks on the woman's back, especially since the woman was a dead ringer for Rox. She shook her head. *My imagination is working overtime; I'm sure there's nothing to worry about. Besides, except for a couple of e-mails, I don't even know Rox. Darned subconscious is playing games.*

Her thoughts didn't stop Cass from switching on her computer to see if Rox had replied to her message. She watched the screen intently, and the logon process seemed to take longer than usual. Finally, a message appeared on the screen: "Failed to make connection. Try again later."

"Goddamned son of a bitch!" Cass screamed. "Frickin' technology! Can't even connect to the Internet without an act of Congress." She slammed her hand on the desk, then shook her fist at the monitor. "I'm gonna take a shower. If you don't work by the time I come back, you're out the fucking window, understand?" The monitor remained blank, mutely defiant, as Cass stomped off.

Luckily for the computer, the program connected fairly quickly when the freshly showered Cass sat in front of it. "That's better," Cass mumbled, and her attitude improved even further as her inbox came up and displayed one new message… from Rox@Starship.com.

Cass was suddenly very nervous. *Get a grip, Cass. She's just a chick who lives three thousand miles away. You're acting like a schoolgirl, here. Christ, grow up, will you?* As Enforcer scolded, Cass gathered the courage to open the note.

> *Hi again, Cass.*
>
> *Your job sounds very interesting. I hear Mexico and Central America are beautiful. Do you get a chance to do any sightseeing, or do you just fly in and out? Someday I would like to travel, to see the world and to experience the beauty the Earth has to offer. You are very fortunate to have that opportunity.*

I live in the town of Rockland, Maine, and yes, my home sits directly on the ocean. I love the ocean, and like you, I especially love it during a storm.

Thank you for the compliments on my work and my appearance. I'm afraid that circumstances don't always allow me to look as attractive as that picture might suggest. Also, I'm glad you weren't disappointed by the story. It was written during a time of traumatic upheaval in my life, and quite frankly, I'm surprised it turned out as well as it did. I'm currently engaged in writing another science fiction story, which also has a romantic theme. I'm afraid this one will be equally difficult to write.

Sometimes my writing provides an escape from reality, into a world where truly loving and dedicated relationships exist, and where love is so intense and so real that it becomes tangible; a world where people never hurt the ones they profess to love. It's a pity that print doesn't always emulate life, Cass. If you ever meet the woman of your dreams, reach out and grab her, treat her like a queen, and don't ever let her go. She will love you forever for it.

Look at me, philosophizing. I'm certainly in no position to give advice on love, and writing love stories certainly doesn't make me an expert on relationships. Forgive me for overstepping my bounds.

Well, you are probably very busy, and I have a book to write, so I will say 'adios' for now.

Sincerely,
Rox

"Oh, my God," Cass whispered. She re-read Rox's words.

What is it, Cass? Enforcer asked, feeling Cass's gut-wrenching reaction to Rox's note.

I'm not sure. Something isn't right here. She's in trouble. I can feel it.

What the hell do you mean, she's in trouble? How can you tell that from a frickin' note?

Look, E.! She says her life is in an "upheaval." She writes about fantasy worlds where everyone is loving and gentle and kind, and then says that "it's a pity that print doesn't always emulate life." Can't you see it?

Be careful, Cass, this dame could be trouble. Be afraid... be very afraid. Remember what happened with Patti. Take this one slow and easy, pal, okay?

Cass nodded as she read the note yet again. *Okay. Now, what to write back?*

For several minutes, Cass paced back and forth in front of the computer. What was it about Roxanne Ward that had her so worked up? She didn't even know the woman. Why was she so concerned about the well-being of a person she didn't even know? Why this overwhelming need to communicate with the woman? Cass didn't know, but the need was real... as real as the loneliness that fed it. She resumed her seat, and decided to be up front and honest.

> *Hi, Rox.*
>
> *I must say that I'm a bit concerned by your last reply. You seem troubled, or maybe depressed. Call me paranoid, since I've never met you, but I sense that you're troubled by something... or someone. If you'd like to talk, I'd be glad to listen -- I'm a good listener. I don't want to intrude on your life; I just thought maybe you could use a friendly ear.*
>
> *Please don't be angry with me for expressing my concern. If you'd rather not discuss it, just let me know and I'll never bring it up again. I will continue to be an avid fan of your writing, and of your beauty, regardless.*
>
> *I am here to help if you need me.*
> *Yours always,*
> *Cass*

Cass hit "Send," then re-read Rox's note several times. Each time, she felt an underlying sense of sadness, of desperation. She hoped she'd done the right thing by offering a friendly ear. Just as she was about to start the shutdown process, the new mail indicator flashed on the lower right-hand corner of the screen.

* * *

Rox had come in from the storm drenched to the skin, but on an emotional high that she knew would carry her through the night. She made her way down one flight of stairs, stripped off her clothes and jumped into the shower, wincing as the spray stung her tender back.

After finishing her shower, she donned a clean nightshirt and returned to her office to resume writing.

At nearly one a.m., she decided to take a much-needed break. Standing, Rox stretched her body as much as her bruises would allow. She heard her back crack in several places as she clasped her hands behind her and pulled them up and backward. After shaking out the kinks, she went to the corner kitchenette and made a cup of hot chocolate. She carried it over to the computer and set it down next to the keyboard, then sat down to resume writing. As her hands hovered over the keys, she noticed the exclamation point next to the tiny envelope in the bottom right corner of her screen. She had mail.

"Who would be sending mail this late in the evening, Gerald?" A puzzled expression on her face, Rox clicked on the icon. She watched with interest as a message from CConway@Flyboy.com appeared in the inbox. *That was fast*, Rox thought. She hadn't expected a reply until the next day. She opened the note, read the text and immediately went into panic mode.

Oh, my God! I didn't expect him to pick up on my distress like that. Now what do I do? She pushed herself away from the computer and started to pace. *What do I do? What do I do?* Her mind kept repeating. *Okay, Rox, calm down. It's only a concerned reader. So you gave a little more away in that last note than you intended. So what? So the guy wants to help. He's probably lonely and sees you as someone he can talk to from a safe distance. What can it hurt?*

Rox read the message again and made a hasty decision as she resumed her seat.

* * *

Cass stared at the new mail indicator for several moments before clicking on it and refreshing her inbox. There on the screen appeared the address Rox@Starship.com.

"Huh? I just e-mailed her."

Cass was thoroughly surprised that she had received a reply so quickly. She hesitated to open it, afraid it would be a "Dear John" letter of some sort, and would ask her to end her correspondence with the author. Finally, she built up the courage to open the note, and read:

Hi, Cass… Do you have time to meet me in chat?

Chapter 9

Cass sat staring at the message. *Chat? She wants to meet me in chat?* Her stomach felt queasy. *Oh, my God, I didn't expect this. Okay, Cass… it's just chat. Stop being such a baby.* She sent a reply:

Hi, Rox
> *I didn't expect a reply so soon. Sure, I'd love to chat. Name the place and I'll be there.*

Moments later, the new mail message flashed again.

Cass:
> *Go to this url: www.alienchat.com. I'll meet you there in a jiff.*

With shaking hands, Cass entered the chat room and logged in as "Flyboy." *Come on, Rox. Damn, I'm nervous.* Trying to be patient, she waited for the author to enter the room.

Within moments, the name "Alien" appeared on the screen.

"Rox?" Cass typed.

"Hi, Cass," came the reply.

"Hi, yourself," Cass returned nervously, her heart beating furiously.

"How are you?" Rox asked.

"Fine, and you?" Cass felt really stupid typing the polite, nerdy responses.

"I've been better," Rox typed.

"I sensed that from your last e-mail," Cass commented. *"Are you all right?"*

"For the time being," came the vague reply.

"Look, I know you don't know me, but I'm a really good listener if you want to talk about it." When there was no response, Cass typed, *"Rox?"*

Several moments later, Rox replied, *"Cass, I'm having a bit of a problem right now that I need to work through, that's all."*

"Is there anything I can do to help?" Cass asked.

"No, not really. It's kind of complicated. Let's just say that it's a situation I have to live with for a while," came Rox's reply.

"Well, if you need someone to talk to, you have my address."

"Thanks, Cass, I really appreciate it," Rox said.

"So you're working on a new book, huh?" Cass asked, changing the subject.

The sigh of relief was almost evident in Rox's words as she typed, *"Yes, and I'm making pretty good headway. I had a bit of a setback due to an injury, but things are moving forward steadily now."*

Cass frowned at the mention of an injury, but didn't pursue the matter.

"I'm always curious about how people get started in their careers. Want to share?"

"I've always loved to write. I started by enrolling in creative writing and poetry classes in high school. Pretty soon, I was the editor of the high school yearbook. I was also involved with the campus newspaper in college, where I majored in Journalism," Rox supplied.

"Did you start writing as soon as you graduated from college?"

"Not exactly," Rox began. *"I actually moved to Portland and landed a job as a copywriter in the local newspaper office. It was an okay job, but I felt stifled, so I quit and moved back in with my parents. Living at home when you're 24 years old isn't much fun, but it gave me the financial freedom to write without having to worry about paying the bills."*

Cass smiled. *"Can't beat that. Was* Starflight *your first book?"*

"Yes, it was. I guess I got lucky. It made it to the top of the Sci-Fi best-seller list within months of being published."

"Luck had nothing to do with it. If Starflight *is as good as the* Stargazer *series, it's got to be a great book,"* Cass insisted. *"I can't wait to read it. I'm awestruck at how well you're able to combine science fiction and romance."*

For the next hour, Cass and Rox chatted about recent science fiction novels and their lack of romance. At the end of that time, Cass was truly captivated by this woman, whom she knew only in print. She was bright, intelligent, kind and warm-hearted, and had a bubbly, outgoing personality.

Rox felt giddy inside. She tried to analyze the feeling several times during the chat session, and wondered why this person had captivated her so quickly. After all, she had only exchanged a few e-mails with him, but he seemed bright, intelligent, kind and warm-hearted—traits she had seldom seen in the men she had associated with in the past.

Rox yawned. She realized that it was nearly two a.m., and steered the conversation toward an end.

"Well, Cass. I must say I've enjoyed your company, but the hour is late, and I really must get some sleep if I plan to be productive tomorrow," she typed.

Cass looked over at the clock and was shocked to see that it was eleven p.m. *Jesus, it's two a.m. where she is.* She typed, *"Rox, I am so sorry! I didn't realize it was so late. This three-hour time difference can certainly fool you. I'd better let you go so you can get to bed. I really enjoyed our chat. I'd like to do it again sometime, if you have time."*

"I'd like that, Cass. Until later, then. Good night," Rox typed.

"Good night, Rox."

Cass watched the monitor as the words "Alien has left the chat room" appeared on the screen. Sighing deeply, she shut down her computer and sat back in her chair. She picked up *Stargazer II* from her desk, turned it over and looked at the picture. A smile came to her lips as she savored the warm feeling she had from spending the past hour with this beautiful woman.

Rox logged out of chat and returned to her manuscript. It was difficult to concentrate, so she picked up her cup and walked out onto the widow's walk and leaned against the railing. The storm had ended. The night was now cool, but clear, and the stars seemed to hang so low in the sky that she could almost touch them. Looking out over the dark ocean, she sipped her drink and savored the warm feeling she had from spending the past hour with her new friend.

* * *

Wednesday morning, the sun shone through the open shade and onto Cass's face. The heat from its rays woke the sleeping woman. She opened her eyes, looked at the clock, and groaned. "Seven a.m.?" She was scheduled for another two-day trip into Mexico, starting Thursday, and she'd really been looking forward to sleeping in. "Why can't I ever sleep late on a day off?"

As she lay in bed, Cass's thoughts soon turned to the chat session from the previous night. She couldn't keep the smile from her face as memories of her conversation with the author filled her mind. *God, that woman is something else—beautiful, intelligent, beautiful, intuitive, beautiful, informed, beautiful.*

Her grin widened and a warm feeling spread through her stomach. Her eyes widened at the sensation. *Wow! I haven't felt that... I mean,* really *felt that since... well, since Patti.*

Cass stretched her arms over her head and arched her back into the mattress, her breasts thrusting toward the ceiling as a whimper of satisfaction escaped her throat. After climbing out of bed, she donned her running clothes and headed out for her usual five-mile trek. At its end, she arrived at Angie's for breakfast.

Cass walked into the diner, threw her arms around Angie, and gave the older woman a big hug.

Angie was taken aback by the overt gesture, and looked into Cass's face questioningly.

"What?" Cass asked mischievously, looking for all the world like a child anxious to share a secret.

"What are you up to, Cassidy Conway? You look like the cat that ate the canary,"

Cass smiled broadly. "Now, that's one canary I would definitely like to eat." She blushed at her own brashness.

Way to go, Cass! I like the way you think, Enforcer cheered.

Angie noticed the blush as she walked the younger woman to her usual table, and chuckled. "New lady friend, Cass?"

Cass sat down and held the menu in front of her face to hide her continuing blush.

Angie wasn't deterred. She pulled the menu down and leaned over in Cass's face. "You know I won't go away until you 'fess up."

Cass was trying to repress her excitement; she was dying to tell someone about Rox. She grinned, and leaned in to meet Angie nose to nose. "Coffee first, gossip second." She sat back and held her cup up to the waitress.

Angie grabbed the cup. "Be right back." She hurried off, and came back with two cups of coffee. She sat down, and slid one cup over to Cass.

Cass took her time stirring, and then tasting the flavorful brew.

The waitress was bursting with anticipation. "Caaaaassssss," she said menacingly.

Finally, feeling sorry for her friend, Cass gave in. "Rox."

Angie's brow furrowed. "Rocks? What do rocks have to do with anything?" she asked, confused.

Cass threw her head back and laughed. "No, no. Rox, as in 'Roxanne.'" She placed a large hand over Angie's.

"Roxanne," Angie stated flatly. "Roxanne... who? Come on, Cass. A little more information would be good."

"Angie, *Stargazer*? You know—Roxanne Ward?"

"Roxanne Ward, the writer?" Angie's mouth dropped open. Seeing Cass grin and nod her head, she added, "Just how did you meet *her*?"

"Well, I haven't actually *met* her yet, Ang. We've traded e-mail a few times, and last night we talked for an hour in chat."

Angie's eyebrows went up. "What kind of relationship is that?"

Cass smiled. "A safe one. Don't you see, we get a chance to know each other a little better before we meet face to face. It's perfect." She took another sip of coffee.

"Weird, is what it is," Angie exclaimed. "Cass, whatever happened to boy meets... er, sorry. Girl meets girl, girls get to know each other, girls falls in love? You know, the old-fashioned way to meet your mate."

"Progress, Ang, progress." Cass's stomach rumbled, and she gave Angie a slightly embarrassed look.

"I guess I'd better *progress* my butt into the kitchen and feed that beast, huh? How about the special this morning?"

Cass glanced over at the Specials board and saw French toast, sausage and home fries listed. "Sounds good to me," she said, which sent Angie on her way.

Cass crossed her long legs under the table, picked up her coffee cup and brought it to her lips. *I wonder what you're doing right now, Roxanne Ward.*

* * *

Rox carefully rolled onto her side to look at the clock. *Eleven-thirty a.m. Geez, half the day's gone already,* she admonished herself. *Rox, why do you do it? You get to bed in the wee hours of the morning, then sleep half the day away.*

She rolled onto her back and tried to remember what had kept her up so late. A sudden smile flitted across her face. *Cass,* she thought. *Wow! I can't believe we spent an entire hour talking like we were long-lost friends. He really seems like a nice guy. I wonder what he looks like?*

A few minutes later, she climbed out of bed and padded gingerly to the bathroom to take care of morning necessities before heading to her office. *Damn, I can't believe I'm still so sore. Nikki's right—I really need to do something about Chris.*

Rox pressed the power button on her hard drive to boot up the computer. While it powered up, she set a pot of coffee to brew and took a container of fat-free yogurt from the refrigerator. She stood in front of the computer eating, and wondered what Cass would think if he could see her now. She was sure she looked a sight, with her hair standing on end and a collection of blue, purple and green bruises covering her face and body. She could only imagine what her back looked like after the other night's whipping.

When the coffee was done, Rox poured herself a cup and logged on to the Internet. After accessing her mail program, she started composing.

> *Hi, Cass.*
>
> *I wanted to drop you a line to say that I really enjoyed our chat last night. It's been a long time since I had such an interesting discussion about my work. My typical audience isn't usually interested in such things. I would very much like to chat with you again some time.*
>
> *BTW, you have an advantage -- you know what I look like, but I am at a loss. Want to share?*
>
> *Drop me a line and let me know when it's convenient for you to chat again. I work from home, so nearly any time is okay for me.*
>
> *I'll talk to you later.*
>
> *Rox*

While she was rereading the message, she heard a voice call to her from below. "In the office, Nikki," she yelled back.

Moments later, the small blonde appeared at her left shoulder, out of breath from climbing two flights of stairs.

Rox looked at her friend. "You know, you really need to go to the gym. You're out of shape, girl. Although the way you and Jerri go at it all the time, you shouldn't need exercise!" she teased.

Nikki swatted her on the shoulder, which made Rox wince.

"Ooohhh, sorry, Rox! I forgot about the bruises. Sorry." She looked over her friend's shoulder at the computer screen. "Cass?" she asked. "Who's that?"

Rox looked up at her friend and blushed. "A new e-mail friend. We've been trading notes for about a week now and met in chat last night. He seems like a very intelligent person."

Nikki placed two fingers under her friend's chin. "You look pretty in pink, Rox," she said. "You must like this guy. I haven't seen you blush like this since you first met Chris." Nikki looked at the screen again. "By the looks of it, you're planning on 'seeing' him again," she said, her tone cautious.

Rox's eyes went to her note, which was still on the screen. "Yeah, I guess I am," she admitted, smiling.

Turning her friend to face her, Nikki looked into green eyes. "Rox, you know if Chris finds out about this, you're in big trouble. The whip marks on your back will feel like mosquito bites compared to what would happen then."

Rox became serious. "I know, Nik. That's why Chris can't ever know, okay?"

"I'll take it to my grave. You know that, don't you?"

In response, Rox just nodded and hugged her friend.

Nikki pushed the bangs off Rox's forehead and brushed her palm against her friend's cheek. "Okay, so tell me about Cass."

"There's not much to tell. We've only chatted once, and we spent most of the time talking about my writing. I didn't even get a chance to ask him what he looks like. The only thing I know for sure is that he's a pilot. See, his user ID is CConway@Flyboy.com. Oh, and I know that he flies mostly into Mexico and Central America."

"Well, that's certainly enough to base a relationship on," was Nikki's sarcastic comment.

It was Rox's turn to swat her friend on the shoulder. "Nikki! No one said anything about starting a relationship. At this point, we're just friends."

"Just friends—that's what you said about Chris, two years ago."

Chapter 10

It was early afternoon before Rox could talk Nikki into going home so that she could get some writing done. They didn't know when Chris was coming home, and Nikki didn't want Rox to be in the house alone when the bastard came back.

At last, Nikki left. She went straight home, then called Jerri to fill her in on the Cass situation. She waited patiently as the ER nurse located her partner, and Jerri finally answered the phone.

"Hello, this is Jerri Lockwood."

"Hi, hon! I just came from Rox's, and boy, have I got some news for you! It seems that she's met a new friend on-line. The guy's name is Cass, and she's been trading e-mails with him for a few days now."

Jerri was surprised. "Are you serious? Did she tell you anything about him?"

"Not much, except that he's a pilot."

"I don't know about this, Nik. I hope this guy is being straight with her."

"Me too, Jer. Me too. He's got to be better than Chris. Hell, *anyone* would be better than Chris. Speaking of him, he's due back soon. I'm really afraid she'll be alone when he gets home, Jerri, but I don't know what to do about it. She's so damned stubborn! She absolutely refused to stay with us and have him arrested."

Jerri thought for a moment before replying. "Sweetheart, call Rox and invite her to dinner tonight. We'll keep her out late. If Chris does come home today, maybe the jerk will be sleeping by the time she gets there."

"Jerri, my love, I knew there was a reason to keep you around." Nikki smiled against the receiver. "Well, that and other things," she added coyly.

"Yeah? Well, you can demonstrate those 'other things' when I get home tonight, okay?"

"Are you sure you want to keep Rox out late? I mean, it might eat into some of our quality time together," Nikki said suggestively.

"There's only one thing I want to eat into tonight, short stuff, and you know what it is," her partner teased.

"You are such a pig."

"Oink!" was the immediate reply. "Look, we'll keep Rox out till a respectable-but-late hour, then we'll drive her home and make sure the house is safe before she goes in. Okay?"

"Respectable hour. Right. Okay, Jer. I love you, sweetheart. Hurry home, okay? Maybe we can have appetizers before dinner," Nikki's sultry voice left no doubt as to what she meant.

After hanging up, Nikki sent an e-mail to Rox.

Hey, Girl.
Are you free for dinner tonight? I just spoke with Miss Gorgeous and she suggested I invite you over.
Let me know, okay?
Love ya!
N

* * *

Rox made significant progress on her story before taking a coffee break late in the afternoon. As was her habit, she carried her coffee out onto the back deck and sat in the glider to look out over the ocean as she drank. She loved to spend time here, where the only sounds were crashing surf and seagull cries. Her journal entries and most recent novel had their origins here, and it was here that the sparks of romance between her alien lovers had blossomed into a raging fire. The atmosphere inspired her creativity. It was part of what she loved about her home.

A gamut of emotions running through her, Rox sat staring at the ocean long after she had seen the bottom of her coffee cup. She felt trapped, caught in a relationship that was cruel and controlling. She didn't love Chris any more, not since the beatings began, six months ago. At about that time, Rox began to suspect that Chris was having an affair. Perhaps the abuse was his way of soothing his guilt, of transferring the blame to her. Rox didn't really care. She had threatened to leave the relationship many times, but Chris would always dwell on how their separation would break her father's heart. Rox couldn't do that. She loved her parents deeply, and would make her father's last few months as happy as she could, even if her personal life became a nightmare.

Heaving a deep sigh, Rox wiped a tear from the corner of her eye. She rose stiffly from the glider and headed back to work, refilling her coffee cup on the way. As she sat down at her computer, Rox decided to check her e-mail before beginning to write. She had two new messages—an advertisement from her local server, and one from Nikki. She clicked on Nikki's note and read it quickly.

Dinner, huh? Sounds good to me. I haven't seen Jerri in a while, so it should be a good visit. She clicked on "Reply."

Hey, Nik,

I'd love to come to dinner, but are you sure you two can tear yourselves away from each other long enough to entertain a visitor? After all, my little mattress queen, you and the big guy have the most active libidos in Maine! You two spend more time in each other's personal space than outside of it. Hell, nearly every time I call you, you're in the middle of playtime. Enough is enough! No more playtime for you until you find someone for me to love like that.

Let me know what time.

Love ya back,

R

Roxanne clicked on "Send," then sat back to see if Nikki was monitoring her mail. Sure enough, a reply appeared. Rox grinned as she read her friend's response.

Roxanne Ward, you are almost as bad as my wife. If I told you what she said to me earlier, I bet I'd see you blush right over the phone. So, Big Guy and Mattress Queen, huh? Do I sense some jealousy here?

Dinner's at 6 p.m. Jerri will pick you up around 5:30 p.m., on her way home from work.

See you then,

N

Rox couldn't resist. As straightforward as Nikki could be, she still blushed easily when confronted with her hyper-active sex life. Clicking on "Reply" again, she wrote:

Hi again, Nik!

Oh, yeah... Big Guy and Mattress Queen. I like it. BG and MQ for short. Hey! Maybe I can write a comic strip about the two of you. No, no... better yet, I'll write a full-length novel. Yeah, that's what I'll do. MQ can walk around with a self-inflating mattress in her pocket. Whenever she gets the urge (say, a minimum of 10 times a day), she just whips out the mattress, pulls a cord and poof! Instant playground. Of course, BG would have to be available and ready at a moment's notice, but somehow I don't think that'll be a problem. And no toys with pointy edges, don't want to pop the playground.

BG could carry a pager, so she'd know when MQ was 'wanting her woman'. No, wait, I have a better idea. BG could have super hearing, like Supergirl or the Bionic Woman or someone. Then she could hear MQ pull the ripcord and know exactly when she was needed. Oh, oh! Another good idea—maybe BG could even blink herself places. You know, like in I Dream of Jeannie. Cool idea, huh? Then, as soon as she hears the ripcord, she could just blink and whammo... she's jumping MQ's bones in an instant! That'll save BG some time trying to find a phone to call the little hussy.

Now, let me see... BG needs a costume. Supergirl, Wonder Woman... nah, those costumes are too dorky... Hey! What about a skimpy little dominatrix outfit, instead?? That would be cool. Yeah, yeah... I can see it now: a leather bikini with a skimpy halter top that just barely covers the essentials, high-heeled boots that go halfway up her thighs, whip, spiked dog collar, leather wrist bands... chains all over the place. Shit... one look at her and ziiiippp... it wouldn't take more than that for MQ to pull that ripcord. Oh, boy... this will definitely make the best seller list!

So, tell me, Nik—which one of you wants to be the alien?
R

Rox sat back and chuckled to herself as she waited for her friend's reply. It didn't take long.

Jesus, Rox, what have you been smoking? Whatever it is, save some for me, huh? This is hysterical. Wait until Jer sees it! Shit, woman, I am red to the roots of my hair right now, but—Wow! What an imagination you have, my friend.

Seeing as BG has the super powers (hearing, blinking), then she should be the alien. I'll let her know when she comes home. Just do me one favor -- when you write this story, make sure BG has REALLY long tentacles, okay?

Jeeeeesus Chrrrrrist! I can't believe I just wrote that! I'm becoming an evil, corrupt little hussy, aren't I? Must be the influence of a certain GIRLFRIEND of mine. :-)

I'm going to log off now before I get myself into MORE trouble! Jerri will pick you up around 5:30 p.m., okay?

We're having lobster, so bring a bib. Oh, and bring the salve with you. I'll rub it into your bruises again while you're here.

I'll see you in a few.

Love you,

Nikki

Rox smiled at her friend's reply. *Nikki certainly is a study in contrasts,* she thought. *One moment she's all fire and passion, the next she's blushing like a schoolgirl. That's why I love her.* Rox logged off e-mail and returned to her writing.

* * *

It was nearly noon by the time Cass left Angie's diner. After eating a leisurely breakfast, she hung around and visited with the older woman for over an hour. She simply didn't want to be alone, so returning to her empty condo was not appealing. When she had worn out her welcome by keeping Angie from her customers, she headed to the gym to work out and get in some Tae Kwon Do practice. She had taken martial arts instruction for the last three years. After Patti, she never wanted to be defenseless again. Cass was an apt pupil, and had earned her first-degree black belt a few months earlier.

Cass loved the physical catharsis of working out. Her gym was located in the heart of San Jose, and was open 24 hours to cater to Silicon Valley clients who worked odd shifts. She had spent many a night there, escaping nightmarish memories and working off her nervous energy until she was tired enough to sleep. Her job required her to be alert, so the gym was a godsend, allowing her to get the sleep she needed to be fresh for her next flight.

She spent a couple of hours working out on the Nautilus machines that afternoon, enhancing her already toned muscles. In times like these, Cass could understand Patti's preoccupation with weight lifting. Her workout gave her such a sense of euphoria that she pushed her body further by running through her Tae Kwon Do forms. By the time she had finished, her workout clothes were drenched with sweat and her bangs were plastered to her forehead.

As she left the gym, she ran into a man she had met a few years earlier.

"Hi, Cass," he said. "Looks like you've had quite a workout."

Cass smiled. "Good to see you, Jason." She shook his hand and then wiped her forehead with her gym towel. "Where have you been? I haven't seen you around the gym lately."

"Oh, I've been around. Still flying?"

"Yeah. I'm working for Southern Lights Airline now. No real complaints," Cass answered.

"Southern Lights? Where do they fly?" asked Jason.

"Mostly on the West Coast, some Midwest locations, and into Central America. That's my normal route," Cass explained.

"Central America? Wow, that must be interesting. Why there?"

Cass ran the towel over her neck. "Well, I'm fluent in Spanish, and the flight schedule keeps me home on weekends, and I get an occasional day off during the week, like today," she said, grinning.

"Sounds like you've got it made," Jason replied. "Hey, um… would you be interested in dinner?"

Cass raised her eyebrows. Jason knew that she and Patti had been a couple.

Seeing the silent question, Jason clarified. "Oh! Oh, no, Cass. I'm sorry. All I want is dinner. Just between friends, okay?"

Cass immediately relaxed and smiled. "I'm sorry, Jason. I'm afraid I haven't gotten out much since… well, you know. Anyway, dinner sounds great. Can I meet you somewhere?"

"Why don't I pick you up at your place? Say, six o'clock?"

"Okay. I'm in the Hillside Condos, Unit 3, on Maycoumber Parkway. I'll see you at six," Cass said, heading to the door.

"At six," Jason replied, as he watched her retreating form.

The desk attendant looked at Jason with a smirk. "You don't have a chance with her, you know. You won't get within two feet of that gorgeous body."

Jason looked at the man. "It's not her body I'm interested in." He was grinning as he headed to the weight room.

* * *

Cass arrived at her condo around three p.m. and headed straight for the shower. Her body heavy with the fatigue of her extensive workout, she stood under the needle spray. She had overdone it again.

Cassidy Conway, when are you going to learn that you can't replace sex with exercise? Enforcer scolded. *Damn it, girl, you do this every time. Now you'll walk around for the next several days so sore that you can't move. Shit, woman, a little sheet action is what you need. That guy you've got a date with tonight is kind of cute. So what if the equipment is wrong, the desired result is the same. Go for it, girl!*

E., please back off. Jason is just an acquaintance. Beside, you're right—the equipment is wrong. I'm not interested.

Well, then, it's time to break down and buy some toys, don't you think? Enforcer suggested boldly.

Cass shook her head and blushed at the direction her alter ego's libido was heading, and shut off the shower. She toweled dry and headed to her bed. *Plenty of time to take a nap before dinner,* she thought as she lay naked between the cool sheets. She drifted off to sleep almost immediately.

Cass approached the mystery woman in the field of flowers. She walked straight up to her, reached out and cupped the woman's face in her hands, and leaned in to place a soft, delicate kiss on her lips. Her heart fluttered as bolts of electricity shot through her body at the contact.

"I want you," Cass heard herself whisper in the woman's ear.

The woman whimpered softly in response. Standing in Cass's gentle embrace, she closed her eyes and tilted her chin up for more, and a look of arousal crossed her features.

Cass lowered her head again. Their lips touched, this time with more ardor, parting to admit invading tongues. Cass marveled at the wondrous taste of the woman as her tongue ventured deep into the proffered mouth.

The smaller woman moaned with pleasure as she eagerly welcomed the intrusion, and the flowers she was holding were forgotten. They fell, scattering on the ground around their feet as her hands moved to circle the taller woman's waist and pull her close.

"Let me love you," the woman said, as Cass released her mouth. It was Cass's turn to moan as she threw her head back and allowed the woman's lips access to her throat. Her hands moved to the woman's shoulders and pulled her in tightly.

She tore open Cass's gown, exposing full, firm breasts, upon which she hungrily feasted. Cass writhed in bliss. She was so caught up in her sexual haze that she didn't feel her gown being lifted to expose the heated skin beneath. All at once, bare hands were caressing her thighs.

"Oh, my God!" Cass exclaimed, as eager hands slipped inside the lace panties she wore, squeezed her buttocks firmly, and pulled her even closer. Soon the panties were gone, as was the gown, and small hands caressed the taut mounds, tracing circular patterns on Cass's skin.

The woman moved around Cass to stand behind her, wrapping her arms around the tall woman's waist and slipping her hands lower over her abdomen, closer and closer to the triangle of dark hair that stood guard over her treasure.

Cass arched back against the woman, and her breath caught in her throat as deft fingers slipped between dark curls.

"Ahhhhhh!"

Cass bolted awake and sat straight up in bed, covered in sweat and vibrating with sexual desire. She looked frantically around for her lover, then realized that she'd been dreaming. She dropped her head into her hands and took several deep breaths. *Oh, my God; oh, my God,* she chanted, knowing that her body needed sexual relief like a drug addict needed a fix.

Realizing also that she was drenched in sweat, Cass climbed off the bed and headed back to the shower. As she stood under the cool spray, she replayed the dream in her mind, her hands moving over her body. She leaned back against the shower wall and lathered her body, raising the level of her sexual desire exponentially. Finally, when the stimulation was more than she could take, she plunged her fingers between her legs and brought herself to fulfillment. As she leaned heavily against the shower wall, knees weak with relief, her dream lover's face filled her mind and her heart.

After her shower, Cass dressed for dinner, then powered up her computer to see if Rox had sent her e-mail. She had. Double-clicking on the icon next to Rox's note, she read:

> Hi, Cass,
>
> I wanted to drop you a line to say that I really enjoyed our chat last night. It's been a long time since I had such an interesting discussion about my work. My typical audience isn't usually interested in such things. I would very much like to chat with you again some time.
>
> BTW, you have an advantage—you know what I look like, but I am at a loss. Want to share?
>
> Drop me a line and let me know when it's convenient for you to chat again. I work from home, so nearly any time is okay for me.
>
> I'll talk to you later,
> Rox

Cass smiled as she read the note. *Yeah, I had a good time too,* she thought. *So, she wants to know what I look like. Okay. I'll just power up the scanner and send that picture of me and Brian. It's the best one that I have. Hope she isn't disappointed.*

Cass wrote:

> Hi, Rox,
>
> I really enjoyed our chat session too. I can't believe how fast the time flew. I hope I didn't keep you up too late.
>
> I'm sorry to hear that you don't have someone to discuss your work with more often. I find science fiction captivating and stimulating. I can't imagine why someone wouldn't want to discuss it -- especially with a talented writer like you.
>
> So you want a description of me, huh? Okay, I hope I don't disappoint you. I'm nearly six feet tall, relatively slim, somewhat muscular from working out and from Tae Kwon Do. (I earned my black belt a few months ago). I have dark hair and blue eyes. That's about it. I'm attaching a scanned photo of me and my co-pilot so you can see for yourself. If you want to know more, just let me know.
>
> I would like to chat with you again, too. I find myself quite enchanted with you, Roxanne Ward. You invade my thoughts at the oddest moments. It's a welcome invasion,

mind you. I haven't had any real companionship since the woman I was seeing passed away, nearly three years ago. I have guarded my heart closely ever since. It feels good for it to be invaded again.

Well, I'm on my way to dinner, so I will bid you adieu for now.

I'm looking forward to chatting with you again, whenever it's convenient for you.

Cass

Cass hit the "Send" button, then powered down the computer. She grabbed a light jacket and headed out the door to wait at the curb for Jason.

Chapter 11

As promised, Jerri picked Rox up at exactly five-thirty. She climbed into the car and leaned over to kiss her friend hello.

Immediately, Jerri noticed the bruises. She took Rox's chin in her hand and turned the author's head from side to side. "Damn it, why does Chris feel the need to hit you like that? One of these days, I'm going to corner that son of a bitch and return the favor."

"Jer, please. Let's not get started on that, okay? I'd really like this to be a nice evening," Rox said softly.

Jerri looked at her affectionately. She took a deep breath and forced a smile. "All right, Rox. I'll behave, but I meant what I said. Nikki and I love you very much, and it kills us to see that bastard do this to you." Jerri saw a flash of anger in Rox's eyes and threw up her hands in defeat. "All right, all right! Enough said. Let's go have some lobster, okay?"

Her crooked smile instantly dissolved Rox's anger. "Okay," she replied, smiling back.

Jerri and Nikki were as different as night from day. Where Nikki was petite, with short blonde hair, blue-green eyes and a fiery temper, Jerri was about five foot ten, with dark shoulder-length hair, olive-colored skin, brown eyes and a laid-back disposition. That is, unless someone she loved was hurt. That was the case today. Jerri's temper smoldered, yet, even through her anger, she tried to lighten the situation.

"So, tell me about the book," Jerri said, as she guided the car through traffic.

"It's coming along nicely. I managed to get quite a bit written with Chris being gone."

Jerri looked at Rox impatiently. "That's it? 'It's coming along nicely?' Details, woman, give me details! You know I'm chomping at the bit to read it. Sci-fi is like, bitchin' cool!"

Rox laughed at her friend's expression. "'Bitchin' cool,' huh? Well, I hope the reading public agrees with you."

"So spill it. Give me the scoop," Jerri demanded.

"Okay. The main character is an alien from the year 3029, who transports himself back through time to the year 2005. He finds himself in Rockland, Maine, where his transporter malfunctions and lands him smack dab in the middle of the emergency room at Mercy General Hospital."

Rox spared a glance at her friend, who was trying desperately to focus on the road and the narrative at the same time. She had caught Jerri's attention, and she chuckled to herself under her breath.

"So, he materializes out of nowhere, right in the emergency room, and the first person he sets eyes on is a petite, blonde, curly-haired nurse with blue-green eyes. It's love at first sight, only he's not the prettiest baby in the crib, and he scares the bejeezus out of everyone in sight." Rox paused for effect.

Jerri glanced at her quickly, then returned her eyes to the road. "Go on," she insisted.

Rox's smile widened. "Okay, where was I? Oh, yeah—Mr. Alien isn't exactly Brad Pitt, and his appearance has caused doctors and nurses to scatter in every direction as they try to get away from him. In her haste to join the crowd, the blue-eyed, curly-haired blonde nurse trips over her own feet and falls on her face—right in front of Mr. Alien, who immediately reaches down to help her up."

"Jesus Christ! I'll bet she just about shits her pants!" Jerri exclaimed, totally captivated by the story.

"Actually, no," Rox replied. "You see, his face could stop a freight train, but he was able to totally captivate the young nurse with his touch. All his emotions flow through his fingertips… er, make that tentacle-tips, and his love was transmitted right into her arm and straight to her heart. She's so enthralled that she can't take her eyes from him."

"Holy shit, Rox! What happens next?"

"Well, the alien can sense the nurse's reaction to him, and he thinks to himself, 'I've got this chick in the bag' as he cups her face between his hands and lowers his slimy lips to hers." Rox tried desperately to control the laughter that threatened to erupt as she watched the play of emotions cross Jerri's face.

"Oh, my God, I'm going to puke! Does he really kiss her?" Jerri asked incredulously.

"Oh, yeah… dripping slime all over her nurse's uniform all the while."

At this point, Jerri's brow was deeply furrowed. "I don't think I'm going to enjoy beta-reading this one, Rox," she complained. "Please tell me it gets better."

"Oh, it gets tons better. After the wet, slimy kiss, the alien looks the nurse in the eyes and says, 'Orczarki uqhilu ydspfanm.'"

Jerri drove over the curb as she rounded the corner of her street. "Damn it, Rox, see what you made me do?" she complained as she corrected her steering. "So what the hell does 'Orczarki uqhilu ydspfanm' mean?" Jerri maneuvered the car into her driveway, threw the transmission into park, then turned the engine off.

"It means, 'What's your name?'" the author supplied. "Anyway, the alien says 'Orczarki uqhilu ydspfanm', and the nurse replies, 'My name is Nikki Davenport.'"

Jerri's eyes flew open wide. "Why, you teasing little bitch!" she exclaimed, playfully reaching forward as if to grasp Rox by the throat.

Rox threw her head back and laughed. "Do you really think I'd give the plot away before you had a chance to read it? Think again, my friend. You'll have to wait until it's finished before you get to lay those beautiful brown eyes on it."

"You are so lucky I love you, Roxanne Ward! Otherwise, you'd be dead meat. So, when will this one be ready for beta?"

"Well, if I keep writing at my current pace, it should be done in a month or less. Getting a little anxious, are we?" Rox teased.

"Anxious isn't the word for it, Rox, and you know it, you little tease," Jerri shot back.

Rox reached over and patted the side of Jerri's face. "Patience, dear heart, patience," she said, and reached for the door handle.

Jerri and Rox went into the house and followed the sounds and scents of cooking into the kitchen. There they found Nikki, working on dinner.

Nikki wore an apron with a huge, obviously female lobster on the front. The head of the lobster was replaced by the head of the wearer, and its claws were curled upward and pinching its own nipples. The caption below the lobster said *Lobsters Do It In A Pinch.*

"Hi, honey, we're home," Jerri said playfully.

Nikki accepted a kiss from Jerri and then engulfed Rox in a loving hug.

When Rox stood back and took a good look at her friend, she laughed heartily. "Nikki, you look like you belong at a carnival," she said, still chuckling. "So, lobster-woman, what can I do to help?"

"You can set the table, if you'd like. Dinner will be ready in about fifteen minutes." She pointed Rox in the direction of the cupboard. "Oh, by the way, did you bring the salve?"

"Yes, I did. It's in my purse." Rox gathered the necessary dinnerware and took it into the dining room.

While Rox was setting the table, Jerri was ogling Nikki as she took butter from the refrigerator. Seeing Nikki bent over to reach the lower shelves was more than Jerri could stand. She spooned herself behind her wife, reached around and cupped Nikki's breasts, and pinched her nipples firmly while whispering in the blonde's ear, "Can *I* do it in a pinch, sweetheart?"

Nikki moaned and pressed herself back into Jerri, holding on to the open refrigerator door for support. Just then, Rox came back into the kitchen for napkins.

"You'd better close that door before your body heat melts everything in there," Rox said dryly. She got the napkins and nonchalantly sauntered by, acting as if seeing her two friends in the midst of foreplay in front of an open refrigerator was an everyday event.

Nikki blushed and Jerri grinned.

"That's a pretty shade of pink, Nikki," Rox said as she returned to the dining room.

Nikki buried her face against Jerri's shoulder, awash with embarrassment.

Dinner was very pleasant. The three ladies complemented each other well—each of them trying to outtalk the other two.

"So, tell me about Cass, Rox," Jerri asked, as she cracked open a lobster claw and spewed watery juices all over herself. This sent her two companions into a fit of laughter. "Jesus!" she exclaimed, wiping the splatter from her face.

Rox picked up her napkin and reached across the table to wipe away a stray drop before replying. "Cass... where to start?" she mused. "Well, he lives in the San Jose area, and he's a pilot."

"And?" Jerri asked when it became apparent that Rox wasn't going to continue.

"And... I guess I don't know too much more yet," Rox said, feeling the need to defend her interest in this unknown entity. "I do know he's very polite and he loves Sci-Fi, so I guess he can't be all bad."

Jerri watched Rox's face light up as she described her new e-mail friend, and immediately became worried that Rox was jumping in too fast. "Rox, you do realize that Cass lives three thousand miles away, right?"

"I know that, Jer." Rox sighed deeply. "Look, we've only exchanged a few e-mails and met in chat once. I don't know what it is about this guy, Jerri. Something clicked between us. I'm not saying it will develop into anything more substantial, but it just feels really good. I need that right now."

Nodding, Jerri covered her friend's hand with her own and squeezed. "Yes, you do," Jerri agreed, looking pointedly at the bruises on Rox's face. "I just worry about you, that's all."

Rox reached out to pat her friend's hand. "Well, don't. I'm fine. I'm not about to take on another love interest, especially when I haven't figured out how to get rid of the jerk I'm with currently. Besides, I intend my next relationship to be totally different than any I've ever had in the past."

Nikki's interest was piqued by Rox's comment. "Different how?"

Rox wiped her mouth with her napkin and placed it on her now-empty plate before answering. "I intend to find someone who's loving, patient, and understanding. Someone who will be empathetic, not confrontational. In the past few months, I've worn the evidence of confrontation on my face. It's time to switch to a new line of cosmetics, don't you think?"

After dinner, the friends worked together to clean up the kitchen. When the chores were done, Nikki turned to Rox. "Okay, sweetling, time to apply the salve. Strip!"

Jerri raised her eyebrows at Rox. "Pushy broad, isn't she? She bosses me around all the time, too. You two go ahead, I'll pour us each a glass of wine to enjoy while we watch the movie."

As they went into the living room, Rox was laughing at Jerri's comment. She stripped off her t-shirt and lay down on her stomach on the floor.

Nikki straddled her friend's backside, unhooked Rox's bra, and pushed it off her shoulders.

At that very moment, Jerri came into the living room and got her first glimpse of the markings on Rox's back. Even knowing the damage was there, she was still so shaken by what she saw that she almost spilled the wine on the carpet. Trembling with rage, she managed to put the wine down before she started pacing back and forth, sputtering obscenities about Chris.

"Jerri!" Rox said firmly, from her position on the floor.

Jerri stopped pacing and looked at her friend.

"C'mere, Big Guy. Keep me company while your wife tortures me, okay?"

Jerri lay down on her stomach so she was face to face with Rox. They were both lying with their arms in front of them, hands overlapped and chins resting on top of them, their faces inches apart. Nikki worked the salve into the bruised skin on Rox's back, and Jerri held Rox's hand when she winced at the pressure of Nikki's hands.

Nikki bent over Rox's back. "I'm sorry," she whispered. "But we're all done now and the salve really will help the healing process."

Rox sat up and gave her a grateful smile. "Thanks, Nik. It does feel better. Could you help me with the shirt?"

Nikki tossed the bra aside and helped Rox don her t-shirt, then all three women took seats on the couch to watch the movie—Nikki wrapped in Jerri's arms, and Rox with her head on Nikki's leg.

As the film played, Nikki ran her fingers through Rox's red-gold hair until she was fast asleep. Nikki smiled as she looked at Rox, then up at her wife. "Poor baby," she said softly.

Jerri leaned in to kiss her wife. "Let's not wake her. She can stay here tonight."

Nikki nodded her agreement as she carefully raised Rox's head and moved her leg out from under it, then quietly rose from the couch. She fetched a pillow and blanket, and together they made Rox as comfortable as they could before turning out the lights and going to bed.

* * *

Jason arrived promptly at six, driving a brand-new Corvette convertible.

Cass walked around the cherry-red car and whistled. "Wow, Jason, you must be doing really well for yourself. I'm sure this car didn't cost peanuts."

"Yeah, I'm not doing too badly." He held her door open for her.

Sitting next to him in the car, she turned and asked, "So, just what *are* you doing for work these days?"

"Still working for the old man, selling used cars."

Cass turned to look out her window and frowned. *I didn't know selling used cars paid so well. He's got to be making a mint to afford a car like this.*

As if he was trying to impress his "date," Jason bragged about his assets all the way to the restaurant: a beach house in Malibu, stock and bonds, the new car.

After he described his thirty-foot yacht, Cass decided to call his bluff, if bluff it was. "I guess the used-car business is more lucrative than I thought."

"Oh, it's not just the used cars. I've gotten involved in some investments and business ventures," he bragged. "That's where the big money is."

"Indeed?" Cass didn't know what else to say to the blowhard, and she was beginning to regret accepting his invitation. *If he even suggests I hit the sheets with him, I'll kick his assets good and hard.*

What seemed like an interminable time later, they arrived at the restaurant. Cass raised her eyebrows when Jason pulled the car up to the valet-parking facility. As she read the menu, with its hundred-dollar entrees and even pricier wines, Cass began to feel very uncomfortable. When Jason ordered the most expensive bottle of wine, her uneasiness intensified.

E., where are you when I need you? What's going on here? she asked her alter ego. E. remained silent.

All through dinner, Jason quizzed Cass about her job.

"So, Cass, I've told you about my job. Now it's your turn."

Cass's eyebrows lifted. "My turn?" she asked. "I'm afraid my job isn't very interesting."

"I beg to differ. It's got to be more interesting than selling used cars," Jason insisted.

You got that right! This guy is a major bore! "Okay. Where should I start?"

"Well, you said you fly to Mexico and South America quite often. Are they special flights, or are they part of the commercial routes?"

"Southern Lights has both commercial and cargo routes in and out of the Southern Hemisphere. Occasionally I fly commercial routes, but for the most part, my flights are goodwill missions."

"Goodwill missions. You mean, like disaster relief?"

"Something like that. Disaster relief, medical aid, food and water deliveries; stuff like that. Some of the poorer countries have been devastated by drought this past year. Thousands of people depend on the service we provide."

"So that must mean you carry mostly cargo and no passengers," Jason reasoned.

"Some of the flights include passengers, but it's usually no more than a couple of dozen people. The bulk of what we carry is cargo."

"Do you fly into Central America regularly?"

Cass frowned. "Every week," she replied. "So tell me, Jason, why the sudden interest in flying?"

Jason reached for his wine glass and downed its contents. Then he donned what he believed was his most charming smile. "No special reason. I guess I'm just fascinated that such a beautiful creature makes her living flying a plane. I've never met a woman pilot before. The airline must take special precautions, like sending extra security on your flights. You know—so you aren't taken advantage of by anyone."

"I think I'm more than capable of taking care of myself," Cass replied, insulted at the implication that she was helpless because she was a woman.

"Oh, I'm sure you can; I'm sure you can. So, Cass, tell me about..."

Jason wanted to know every detail about her flights, right down to her safety check routine.

Finally, sick of the questioning, Cass said, "Really, Jason, if you're thinking of applying for a job with the airline..."

Jason flushed. "No, just interested in what you do, that's all."

"Well, the answers to most of your questions about flight schedules and such are on the company's website. I'd just as soon not talk about work anymore."

Shortly after Cass brushed off his inquiries, dinner ended rather abruptly. Jason called for the check. The tab came to several hundred dollars, and he added a $100 tip for the waitress.

Cass looked at him with disgust as he made a show of tucking the tip into the waitress's cleavage. *What a pig.*

I'll say, Enforcer piped in. *The man's a pimp. Why'd you go out with him, anyway?*

Oh, so now you show up. Look, you're the one who wanted me to jump into the sack with him, so don't give me any shit about this date. You got it?

Hey, I've got needs too, you know? If you'd only buy those toys I've been bugging you for, I'd back off, Enforcer reminded her.

E., go back into whatever hole you were hiding in when I needed you, okay? I can do without this kind of help.

At last, the valet brought the Corvette, and Jason and Cass drove in silence toward her condo. He pulled up in front, shut off the engine, then turned in his seat to face her. "So when is your next flight?" he asked. "I'd like to take you out again."

Cass nearly choked. She had no intention of seeing Jason again. "Uh, I'm booked up for quite a while. I fly to Durango for the next two days, and then I have a couple of commercial flights."

He persisted. "What about next week, then?"

"Sorry, I make weekly trips to Mexico every Monday, domestic flights sometimes on Wednesdays, Guatemala on Thursdays. I'm really very busy," Cass said.

"All right, I'll leave my business card with you. Why don't you call me when you're free?" Jason handed her his card, from his father's used-car business.

Cass gave him a nervous smile and nodded reluctantly. "Thanks for dinner." As she reached for the door handle, Jason grabbed her arm. Cass raised an eyebrow. "Is there a problem?"

"Can't a guy get a kiss from his date, especially after dropping a few hundred on dinner?" he asked, with a smug smile on his face.

Cass leaned closer to him, so that her nose was a mere inch away from his. "You seem to have forgotten that I'm gay, Jason, *and* that I have a black belt in Tae Kwon Do. Now, I suggest you take your hand off me. Immediately."

Jason was startled, and quickly removed his hand.

Cass was heading for her front door when she heard the Corvette peel away from the curb. "Neanderthal asshole," she muttered.

Chapter 12

Rox woke up at around nine a.m., not immediately aware of where she was. She opened her eyes, looked around, and finally realized she was on Nikki and Jerri's living room couch. She also smelled coffee. She rubbed the sleep out of her eyes and got to her feet, then stretched as far as her bruised body would allow.

"First stop, bathroom," she said under her breath as she padded in that direction.

As she made her way into the kitchen, she saw a note on the table. She picked it up and read:

Hey, Sleeping Beauty,
Some of us work for a living and can't sleep all day.

That made Rox smile.

Help yourself to coffee and whatever you can find for breakfast. If anything in the refrigerator looks like a science project, or snaps at you when you touch it, best leave it alone.
I'll give you a call later this morning. Please don't leave. I'll be home for lunch, so I'll drop you off at your house on my way back to work. Okay?
We love you, chickie,
Talk to you soon,
MQ
PS. I shared your new story idea with Jer. She likes the idea of being the alien, and she especially likes the dominatrix costume. You are a nasty, wicked woman. Don't ever change; we love you just the way you are!
N.

Rox chuckled at her friend's easy banter, then sighed enviously. *Will I ever have a relationship like theirs? I hope so.* She poured herself a cup of coffee and sat down at the kitchen table. Leaning on her elbows and holding her cup suspended in front of her, she thought about the intense, loving relationship her friends shared.

They were true soulmates; a blind man could see it. Nikki was a nurse, and Jerri an EMT on an ambulance crew. Many times, Rox had heard how they would sneak kisses on the elevator or meet on the loading dock of the hospital for secret make-out sessions. They were like teenagers in love, constantly touching, caressing, and expressing their love for each other. Rox longed for someone with whom she could share that level of intimacy; someone she could call her own.

Sighing grimly, Rox thought of her relationship with Chris. *I thought we were soulmates, but then he changed.* She absently lifted the cup and sipped her coffee. Closing her eyes, she recalled the first kiss she and Chris had shared.

They were walking along the beach at night—Rox with a t-shirt thrown on over her bikini, Chris wearing rolled-up blue jeans and a muscle shirt. Barefoot, they walked along in the surf. The moon was very bright overhead in the starless sky, and a slight breeze blew Rox's then-long hair around her face. As they walked, hand in hand, Chris abruptly stopped and pulled Rox close. He cupped her face in his callused hands and tilted it up. Lips met, tongues invaded moist crevices, and Rox melted.

She shuddered at the recollection. *So much has changed since then. Thank God for Nikki and Jerri.* Rox couldn't help but recall the numerous times over the previous six months that she'd called her friends for comfort, after Chris had beaten her and then left to hit the bars with the guys from work. He hadn't harmed her severely enough that she had been forced to seek medical attention yet, but Rox knew it was only a matter of time.

She lowered her head and allowed a tear to fall onto the table. Life was so unfair. She was trapped in an abusive relationship, and the only thing that would free her from it was her father's death. *Life sucks,* she thought, then hardened her heart to her circumstances and rose to refill her coffee cup.

* * *

Cass rose bright and early on Thursday morning. She checked her e-mail before she started her workout, and was disappointed to find that Rox had not replied to her previous message. Her shoulders slumped in defeat.

Damn, I hope I didn't scare her away with that last note. I'm such an idiot for telling the woman she enchanted me. She's probably married, with a bunch of kids. Why am I wasting my time here? Go ahead and say you told me so, E.

Not necessary, Enforcer replied. *You're doing a good job of beating yourself up; you don't need my help.*

Yeah, well, after what happened with Patti, you'd think I'd know better than to think I could form a new relationship successfully.

As she turned back to the keyboard, Cass made a decision. "Okay, Roxanne Ward, one more note, then I'll leave you alone." She selected "New Message."

> *Hi, Rox,*
> *Look, I'm sorry I was so forward in my last post. I don't want to push you into anything. It's just that I have never before felt such an instant connection with anyone the way I did with you, and I was hoping that you felt the same. I'm sorry if I've overstepped my bounds. You're probably involved in a loving relationship already, and I certainly don't want to interfere with your happiness.*
> *Please forgive me?*
> *Cass*

After sending the note, Cass headed to her treadmill. She powered up the machine and started working off her anger and disappointment. Enforcer was right there to keep her company.

What are you going to do if she brushes you off, Cass? Enforcer asked, as she jogged along at an easy pace.

Throw the computer out the window.

Throw it out the window? What will that accomplish? It's not the computer's fault you've got bad taste in women, Enforcer said bluntly.

Cass sighed deeply. *God damn it, E. I don't have bad taste in women, I've just been unlucky in love. My taste in women is just fine, thank you very much. Tell me you don't think Rox is beautiful.*

Well, maybe you're right. Yeah, she's very beautiful. Patti was quite a looker, too. Too bad she was a psycho bitch.

Demon bitch from hell is more like it, E. If I'd only been smart enough to see that she was into steroids and drugs, maybe I could have helped her... maybe I could have prevented her death.

For once, Enforcer was encouraging. *So you're finally starting to realize that her death wasn't your fault, huh? It's about time you lost that guilt and moved on, Cass. It will interfere in any future relationship if you don't.*

E., I can't help it. I will never forget how it felt to be so helpless, and I will never allow myself to be so dependent and vulnerable again. Nor will I ever forget how devastated she was when I left her.

Not everyone is like Patti, Cass. If you keep looking behind you, you're going to stumble past what's in front of you. Get over it and move on. It's been almost three years.

Cass shut off the treadmill and stood leaning over the control panel breathing deeply, sweat covering her body. Several minutes later, she lifted her head again and grabbed her towel. She wiped the sweat off her forehead, reached for the water bottle, drank half its contents, then headed toward the bathroom.

Cass, stop ignoring me. You know I'm right.

Entering the bathroom, she stripped off her workout wear and threw it in the hamper by the sink. She turned on the shower and stood in front of the sink looking at her reflection in the mirror.

Damn it, Cass, wake up and smell the coffee, E. scolded. *Look, we haven't been laid in eons. I have needs too, you know. That little episode of self-gratification in the shower yesterday wasn't enough; we need tenderness. We need to be held and caressed and told that we're loved. Cass, if the cute little author rejects you, find out why. A few well-formulated questions will tell you whether or not she's married. Shit, woman, you don't even know if she's into chicks! You've got a lot of homework to do, my friend, and these polite little notes you've been sending are not going to get you anywhere. Capisce?*

Cass lifted her hands to her face and rubbed vigorously. *I've got to get a hold of myself. Maybe E.'s right and I should take a chance. She's almost three thousand miles away; she can't hurt me.*

Determined to stop looking back, Cass stepped into the shower and washed the sweat from her body. The two-day flight to Durango would allow her time to think. *By the time I return on Friday afternoon, I should have some reaction from Rox, which will give me some indication about whether or not to pursue the connection.*

Cass dressed in her airline uniform and headed out the door with higher spirits and a determined heart.

* * *

Rox made herself a fried egg and cheese sandwich for breakfast and sat curled up on the corner of Nikki's couch, watching the Weather Channel as she ate. She watched with interest as they recapped the weather for the West Coast, specifically California, and wondered what Cass was doing. Glancing at the time display in the bottom corner of the screen, she noted that it was ten-thirty a.m. *Seven-thirty in California. He's probably on his way to work,* she said to herself. *Just like I should be. That story will never be finished if I keep allowing interruptions like this.*

She finished her sandwich, stood up and stretched, then went into the kitchen to clean up after herself. As she wiped her hands on a dishtowel, she looked at the clock again. Time was crawling by; it was only eleven a.m. Rummaging through the refrigerator, she found the fixings for salad and went to work fixing something to feed Nikki for lunch. She opened a can of chicken noodle soup, poured the contents into a pan and set it on the stove on low, and then checked the time again. "Looks like I have time for a shower." She went into Nikki and Jerri's room to find something of Nikki's to change into. *The pants will be a little too short, but it's better than wearing the same clothes I wore yesterday.*

The first thing she noticed was the state of disarray their bed was in. The pillows were pushed up against the headboard and were nearly on top of one another. Her friends obviously slept very close together. For some reason, that simple arrangement of pillows struck a pang of loneliness in Rox's heart as she imagined her friends spooned together, wrapped around each other in a braid of love.

Her bed never looked like that. Chris simply retreated to the far reaches of the mattress after satisfaction was taken. No tender caresses, no vows of love and devotion; just "wham, bam, thank you ma'am," then roll over and go to sleep. Rox pushed those thoughts from her mind as she made her friends' bed and then found clean underclothes, t-shirt and shorts to wear after her shower.

"Rox?" Nikki shouted as she came into the house through the kitchen door.

"In the bathroom, Nik," Rox called back.

Nikki walked through the living room into the downstairs bathroom and leaned against the doorframe to watch Rox finger-comb her short, strawberry-blonde hair loosely into place.

"I like your outfit," Nikki said, noting the familiar clothing.

Rox grinned. "Thanks. I've got good taste in clothes, huh?"

"Very good. Looks like something I'd buy for myself."

"Are you hungry?" Rox asked, brushing the last errant lock into place.

"Very."

Rox threw her arm around her friend's shoulder, led her back to the kitchen, and sat her down in a chair. Moments later, Nikki had a bowl of hot soup and a crisp garden salad in front of her.

Nikki looked at Rox. "Aren't you going to eat?"

"No. Believe it or not, I had an egg sandwich less than two hours ago. I'm really not hungry."

"Don't tell me—you slept until what, nine o'clock?" Her friend nodded, and Nikki said, "Jesus, Rox, how can you sleep so late? You fell asleep on the couch about ten last night. Do you realize that's eleven hours of sleep?"

"I don't know, Nik. I've always been a late sleeper," Rox said defensively.

"Bullshit. You slept so late because you don't take care of yourself. Rox, you're so torn between your work and your home and Chris that you don't make time to take care of your physical needs. You're going to run yourself right into the ground if you're not careful."

Rox looked down at the table and endured the lecture. She knew her friend was right.

Nikki set down her fork and reached over to take Rox's hand. "Honey, I'm sorry for yelling, but damn it, girl, I care about you and I know you're not taking proper care of yourself." Her voice was tender. "You need to make some changes before you become seriously ill. Okay?"

Avoiding her friend's eyes, Rox just nodded.

A short time later, lunch was out of the way and they were in the car, heading toward the ocean. Their conversation became animated as Rox talked about some of the ideas she had for her book.

"I teased Jerri about the whole scene in the emergency room, but the book really is about an alien who travels from many, many years in the future to the year 2005. I just couldn't resist teasing her; she's such an easy target." Rox laughed as she recalled her tall friend's reaction to being duped.

Nikki smiled broadly as she shook her head. "Only you could get away with it, Rox. If I tried a stunt like that, I'd get the silent treatment for a month. So, really, tell me about the story."

"Well, I've already said that it's about an alien from the future. I'm kind of basing the storyline on my relationship with Chris— complete with abuse. The alien stumbles across the female lead after she has a rather distasteful encounter with the antagonist."

"Wait, wait... don't tell me... The alien walks in on Chris beating up on our lady and zaps his sorry ass into the middle of next week. Am I close?"

Rox smiled sadly. "Something like that. Anyway, I'm still in the middle of writing that particular encounter, and I must admit that I'm struggling with it. I feel Chris's belt on my back with every word I write. I was hoping that writing this part of the book would give me the strength to..."

As Rox's voice trailed off, Nikki cast a worried look in her friend's direction, then stared at the road ahead. Her knuckles went white on the steering wheel as she fought to control her temper. "Honey, you don't have to say any more. I get the picture, and I truly hope that someday your alien does pay a visit. It sounds like you need him in more ways than even you realize."

Rox nodded, and reached up to wipe a tear from the corner of her eye. Making a conscious effort to change the subject, she soon fell into a lively debate with her friend on whether or not the alien should fall in love with the heroine and whisk her away to the future.

Nikki glanced at the exuberant look that appeared on Rox's face as she talked about her work. Of late, times like these were the only occasions when she saw any passion there. She was grateful that Rox had at least *that* escape from her nightmarish life.

As she pulled into the driveway of Rox's home, Nikki looked around carefully. *No other car besides Rox's. Thank God Chris isn't home yet.* There was no telling what would happen if that bastard came home to an empty house. Nikki kissed her friend goodbye, and then Rox got out of the car.

Rox waved to Nikki as she drove away, then climbed her front steps and unlocked the door. The moment she stepped into the house, a hand circled her throat and Rox felt a bolt of fear as she was slammed up against the wall next to the door. She looked up frantically into piercing brown eyes.

"Where the fuck have you been?" Chris said, between clenched teeth.

Rox could barely speak, he was constricting her throat so tightly. She grabbed his hands, desperately trying to pry them loose as she began to lose consciousness.

Realizing that Rox was about to pass out, Chris released his death-grip on her throat and watched her slide down the wall to the floor.

"Answer me, bitch!" he screamed, looming over the defenseless woman.

"I... I was at Nikki and Jerri's. They invited me to dinner last night. I... I fell asleep on their couch," Rox explained in a raspy voice.

"Liar!" Chris yelled, and a booted foot landed against Rox's left side, doubling her over in pain. "You were screwing around with them, weren't you? I saw you kiss that bitch before you got out of the car. You whore!" Another kick connected with her side.

"No... Ch... Chris, please," Rox tried to protest, between gasps. "No... "

Chris reached down, grabbed the front of Rox's shirt and pulled her back to her feet. He slammed her up against the wall again, and got right into her face. "Don't you fucking lie to me, bitch. You couldn't wait until I left, could you? I'll bet you've been over there fucking their brains out for the last four days, haven't you? I've seen the way you look at them, Rox. Don't you dare fucking lie to me!" he accused. "You didn't think I was home, did you? *Did you*? No. You didn't see my car, so you thought it was safe. Well, I've got news for you, Miss High and Mighty—my car's at the jobsite, broken down. I had to catch a ride home with one of the guys yesterday because my girlfriend wasn't home to answer the goddamned phone!" His voice was a howl of hatred and disgust.

Rox was terrified, and her side ached so badly that she could barely stand. She was crying, and her breath came in painful gasps as she held her left arm across her body to protect her bruised ribs from further injury.

"Chris... I've been h... home wr... writing since you've b-b-been gone... except for last night," she said through her tears.

Chris backhanded her across the face, sending her sprawling across the floor.

As blood flowed from her mouth and nose, Rox curled up tightly, still protecting her ribs. "Oh, God... Oh, God," she moaned as Chris attacked again.

Chris grabbed her wrist and twisted, lifting her off the floor in the same motion. An audible snap accompanied Rox's shriek of pain. "Shut up, bitch, before the whole neighborhood hears you!" Chris shouted in her face. When Rox continued to cry, he became even angrier. "God damn it, I said shut up!" He hauled back and punched Rox in the face.

She fell against the stairs and hit her head on the newel post. Unconsciousness was a welcome relief.

Chapter 13

Jerri was relaxing in the ER lounge and enjoying her lunch when Mike, her partner, motioned her over. He was on the phone taking an emergency call from the dispatcher.

"What is it, Mike?" she asked.

"Domestic battering, woman unconscious. 1163 Oceanview Terrace. Dispatch says that the victim was found unconscious by the mailman. Let's go."

Jerri's stomach churned and for a moment she was afraid that she might lose her lunch. "Oh, my God—Rox!"

Moments later, Jerri and Mike were on their way to the scene. Mike looked at his partner from the corner of his eye as he maneuvered the ambulance through the streets. "You know her pretty well, don't you?"

Jerri nodded solemnly. "She's my best friend."

"Abusive husband?" Mike asked.

Jerri sat in the passenger seat looking straight ahead, fists clenched and mind seething with anger. "Boyfriend. A dead one, if I ever get my hands on the bastard."

Mike pulled into the driveway of the three-story Victorian, and Jerri jumped out of the ambulance before it came to a complete stop. She ran up the steps into the house, calling frantically, "Rox, Rox!"

She pushed her way past the policemen who were already present and saw her friend lying at the foot of the stairs. "Rox!" Jerri knelt next to her friend and assessed her condition, immediately noting her pallor, the clamminess of her skin and her uncontrollable shivering—all signs that Rox was going into shock. Looking up at the nearest officer, she said, "Get me a blanket, quickly!"

An instant later, Mike appeared with their equipment from the ambulance. He looked at his partner with deep concern. "She's in rough shape, isn't she?"

Jerri's eyes filled with tears as she looked at Mike and nodded. She reached over and cupped the side of her friend's face. "Rox... Rox, honey, can you hear me?"

Rox's eyes fluttered open and she tried to smile when she saw her friend's face. "Jer,?" Her voice was faint.

"Don't talk, sweetheart. Try to lie still; we'll have you taken care of in no time." She tucked the blanket around her friend, and then she and Mike went to work taking Rox's vital signs and assessing her injuries.

Jerri noted the bruises around Rox's neck: four parallel lines on the right side, one on the left. The attacker was left-handed. The purple bruise around her right eye was further testimony to that fact, as was the split lip on the left side of Rox's mouth, which was consistent with a back handed blow from a left-handed person. *Chris is left-handed.*

"Where was she found?" Jerri asked the officer.

"She was lying half on and half off the stairs, right behind you." He pointed to an obvious spattering of blood on the bottom runner of the carpeted stairs.

Jerri reached beneath Rox's head and gently explored the back of the skull, which made Rox moan. As she had expected, Jerri found a large lump on the back of the head. She looked up at the officer. "The injury is consistent with her impacting the newel post at the bottom of the stairway, and the resulting fall would account for the bloodstains found on the bottom runner."

"Jer, her condition is worsening. We need to get her transported to the hospital as soon as possible," Mike interjected, as Rox began to shake violently.

Jerri turned her attention back to him. "Okay, Mike, I'll need a c-collar and backboard, stat." As Mike ran to the ambulance to retrieve the requested items, Jerri leaned in close to her friend. "How are you doing, Rox?"

"My wrist... ribs... hurts to breathe. I'm so cold."

Jerri looked at the large welts on the left side of Rox's chest, then tucked another blanket around her. "Rox, you're going into shock." Turning to look out the open front door, she called loudly to her partner, "Mike, bring a straight board and an Ace bandage to secure her wrist." Turning back to Rox, she tried hard to give her a reassuring smile. "We'll be on our way in no time, love. Hang in there, okay?"

"Chris," Rox whispered.

"Chris... Chris did this to you, right?" Jerri said, trying not to lose her temper. "Chris was here when you got home?" She looked around. *He obviously split after he knocked Rox out. The bastard probably thought she was dead.*

Rox tried to nod. When she couldn't, a tear escaped her eye.

"Lie still. You're safe now, Rox. I'll be by your side the whole way, okay?"

Soon, Jerri and Mike had Rox strapped down to the backboard with her neck in the cervical collar and her head taped securely to the board. Jerri was especially careful to be mindful of Rox's ribs as she tied her down, immobilizing the injured woman for the ride to the hospital.

* * *

Just as she was going on break, Nikki felt her pager vibrate. She checked its display and stopped at the nearest phone to call the emergency room. Nikki had a standing agreement with the dispatcher that she be paged whenever Jerri was coming in with a patient. Depending on how much time they had, she liked to meet Jerri for coffee before she headed back out, or perhaps make a quick trip into a broom closet for an impromptu make-out session. It was rare for them to have an actual break together, and Nikki smiled at the good timing.

Mike backed the ambulance into the emergency room bay just as Nikki came through the swinging doors into Triage, and Jerri spotted Nikki from the corner of her eye as they rushed the stretcher in. She quickly recounted Rox's status to the attending physician, and then tried to intercept her wife before she saw the condition their friend was in. She was too late.

When Nikki saw the familiar red-gold hair of the person on the stretcher, she lunged forward. "Rox! Oh, God, no! Rox!"

Jerri grabbed her wife by the shoulders and pulled her in for an embrace, blocking her view of the battered woman. "Nikki, no. You don't need to see her just yet. She's going to be all right," Jerri whispered into Nikki's ear as she fought to keep the smaller woman from looking over her shoulder at their friend.

"Jerri, please, she needs me," Nikki cried, fighting against her bigger and stronger partner. "Please let me go," she begged.

"Nikki, please don't fight me on this. Let the doctors do their jobs, sweetheart," Jerri said, pushing her away from the scene despite her continued struggles. Finally, Jerri just took her by the arm and dragged her out of Triage and into the nurse's lounge. She sat Nikki in a chair, then leaned in until their faces were only inches apart. Jerri looked into her partner's green eyes, which were filled with such pain she had a difficult time composing herself.

"Nikki," she said, "Rox will be all right. As far as I could tell without X-rays, she has a broken wrist and maybe some fractured ribs. Possibly a concussion, too, but she *will* be all right. Okay?"

Fighting back tears, Nikki nodded, then rested her forehead against Jerri's and closed her eyes. "Chris?"

"Yes."

Nikki started to cry. "It's my fault."

Jerri dropped to her knees in front of Nikki and took the smaller woman into her arms. "No, Nik. How can this be your fault?"

"I left her there, Jerri. Don't you see? Chris must have been hiding in the house. The only car in the driveway was Rox's. I didn't know!"

Nikki felt Jerri stiffen. The change in her partner caused Nikki to draw back and look at the hard set of Jerri's face as the taller woman stood erect and started pacing. "Jerri?"

Jerri's jaw and fists were clenching as she paced. "Nikki, you could have been in the house when all this happened. You could be out there lying next to Rox right now," she said, pointing to the door to Triage. "I'm going to kill that bastard, Nik. There will be no hiding from this. Chris will rue the day Rox hired the outfit that son of a bitch works for. He will not get away with this!" Her voice became louder with each word she spoke.

Nikki rose to her feet and intercepted Jerri's path. Taking her by both arms, she forced Jerri to look at her. "Now, you listen to me. You are *not* going after Chris. I need you with *me*, not rotting away in some jail cell. Do you understand? Look, you want me to let the triage crew do their jobs—right? Well then, *you* let the police do theirs. Promise me, Jer."

Jerri looked over Nikki's head at the wall behind her, her jaw set stubbornly and her hands on her hips. She refused to meet Nikki's eyes.

Nikki shook her lightly. "Promise me, Jerri!" she demanded. "Please," she added in a soft voice.

Jerri took a deep breath, closed her eyes, and lowered her chin to her chest. Dropping her hands from her hips, she wrapped her arms around her wife and held her close. "All right, I promise," she whispered.

"Thank you," Nikki whispered back. "Now, do you think we can check on Rox?" Jerri nodded and gave Nikki a quick kiss. They headed back to Triage.

* * *

"We'll need a cross table and lateral c-spine, abdominal, and chest films here. I don't like the looks of that bruising on her side. Oh, and a CT scan for the head injury, too. She's conscious and her pupils look good, so the scan can wait until we take care of that nasty gash on her brow," the attending physician ordered as he removed the cervical collar from Rox's neck. "What's the name of the brick wall you ran into?" the doctor joked as he looked into Rox's bruised face. Being careful not to move her neck, he examined the bruising pattern on her throat before meeting Rox's eyes.

Rox was silent, knowing she would cry if she tried to speak. Any movement of her body caused sharp, stabbing sensations in her ribs. She was already in enough pain; she didn't need to add more by sobbing.

"What's your name, young lady?" the doctor asked as he replaced the collar.

"Roxanne Ward." Her voice was just barely above a whisper.

"Well, Roxanne Ward, I'm Dr. Syverson. Can you tell me what happened?"

When his patient started to shake her head, the doctor reached out to stabilize it. "Don't move your head, okay? We need to see if there's any spinal damage in your neck first. The technician should be here in a moment to take you to x-ray. Now, I'll ask you again—can you tell me what happened?"

"Rox!" Nikki exclaimed, as she and Jerri approached Rox's bedside.

Rox's gaze, with the one eye she could open, darted to the left. Her right eye was swollen nearly shut from the impact of Chris's fist. She teared up and reached out for Nikki with her unbandaged hand. Dr. Syverson took Jerri aside to ask her about the procedures done at the scene, giving Nikki and Rox a few moments of privacy.

Nikki reached over and touched the left side of Rox's face, cradling her bruised jaw in a tender caress. Making no attempt to hide her tears, she leaned over and kissed Rox on the uninjured side of her mouth. "I'm sorry," she whispered.

Rox's brow furrowed in confusion at Nikki's apology.

"Roxanne Ward?" the x-ray technician said from the doorway.

Nikki turned to the man, wiping her tears away at the same time. "Right here," she said, waving him over to Rox's gurney.

Moments later, Rox was wheeled to x-ray, where the necessary films were taken. Some time later, she was returned to the ER, where she found Nikki still waiting for her.

"Where's Jer?" Rox asked as Nikki took her hand.

"She's gone on another call. Rox, Chris did this to you, right? He was waiting for you in the house? God, Rox, I'm so sorry." She started to cry again.

Rox squeezed Nikki's hand. "Nik, Chris did this, not you. You have nothing to be sorry for," she said through clenched teeth, trying to ignore the pain in her side, jaw, and head.

"But I left you there, Rox," was Nikki's tearful explanation.

"Nik—" Rox began.

Dr. Syverson interrupted. "Okay, while we're waiting for those films, let's take care of this cut near your eye." Looking at Nikki expectantly, he asked, "Are you here to help, or to hinder?"

Shocked into action, Nikki replied, "To help, of course!"

"All right, then," he said, giving her a brief smile. "We need to suture this wound."

Nikki immediately went after the necessary supplies, returning with 3.0 silk, suture needles, and Lidocaine.

Rox took one look at the syringe of Lidocaine and passed out.

Nikki smiled at her friend. "You big baby," she said under her breath as she assisted Dr. Syverson with closing the wound.

"It shouldn't scar too much," the doctor said, as he placed four tiny sutures along the length of the split. Glancing up at Nikki, he added, "You evidently know her. Do you have any idea what happened?"

Nikki nodded. "She's my best friend," she said, her voice cracking. Taking a deep breath, she continued. "She lives with this asshole who brutalizes her whenever the mood strikes him, which is more and more frequently these days," she said sadly.

"Why doesn't she just leave?" the doctor asked, putting in the last stitch.

"I can't tell you how many times I've asked her that very question. It's a long story," Nikki replied.

"Ah, excuse me. I'm looking for a Roxanne Ward," a voice said from the doorway.

Dr. Syverson looked up at the uniformed police officer. "This is Roxanne Ward, but I'm afraid she won't be able to answer your questions right now."

"All right then, is Mike Schmidt or Jerri Lockwood around?" he asked politely. "I understand they were the EMTs who responded to the domestic violence call."

Nikki stepped forward. "Jerri and Mike are on a call right now. They should be back soon, and you're welcome to wait in the lounge."

The x-rays arrived just as Nikki finished sponging the blood from Rox's split lip.

"Okay, let's see," Dr. Syverson said, examining the films carefully.

"Lungs look all right. However, two of the ribs are fractured. No fluid buildup in the abdomen. No obvious fractures in the vertebrae. Good. Looks like she was lucky this time." He took the films off of the light board. "We'll have to set and cast that wrist after the CT scan, though."

Nikki cringed at the doctor's words: "She was lucky this time." *He's right. One of these times, that maniac is going to kill her.*

About an hour later, the CT scan had been completed and a now-conscious Rox was wheeled back to the ER to await any additional treatment. Nikki had gone back to work and Jerri was there waiting for her. She managed a wan smile for her friend as she was placed in one of the examination rooms.

Jerri brushed back a lock of hair as she looked at Rox with a professional eye. Her color was good and she seemed stronger. "I know this sounds like a silly question, but how are you feeling?"

"I'm so glad you're here. I hate hospitals!" Being surrounded by reminders of the frailty of human flesh made Rox think about her father's illness, and that it wouldn't be long before he would take his final breath. Tears formed in her eyes at the prospect.

"I'm glad I'm here, too," Jerri said. "But what I meant was, how are you feeling physically?"

Rox was too tired to equivocate. "Miserable. My entire body hurts so badly. I've never felt anything like it before, not even..." She stopped abruptly, not having to say that she was referring to the whipping she had received earlier in the week.

Jerri nodded. "Hey, I can ask for some painkillers for you if you'd like," she said, leaning in close to her friend.

"Drugs? Drugs would be good." Rox was fighting to hold back the tears. When Nikki was around, all she wanted to do was cry and be held, but when Jerri was with her, she felt a driving need to put on a brave front.

As if she knew what Rox was thinking, Jerri whispered in her ear, "You know, Rox, you *can* cry in front of me. I won't tell, okay?" She grinned and winked conspiratorially.

Rox chuckled, then grabbed her ribs. "Oh, God, don't make me laugh," she said. After a moment, she caught her breath and looked up into her friend's concerned face.

With her good hand, she touched the side of Jerri's face and said, "I'm sorry, Jer. It's just that I'm so used to being the caretaker, it's tough to be the one who needs taking care of. It makes me feel so weak to cry."

"I know. Nikki is such a girl when it comes to crying. I, on the other hand... well, I avoid it when I can, but sometimes it's necessary. Like now." She brushed the bangs away from her friend's eyes, which were now closed. As Jerri played affectionately with Rox's hair, the tears began. They escaped from beneath the closed lids, ran down pale cheeks and spilled over onto the pillow.

"That's it, love, let it out," Jerri cooed as she continued to run her fingers through Rox's hair.

Rox grasped Jerri's other hand and squeezed it tightly as she cried. Soon, the crying subsided as Rox took a semi-deep breath, gasping at the pain in her side.

"Feel better?" Jerri asked.

"A little."

"Good."

At that moment, the orthopedic surgeon entered the cubicle and smiled at the patient. "I understand we have a wrist to set."

Jerri accompanied them into the cast room and held Rox tightly as they first numbed and then set the wrist. Rox came right off the gurney as they pushed and prodded the bones back into place, crying out in pain from the procedure. At last, it was time for the fiberglass cast to be applied.

"How long am I going to have to wear this clunky thing?" Rox asked petulantly.

Jerri smiled. It was a good sign that Rox was able to focus on something other than the pain of her injuries.

The doctor answered, "In order to allow the bones a good start at setting, about six weeks."

"Six weeks! I can't be out of commission that long, I've got a deadline."

"Six weeks is the minimum," the doctor cautioned. "You don't want any permanent disability, I'm sure."

Rox considered this for only a moment before she agreed. "Then you have to be sure that all of my fingers and my thumb are as mobile as possible," she insisted.

The doctor shook his head, but a wry smile flitted across his lips. "I'll do my best," he said, and began applying strips to form the cast.

Eventually, Rox and Jerri returned to the ER. Dr. Syverson was waiting for them with the results of the CT scan.

"Okay, Ms. Ward, you have a small subdural hematoma—a little blood gathering beneath the skull, near the point of impact. It's minor, but the risk remains for a cerebral hemorrhage or embolism. Several days of complete bed rest should take care of it." He saw the panicked look on Rox's face at the mention of several days in bed. "Most of which can be done at home," he added. "As long as you have help."

"She has help."

Jerri's immediate declaration drew a teary smile from Rox.

"Good. I would like to keep you overnight for observation. If things look all right in the morning, we'll send you home. Okay?"

Rox nodded. "Thank you, doctor."

He smiled at her. "You're very welcome. Now, we've got you patched up, but the healing part is up to you. Be sure you follow the discharge orders you'll be given." Receiving another nod of acknowledgement from Jerri, he said, "A nurse will be in shortly to escort you to your room. I'll be by to see you in the morning." With that, he left.

Jerri turned to Rox with a serious expression. "There's one more thing."

Rox looked up in question. "Those painkillers you mentioned, I hope."

"We'll see what we can do about that shortly, but no. The police are here. They've already talked to me about what we found at the scene, and they're waiting to interview you."

Rox sighed and closed her eyes. There was no escape.

Chapter 14

Cass ran from her car to the terminal, cursing herself for leaving her umbrella at home and cursing the weatherman for an inaccurate prediction of the morning's weather. *Now I'll have to sit in that cockpit in damp clothes for the next few hours,* she grumbled to herself as she entered the terminal, shaking the excess rain from her clothing.

"Nice day to travel, huh?" The sarcasm-laced voice came from her right as she stood at the control desk, filing her flight plan. Glancing over, Cass saw her co-pilot, Brian Anderson, standing there, also quite damp around the edges. "Forgot your umbrella too, huh, Brian?" she asked, chuckling.

"Damned weatherman couldn't predict rain if he was standing in the middle of a thundershower," he replied irritably.

"God, I hate flying in this kind of weather." Cass handed the paperwork over to the flight controller. Looking back at Brian, she asked, "Have they loaded the cargo yet?"

"Just about finished," he said. "You know, Cass, these goodwill missions are starting to wear thin—all cargo and not many passengers. Not a lot of action on board, if you know what I mean." He winked at his ranking officer. Brian was tall, dark and handsome, and considered himself to be quite a ladies' man, so he couldn't figure out why Cass wasn't interested in him. "But then, if I could just talk you into sharing more than a cockpit... " He grinned and left the rest of the sentence hanging.

Cass reached up and patted the side of his face. "In your dreams, Brian." She turned and headed out to the runway.

Brian threw his hands up and whined, "Aw, come on, Cass. How can you resist this handsome face?" he asked, only half in jest.

Cass was very tempted to answer his question, but decided against it. The fewer people who knew, the fewer questions she would have to field. "Let's just say you're not my type, and leave it at that, okay?" she said over her shoulder as they dashed from the terminal to the plane.

Brian boarded the plane before Cass, and went directly to the cockpit to start entering their flight information into the computer, while Cass checked the cargo status with the rest of the flight crew. As she climbed the last two steps and boarded the plane, she was met by Ginny, the attendant from her flight to Veracruz the previous week. Stopping just inside the entryway, she looked at the woman and smiled broadly. "Hi."

"Hi yourself, Captain Conway."

"Cass," the pilot corrected.

"Cass," Ginny repeated, handing her a towel.

"Thanks." She accepted the towel and wiped the rain from her face. "I missed you on last week's flight home. I hope things are all right with your family," Cass said sincerely.

Ginny smiled. "Yes, thank you. My mom rushed Dad to the hospital with chest pains, but it turned out to be heartburn." She blushed under Cass's intent gaze.

Cass placed her hand on Ginny's arm. "Good. I'm glad things worked out." She turned toward the cockpit.

"Can I get you anything once we're airborne?" Ginny asked hopefully.

Cass smiled disarmingly. "Coffee would be great."

"Black, right?" Ginny asked, raising her eyebrows expectantly.

"Black," Cass confirmed. She stood there for a moment and watched Ginny's hips sway back and forth beneath the tight uniform as she walked away. With an uncomfortable ache in her groin, she turned and entered the cockpit.

Cass, old buddy, old pal... we're gonna score tonight! Enforcer exclaimed gleefully.

A crackly voice came over the radio. "Flight 203, you are cleared for takeoff."

"It's about time," Brian complained as Cass taxied the plane to the runway.

"Ladies and gentlemen, this is your captain speaking," Cass said into the microphone, addressing the small group of passengers. "We have been cleared for takeoff. Please be sure that your seatbelts are fastened and your tray tables are locked in their upright position. Be advised that we'll be flying through a storm, and we expect to hit a little turbulence. It is highly recommend that your seatbelt remain fastened throughout the flight, or at the very least, while the seatbelt sign above your heads is illuminated. The flight attendant will review safety and evacuation procedures with you in the unlikely event of an emergency. As always, thank you for flying Southern Lights Airline, and have a nice flight."

"Th-th-th-that's all, folks!" Brian said in his best Porky Pig voice.

"Let's rock and roll, kiddies." Cass opened the jet engines to full throttle and propelled the aircraft down the runway. Within moments, they were airborne.

Their ascent into the clouds was a rocky one. The 737 was a mid-sized jet, and wasn't as immune to turbulence as the jumbo jets were. Soon, however, they were at a safe altitude above the storm, which increased the comfort of the ride significantly. Cass turned control of the plane over to Brian and left the cabin to use the ladies' room. Coming out of the washroom, she ran into Ginny.

"Captain," Ginny said shyly as she prepared the snack cart.

"Hi, Ginny."

The two women stood there in awkward silence for a few seconds. Shifting from foot to foot, Cass finally spoke. "Uh, Ginny, would you be interested in having dinner with me when we land in Durango?"

Ginny smiled and pushed an errant lock of hair behind her ear. "I'd like that very much, Captain."

"Cass. Please, call me Cass," she reminded the flight attendant as she reached forward and tucked that same stubborn lock of hair away from Ginny's face.

Flustered by the intimate gesture, Ginny giggled and blushed.

"All right then," Cass said. "I assume the airline has us all booked into the same hotel. Which room are you staying in?"

"304," replied Ginny.

"304. Okay. I'll pick you up at… six p.m. Is that all right?"

Ginny smiled. "Six o'clock is fine, Cap… I mean, Cass. I'll see you then."

"I'm looking forward to it," Cass said.

"Me, too."

The two women stood there awkwardly again, looking at each other. Finally, Ginny excused herself. "I've got to get back to the passengers. Until tonight?"

"Tonight," Cass replied, heading back to the cockpit, very proud of herself.

In her seat again, Cass checked the weather conditions along the route to Durango. It appeared that the West Coast, from Washington State through Central America, was being hit by a severe storm front and that they were about to fly into the worst of it. They were in for a bumpy ride

About an hour into the flight, an especially bad patch of turbulence rocked the mid-sized airplane.

"Shit!" Cass exclaimed. "Why they make us fly in weather like this is beyond me."

"Anything for the almighty dollar, Cass," Brian said.

Cass flipped on the seatbelt sign and reached for the microphone. "Ladies and gentlemen, please fasten your seatbelts and stow all loose pieces of luggage. As I'm sure you've noticed, we are experiencing turbulence at this time." She clicked off the microphone and hung it back up. "Goddamned weather!" she exclaimed as the plane was tossed around.

A loud crack echoed through the air, and the plane shuddered and dipped.

"What the fuck?" Brian exclaimed.

Quickly checking the controls, Cass determined that they had indeed lost altitude, and that one of the rudder controls was not functioning. "Shit! I think we've been hit!"

"Hit? You mean by lightning?"

"Of course, by lightning. What else could we hit up here, a UFO?" she said sharply, suddenly thinking of Rox. "Damn!" The closest airport was in San Diego. *Okay, don't panic.* Just as she reached for the microphone, the door to the cockpit flew open.

"What happened?" Ginny shouted.

"We've been struck by lighting, Ginny. Make sure the passengers are secure," Cass instructed. When Ginny hesitated, Cass shouted, "Now!"

Ginny turned and hurried out of the cockpit.

"Brian, hold her as steady as you can," Cass said. She reached for the microphone and switched the radio over to the emergency channel.

"Jesus Christ, Cass! Jesus Christ!" Brian struggled to keep the plane level.

"Mayday, mayday. This is Flight 203 out of San Jose, California en route to Durango, Mexico. We have been struck by lightning. I repeat, we have been struck by lightning." Cass's voice sounded much calmer than she felt.

The radio crackled to life. "Flight 203, this is the San Diego control tower. We have you on radar. Please state your condition."

Cass closed her eyes and thanked the powers that be for the response. "We are losing altitude and rudder control." She looked out the window on Brian's side of the plane and saw ragged pieces of metal where the wing tip had been. "As far as I can tell, the strike hit our right wing section only."

Suddenly, another jolt hit the plane and caused it to drop sharply. Cass dropped the microphone and grabbed the controls, helping Brian stabilize the plane.

Afraid to release the controls for any length of time, Cass switched from the microphone to the speaker box so she could talk and keep both hand on the controls.

The radio crackled again. "Flight 203, we show a sudden drop in your altitude. What is your condition?"

"We've been hit again, San Diego," Cass confirmed. Checking out the controls, she realized they had very little control over the steering. "Looks like—"

The cockpit door swung open and a visibly panicked Ginny stood in the doorway. "Oh, my God, Cass, we've been hit again!"

"God damn it, Ginny, I know we're usually only cargo, but you're supposed to be seeing to the passengers. Now pull yourself together and get your ass out there!"

Ginny turned and left.

"San Diego," Cass said, getting back to her damage report, "we have lost directional control. It appears we have been hit again, this time on our tail fin."

"Flight 203, you are approximately 90 miles north of the San Diego airport. If you can continue along this flight path and maintain your altitude, your arrival time should be approximately 20 minutes," came the reply. "We are preparing emergency crews for a potential crash landing."

"On a wing and a prayer, we'll make it," Cass muttered. Turning to Brian, she said, "Okay, all we need is twenty minutes. We need to hold her as steady as possible."

Cass reached up and switched on the microphone to the passenger cabin. "Folks, this is your captain speaking. As I'm sure you're aware, we have been hit by lightning. We've radioed the airport in San Diego and are now redirecting our flight to that destination. I ask that you remain as calm as possible, and remain seated and securely belted into your seats. In the event of a crash landing, you will be instructed to remain seated and to lower your head into your laps and wrap your arms around your legs. In the event of an ocean landing, your seat cushion can be used as a flotation device. Our estimated time of arrival is twenty minutes. Once again, please remain calm. We will do our best to land the plane as safely as possible. Thank you."

Taking a deep breath, Cass looked over at an ashen-faced Brian, who was holding onto his controls with white knuckles.

He glanced at her and smiled nervously. "We're going to make it, right, Cass?"

"We're certainly going to try."

Fifteen minutes later, they were making their descent into the San Diego airport.

"So far, so good." Cass reached for the lever to lower the landing gear. Nothing happened. "Shit! No landing gear. God damn it!" She reached for the radio to report their latest failure. "San Diego, this is Flight 203. We have landing gear failure. I repeat—we have landing gear failure. Please be prepared for a crash landing."

"We read you, Flight 203. Emergency preparations are underway."

Cass spotted the airport in the distance. "Okay, Brian. We've prepared for this eventuality. We just need to take her in easy. She's going to slide in on her belly, so we have to reduce speed as much as possible without allowing the nose to drop." Cass saw her co-pilot nod nervously in response to her instructions.

She switched on the microphone to the passenger cabin. "Folks, this is your captain speaking. The lightning strikes have affected our landing gear, so a crash landing will be necessary. Again, I ask you to remain calm, securely belted into your seat with your head in your lap and arms wrapped around your legs. Please take that position now, and remain that way until the plane comes to a safe stop. Flight attendants, take your seats and prepare for landing."

Cass's heart was in her throat as she watched the airport loom larger and larger. She reduced their speed dramatically, to the point where she felt as if they were floating above the ground, while she and Brian struggled to keep the nose pointed slightly upward. Closer and closer they came, slower and slower the plane flew, almost drifting toward the runway. She could see the emergency trucks and the ground crew applying layers of foam, then scrambling out of the way of the approaching aircraft. Finally, the tail end of the plane touched the ground, and the impact threw them all forward in their seats. The force was so great that it propelled Cass against the control panel in front of her, opening a deep gash above her right eye before she was whipped backward into her seat again.

The plane shuddered and then rolled from side to side as its entire belly made contact with the ground. What was left of the wing tips hit the ground alternately, breaking off in pieces and scattering all along the runway. Momentum kept the plane moving forward, counteracted only by the friction of metal against concrete as the injured bird slid through the foam that the emergency crews had spread moments earlier to prevent the plane from igniting into flames.

After what seemed like an eternity, the plane came to a stop near the end of the runway. For a long moment, Cass and Brian both remained in their seats, hands glued to the controls, looking straight ahead. An eerie silence ensued as the passengers looked at each other, amazed that they were still alive and uninjured. Finally, a collective sigh of relief was released and a cheer rose from the passenger cabin.

The cockpit door slammed open again and a very ruffled Ginny entered, tears running down her cheeks as she hugged and kissed Cass and then Brian. Moments later, the emergency crews began evacuating the plane. Cass insisted on remaining on board until all the passengers had safely deplaned, assisting in rescue efforts as much as possible. She brushed off the paramedics' attempts to look at the cut above her eye until all of the passengers had disembarked. By the time she did allow treatment, she had blood spattered over the right side of her face and shoulder.

The instant her feet touched the ground, Cass was surrounded by TV crews vying for an interview, and the paramedics finally forced her to sit still long enough for them to treat the cut on her forehead.

It was nearly five p.m. by the time the crew was debriefed by airport officials, and a special flight was arranged to fly them all back to San Jose.

Chapter 15

"Nikki, that isn't necessary," Rox said to her friend, who was sitting on the side of her hospital bed.

"Yes, it is. Dr. Syverson said you could go home tomorrow *if* you had help. Now, either you accept it, or you stay here. It's your choice."

"Niii-iik," Rox whined.

"Don't you, 'Nik' me. Jerri and I discussed it, and we both agree. If you won't stay with us, then we're moving in with you until you're able to take care of yourself." Nikki's tone was matter of fact.

Rox looked at Jerri, who was leaning against the windowsill.

"Don't look for any sympathy from me, Rox. I agree with Nikki."

Rox threw her good hand up into the air. "I can't win with you two, can I?"

Nikki leaned in and kissed Rox on the cheek. "No, you can't, so get over it. Jerri and I both took the day off tomorrow, so we'll be by early to get you. Okay?" She rose to leave.

Rox feigned indignation. "All right. I guess I don't have any choice, do I?"

"No, you don't. Now scoot down there so I can tuck you in," Nikki commanded as Jerri chuckled from her seat on the windowsill.

She's such a mother hen, Jerri thought as she watched her wife taking care of their friend. She walked over to Rox's bedside and leaned in to kiss her. "Sleep well, girlfriend. The night nurse should be by soon with something to help you sleep, and we'll be here bright and early tomorrow."

Rox nodded, trying hard not to cry. *I feel like such a big baby.* At times like this, she wished she had her own Jerri. Someone who would hold her and comfort her while she cried. Someone who would chase away her doubts and fears. Someone who would make love feel good, not painful. *Someone… some day.*

"I love you guys," Rox said as a tear rolled down her cheek.

"We love you too, sweetie," Nikki said from the doorway.

Jerri smiled. "We'll see you in the morning."

The night nurse came in as Nikki and Jerri left. Soon, the meds she administered kicked in, and Rox fell into a restless sleep.

Rox awoke in the middle of a forest. She sat up and looked around; she was alone, in what looked like someone's camp. She rose to her feet, then looked down at herself. She was wearing leather trousers tucked into knee-high boots and a long white muslin shirt with a wide, pointed collar and billowy sleeves that were cuffed at the wrists. A sash circled her waist twice and tied at the side. The attire made her think of the Three Musketeers.

This all looks so familiar, she thought as she walked around the campsite.

In the distance, she heard a moan. She stopped and strained to listen. She heard the moan again, this time louder. Following the sound, Rox came upon a figure lying on the ground, moaning in pain. She reached down and turned the person over; it was a dark-haired woman. She wore an outfit similar to Rox's, except her shirt was loosely held together with thin leather laces.

Brushing the hair off the woman's face, Rox saw a deep gash above her right eye. Rox went to a nearby stream, tore off a piece of her shirt and soaked the material in the cool water, then returned to cleanse the wound. As she was washing away the blood, the woman stirred.

"Rox."

Startled that the woman knew her name, Rox said, "Do I know you?"

"We have only met in our hearts, but we have spent many lifetimes together," the injured woman replied.

Thinking the woman was delirious, Rox ignored her ramblings. "Can you tell me how you were injured?"

The woman looked confused for a second, then replied, "I fell from the sky."

Rox suddenly woke, and sat up in her hospital bed so quickly that she felt dizzy, and was forced to lie back down for fear of toppling out of bed. Placing her good hand on her forehead, she breathed deeply until her heartbeat returned to normal. *Fell from the sky?* Rox thought as she tried to remember her dream. Almost immediately, she succumbed again to the effects of the medication and fell into a deep sleep.

* * *

Cass's return flight landed in San Jose at eight p.m. Thursday evening. What had started out as a routine two-day flight into Mexico had turned into a nightmare. Though crash-landing a plane was a required exercise in simulated flight training, most pilots lived a lifetime without actually having to go through it. In the ten years Cass had been flying, she had never before had to ditch a plane. The experience had left her shaken to the depths of her soul.

The San Jose airport was mobbed with reporters and TV crews, all wanting to get a first-hand account of the crash landing and to get an interview with Cass, who had quickly become a local hero.

She was essentially a private person, and the notoriety was making her uncomfortable. After trying to get away from the throng for twenty minutes, she finally decided that the fastest way to escape was to do the interview. Perhaps then would they leave her alone. Ten minutes later, after the local TV stations had taped the joint interview, the press reluctantly allowed Cass to leave.

She had almost made it to her car, when she heard a woman's voice calling after her. "Cass! Cass, wait up."

Cass turned and saw Ginny walking quickly toward her. She sighed impatiently. After the day's harrowing experience and Ginny's lack of composure during the crisis, Cass didn't much feel like entertaining her. She had a pounding headache and the stitches in her forehead stung and itched. On top of everything else, she was still wearing her bloodstained uniform and desperately wanted a shower. Nevertheless, Cass summoned the shreds of her patience and stopped to wait.

"Hi, Ginny."

"Hi. Are you still interested in dinner?" Ginny asked hopefully.

"Truthfully, after today's flight, all I want to do is go home, shower, and climb into bed," Cass replied.

"Sounds like a plan to me," Ginny replied suggestively.

"Alone." Cass saw the disappointment on the woman's face and tried to soften the letdown. "Look, I'm sorry, Ginny, but my head is killing me and I need to sleep. Some other time, maybe?"

Obviously disappointed, Ginny pouted and nodded.

"All right then. Good night."

Cass turned resolutely, walked to her car and climbed in. Ten minutes later, she was walking through her condo toward the shower, stripping off her clothes and discarding them wherever they happened to fall. Standing under the spray, she gradually released the nervous tension that had built up since that first lightning strike, when the realization of her own mortality had rushed in on her. A shudder ran through her body and a sob escaped.

No, Cass, you're not going to live forever, E. confirmed. *We would have died today, if it hadn't been for your piloting skills. Girl, life is too short to go on living it alone. Why don't we do something about that? Let's e-mail the chick from Maine and ask her to marry us.*

Cass chuckled at her alter ego's boldness. *Oh, E., if it were only that easy.* She rinsed soap and blood out of her hair. *I will e-mail her, though. Let's hope she's had time to respond to my last two messages.*

Feeling much better after her shower, Cass sat in front of her computer, waiting impatiently. When it finally booted, she tried to log on to the Internet. Three failed attempts later, she called her ISP's help line and learned that her Internet server was down and not expected to be back up for several hours. She slammed the phone into the cradle, shut down the computer and stomped off to bed.

* * *

Rox was up and dressed long before Nikki and Jerri arrived to drive her home. The doctor had examined her and declared her well enough to go home, as long as she had help around the house for the next few days. She had also been given strict orders to remain in bed and get plenty of rest. Leaning back against an array of pillows, Rox surfed through the TV channels with the remote control as she waited. Just as she began to take interest in a newscast about a downed airplane in San Diego, she was interrupted by a police officer who knocked at the door.

"Miss Ward?"

Clicking off the TV, Rox turned to the officer. "Yes. What can I do for you, officer?"

"Miss Ward, I'm Officer Richmond, and I'm following up on the domestic abuse report we received yesterday from emergency room personnel. May I have a few moments of your time?"

Rox was suddenly nervous. She had not considered the legal entanglements that could result from Chris's attack, and she wasn't sure she was prepared to pursue action against him. "Yes, of course. Please have a seat." She gestured him to a chair by her bedside.

"Miss Ward, do you live at 1163 Oceanview Terrace?"

"Yes, I do."

Officer Richmond glanced at his notepad. "And were you assaulted in your home yesterday by one Chris Dalton?"

Roxanne hemmed and hawed. "I... uh... I wouldn't exactly say assaulted. Yes, we argued," she said, quickly fabricating a story. "But 'assault' seems a little strong," she equivocated, not meeting the officer's eyes.

"Miss Ward, your injuries are consistent with domestic violence. Based on the information we received from the paramedics yesterday, we have reason to believe Dalton assaulted you," he insisted.

Rox felt as if she were being backed into a corner, and she lashed out defensively. "Officer Richmond, we argued, okay? We were at the top of the stairs... Chris grabbed me... I pulled away, lost my balance, and fell down the stairs. That is what happened," she lied.

"Miss Ward, are you saying that you don't want to press charges against Dalton?"

"That's exactly what I'm saying."

Officer Richmond looked at her for several long moments before he took a deep breath and shook his head. "All right, then, I guess I'm finished here." He stood and closed his notebook, and slipped it and his pen into his shirt pocket. He retrieved his hat from the bedside table and looked down at Rox. "Miss Ward, if you suddenly remember any new information, please call the precinct and ask for Officer Doug Richmond, all right? Here's my contact information." He handed her a card.

Rox took it with her good hand, then glanced down at the casted arm lying in her lap. "All right, thank you," she said in a small voice.

"Have a good day," Officer Richmond said as he left the room, passing Nikki and Jerri on his way out.

"Hey there, love." Nikki planted herself at the side of Rox's bed and kissed her on the cheek. "How are you feeling this morning?"

Rox didn't meet Nikki's eyes, continuing to stare at her broken wrist. "Fine," she mumbled.

Nikki lifted Rox's chin to force eye contact. "Roxie, what's wrong?"

Jerri, who had remained in the doorway watching the police officer walk down the hall, answered for her. "You told him it was an accident, didn't you, Rox?"

Roxanne shook her chin free of Nikki's hand and looked down without answering.

Jerri threw her arms up into the air. "Well, that's great, just great! God damn it, Rox, do you have a death wish? Why are you protecting that asshole?"

"My father… " Roxanne began.

Jerri was at the foot of Rox's bed in two long strides. "No! I don't want to hear about how you're protecting your father, Roxanne. How about protecting yourself for a change, huh?" She leaned over the bed to emphasize her point.

"Jerri, honey, please calm down." Nikki turned to Rox. "Is that right, Rox? Did you tell the police it was an accident?"

Rox closed her eyes and tears trickled down her cheeks as she nodded.

Nikki looked up at Jerri, who raised an eyebrow. Taking a quick breath, Nikki closed her eyes and massaged her forehead. "Roxie—"

"Look, I know you mean well, and I love you both for it, but it's my life, okay? Now, please, I just want to go home."

Nikki stood up beside the bed. "All right." Her voice had a defeated sound. "Let's go."

The ride to Rox's house was quiet and heavy with tension. Jerri drove as Nikki sat sideways in the passenger seat, watching Rox in the back seat. Rox spent most of the drive looking solemnly out the side window, avoiding her friend's gaze.

As they stepped into the large, open entryway, Rox turned to her friends. "Look, I really appreciate what you're willing to do for me, but it isn't necessary for you to stay."

"We're staying, Rox," Jerri said. "Nikki's already arranged to take the week off so she can care for you, which is more than you seem to be willing to do for yourself. I don't want to hear another word about it." She grabbed the two suitcases that she and Nikki had brought along and headed up the stairs to settle into one of the guest rooms.

"Let's go make a pot of coffee before we tuck you into bed."

"I don't need to go to bed, Nik."

"Your doctor said 'plenty of rest,' Rox. Now, who is the nurse here; you or me? Come on, it'll be fun. Jerri and I will join you there for coffee and girl talk. What do you say?"

Rox reluctantly agreed as she allowed Nikki to steer her into the kitchen. Along the way, Nikki tried to explain her partner's behavior. "Please don't be angry with Jerri. She cares so much about you. She's just trying to protect you."

Dropping heavily onto one of the kitchen chairs, Rox placed her broken wrist gingerly on the table and sighed. "I know, but I... damn it, Nik, my father only has a few months left to live. It'll be all over then, I promise."

Nikki walked over and wrapped her arms around her friend, pulling her head in to rest on her own chest. She placed a long, firm kiss on Rox's head, then said, "You don't have to let the end of your father's life signal the beginning of yours. Sweetheart, if he only knew you were living in such pain, he'd be the first to tell you to escape from it, and he'd be the first to kick Chris's ass. If you want your father to die happy, then let him die with the knowledge that you are truly happy, not living behind a facade of happiness."

Rox wrapped her good arm around Nikki's waist and hugged her as tightly as her broken ribs would allow. Her body shuddered as she sobbed in her friend's embrace. Then she felt another pair of arms wrap around her as Jerri joined them, holding the two women who meant the world to her.

After several moments, Rox broke the embrace, feeling foolish for crying like a helpless child. Wiping her eyes, she started to rise. "I've got to pick up the mail, get the paper—"

"Sit. I'll get it," Jerri said. She gently pushed the smaller woman back into the chair, then went to gather the mail and the newspaper that were lying in a heap on the living room floor where they had been shoved through the mail slot in the front door. She returned to the kitchen and tossed the mail on the table, then unfolded the paper and laid it flat in front of Rox.

Rox scanned the front page. The banner headline read, "Boeing 737 Crash-Lands in San Diego."

"Hey! This was on the news while I was waiting for you two this morning," Rox said as she continued to scan the article.

A skilled Southern Lights Airline pilot guided Flight 203 through an emergency landing in San Diego yesterday afternoon after the plane was struck twice by lightning. The aircraft was en route from San Jose to Durango, Mexico to deliver much needed medical supplies to the drought-stricken area. Airport officials attribute the safety of the flight crew and passengers to the skillful flying of pilot Cassidy Conway...

"Oh, my God, Cass!" Rox exclaimed. She felt dizzy and nauseous. "Oh, my God!"

Nikki put a cup of coffee in front of Rox, then continued reading aloud from the article while Jerri rubbed Rox's back in an effort to calm her.

"Airport officials attribute the safety of the flight crew and passengers to the skillful flying of pilot Cassidy Conway, who was forced to land the plane without landing gear. Witnesses say the plane slid onto the runway and glided several hundred yards, rolling side to side while pieces of the wings broke off and scattered in its wake. When the plane came to a stop near the end of the runway, Captain Conway refused to exit the plane and refused medical help for a wound on the forehead until all the passengers had safely disembarked."

Nikki put the paper down on the table and looked at Rox. "Wow! Looks like your Captain Conway is a hero." She saw the ashen hue of her friend's face and asked, "Are you okay, Rox?"

Rox just stared at the paper on the table. Finally, she looked at Nikki and then Jerri. "I have to get online," she said. "I need to send him an e-mail."

"Rox, you're supposed to be resting," Nikki said, "not spending hours on the Net."

"I won't spend hours. Nikki, I've got to do this. He almost died! I want him to know that I'm thinking about him." *And that I'm proud of him.*

"Come on, I'll help you with the stairs," Jerri said.

"Jer," Nikki whined, exasperated with both Rox and her wife.

"Nik, if it were me in that situation, wouldn't you do the same?" Jerri asked, immediately quashing Nikki's objections.

Nikki frowned, knowing she was outvoted. "All right, all right," she said. "But you're going to bed right after that, okay?" She gave Rox a pointed look.

"Okay," Rox agreed. "I'll sleep on the hide-a-bed in my office."

"What am I going to do with you?" Nikki exclaimed, throwing up her hands.

Jerri and Rox tried to hide their grins as they made their way to the stairs.

"Well, it's already noon. You have one hour, then I'm bringing lunch up. You got it?" Nikki watched her wife and best friend head for the stairs. "Kids today," she muttered as she went into the kitchen to fix something for lunch.

* * *

"Oh, my God. Did someone get the name of the guy that ran over me?" Cass struggled to sit up in bed. "Gee, it feels like I was in a plane wreck," she muttered. Every muscle in her body ached. Her legs hurt worst of all. *Must be from when I braced them for the impact.*

Cass, do you realize you're talking to yourself again? Enforcer asked.

E., I've decided to live life to the fullest. After that near disaster yesterday, I really don't give a damn if I talk to myself anymore or not. At least I'm alive.

Just as she managed to maneuver her feet to the floor, the telephone rang. She reached over to pick up the receiver and brought it to her ear. "Hello?"

"Cassidy Conway, I'm going to kick your ass from here to kingdom come! Damn it, young lady, why didn't you call me last night when you got in? For Christ's sake, I pick up the morning paper and there, across the headlines, it says, 'Local Hero Cassidy Conway Crash-Lands Plane.' Roger nearly had to pick me up off the floor. What do you have to say for yourself?"

"Good morning to you, too, Ang," Cass said dryly.

"I'll 'good morning' you. You get your ass dressed and over here to the diner this instant, do you hear me? I need to see for myself that you're all right."

"Can I take a shower first? It seems like my muscles aren't cooperating today," Cass said, mirth brightening her voice.

"I'm glad you think this is funny. You've got one hour. I'll have today's special waiting for you, all right?"

Cass smiled to herself. "All right, Angie. One hour."

An hour later, Cass was sitting at her usual table, head in her hands, waiting patiently as she got reamed out for the second time that morning.

Angie paced back and forth in front of her table, her hands flailing as she vented her anger. Finally, she stopped in front of the table, put her hands on her hips and said, "Well?"

Cass looked up sheepishly. Sitting back in her chair, she threw up her hands. "All right, Ang. You're right—I should have called. I'm sorry. The next time I have to crash-land a plane, I'll call you, okay?"

Having purged her worry along with her annoyance, Angie softened. "All right, you remember that. Now, as soon as you've finished your breakfast, I want you to tell me about this landing that's made you such a hero, okay?"

Smiling, Cass said, "Yes, mommy. May I eat now?"

Angie swatted Cass on the arm and the younger woman grasped the point of injury and howled in mock pain. Angie swatted her again. "There's another one for good measure," she said, then headed to the kitchen for Cass's breakfast.

Cass grinned as she watched her go.

Chapter 16

Jerri could see that the two flights of stairs took more out of her friend than Rox cared to admit. She sat her down at the computer and booted up the machine for her as Rox caught her breath. While she logged on, Jerri went over and pulled the hide-a-bed out of the couch, then went down to the linen closet in the second-floor bathroom to get clean sheets and a blanket. She returned to the attic and made the bed, keeping watch from the corner of her eye.

Rox was massaging her ribs with her uninjured hand as she waited for the network to connect.

"Are you all right?" Jerri asked.

Rox nodded, not taking her eyes off the monitor. "Ribs ache. I'll be fine."

Finally, she was in, and she went directly to new mail. She hadn't checked her mail since Wednesday afternoon, and now it was Friday morning. The system retrieved a total of seven new messages. Two of them were from Cass. Bypassing the other five, she went directly to Cass's first note.

Hi, Rox,

I really enjoyed our chat session too. I can't believe how fast the time flew. I hope I didn't keep you up too late.

I'm sorry to hear that you don't have someone to discuss your work with more often. I find science fiction captivating and stimulating. I can't imagine why someone wouldn't want to discuss it—especially with a talented writer like you.

So you want a description of me, huh? Okay, I hope I don't disappoint you. I'm nearly six feet tall, relatively slim, somewhat muscular from working out and from Tae Kwon Do. (I earned my black belt a few months ago). I have dark hair and blue eyes. That's about it. I'm attaching a scanned photo of me and my co-pilot so you can see for yourself. If you want to know more, just let me know.

I would like to chat with you again, too. I find myself quite enchanted with you, Roxanne Ward. You invade my thoughts at the oddest moments. It's a welcome invasion, mind you. I haven't had any real companionship since the woman I was seeing passed away, nearly three years ago. I have guarded my heart closely ever since. It feels good for it to be invaded again.

Well, I'm on my way to dinner, so I will bid you adieu for now.

I'm looking forward to chatting with you again, whenever it's convenient for you.

Cass

Roxanne sat stunned as she read the note. *He's enchanted with me?* She felt her heart flip-flop in her chest. *Tall, dark, blue eyes. Wow, sounds like a dream come true. It looks like he's had a pretty rough life though. His companion passed away three years ago. I wonder if he loved her.* Rox scrolled to the attached photograph.

"Wow, he *is* good-looking," Rox said, looking at a picture of a tall, dark-haired man in a pilot's uniform posing with an attractive woman, also dressed in flight blues. *Hmmm, she's quite good-looking, too. I wonder if they have a history.*

Jerri couldn't resist taking a look at the mystery man over Rox's shoulder. "Yeah, he's good-looking, all right, but I'm kind of partial to the lovely lady with him."

"You would be." Rox gently elbowed her friend in the stomach. "You'd better not let Nikki hear you say that. You'll be sleeping on the couch for a week."

Jerri laughed. "Fat chance of that. She can't resist my beauty and charm."

"Oh. puh-lease," Rox said, taking a closer look at the picture. *She looks really familiar; where have I seen her before?* she thought. *She certainly is beautiful.*

Shrugging off the feeling of familiarity, she decided to read the second post before answering either. Maneuvering the mouse with difficulty, she closed the note and struggled to align the pointer to the next piece of mail. "Damn it."

"You okay?"

"Yeah, it's just hard to do things left-handed. Damned cast. How am I going to write with my hand in this contraption? And look, my fingers are all swollen. Will it be like that for the whole six weeks?"

"No. The swelling will be gone in a few days. Do you want some help typing a reply?"

Rox looked at Jerri as if to say, "you're kidding, right?" After she gave the offer some logical consideration, her eyebrows drew into a frown.

"That was an interesting play of emotions," Jerri said, watching the expressions parading across her friend's face.

Rox grinned. "I'm sorry, Jer. I just feel so damned helpless. Yeah, I might need some help. Let me read this next one first, okay?"

"I'm in no hurry. Got the day off." Jerri settled herself on one of the overstuffed chairs and crossed her legs.

Rox turned back to the monitor and clicked on Cass's second post.

> *Hi, Rox,*
>
> *Look, I'm sorry I was so forward in my last post. I don't want to push you into anything. It's just that I have never before felt such an instant connection with anyone the way I did with you, and I was hoping that you felt the same. I'm sorry if I've overstepped my bounds. You're probably involved in a loving relationship already, and I certainly don't want to interfere with your happiness.*
>
> *Please forgive me?*
> *Cass*

Rox stared at the note. "Nothing could be further from the truth, Cass." Without turning around, she said, "Jer, I guess I need to take you up on that offer."

Jerri rose to her feet and stood behind her friend. She looked at Rox for permission, then scanned the screen. When she was through, Rox clicked on the first note and allowed her friend to read that one as well.

"Go back to the second note," Jerri said. After reading it again, she looked at Rox. "Sounds like this guy is pretty taken with you. How do you feel about that?"

"I don't know, exactly," Rox said, flustered. "I got a tingly feeling in the pit of my stomach when I read it... kind of like butterflies."

"Well, what do we know about him?" Jerri asked, trying to take an analytic approach.

"Well, I know that he's nearly six feet tall and he has dark hair and blue eyes; he's muscular, works out, and has a black belt in Tae Kwon Do. He's a pilot for a commercial airline, lives in San Jose, California, is apparently very skilled in flying a plane—and crash-landing one, by the looks of it—so he's probably cool under pressure. Considering that he refused medical help until all the passengers were safe, he must be pretty gallant. That's about it. Oh, oh—he said he was in a relationship and that she died three years ago."

Jerri listened carefully then recapped what she had heard. "Okay—single, tall, dark and handsome, good job, even-tempered, smart and respectful. Sounds like the perfect guy. He's also a safe distance away, so that will give you time to get to know him before he physically invades your life. I'd say go for it."

Rox grinned. "I was hoping you'd say that." When Jerri just looked down at her expectantly, Rox became confused. "What?"

"I can't type if your butt is in the chair," Jerri teased.

Rox chuckled and gingerly rose from her seat, taking the chair Jerri had pulled alongside the desk.

Jerri settled down in front of the computer, selected "Reply," and sat with her fingers poised over the keys. "Shoot."

"Ah… ah… okay… let me think," Rox said. "Okay, type this… She proceeded to dictate, then read the resulting message.

> *Hi, Cass,*
>
> *I picked up the paper this morning and read about a heroic pilot named Cassidy Conway, who skillfully saved a plane full of people from probable death. Know anyone by that name?*
>
> *I can't tell you how it made me feel to know your life was in danger. I know we haven't gotten to know each other very well yet, but I also feel the connection you mentioned in your last message. I thank the powers above that I didn't lose you so soon after finding you.*
>
> *Please don't feel that you have overstepped your bounds. I am not currently in a loving relationship.*

Rox blinked at the following words, which she had not dictated:

In fact, I live with a brutal, motherfucking, abusive son of a bitch whom my friend Jerri wants to pulverize.

"Jerri, erase that! Jesus Christ, woman, this is *my* note, remember?" Rox scolded.

"Gee, Rox, you're no fun. I vote for telling it like it is. Maybe Cass will fly out here and kick Chris's ass for all of us."

"Jerri!"

"All right, all right, I'm erasing it. Sheesh." Jerri deleted the last sentence.

"All right, moving on…" Rox said.

In fact, I'm just ending a very dark and disturbing relationship with someone I'm sure is being unfaithful to me. I will guard my heart carefully from this point on. However, somehow I feel that it would be safe in your hands. I'm looking forward to knowing you better and seeing if my assessment is correct.

"Don't you think 'assessment' sounds a little clinical? It's like you're telling the guy you want to do his tax return or something."

"Jerri!"

"Well, it is," Jerri said defensively.

"Okay, okay. Change it to… 'I'm looking forward to knowing you better and finding out if my feelings are correct.' How's that?"

"Much better," Jerri commented, typing the amendment.

"All right, just a bit more." Rox read the last section of the draft.

You say that you're enchanted with me, and that I invade your thoughts. I'm enchanted with you, too. I long to know the sensitive, caring and compassionate person described in the news article in this morning's paper. I am truly impressed by your gallant nature, Cass Conway. I look forward to becoming your friend, and to whatever develops beyond friendship.

Please write soon. I await your reply in hope of beginning a new and wonderful relationship… one that is mutually satisfying and enjoyable.

You are in my thoughts,

Rox

"What do you think?" Rox asked her friend.

"Well, it doesn't make me cream my jeans, but it's a start," Jerri replied.

"What do you want me to do—tell the guy I want to jump his bones? Christ, I haven't even met him yet!" Rox's voice was shrill.

"Whoa! Calm down there, tiger, I was only kidding. It sounds good. Not too pushy, not too desperate, but definitely interested. It's good," Jerri said, trying to sound soothing.

"Do you really think so, or are you just saying that to shut me up?" Rox asked seriously.

"I'm just saying that to shut you up. No, no, Rox, really, it's good," she quickly repeated when she saw her friend's temper begin to rise.

"Okay, then, send it," Rox said.

Grinning, Jerri moved the mouse over to "Send" and clicked the button. An instant later, the note was gone.

* * *

Angie sat and talked to Cass all during her breakfast, feeding her coffee after coffee, keeping her there long enough to get all the crash details out of her.

Finally, after Cass had given the woman every detail at least three times, she called a halt to the cross-examination. "Ang, I'd love to stay and talk to you all day, but I really need to go home and soak in a hot tub. My entire body is aching."

Angie was on her feet in an instant to help Cass out of her chair. "That's a good idea, sweetie. Go home, soak and relax. You certainly deserve it after what you've been through. Why don't you call me later and let me know when you'll be ready for dinner, and I'll run it over to you. Okay?"

"Thanks very much. And thanks for breakfast." Cass accepted one last hug, then walked toward the door.

Angie's heart broke with each halting step she watched. "Honey, do you want me to take you home?"

"Nah, I'll be fine. I'm just a little sore. Nothing a nice soak in the hot tub won't cure."

Halfway home, Cass was cursing herself for walking instead of driving to the diner, or at the very least, for not accepting Angie's offer of a ride home. *Damn! And here I thought I was in good shape.*

Not enough sex. That's it, you know. Not enough sex, Enforcer interjected.

What the hell are you talking about? What does sex have to do with a plane crash?

Well, what hurts the most? Your legs, right? Enforcer asked.

Yeah. And your point is?

Your legs would be in better shape if you spread them more often.

Oh, for Christ's sake, will you take a chill pill and crawl back into your corner, please?

Hey, don't shoot the messenger. I'm just trying to help, Enforcer protested.

Your kind of help I don't need.

Cass unlocked her door and stepped inside. She went directly to the bathroom and started filling the tub with hot water and scented bath oils. She stripped off her clothes and stretched her arms straight over her head, leaning her body from side to side in an attempt to loosen the sore muscles before immersing herself in the hot water. Cass turned her back to the mirror and looked over her shoulder to evaluate the shape her body was in, relatively pleased with her reflection until she saw the large bruises that extended from her left shoulder blade to her hipbone, and then again from the top of her thigh to her knee.

"Holy shit!" Cass closed her eyes and lowered her head, trying to remember any kind of impact. She remembered being thrown forward into the control panel and cutting her forehead, and then roughly to the left against the side of the cockpit when the plane rolled that way. "No wonder I'm all bruised and sore."

Finally, the tub was filled and Cass slipped gingerly into the hot water. She groaned at the heat as first her feet, then legs, buttocks, back, breasts, and finally, her arms and shoulders were immersed. She struggled to breathe, taking short, gasping breaths until her body acclimated to the water's temperature. Finally, she was able to relax and lean her head against the headrest as the massaging action of the churning water began to alleviate her soreness. Closing her eyes, Cass found herself wishing for something to read. That led her thoughts to Rox.

"Roxanne," she whispered into the air, savoring the sound of the name as it rolled off her tongue.

Cass imagined what it would be like to hold the petite woman in her arms... to caress her skin... to kiss her lips. Closing her eyes, she pictured their bodies entwined—one light, one dark; one tall, one short; green eyes and blue locked in a gaze of love. By concentrating very hard, Cass felt that she could almost hear Roxanne call out her name in the throes of passion as she pushed her closer to the pinnacle.

This isn't fair, Cass, Enforcer said, snapping her back to reality.

What isn't fair?

You're trying to drive me crazy, aren't you? You'd better buy those toys real soon, before I do something to embarrass you. Capisce?

Give me a break, E. I take care of you when it's necessary, don't I?

Your definition of necessary and mine are not the same, unfortunately, Enforcer groused.

Well, my friend, I'm starting to agree with you, and that in itself terrifies me. Cass reached forward and flicked the drain switch.

Chapter 17

Nikki carried the lunch tray up to the attic, arriving just as Jerri helped Rox settle into the hide-a-bed.

"Did you send your note?" she asked as she placed the tray on the end table next to the bed.

Rox nodded, and Jerri went over to see what was on the tray.

"That looks heavy. You should have yelled; I would have given you a hand," she said, taking in the assortment of fruit, breakfast cereal, pastries, milk, coffee and dinnerware.

"Hey, I'm stronger than I look. I lug patients all day, remember?" Nikki said.

"I've got something you can lug," Jerri said, wicked eyebrows waggling up and down. Her arms circled her wife's waist as Nikki grinned.

"Uh, guys... Yoo-hoo! Over here?" Rox waved her uninjured hand at her friends. "Can you save that for later? I'm kind of starved here."

Still holding Nikki in her arms, Jerri looked down at Rox. "You're just jealous," she said.

"You're damned right I am. Now cut that out and feed me."

Nikki looked up at Jerri. "She's a bossy little thing, isn't she? Are you sure you want to stay here with her?" she asked with a straight face.

"Aarrgghh!" Rox yelled.

"All right, all right, Your Highness, we'll feed you," Jerri said.

Soon, all three women were sitting on the bed with plates of food in their laps.

"So what did the note say?" Nikki asked, popping a strawberry into her mouth.

"It said that Rox wanted to fly to California and jump this guy's bones," Jerri volunteered. "Ow!" Jerri yelped as a well-directed grape hit her in the side of the face.

"It did not," Rox said, grinning at her surprisingly accurate left-handed aim.

Nikki gave Rox a high-five for her marksmanship.

"Hey, you're supposed to be on my side," Jerri complained to her wife.

"It was a good shot, even you have to admit that. Can't let good work go unrewarded, now, can we?" Nikki replied. "So what did the e-mail say?"

"Well, Cass was concerned that I might already be involved in a happy relationship, and he didn't want to do anything to disrupt it. I told him that wasn't the case, and that I was very interested in getting to know him," Rox said. "Oh, and he sent a picture of himself with his co-pilot. He's really very good-looking."

When Jerri looked at Rox pleadingly, silently begging her not to divulge her comment about the co-pilot, Rox couldn't resist. "And his co-pilot is quite a looker too. Right, Jerri?" She grinned.

Nikki quirked an eyebrow and looked expectantly at her wife.

"Uh, yeah, a real looker," Jerri replied, giving Rox a dirty look.

"Mind if I see?" Nikki asked, rising to her feet.

"We shut it down already," Jerri said quickly.

Rox maintained eye contact with a squirming Jerri. "No, I don't mind at all. Just log back on; you know my password."

Jerri scooted over beside Rox. "You're lucky your wrist is already broken, little one," Jerri said with an evil smile.

Nikki turned from the computer screen to look at her wife, who wore the saddest pair of puppy dog eyes she had ever seen. Nikki began to chuckle. She just couldn't stay mad at Jerri when she looked like that. "You are in so much trouble, Big Guy," she said to her dark-haired wife.

Jerri began to whimper like a puppy dog.

"Jerri, it won't work!" Nikki said, trying to act angry but failing miserably.

"What if I roll over and play dead?"

"Nope. Still angry."

"What if I sit up and beg?" Jerri offered

Nikki shook her head, and covered her mouth to hide a grin.

"How about... how about if I ride your leg?" Jerri said, eyebrows dancing up and down.

Nikki's eyes widened. Without breaking eye contact with her wife, she said, "Uh, Rox, will you be all right here by yourself for a while?"

"Sure. There are three guest rooms; just pick one," Rox said with a knowing grin. "I'm going to take a nap. Keep the noise down, will you?"

Jerri was off the hide-a-bed in a jiffy. She picked Nikki up and threw her over her shoulder, then carefully negotiated the stairs. Nikki held on tightly and squealed all the way down.

Rox grinned as she slowly settled her aching body under the covers. *Those two are just way cute. Some day I'll know that kind of love. Some day,* she thought, just before she drifted off to sleep.

* * *

After she got out of the tub, Cass toweled herself dry, slipped on a matching pair of blue briefs and sports bra, and suffered through fifteen minutes of stretching exercises. Feeling a hundred percent better than when she'd stepped into the hot water, she went to power up the computer. A glance at the clock told her that it was almost noon.

While she waited, she picked up the phone and called pizza delivery, then went to her room to slip on shorts and a t-shirt. The last time Cass had answered the door in her underwear, the elderly gentleman who lived in the end unit had been collecting association fees and she had nearly given him a heart attack. The condo association had put her on notice for indecent exposure.

After logging on, Cass waited nervously while the server went out to retrieve new posts. She was hoping that Rox had responded to her previous two e-mails. Finally, one new message was displayed, from Rox@Starship.com.

"Yes!" Cass hurriedly double-clicked on the icon.

> *Hi, Cass,*
>
> *I picked up the paper this morning and read about a heroic pilot named Cassidy Conway, who skillfully saved a plane full of people from probable death. Know anyone by that name?*
>
> *I can't tell you how it made me feel to know your life was in danger. I know we haven't gotten to know each other very well yet, but I also feel the connection you mentioned in your last message. I thank the powers above that I didn't lose you so soon after finding you.*

Please don't feel that you have overstepped your bounds. I am not currently in a loving relationship. In fact, I'm just ending a very dark and disturbing relationship with someone I'm sure is being unfaithful to me. I will guard my heart carefully from this point on. However, somehow I feel that it would be safe in your hands. I'm looking forward to knowing you better and finding out if my feelings are correct.

You say that you're enchanted with me, and that I invade your thoughts. I'm enchanted with you, too. I long to know the sensitive, caring, and compassionate person described in the news article in this morning's paper. I am truly impressed by your gallant nature, Cass Conway. I look forward to becoming your friend, and to whatever develops beyond friendship.

Please write soon. I await your reply in hope of beginning a new and wonderful relationship... one that is mutually satisfying and enjoyable.

You are in my thoughts,
Rox

Cass stared at the screen, then scrolled back to the top of the note and read it again.

"Oh, my God! E., did you read what I read?"

What, did you forget how to read English? Get a grip, woman. What I read is someone who's interested in getting to know you. Maybe you'll even score—you think?

Cass read the message a third time.

Hellllloooo! Anybody home? Earth to Cass! Okay, it's real easy. Step 1, pick up the mouse. Step 2, click on "Reply." Step 3, type "I want to jump your bones. What time do I pick you up?" Okay? Very simple, Cass. Move your ass!

Cass shook off the voice and poised her hands over the keyboard.

Hi, Rox,

I can't tell you how much your words mean to me. I was so afraid that I was pushing this interaction too fast and too far. For all I knew, you were married with children. The last thing I want to do is break up a relationship that is happily working. I'm sorry for your heartbreak, but at the same time elated that this opens a

*realm of possibilities for us. You have been in my mind
night and day. You invade my dreams, Roxanne Ward.*

*I'm afraid the newspaper articles are way overstated. I
don't consider myself a hero; I was just doing my job. It's
my responsibility to ensure the safety of the passengers, no
matter what it takes. Of course, it would have been a lot
easier if I'd had landing gear, but a bellyflop was the only
recourse. I thank the powers above that allowed me to live
another day so I would be here for you.*

*Do you believe in fate, Roxanne? I do. I believe that
people are destined to be together. I believe that you and I
have known each other in past lives, and will meet again in
the future. Our karma dictates it. I know this probably
sounds like a bunch of mumbo-jumbo to you, but it's real. I
feel strongly that our souls have met before. The connection
we've both mentioned is evidence of that.*

*I want to know your heart and your mind, Rox, and I
want you to know mine. If we're destined to be together, as
I believe we are, we will cross the barriers of distance and
time and our souls will be one. Open your heart to me, Rox.
I promise to hold it lovingly, and protect it with my life.
Trust in me, Rox. I will not hurt you.*

Please write again soon.
You are in my heart,
Cass

Cass sent the message. Her heart was filled with such an intense
feeling of happiness and anticipation at the unexpected turn of events
that she felt like running a marathon, sore body and all. Holding her
breath, she closed her eyes and allowed her heart to savor the
sensation.

Suddenly, her eyes snapped open and she jumped to her feet and
stared at the computer. Pressing her hands against her heart, she took
a deep breath and just stared at the screen. "How can it be? I've only
known—it's not possible." She paced back and forth for long
moments before finally admitting to herself that no amount of pacing
would change the obvious. *I'm in love.*

* * *

Rox fought the urge as long as she could, but finally had to give
in and tried to get out of bed. After three failed attempts at convincing

her broken ribs to let her sit up, she lay back down and yelled, "Nikki! Jerri! Guys, I could use some help here." She waited as patiently as she could. When no response came, she called again.

"Nikki? Jerri? For the love of God, if someone doesn't give me a hand, we're going to have a bed to change."

"Geesh, woman, hold your water, will you?" Jerri called back, taking the stairs two at a time.

"What do you think I've been trying to do?"

"All right, come on," the taller woman said, helping Rox to her feet.

"Some nurses you guys are—leaving your patient all alone like that," Rox fussed, half grinning while she teased her friend.

"I'm not a nurse, I'm an EMT. Blame it on Nikki, if you like. She's a nurse."

"All right, I will," Rox agreed as she allowed her friend to help her. "I really need to have a bathroom installed in the attic," she mumbled as they slowly made their way down the stairs. When she reached the second story, she inhaled as deeply as her injured ribs would allow. "Wow, that smells good. What is it?"

"Chicken with mushrooms and wild rice, and asparagus with garlic. It's one of Nikki's specialties," Jerri answered as Rox went into the bathroom. "It's just about ready, too."

"What time is it?" Rox called out.

"Nearly six p.m.," Jerri said. "You must have been tired. You slept for three hours."

Rox washed her hands then opened the bathroom door. "Three hours? Damn!"

"Ready?" Jerri asked, taking her arm for the descent to the first floor.

Nikki met them at the bottom of the stairs, where Rox had to pause to regain her strength. "Roxie, maybe we should move your computer down to the living room until you manage the stairs without so much pain," Nikki suggested, reaching up to brush the hair out of her friend's eyes.

"No, that's too much work. But I can use the laptop. I'll just sleep on the couch for the next few nights."

"That'll work. Then you won't have to worry about walking down two flights of stairs every time you want to eat," Nikki agreed.

"Actually, I was thinking more along the lines of using it on the deck," Rox said. "You know how I like to sit out there and work."

"That'll work too." Nikki took Rox's arm and led her to the kitchen table. "Sit. You need to eat to keep up your strength."

Soon the women were enjoying dinner and sharing friendly conversation. Midway through the meal, the topic turned to Chris.

"Where do you think Chris is?" Nikki asked.

Rox shook her head. "I don't know. I suppose I could call the jobsite tomorrow."

"What for? You aren't pressing charges. Once Chris realizes that he's gotten away with it again, it won't be long before he finds his way back here," Jerri replied.

Rox hung her head, wondering if she had made a mistake by letting Chris off the hook for the assault.

Nikki saw her friend's distress and reached over to take her hand. "Honey, we won't let you out of our sight, okay? Chris won't be able to get near you without one of us knowing it."

Rox nodded, but she'd lost her appetite. She chased the food around her plate with her fork for a while, then set it down. "I guess I'm done," she said, and painfully pushed her chair away from the table. She rose, picked up her plate, and headed to the counter with it.

"Oh, no, you don't, Lady Jane. Jerri and I will take care of the cleanup. You need to rest. Remember, the doctor said total bed rest for a few days." Nikki got up and led her friend to the couch in the living room.

"But I want to do my e-mail," Rox complained.

"Does your laptop have a modem?" Jerri asked.

Seeing Rox's nod, she asked for the location of the Internet software, then sprinted upstairs to get the laptop and disks. For the next hour, Jerri and Rox sat side by side on the couch, setting up the laptop to accept e-mail. When they finished, Rox reclined happily against the arm of the couch, legs covered with a quilt, surrounded by fluffy pillows and supporting the lightweight computer on her lap.

Nikki brought a glass of iced tea, which she set within reach on the coffee table, then kissed Rox on the forehead.

Rox grinned at her friend. "A girl could get used to this."

"Enjoy it while you can, sugar," Nikki said. She curled up in the overstuffed chair and started reading a book she had found in the bookcase in the guest room.

Jerri was lying on the floor of the living room, off in her own little world. She had brought her collection of Legos and was happily building an airport, complete with Cass's plane making a crash landing on the runway.

Rox went immediately to her inbox. She tapped the keyboard nervously as she waited. The laptop was much slower than her desktop computer, as it had only a fraction of the memory and processing power. Taking a deep breath, she tried to quell her impatience, surprised at the way she felt. She was usually a very patient person. *Christ, you'd think I was a schoolgirl in love,* she said to herself. *Whoa! Where did that come from?*

Finally, the server delivered two new messages into her inbox: one from her agent and the other from CConway@Flyboy.com. She guiltily skipped the note from her agent and immediately clicked on Cass's note.

> *Hi, Rox,*
>
> *I can't tell you how much your words mean to me. I was so afraid that I was pushing this interaction too fast and too far. For all I knew, you were married with children. The last thing I want to do is break up a relationship that is happily working. I'm sorry for your heartbreak, but at the same time elated that this opens a realm of possibilities for us. You have been in my mind night and day. You invade my dreams, Roxanne Ward.*
>
> *I'm afraid the newspaper articles are way overstated. I don't consider myself a hero; I was just doing my job. It's my responsibility to ensure the safety of the passengers, no matter what it takes. Of course, it would have been a lot easier if I'd had landing gear, but a bellyflop was the only recourse. I thank the powers above that allowed me to live another day so I would be here for you.*
>
> *Do you believe in fate, Roxanne? I do. I believe that people are destined to be together. I believe that you and I have known each other in past lives, and will meet again in the future. Our karma dictates it. I know this probably sounds like a bunch of mumbo-jumbo to you, but it's real. I feel strongly that our souls have met before. The connection we've both mentioned is evidence of that.*
>
> *I want to know your heart and your mind, Rox, and I want you to know mine. If we're destined to be together, as I believe we are, we will cross the barriers of distance and time and our souls will be one. Open your heart to me, Rox. I promise to hold it lovingly, and protect it with my life. Trust in me, Rox. I will not hurt you.*
>
> *Please write again soon.*

You are in my heart,
Cass

Rox smiled and tears sprang to her eyes as she read the tender passage.

Open your heart to me, Rox. I promise to hold it lovingly, and protect it with my life. Trust in me, Rox. I will not hurt you.

"I will not hurt you." My God, that sounds too good to be true. She closed her eyes as tears tracked down her cheeks. Suddenly, she felt a pair of arms circle her neck from behind, and a cheek pressed up against hers.

"Are you all right?" Nikki asked tenderly.

Rox reached up and patted the arms around her neck. Leaning into Nikki's cheek, she nodded. "I'm okay, love. Thanks," she said. "Nikki, he wrote back. Look." She scrolled to the top of Cass's note.

Nikki read the note over Rox's shoulder, sighing deeply as she read the last line. "God, Rox, this guy is a real romantic, isn't he? How do you feel about this? Do you think you can trust him?"

Her brow furrowed, Rox thought for a moment before answering. "I don't know, Nik. It feels right... from this distance, anyway."

Nikki nodded, her cheek still pressed up against Rox's. "Are you going to send a reply?"

Rox nodded.

"Need some help?"

"Yeah, I think so," Rox answered.

"Okay." Nikki released her friend and pulled the coffee table up to the edge of the couch so that it was directly next to Rox. She took the computer out of her friend's hands and placed it on the table within comfortable reach of her own hands, but still within viewing range for Rox. "All right, what would you like to say?"

Again, Rox dictated her message. Nikki diligently typed word for word.

Dear Cass,
It amazes me that we're so far apart, yet I feel so close to you. What is it about you, Cass Conway? Why does this feel so familiar, so safe?

Do I believe in fate? I believe in destiny. Kismet, if you will. And what I feel for you is too familiar to be anything but fate. My friend Nikki asked how I feel about you. I told her that this feels right. I also feel like I have known you before; that we share a connection of some sort.

Do I believe that we have known each other in past lives? I don't know. It would be one explanation for the sense of familiarity that I feel when I read your notes. I do believe our souls are bonded in some way, across distance... across time.

As I've told you previously, I'm currently involved in a very dark relationship. I'm bound to this person at the present time, only to bring peace to my father, who is dying. He wants so badly to see me happy, and he believes that I am. I will continue to foster that belief until he is gone. Until then, I will endure the darkness and wait for the light. I wonder if you are that light, Cass. I feel in my heart that you are. I long to reach into the light, to embrace it, to let it guide me and protect me.

You've asked me to trust in you, Cass. That's very difficult, but I find my inner voice telling me to do just that. I will listen to that voice. I will take the risk and I will learn your heart. I will offer you a piece of mine; a piece that I have never given another living soul. I ask that you protect it carefully, for it bruises easily. I do trust that you will not hurt me.

I'm looking forward to hearing from you again.
Rox

"This is exactly why you're the writer and I'm not," Nikki said, reading the note over again. "Rox, this is so eloquent, so intimate. Damn, girl, you're good."

"That's enough for me," Rox said. "Send it."

Chapter 18

Shortly after Cass hit the "Send" button, the doorbell rang.

"Who can that be?" Cass said aloud.

You ordered pizza, remember? Enforcer reminded her, spurring her into action.

She grabbed her wallet and went to the door. Through the peephole, she saw the pizza delivery boy standing there, looking around impatiently. Cass swung the door open and Pizza Boy's eyes took her in.

"Hi," she said, flashing him a smile. "What do I owe you?"

"Uh... uh... "

"Hello," Cass said, waving her hand in front of his face.

Pizza Boy turned several unbecoming shades of red before focusing on the business at hand. "Uh, $7.95."

"Here you go. Thanks." Cass shoved a ten-dollar bill into his hand and grabbed the pizza. He was still standing there staring when she closed the door.

Since she didn't want to venture too far away from the computer, Cass carried the pizza into the office to eat. She even left herself logged on, glancing at the screen periodically to see if Rox would reply immediately. Half an hour later, Cass finished her lunch and made a quick trip to the kitchen to discard the pizza box, then returned to her e-mail vigil.

After another half hour spent pacing in front of the screen, Enforcer lost patience.

You are pathetic.

What do you mean?

Look at you. You're acting like a pubescent teen waiting for the phone to ring. Have you no pride, woman?

E., I... I... Oh, hell. Who am I kidding? I'm going out of my mind waiting to see if she'll write back. What if I pushed it too far this time?

Cass, this one's a sure thing! A done deal! This chick is like putty in your hands. What are you fretting about? Look, if you seem too anxious, you might scare her away. You need to shut the computer off and go do something else.

Cass's brow furrowed into a frown. *Like what?*

Well, Rox is into sci-fi, right? How about we go to the new Star Wars movie? Heaven knows your nervousness can screw up a wet dream. At least you'll be prepared to talk intelligently about something when she finally responds, Enforcer suggested.

Cass contemplated the suggestion.

Well? Enforcer urged.

She threw up her hands. "Okay, okay. You win. Let's go." She grabbed some money and her car keys and shoved them into the pocket of her shorts, shut the computer down, and headed out the door.

It was nearly five p.m. by the time Cass returned home. She could hardly remember what the movie was about, since she'd spent nearly the entire two hours daydreaming about Rox.

I've been alone way too long, E. This woman, who also happens to live three thousand miles away, pays me a little attention, and whammo, I'm hooked. I can't think of anything but her. She invades my dreams; she's in my mind constantly. E., this is only Friday. What am I going to do for the next two days? I'll be a basket case by Monday morning if I keep this up.

You know what I think, Cass. It's all that nervous energy. You need to get lai—

Don't even go there, E. I don't want *to get laid. Well, I do, but only... but... Damn! Now look where my mind is going. Aarrgghh!* She shook her head to try to clear it of the vision of Rox. *Maybe a nice cold shower. Yeah, that should do it.* She charged into the bathroom, stripping off her clothing along the way.

Fifteen minutes later, Cass was sitting in front of her computer , shivering, hair still dripping as she waited for it to power up.

D-d-d-did you h-h-have to m-m-m-make the w-w-water s-s-so c-c-c-c-cold, Cass? Enforcer asked.

Cass just stared at the screen, a terrycloth robe pulled tightly around her body.

When she was connected to her e-mail server, Cass clicked to download new messages and waited again. "I could reach her faster if I jumped in a jet and *flew* to Maine," she shouted at the computer.

You're dripping on the keyboard, Cass. Remember what happened last time, when you spilled your coffee on it? That was an expensive cup of coffee. You'd better go towel-dry your hair.

Exasperated, Cass did just that, returning with a towel over her head. To her delight, her inbox contained an e-mail from Rox@Starship.com. Checking the time of the post, she noted that it had arrived about ten minutes earlier. With a shaky hand, she guided the mouse to the "New Mail" icon and clicked on it.

> *Dear Cass,*
> *It amazes me that we're so far apart, yet I feel so close to you. What is it about you, Cass Conway? Why does this feel so familiar, so safe?*

"She feels safe? E., she feels safe with me. Wow! That's more than I hoped for at this point. Cool."

> *Do I believe in fate? I believe in destiny. Kismet, if you will. And what I feel for you is too familiar to be anything but fate. My friend Nikki asked how I feel about you. I told her that this feels right. I also feel like I have known you before; that we share a connection of some sort.*

"Oh, yes, we have definitely known each other before, Rox. We are soulmates. I can feel it."

> *Do I believe that we have known each other in past lives? I don't know. It would be one explanation for the sense of familiarity that I feel when I read your notes. I do believe our souls are bonded in some way, across distance... across time.*

"E, she says she can feel the connection."
I can read, Cass. Geesh. You are a whipped puppy already, my friend, Enforcer teased.

> *As I've told you previously, I'm currently involved in a very dark relationship. I'm bound to this person at the present time, only to bring peace to my father, who is dying. He wants so badly to see me happy, and he believes that I am. I will continue to foster that belief until he is gone. Until then, I will endure the darkness and wait for the*

light. I wonder if you are that light, Cass. I feel in my heart that you are. I long to reach into the light, to embrace it, to let it guide me and protect me.

"Oh, Rox, I'm so sorry," Cass whispered. "Rox, I *will* be your light. I promise."

You've asked me to trust in you, Cass. That's very difficult, but I find my inner voice telling me to do just that. I will listen to that voice. I will take the risk and I will learn your heart. I will offer you a piece of mine; a piece that I have never given another living soul. I ask that you protect it carefully, for it bruises easily. I do trust that you will not hurt me.

She shoots, she scores! Raahhhhh, yeeeeaaahhhhh, Enforcer cheered. *This chick can't be that bad if she has an inner voice of her own. We both know you'd be lost without yours, AKA—me! I wonder if her voice is as cute as I am.*

"E, calm down, will you? She writes so eloquently, so passionately. Damn, Rox, what these simple words do to me." Her stomach clenched in anticipation of writing a reply. She sat back in her chair and took a deep breath, surprised to find her eyes welling with tears. *Rox, why am I so enchanted by you? How is it that you can affect me this way?*

Sitting up straight, Cass reached over to the keyboard and started to type.

My dearest Roxanne,

I knew from the minute I saw your picture that you would change my life in some way. You've never been far from my thoughts since that day, just two short weeks ago.

Fate has most definitely brought us together, dear heart. Yes, this does feel right, and safe and warm, and very, very familiar. I feel as though I have always known you, Rox. I feel as though you have always lived in a slumbering part of my heart that was suddenly awakened when I saw your eyes on the back cover of your book.

No amount of distance or time will keep us apart. Not in our hearts. Just think of me, Rox, and my spirit will be there -- in your mind and in your soul.

Rox, it pains me to know that you're living under a veil of darkness. Please tell me what I can do to help. Please tell me that you're safe and well.

I'm sorry that your father is ill, and that you're living out a pretense of happiness so as not to dispel his illusions. Roxanne, your life and your future are so much more important than that. I am sure your father wants to see you truly happy, not just projecting a façade of happiness. Let me help you, Rox. Tell me how to free you from this pain. Let me be that light you speak of. I want to be the one to guide and protect you, Rox. Please let me.

I will never give you a reason to mistrust me, Rox, and I will never hurt you. I am honored to have been given a piece of your precious heart, a part that you haven't given to anyone else before... and yes, I shall guard it and honor it with love. Thank you for entrusting me with such a wonderful gift.

Every moment that I wait for you seems like an eternity. Please speak your heart to me, Roxanne. I am here to listen, to help. I am so looking forward to hearing from you again. Please write soon.

With love,

Cass

You are one six-foot tall mush-ball, you know that? Enforcer said. *Don't ever change, buddy. I love you just the way you are.*

Cass clicked on "Send."

* * *

As soon as Rox replied to Cass's note, she went on to answer her agent's e-mail, sending him the bad news about her broken wrist. She warned him that she might require a two or three-week extension on the deadline for the book, and promised to work as hard as possible to shorten the delay. That task out of the way, she decided to start outlining the next chapter, typing one-handed so Nikki could return to reading her book.

Just as she was about to log off, the mail icon flashed, indicating the delivery of new mail. Awkwardly moving the mouse with her left hand, Rox managed to query the server and discover that Cass had already replied to her post.

"Oh, my." Rox's exclamation drew the attention of her two friends. "He's responded already. I only sent the note fifteen minutes ago."

The quick response piqued Jerri's and Nikki's interest, and they clambered up from their respective positions to come over and read along with her.

> *My dearest Roxanne,*
> *I knew from the minute I saw your picture that you would change my life in some way. You've never been far from my thoughts since that day, just two short weeks ago.*

Roxanne looked at her friends. "Has it only been two weeks?" she asked. "It feels like I've known him forever."

> *Fate has most definitely brought us together, dear heart. Yes, this does feel right, and safe and warm, and very, very familiar. I feel as though I have always known you, Rox. I feel as though you have always lived in a slumbering part of my heart that was suddenly awakened when I saw your eyes on the back cover of your book.*

"Look, he called you 'dear heart,'" Jerri observed, pointing to the screen. "You've got him hooked, Rox, just reel him in."

> *No amount of distance or time will keep us apart. Not in our hearts. Just think of me, Rox, and my spirit will be there -- in your mind and in your soul.*

"I know, Cass. I feel like you're here next to me right now, instead of three thousand miles away," Rox said softly to herself.

> *Rox, it pains me to know that you're living under a veil of darkness. Please tell me what I can do to help. Please tell me that you're safe and well.*
> *I'm sorry that your father is ill, and that you're living out a pretense of happiness so as not to dispel his illusions. Roxanne, your life and your future are so much more important than that. I am sure your father wants to see you truly happy, not just projecting a façade of happiness. Let me help you, Rox. Tell me how to free you from this pain.*

Let me be that light you speak of. I want to be the one to guide and protect you, Rox. Please let me.

"I like this guy. See, Rox, this is the same advice I gave you earlier this week. Now will you listen to me?" Nikki asked.

I will never give you a reason to mistrust me, Rox, and I will never hurt you. I am honored to have been given a piece of your precious heart, a part that you haven't given to anyone else before... and yes, I shall guard it and honor it with love. Thank you for entrusting me with such a wonderful gift.

Rox covered her mouth to stifle a sob. Nikki and Jerri looked at each other and smiled their approval.

Every moment that I wait for you seems like an eternity. Please speak your heart to me, Roxanne. I am here to listen, to help. I am so looking forward to hearing from you again. Please write soon.
With love,
Cass

Rox looked at her friends, tears rolling down her cheeks.

"Are you going to tell him about Chris, Rox? He's asking you to speak your heart," Nikki pointed out.

"Here, give me the computer. I'll tell him about Chris," Jerri volunteered.

"No, no. I'll tell him when the time is right," Rox replied.

"What do you mean, 'when the time is right'?" Nikki asked suspiciously.

"Nikki, I don't want a knight in shining armor. I want someone who will love me for me, for what I am, not because they have a sense of outrage about domestic abuse." Seeing that they didn't quite understand her point, she continued. "Look, I don't want Cass to come here because he wants to beat the shit out of Chris. I want him to come here because he has fallen in love with me. Understand?"

"So what are you planning to do now?" Nikki asked.

"I'm going to speak my heart, Nikki," Rox replied. "But it's a long road from here to California. That's a road I will not travel at breakneck speed. I did that with Chris, and look where it got me. No, this time I'll take baby steps. If Cass truly is the light, sooner or later his beacon will lead me to him."

"And just what do you mean by 'baby steps?'" Jerri asked, eyebrows raised.

"Chat," Rox said.

"Chat?" Nikki and Jerri chorused.

"Chat."

Chapter 19

"Are you absolutely sure you don't need any help with the typing?" Nikki asked again.

"No problem," Rox insisted. "I can type pretty quickly with just my left hand. You two feel free to go do… whatever it is you usually do at nine o'clock on a Friday evening."

Her knowing look caused Nikki and Jerri to exchange guilty glances. "Well, then, we'll just go upstairs so you can have some privacy," Jerri said.

Rox's smile turned into a grin. "Uh-huh. Right."

Nikki blushed and switched the topic back to Rox. "You know, you're supposed to be resting, and chat can be addictive. Hell, Jerri spends hours at a time in those chat rooms. Promise me you'll keep it short and get some sleep, okay?"

Distracted, Rox mumbled her agreement and wished her friends a good night, her attention already back on the computer screen.

Nikki kissed Rox's head and followed Jerri up to bed, leaving Rox alone on the living room couch.

Using only her left hand, Rox laboriously composed and sent a note to Cass inviting him into a chat session. She brought up a host Internet session and logged into alienchat.com, then sat and waited nervously. It wasn't long before Flyboy entered the chat room.

"Hi!" typed Rox.

"Hi, yourself," came the reply.

"Cass, I've been deeply touched by your notes. It's as though you can see directly into my heart." Rox typed awkwardly, backing up several times to correct mistakes.

"I've been touched by yours, too, Rox. I feel as though I have known you my entire life. In such a short time, you've become an irreplaceable part of my heart."

Rox gasped, then typed a reply. *"My heart is in my throat right now, Cass. I'm a nervous wreck. I've never felt this way before."*

"Rox, you're going to think I'm crazy. We've only known each other for a couple of weeks, but I feel so close to you," Cass wrote. "I've had dreams of you. I see your face every time I close my eyes, like it was imprinted on the inside of my eyelids. I've never felt this way before either."

"You mentioned that the woman you were involved with died three years ago. I'm sorry... that must have hurt you terribly."

"Yes. She died from a drug overdose. I loved her very much, but the situation between us degraded badly just before she died," Cass admitted.

"I'm sorry to hear that. Have you dated much since?"

"Very little. No committed relationships. Patti left some deep scars on my heart, some of which still bleed."

"Cass, why me? Why now?"

"I don't know, Rox. For some reason, I feel safe with you. My heart is willing to take the chance," Cass answered.

Rox looked inward, asking herself if she truly felt safe with Cass. "I've looked into my own heart and seen the truth of your words, Cass. I feel safe with you. Heaven knows I've had reason not to trust anyone, but I trust you."

"Rox, I sense that there's something wrong. You mentioned in your last note that you're in a dark relationship. Talk to me. Please tell me you're safe."

"I'm safe for the time being, since I have two very dear friends staying with me right now. Please don't worry."

Cass very much wanted more information, but she suddenly remembered the way time had slipped by during their previous chat, and glanced at the clock to be certain she wouldn't be keeping Rox up too late. *Six-twenty, so... nine-twenty there.* She fretted over continuing.

Something is wrong here, E. I can feel it.

I hear you, Cass. I feel it too. Go ahead and ask her.

I don't know. I don't want to keep her up too late and I don't want to scare her away, yet I'm afraid for her. Why would she need her friends to stay with her to keep her safe?

Ask her. Notice how long it takes her to reply to your notes? I wonder why? You'd think a writer could type faster than that. She typed a lot faster than that the last time we were in chat with her. This doesn't feel right to me, either.

Making a quick decision, Cass typed, "Rox, I'm worried about you. If you need your friends to stay with you, you must be in danger. Please talk to me."

She watched her note appear at the bottom of their chat log, then waited. After almost a full minute without a reply, she realized that Enforcer was right. It was taking an inordinate amount of time for Rox to send each line of dialogue. *What the hell is going on here?*

"Rox, are you there?" she typed.

"Cass, please don't worry. I am safe. I will tell you about my relationship soon, I promise," came the immediate reply, so quickly that it had to have been in transit as Cass was sending her last query.

Cass stared at the screen intently and waited. About thirty seconds later, another reply came across the screen.

"Yes, I'm here. Wait..."

Cass waited. A full minute later, another message appeared.

"Cass, I owe you an explanation."

Yes, Cass thought as she waited for more.

"I am typing one-handed."

One-handed? She's hurt! Enforcer concluded.

"My wrist is broken."

"Son of a bitch!" *"How?!"* Cass typed.

Long moments passed and there was no response. Cass's fingers flew over the keyboard. *"Rox, my stomach is in knots here. How did you break your wrist? Please talk to me."*

Again she waited.

"Please, Cass, I'm all right. Really, I am," came Rox's reply.

Agitated, Cass typed, *"I'm sitting here imagining all kinds of horrors. Now tell me how you broke your wrist or I'll book myself on the next flight to Maine and find out for myself!"*

Rox read the last line of dialogue from Cass. *Oh, my God. I can feel his anger right through the screen. What have I gotten myself into here? I don't need to leave one abusive relationship just to enter another.*

"Cass, please don't be angry. I've dealt with enough anger over the past several months to last a lifetime."

"Rox, I'm sorry. Please forgive me. I'm not angry with you. Sweetheart, please believe me," Cass replied.

Sweetheart? Rox's stomach did flip-flops at the endearment. Before she could formulate a reply, another line of dialogue came across the screen.

"Rox, I am sick with fear for you. Please talk to me."

"Cass, I'm sorry I upset you. I'm afraid that if I tell you how I was injured, you'll become even more upset. Just be assured that I am safe... please."

"Rox, please..." came the almost immediate response.

Rox sat back and stared at the screen for several moments.

"Rox?"

Rox reached forward and typed, *"I'm here."*

"Are you all right?"

"I'm okay, Cass. I'm sorry for worrying you," Rox said.

Cass made a difficult decision and faced her fears head on. *"You've been beaten, haven't you?"*

Tears welled in Rox's eyes—tears of hurt, anger and indignation. Soon, she was sobbing openly.

"Sweetheart, please talk to me!"

Rox started typing, finding it difficult to see the keyboard through her tears. *"I'm o-"*

"Rox, honey, what's wrong?" Nikki asked, appearing beside her friend. She had been on her way to the kitchen for a glass of milk when she heard Rox crying. Wrapping her arms around her injured friend, she looked over Rox's shoulder at the monitor screen and read the last few lines of dialogue. "Looks like he guessed, huh?"

Unable to speak, Rox nodded.

"May I?" Nikki asked, sitting next to Rox and reaching for the laptop.

Again, Rox nodded.

"Is it okay for me to tell him what's going on, Rox?" Nikki asked.

"Rox! Rox, honey, please answer me!" flashed onto the computer screen.

"Nikki, he called me sweetheart—twice. I... I... Nik, I'm afraid," Rox said, dissolving into tears against her friend's shoulder.

"I understand, love. Let me talk to him," she said. "He needs to know."

When Rox nodded again, Nikki took the computer and placed it on her own lap. She wrote, *"Hi, Cass, this is Rox's friend Nikki."*

Nikki? Cass thought. *Rox mentioned her in one of her e-mails.* Excited that she had someone on the other end who might tell her what was going on, Cass quickly typed her next line of dialogue. *"Nikki, where is Rox?"*

"Rox is sitting right here next to me. She's too upset to type."

"Nikki, talk to me, please. I'm worried sick about her. What happened? How was she injured?"

"For the past couple of years, she's been living with an abusive asshole. Things were fine between them for the first year and a half or so, but lately, the beatings have been pretty damned regular."

"Oh, my God!" Cass exclaimed.

Cass, let's charter a plane. I want to go kick some ass! Enforcer snarled.

"Get her out of there!" Cass typed back.

"We've tried, Cass. Believe me. My wife Jerri and I have been trying to get her to leave for the past several months."

"Why won't she go?"

"The more you get to know Rox, the more you'll realize that she's a very unselfish and dedicated person. Her father is dying and he's under the illusion that she's happy. She won't dispel that belief. Quite frankly, she plans on staying in her current situation until the poor man dies."

"No! She can't do that, Nikki! Please get her out of there," Cass wrote in desperation.

"She won't go. Jerri and I are staying with her right now. We'll stay for as long as it takes."

"Thank you. Nikki, how did she get into this situation?"

"She met Chris when he was doing some construction work on her home. He was kind of a nice guy in the beginning."

"What went wrong?"

"Well, he can be charming when it suits him. The way I see it, he took advantage of the fact that Rox's parents fell absolutely in love with him, and when they realized her dad was dying, he found himself in a nice cushy place."

"What do you mean?" Cass inquired.

"He knew Rox wouldn't disappoint her dad, so he cashed in on his meal ticket and started his 'I'm the man of the house' bullshit, knowing she wouldn't throw him out. Any objections on her part get her a beating, and she has to dedicate every waking moment to waiting on his sorry ass. She barely has time for her writing. He has made her life a living hell. He doesn't need an excuse; he just knocks her around whenever he feels like it."

"That son of a bitch. I'd like to get my hands on him!"

"You'll have to stand in line behind me and Jerri. He's a marked man if he ever shows his face around us."

"Where is he now?"

"Beats the hell out of me. If he's smart, he's as far away from here as he can get, but I wouldn't count on it."

"Please don't leave her alone."

"Don't worry, we won't. Jerri and I will protect her to the best of our ability."

"Thank you. I can't tell you how much that means to me, knowing she has you and Jerri."

"No thanks necessary. I love her like a sister. She's a very special lady."

"Nikki, can I tell you something?"

"Sure."

Cass took a deep breath and let it out slowly, then typed: *"I know this sounds incredible, after knowing her for so short a period of time, but I think I'm in love with her."*

Rox caught her breath when she read what Cass had written. She looked at Nikki, tears of hope and fear rolling down her face.

Nikki was grinning from ear to ear. It might be premature, but she liked this Cass Conway. "What do you want me to tell him, Rox?"

"Nikki?" popped up on the computer screen.

"We're still here, Cass... BRB," Nikki wrote. "Rox?" Nikki asked, looking at her friend. "How do you feel about him?"

"Terrified, excited, exhilarated, and scared. Nik, I don't know for sure. He's so different from Chris, so different from all my past relationships."

"Yes, he is," Nikki replied, remembering some of the idiots Rox had dated while they were in college together.

The computer screen flashed. *"Nikki, you're scaring me. Is Rox all right?"*

"Cass, please be patient. Rox is right here... she's fine. We're having a little girl-talk right now. Just keep your britches on, okay?" Nikki replied. She chuckled as a return query appeared on the screen.

"Did I just get my ass kicked?"

"Yes, you did. Now, be patient, okay?"

"Yes, ma'am!" came the reply, followed by a smiley face.

Nikki grinned broadly at the response. Looking at Rox, she said, "I like him, hon. He seems like a really nice guy."

Rox smiled back. "Give me the laptop, please." She settled it on her lap and began to type.

"Hi, Cass, this is Rox again."

"Rox! Thank God. Are you all right?"

"I'm fine. I love you for caring. Look, it's almost ten o'clock here. I'm under doctor's orders to rest, so I need to sign off," she typed.

"You love me for caring?"

"Yes, I do," Rox replied.

Nikki threw an arm around her friend's shoulder and hugged her close, kissing her temple.

"I love you too, Rox," was Cass's reply.

Rox was crying openly as she dropped her head to Nikki's shoulder.

Nikki reached for the keyboard. *"Hey, Cass, Nik again. I'm afraid that last declaration turned our friend here into a limp dishrag. I need to put her to bed, so I'll sign off for her."*

"I understand, Nikki. Tell her I love her. I'll contact her through e-mail tomorrow."

"Tomorrow, then. Good night, Cass."

"Good night, sweet ladies," Cass responded.

Cass sat back and watched the screen until the message, "Alien has left the chat room" appeared. She scrolled back through the last several lines of dialogue and re-read the conversation.

She loves me, E.

She loves you for caring, Enforcer pointed out, *but does she love you for* you?

Cass frowned. *Good point,* she thought. *Good point. It is a start, though,* she thought hopefully.

That it is, old buddy. Now, what are we going do about this asshole who's been beating her up?

Chapter 20

Nikki shut down the laptop and placed it carefully on the end table next to the couch while she waited for Rox to come back from the bathroom. Watching her friend shuffle painfully across the floor toward her, Nikki rose to her feet and went to meet her. She wrapped her arm around Rox's waist and led her back to the couch. As they neared the stairs, Rox detoured in that direction.

"I thought you were sleeping on the couch," Nikki commented.

"Nah, my bed is much more comfortable," Rox replied. She held tightly to the railing with her right hand and to Nikki's arm with her left. Slowly, they made their way up the stairs.

Rox was out of breath by the time they reached her room, and she sat on the side of the bed. Nikki lifted her friend's feet, swinging them up and under the covers as Rox slowly lowered her head to the pillow.

Nikki pulled the covers up and tucked Rox in, then leaned over and kissed her tenderly. Sitting on the edge of the bed, she crossed her legs, reaching over and brushing the red-gold hair off Rox's forehead.

"What do you think of him, Nik?"

"I like him. He's really worried about you. How long did it take him to guess you were in trouble?"

"About ten minutes."

Nikki nodded and smiled. "Sounds like he's pretty sweet on you already. He won't stand a chance once he actually meets you, you know," she said softly.

Rox frowned. "What do you mean?"

Nikki reached forward and ran her forefinger down the side of Rox's face. "Roxanne Ward, you have got to be one of the most outgoing, friendliest, compassionate people I know. Not to mention smart, talented, and very beautiful. Any man, or woman for that matter, would be a fool not to fall in love with you at first sight."

Rox blushed as she slapped Nikki's hand away. "Cut it out, Nik, you're embarrassing me."

"It's true," Nikki said, leaning in until she was nose to nose with Rox. "And you know it." She dropped a kiss on her friend's lips. "I love you. Sleep well," she whispered. Nikki kissed Rox again before getting up from the bed and heading for the door. Stopping, she turned around and looked at her friend, "Good night, Rox."

"Good night, Nik. I love you too. Kiss the Big Guy for me, okay?"

"I will. See you in the morning." Nikki closed the door behind her and went to join her wife.

Once in bed, she snuggled up close to the taller woman.

Jerri's arms went around the smaller woman as she spooned herself in behind. "Where've you been, love?"

"I just put Rox to bed. She had a pretty intense chat session with Cass. Seems they're falling in love already."

"So much for baby steps. But then, Rox is easy to fall in love with. She's just way too cute for her own good." Jerri pulled her wife in tighter.

"Yes, she is. Kind of like a tall, dark EMT I know and love." Nikki rolled over to face her wife.

Jerri kissed her soundly. "Mmm, you taste good."

"Make love to me, Jer," Nikki whispered.

Jerri rolled them both over so that she was lying on top. Leaning on her elbows, she looked down into Nikki's face. "I love you, Nik." She placed butterfly kisses along Nikki's jaw.

Nikki tipped her head back to allow better access to her throat as her wife slowly moved down, nipping at the tender skin along her collarbone. She reached up and grabbed Jerri's head and pulled her closer. "God, that feels so good," she said breathlessly.

Sitting up and straddling her, Jerri took Nikki's wrists and pinned them to the bed above her head.

Nikki looked up into smoldering brown eyes and knew she was in for a very passionate evening.

Two doors down, Rox smiled and pulled the blanket up over her head to drown out the sounds coming from her guest room.

Soon, Cass, she thought. *Soon.*

* * *

Adrenaline was surging through Cass as she logged off the computer. It was only a little after seven, so she decided to burn off some energy by going to the gym, and then to stop at the diner for a late dessert and a much-needed visit with Angie.

By eight-thirty, she had completed her workout. Gym bag slung carelessly over her shoulder, she was on her way out when she heard someone call her name. She turned sharply and spotted the obnoxious Jason approaching her. "Oh, hi."

"Cass, I wanted to tell you how much I admired your skillful performance in San Diego. A less experienced pilot probably would have crashed the plane and killed everyone on board. You must be very good under pressure."

"It wasn't a performance, Jason, it was a necessity. People's lives were at stake," she said, wanting to stomp him like the bug he was, right there where he stood.

"Well, anyway, I just wanted to congratulate you on a job well done." His manner was cocky and self-assured.

"Gee, Jason, that means so much coming from you."

The sarcasm was lost on him. "Maybe we can go out again?" he asked. "Here's my card. Give me a call when you're free." He handed her a card and then walked out the door.

Cass flipped it into the trashcan on her way out.

"Here you go, love." Angie placed a piece of hot apple pie topped with ice cream in front of Cass.

"Ang, it's a good thing I work out. Otherwise, I'd weigh 300 pounds from all the food you feed me." Cass's seeming complaint was good-natured.

"Oh, quit your whining and tell me about this new lady friend of yours."

Angie didn't miss the way Cass's face brightened at the mention of Rox. "She must be something wonderful to cause your face to glow like that," she observed.

Cass blushed. "Wonderful doesn't come close to describing her." She took a big bite of her pie.

"Well, tell me how it's going! The last time we talked, you'd just sent a couple of e-mails back and forth."

"We're still doing the e-mail and chat thing, but it's no longer just a friendly exchange. Ang, I believe I'm falling in love."

"How can you be in love? You haven't even met her yet," Angie said, disbelief evident in her voice.

"It's true. Don't ask me how; I just know that I am. She's even in my dreams. I've had three dreams in which she's figured prominently. Our chat session last night was so intimate, so enlightening, so personal," Cass continued. "I've never been so sure of anything in my life as I am about falling in love with Rox."

Angie could see the sincerity behind Cass's words just by looking in her eyes. "So, what else did you learn about her in this chat session of yours?"

Cass's face darkened. Putting down the fork, she sat back in her chair and looked seriously at Angie. "She's involved in an abusive relationship. Shit! She was typing to me last night with one hand because the other wrist is broken."

Immediately, Angie was concerned. "Cass, forgive me for saying this when you're so obviously smitten with this woman, but do you really need to be involved in such a volatile situation? I mean, considering what you lived through with Patti, do you really want a daily reminder by your side?"

"There would be no 'daily reminders,' Ang. Look, both of us have come from abusive relationships. The last thing we'd do is abuse each other. No, if we were together, the memories of abuse would make our relationship more loving."

Angie reached across the table and brushed an errant lock of hair from her tall friend's face. "I hope you're right, hon. It's about time you settled down with someone who truly loves you."

"Yes, it is time, and I just know that Rox is the one. I've never felt this way about anyone. She chases away the feeling of longing and regret that was constantly in the pit of my stomach. I feel giddy and excited when I think of her. I thought I was in love with Patti, but what I felt for her is nothing compared to what I feel for Rox, and we haven't even met."

Angie reached out and placed her hand over Cass's. "You know, there are different levels of love, sweetie. I'm sure you loved Patti, but maybe Rox is your true soulmate."

Cass smiled and squeezed her hand. "It's late and I'm tired. I'm going to head home. Thanks for listening, Ang. I really needed someone to talk to tonight." She rose to her feet and gave the older woman a kiss on the cheek and an affectionate hug before turning to go.

"Good night, Cass," Angie said. *She isn't going to like the cold Maine winters.*

At home, Cass went immediately into her office and fired up her computer. Although she had told Rox that she would send her an e-mail in the morning, Cass couldn't wait. *It's already after one a.m. on the East Coast, so she won't see the message until morning.* She sat down at the computer, thought for a moment, then started to write.

> *Hi, love,*
>
> *I want you to know that I've given you a piece of my heart that I never want you to return. I have never felt for anyone else the way I feel for you. You are the other half of my soul; you complete me.*
>
> *It breaks my heart to know you're living in an abusive situation. I thank the powers above that you have two friends who love you, and who are willing to stay with you to keep you safe. I wish I could be there myself, but I don't want to rush you into anything or make you uncomfortable with the pace of this relationship. Know, however, that I will come to you immediately if you need me. My phone number is 408-555-1080. I generally fly Monday and Tuesday, and then again on Thursday and Friday, but I'm home on Wednesdays and weekends. Please call if you need me, Rox. I really want to be there for you.*
>
> *You are a brilliant writer. I can only imagine what it would be like to look inside your mind. I'm sure it's a wondrous and magical place. I desperately want to get to know you better, to see the inner Roxanne Ward. I know, without a doubt, that I will not be disappointed. I want to know your mind as well as your heart. I ask that you share them both with me; I will treat them with care.*
>
> *What I feel for you goes beyond friendship. Don't ask me how it happened, especially since we've known each other for such a short period of time, and especially since we have never met face to face, but I feel it in my heart. I know without a doubt that I love you, and I will cherish you forever. I hope I have not made you uncomfortable with this declaration. I couldn't bear to lose you.*
>
> *I'll let you go for now. Until later, then.*
> *With loving thoughts,*
> *Cass*

"Pleasant dreams, sweet angel," Cass whispered as she sent the message.

Rising, she made her way to the bedroom and she stripped off her t-shirt and shorts. After slipping a nightshirt over her head, she climbed between the sheets and got into bed, releasing a deep sigh as she settled into the soft pillow and closed her eyes.

* * *

Her hair blowing in the breeze behind her, Rox was riding on a horse behind a dark-haired man, galloping through rolling fields. Suddenly, they came to a stop and she slipped off of the horse's back. She walked around for a moment, then turned and looked at the man, smiling broadly at his handsome features. Tall and dark, dressed in faded blue jeans and flannel shirt, he wore cowboy boots with silver-plated toes.

Is this Cass?

Giddy with excitement, she threw herself into the man's arms and hugged him close. She closed her eyes and savored the feel of him as the entire length of her pressed against his tall, firm frame.

She tilted her head back and opened her eyes, surprised to see a woman with smoldering blue eyes staring back at her. There before her stood the woman from her dreams.

Leaning in, the woman lowered her mouth toward Rox's.

Her eyes closed as their lips touched. She felt as though her insides had liquefied. Warmth spread from her chest to her groin. Her heart started to flutter, and her body shook uncontrollably.

The kiss ended far too soon. The tall, dark-haired woman stepped away, and a sudden chill passed through Rox. An instant later, she opened her eyes and found that she stood alone in the field.

* * *

Jerri rolled off her wife and onto her back, pulling the smaller woman along to rest on top of her. Both women were breathing heavily.

Nikki laid her cheek on Jerri's breast. "You're going to kill me one of these days, Jer," she said, panting. "God, that was good."

"I aim to please, love. Had enough?"

Nikki's entire body was throbbing with post-orgasmic relief, and small tremors continued to vibrate through her body. "Oh, yeah," she said breathlessly, unable to move.

Jerri kissed the top of Nikki's head. "Good. Now would you mind sliding off so I can use the bathroom?"

"Can't."

Jerri smiled and rolled onto her side, depositing Nikki onto her back on the mattress next to her. "Some Mattress Queen you are."

Nikki grinned as she watched her wife get out of bed. *God, she's beautiful,* she thought as she watched a naked Jerri head for the door. "Uh, Jer, did you forget something?"

When Jerri turned sleepy eyes back toward the bed and raised an eyebrow, Nikki said, "We're not at home, love. I don't think Rox would appreciate us walking around in our birthday suits."

Jerri tilted her head back. A chuckle escaped her throat as she padded back to the bed and reached for her nightshirt and panties before heading out once more.

Jerri passed Rox's room on her way back to Nikki and heard the injured woman moaning. After quietly pushing the door open, she saw Rox thrashing about on the bed. *She's going to re-injure her ribs if she keeps that up.*

Moving quietly into the room, Jerri climbed into bed and took Rox into her arms, intending to stay just long enough for Rox to settle down into peaceful sleep. As soon as she felt Jerri's arms around her, Rox burrowed into her friend's embrace. "Shh," Jerri cooed to the smaller woman. "Sleep, Rox. You're safe, hon. Just relax and sleep." Soon, both women had fallen asleep.

Some time later, Nikki rolled over and threw her arm over the space her wife was supposed to be occupying. She sat up and looked around, realizing that Jerri was missing. After slipping on her own nightshirt and panties, she went in search of Jerri, finding her and her best friend wrapped in a loving embrace, both asleep.

Nikki stood in the doorway of Rox's room and smiled. *Damn, they look cute.* She tiptoed silently to the bed and slipped in between the covers so that Rox was lying between her and Jerri.

As Nikki settled in, Jerri opened one eye and smiled at her wife. "Nightmare," she said softly.

Nikki smiled back and wrapped an arm around both her wife and her friend. Soon, the three of them were sound asleep.

* * *

Cass was astride a horse that was galloping through rolling fields. Rox was behind her in the saddle, arms wrapped tightly around her waist. Cass brought the horse to a halt and allowed Rox to slide off. She watched for a moment as the woman twirled around in excitement and then dismounted herself, looking up just in time to catch Rox as she threw herself into Cass's arms.

When Rox tilted her head back and smiled, bolts of desire shot straight to Cass's groin. Blue eyes smoldered as Cass looked down at the green-eyed siren. She leaned in and lowered her mouth toward Rox's. Their lips touched and Cass felt as though her insides had liquefied. Warmth spread from her chest to her groin, her heart started to flutter and her body shook uncontrollably.

Finally, she broke the kiss and stepped back. It was a long moment before she could open her eyes. When she did, she was alone.

Bolting awake, Cass sat up and looked around her empty bedroom, trying to get her bearings.

E., did you dream what I dreamed? she asked, attempting to clear the sleep-dazed confusion from her mind.

I sure did. You know, Cass, you really do *need to get—*

Yeah, yeah, I know. I need to get laid. Enough with the broken record, okay?

Go back to sleep, Cass. Maybe you'll get to kiss her again. And this time, don't wake up!

Cass threw herself back down and stared at the ceiling for long moments before she drifted back to sleep.

Chapter 21

Rox awoke to find herself spooned between her two friends. They had her trapped. *How the hell did this happen?* She managed to work one hand free to scratch her nose. "Guys?" she said. "Uh, guys... hello?"

"Go to sleep, Nik. It's too early to get up." Jerri threw her arm across both Rox and Nikki, trapping the hand Rox had worked free.

"Aarrgghh!" Rox exclaimed, turning her head to Nikki. "Nikki, wake up!"

"Rox, go back to sleep." Suddenly, what she had just said registered and Nikki bolted upright. "Rox?" She looked at her friend. "How did you get into our bed?"

Rox grinned. "You're in *my* bed, Nik. And so is Jerri," she pointed out.

Nikki frowned, trying to remember the previous evening. "Oh, yeah. Now I remember." She ran a hand through her short blonde hair. "You had a nightmare and Jerri came to your rescue. I missed her, so I joined the two of you."

"I had a nightmare?"

"Yes, you did," said Jerri, from her position on the other side of the bed.

Rox looked over at her. "Did I say anything?"

Jerri rolled onto her back and rubbed her eyes. "Yeah," she said, looking at Rox. "Lots of moaning and stuff like 'Ooh... harder, Cass... harder,'" Jerri teased.

"I did not!" An embarrassed flush spread across her face. "Did I?" she added timidly.

"No, just kidding," Jerri admitted. "You're just so easy to bait, I couldn't resist."

"Jerri Lockwood, if you weren't my friend, I'd... I don't know what I'd do, but it would be bad!"

"Do you remember any of the dream?" Nikki asked.

"A little. I remember riding behind a man on a horse. He was dressed like a cowboy, and I'm sure it was Cass—he looked just like the picture Cass sent. When we stopped, I got off the horse and hugged him, but when I opened my eyes, I was hugging a woman! She kissed me, then disappeared." Confusion was clearly written on Rox's face.

Nikki gave her an odd look and reached over to feel Rox's forehead. "No fever. Are you all right, Rox?"

"I'm fine, Nik. The dream was so real, though."

"Rox, just how hard did you hit your head on that newel post?" Jerri asked.

"Some friends you are. I invite you into my bed, and this is the way you treat me?" Rox said, smiling.

"Well, this friend could use some coffee and a trip to the bathroom." Nikki climbed out of bed and reached back for Rox. "Coming?"

Rox made her way painfully over to the edge of the bed and took Nikki's hand. She groaned as she rose slowly to her feet. "God, I feel like someone beat the shit out of me."

Jerri was right behind them as they made their way downstairs to feed their caffeine addictions.

Bathroom chores out of the way and a cup of coffee beside her, Rox powered up her laptop and accessed her e-mail. She went directly to her inbox and smiled broadly when she saw the note from Cass. Seeing the date and time the message had been sent, she grinned. *You couldn't wait until morning, could you, Cass?*

She opened the message and read:

> *Hi, love,*
> *I want you to know that I've given you a piece of my heart that I never want you to return. I have never felt for anyone else the way I feel for you. You are the other half of my soul; you complete me.*
> *It breaks my heart to know you're living in an abusive situation. I thank the powers above that you have two friends who love you, and who are willing to stay with you to keep you safe. I wish I could be there myself, but I don't want to rush you into anything or make you uncomfortable with the pace of this relationship. Know, however, that I will come to you immediately if you need me. My phone number is 408-555-1080. I generally fly Monday and*

Tuesday, and then again on Thursday and Friday, but I'm home on Wednesdays and weekends. Please call if you need me, Rox. I really want to be there for you.

You are a brilliant writer. I can only imagine what it would be like to look inside your mind. I'm sure it's a wondrous and magical place. I desperately want to get to know you better, to see the inner Roxanne Ward. I know, without a doubt, that I will not be disappointed. I want to know your mind as well as your heart. I ask that you share them both with me; I will treat them with care.

What I feel for you goes beyond friendship. Don't ask me how it happened, especially since we've known each other for such a short period of time, and especially since we have never met face to face, but I feel it in my heart. I know without a doubt that I love you, and I will cherish you forever. I hope I have not made you uncomfortable with this declaration. I couldn't bear to lose you.

I'll let you go for now. Until later, then.

With loving thoughts,

Cass

So he wants to know my heart and soul, Rox thought. *Well, the only place I really pour that out is in my writing and in my journal. Do I dare send him my journal? Am I ashamed of the feelings I have disclosed in the journal for the past several weeks?* Rox considered for a moment. *No, I'm not. Okay, journal entries it is.*

She double-clicked on the folder labeled "Journal." Once opened, the folder displayed individual journal entries dating back nearly a year.

Let's start with the ones I wrote earlier this week, Rox thought as she waited for the selected documents to open. When they did, she copied them into e-mail message, added introductory and closing comments and then reviewed the contents.

My dearest Cass,

You said in your last note that you wanted to see into my soul. Besides my dreams, there are only two places where I allow my soul to be free. The first is in my writing and the second is in my journal, which I will share with you. Cass, in these notes, I speak my heart... as you read them, you'll see pieces of my soul. Most of them are daily entries; descriptions of my life during dark times. Please don't let them distress you. This is a vehicle I use to vent my emotions, to help me survive the trials of my life. Damn, this is taking forever to type with one hand. I'll be glad when the swelling has subsided enough that I can use both.

I wrote the most recent entry on Wednesday, since I was in the hospital on Thursday and Friday. In any case, here are my notes from earlier this week:

Monday

It's 9:30 p.m. I'm sitting in my glider on the back deck, my legs tucked under me, my laptop where it belongs. John Cougar is playing on the CD on my computer. I'm freezing. It is 80 degrees outside and I'm freezing. I don't feel well... my body aches, especially my back. My nose is a chunk of ice. My toes are cold; goosebumps cover both arms. My fingers are like icicles. I slip them under the laptop where they soak up the warmth radiating from the bottom of the computer. Why am I cold?

Nikki was here this morning. She was extremely upset at my condition and begged me again to leave Chris. I wish I could. I wish it was that easy. It felt good to be held in her warm, loving arms.

Why is it that people need contact? Especially women? What is it about the sense of touch that conveys so much emotion? Touch comes in many flavors—soft and gentle, hard and abusive, rough and callused, sharp and stinging, firm and reassuring, warm and cuddly. Why is it that we want to be held when we are ill? Why is the need so much greater at certain times? Why is the need so great sometimes that one can visualize the act and feel the warmth and erratic heartbeat as though it were actually happening? The need for contact is very powerful indeed.

What am I missing? I ask myself that question a lot. Will I finally realize what I want from life when I'm too old to have it, when I'm too unattractive for others to seek it from me? That thought causes a lump to rise into my throat, making it difficult to breathe. I'm tired. I close my eyes and lean my head against the swing.

- - -

Tuesday

I'm sitting on my deck again. It's mid-morning. I'm enjoying the sounds of the ocean and a strong cup of coffee. I'm feeling a little better today, physically and emotionally. My spirits are a little higher, although I remain contemplative. Sometimes I think I spend too much time thinking, and wanting, and not enough time acting.

Nikki stopped by again this morning. She'd still be here now if I hadn't sent her home to spend time with her wife. She is a good friend, and I love her dearly.

I spent a significant amount of time writing yesterday, and added another chapter to the book. I'm pleased with the way it's turning out. Chris is out of town on a job, affording me the peace and quiet I so desperately crave. The sunrise is painting the sky in a panorama of red. It's a beautiful sight. A dog is barking in the distance. I take a deep breath and release it as a sigh. I'm feeling melancholy... I'm not sure why the mood strikes me, but sometimes it does.

- - -

Wednesday

Woke up at 6:30 this morning... My body is killing me again. Why does it always hurt more on the second day after than the first? The pain was tolerable when I went to bed last night, but this morning it's nearly unbearable. Standing under the hot shower helped a lot, though.

Nikki came to visit again this morning. She is such a mother hen. I know she's afraid for me; afraid that Chris will hurt me again. When my poor father finally finds release from his pain, I too will be free. It breaks my heart to know that he will soon be gone. He's been a stabilizing force in my life and I will miss him dearly.

Well, I'd better get to work... deadlines to meet, publishers to keep happy. I've been invited to dinner at Nik's and Jerri's this evening. I have a lot to accomplish before then.

- - -

That's all I've written this week, Cass. As I said, I was in the hospital Thursday and Friday. I try very hard to keep my journal current, and I will gladly send it to you daily, if you'd like. I want to be open and honest with you. A good relationship cannot be built on lies and suspicion. I'm looking forward to seeing into your soul as well.

I will try to write today. We haven't seen Chris since the beating on Thursday. Nikki and Jerri insist on staying with me, so I am never alone. Please don't fear for my safety.

Until later, then.
Lovingly yours,
Rox

Satisfied, Rox selected "Send" and watched her soul disappear into the recesses of the Internet. She sighed deeply as she shut down the computer.

Jerri came up beside Rox and leaned down to kiss her cheek. "You okay?" she asked.

Rox looked at her friend and smiled. "Yeah." Suddenly, Rox's stomach rumbled loudly, which made both women chuckle.

"Come on, let's go feed that beast," Jerri said, offering her hand to help her injured friend to her feet.

* * *

Cass rolled over and tried to get comfortable, but she couldn't get rid of the urgent pressure. Finally she gave up, climbed out of bed and plodded to the bathroom to relieve herself. She returned to the bedroom and sat heavily on the side of the bed, rubbing the sleep out of her eyes, then sighed deeply and let her chin drop to her chest, scattering her dark hair over her face.

God, I hate mornings. She glanced at the clock; it was nine a.m. Her brow furrowed. *Nine a.m.? I went to bed around eleven. After ten hours of sleep, I shouldn't still be tired.*

You don't remember the dream, do you? Enforcer asked.

Dream? Cass pondered a moment before the memory returned to her. *Oh, yeah. You know, that was really strange. Why would Rox just disappear like that?*

Maybe it's a sign, Enforcer suggested.

A sign? Like an omen, you mean?

Yeah—like maybe it means you'd better get your butt in gear and jump her bones before she loses interest.

Oh, for crying out loud, E.! Where do you come up with this stuff?

Hello? Don't you mean where do you *come up with this stuff?*

"Aarrgghh!" Cass jumped off the bed, stripped off her night shirt, and headed for the treadmill.

Forty-five minutes later, Cass had just finished showering off the sweat from her workout. She stood in the den with a towel around her middle, rubbing a second towel through her hair as she booted up her computer and waited for her wallpaper to appear—a smiling picture of Rox she had scanned from the back cover of *Stargazer II*.

"Damn, that woman is gorgeous," she commented as she sat down and accessed her e-mail program. Her inbox opened, indicating two pieces of new mail. The first message was from the airline, indicating that her flight to Durango that Monday was being rescheduled to depart an hour earlier than usual, which wasn't an uncommon occurrence with international flights and foreign airports. The second was from Rox. Scanning the contents of the note gave Cass a very uneasy feeling. *This is a very unhappy woman, E. God, I wish I could take her away from it all.*

Why can't you? Enforcer asked.

What do you mean, 'why can't I?'

Why can't you? What's stopping you?

For one, I don't even know that she's into women. Like you said during chat, she said she loved me for caring, not that she loved me. *Her friends Nikki and Jerri are obviously a lesbian couple, but that doesn't make her gay. It's possible that all she wants from this relationship is someone she can be emotionally intimate with, but not on a romantic level. Anyway, she made it perfectly clear that she had to stay in her current relationship until her father was gone. What chance do I have?*

Well, you could always knock her father off and get it over with, Enforcer suggested.

Cass slapped her palms to her forehead and shook her head in disgust at where her mind was taking her. *Damn it, just answer the note.* She read Rox's note once more before composing a reply.

> *My dearest Rox,*
> *I feel so privileged to be allowed a glimpse of your soul. Thank you so much for sending your journal. Yes, I would*

very much like to continue receiving daily entries. I feel like you are showing me a secret part of yourself, a part reserved only for those you hold dear. Thank you for trusting me.

You've posed many valid questions. You have the mind of a philosopher and the soul of an angel. I wish I had answers for you, but I don't. Nevertheless, here are my thoughts.

Why do people need contact? I don't know. I suppose we need contact to measure our impact on others, and maybe even to validate our own self-worth. You know -- the more people we physically touch and the more people we have who voluntarily touch us, the greater our sense of worth. That's one theory. I think we draw comfort from touching... we seek refuge in it.

That's why we need contact even more when we are ill. We all want to be taken care of, in one respect or another. Too many of us are the caretakers, never receiving anything in return. Yes, even something as simple as a touch to reward our efforts... a kiss, a hug, a hand cupping your cheek. That type of touch validates us, and tells us that the world is a better place with us in it. I don't know, Rox. These are only my thoughts. They're not based on fact, or on psychological doctrine, they're just my thoughts.

I'm glad to hear that you're making progress with your new book. I'm afraid the cast on your hand will hinder you, though, unless you can get some help. Nikki seemed to do a very good job typing for you last night. Maybe she would be willing to help?

Rox, like Nikki, I'm worried about your relationship with Chris. I want so badly to rescue you from his brutality. Say the word and I will be on the next flight to Maine.

Please feel free to call my home whenever you need me. I've already given you the number, but here it is again: 408-555-1080. My pager number is 408-555-0046.

Please don't let Chris hurt you again, Rox. Please call me, and I will do whatever is in my power to stop it. Nikki is right to be worried about you. What if Chris does return? What then? I am so glad Nikki and Jerri are staying with you. They sound like wonderful friends.

I feel a closeness to you I never thought I would feel again after Patti died. In the three years since her death, I've held a small sliver of my heart in reserve, saving it only for

Patti's memory. I find you invading that sliver, as you have invaded the rest of my heart. I can't stop thinking of you, Rox. I don't want to stop. Please promise that you will call me if you need me. I don't care what time of the day or night it is. If you can't reach me at home, please call my pager. If you need me, I promise I will find a way to get to you.

    Enough said; I'll let you go for now. I'm so looking forward to your next note.

    Lovingly yours,

    Cass

Happy with her note, Cass sent the message and watched it disappear from her screen.

* * *

After a leisurely breakfast, Rox spent the next three hours sitting on the back deck, alternately watching the ocean and awkwardly typing material for her new book. Try as she might, she was unable to erase the picture of the tall, dark-haired man she had seen in her dream. *He looked so much like the picture Cass sent of himself.* She thought he looked quite attractive in blue jeans, exuding a rugged appeal that could not be denied. Redirecting her attention to the written word, she tried to concentrate on the laptop screen in front of her.

The figure behind the tool shed watched as Rox lowered her head and resumed typing. Like a gargoyle standing guard over its gable, it stood unmoving, eyes rarely leaving the woman on the deck. Occasionally a petite blonde or tall brunette would join her, sitting to enjoy a cup of coffee and chat, or bringing her refreshment. When the woman went back into the house, the watcher slipped away.

* * *

Cass stared at the blank computer screen. All she could think about was Rox and her abusive situation. She got to her feet and started pacing back and forth, left hand on her hip, right hand rubbing her chin. As she paced, Cass talked to her alter ego.

    E., I'm worried about her. I have this uneasy feeling in the pit of my stomach. I wish I could be there with her right now.

You realize you won't rest easy until you fly to Maine and check things out for yourself, don't you?

How can I do that? I have to work on Monday. I can't just pack up and go to Maine. Besides, she has her friends there with her, so she's probably relatively safe, Cass reasoned.

Admit it, Cass. You really want to be there because you have this overwhelming need to touch her, hold her, and tell her you love her. It has little to do with your protective instincts.

Cass stopped for a moment, frowning. *I've got it bad,* she admitted, and resumed her pacing.

Chapter 22

Jerri kissed her wife goodbye as she was leaving for work. "I really hate to leave you two alone. You know when I work the noon-to-midnight shift, I don't get home until nearly one in the morning. I could call in."

Nikki shook her head. "You've missed enough work already. Besides, it won't be as bad as it usually is when you're working late—I have Rox to keep me company tonight."

After seeing Jerri off, Nikki returned to the kitchen where Rox was sitting at the table, enjoying a garden salad and a grilled-cheese sandwich. Nikki raised her eyebrows as she saw a place set for her and her own meal waiting. She wrapped her arms around Rox and hugged her affectionately, kissing her cheek in thanks.

"How did you manage to cook lunch with a broken wrist?" Nikki asked as she sat down.

"I'm very talented," Rox said, wiggling her eyebrows.

Nikki gave her a pointed look. "I'll bet you are," she replied. "Speaking of which, how's the story coming?"

Rox's face glowed as she began to talk about her work. "Wonderfully. I managed to write half a chapter this morning. That's pretty good, considering I'm a one-armed bandit right now." She lifted her fiberglass-encased hand for emphasis.

"Do you need some help with the typing? It might move along faster that way."

"No, I don't think so. I'm doing okay. Besides, I have a really strange writing style. I'm forever going back to reread what I've written and tweak things. I jump back and forth so much I'd confuse the hell out of you. I'll be fine on my own. The swelling should go down in a day or so, and it'll be easier then. Thanks for asking, though."

Nikki reached across the table to cover her friend's injured hand. "You know I'd do anything for you, Rox, right?" she asked seriously.

Rox met her friend's eyes and held them for a moment as feelings of affection and love passed between them. "Yeah, I know. I can't thank you enough."

Nikki smiled. "So are you planning to write all day, or can I talk you into a little shopping?" Nikki shoved a forkful of greens into her mouth.

Rox sighed. "I really don't want to go out in public looking like this." She indicated the bruises that were painfully obvious on her face and neck.

Nikki nodded her head in understanding. "Well, how about a walk along the beach a little later? You really should get out of the house."

"I think I might be able to manage that," Rox said with a grin. "But can we make it after dinner? I'm going to do my e-mail after lunch, and then maybe take a nap before writing again this afternoon."

"After dinner's fine. What do you feel like eating tonight?" Nikki asked. "It's just the two of us."

"Nikki, you really don't have to baby me like this. I can cook my own dinner," Rox said.

"Yes, you can, but you won't, and we both know it," Nikki replied knowingly. "Now, don't argue with me. What would you like me to cook?"

Seeing that she had lost the battle, Rox sighed heavily. "I don't know. Whatever you want, I guess."

"And just how do you make that?" Nikki asked, propping her elbow up on the table and resting her chin in her hand.

"Make what?" Rox asked, confusion etched on her face.

"'Whatever you want.' I'm not familiar with that dish," Nikki teased.

Rox grinned, and without breaking eye contact, reached into her salad with her good hand and picked up a piece of lettuce. This she unceremoniously threw at her friend, hitting her on the cheek.

A full-fledged food fight immediately ensued, and by the time they were done, their salad dishes had been emptied all over the kitchen and each other.

Rox waited as the server retrieved her messages. Her eyes brightened when she saw the message from Cass. Clicking on the note, she scanned it quickly then took her time rereading it, stopping short when she saw the phone number. *Do I dare?* she thought, looking at the clock. *Let's see, it's nearly one p.m. here, so it's ten a.m. there. He must be out of bed by now.*

* * *

Cass dressed and waited for Angie to pick her up for a much-needed shopping trip. She hated shopping, but at their last meeting, she'd had to grudgingly admit that she needed some new underclothes and a pair of running shoes. Angie had immediately volunteered to drag her through the mall.

Soon after she'd finished getting ready, Cass heard a car horn and stepped out onto her small balcony, which overlooked the parking lot. *Precisely ten a.m.; Angie's right on time.* Groaning loudly, she grabbed her wallet and headed for the door, only to be brought up short by the ringing of the telephone.

She turned around and looked at the phone hopefully. *Maybe it's work calling. Maybe I can get out of this stupid shopping trip.* She walked the few steps from the door to the end table and picked up the receiver.

"Hello?" There was only silence on the line.

"Hello?" Cass said again, a little louder. An audible click was the response.

She looked at the receiver questioningly, her brow furrowed, then shrugged. "Crank callers." Cass hung up the phone and went out to meet Angie.

* * *

Rox slammed down the receiver.

"Oh, my God," she exclaimed. "A woman answered the phone."

"Huh? Did you say something, hon?" Nikki spoke from the kitchen doorway as she wiped the last dish.

Rox was still looking at the receiver. "I said, 'A woman answered the phone'," she replied, partially in a daze.

"A woman answered whose phone? Honey, maybe you should take that nap now," Nikki suggested, coming into the living room to feel her friend's forehead.

Rox brushed her hand away. "I'm all right. A woman answered Cass's phone. He gave me his phone number in his last message. I called and a woman answered his phone!" she said in an agitated voice.

Nikki raised her eyebrows as she dried her hands on the dishtowel. "I see."

"What do you think it means?"

"It means he had a woman in his apartment. Maybe it was his mother or his sister."

"Or his girlfriend," Rox added. "Nik, what do I really know about this guy? He could be some wacko!"

"Rox, he's an airplane pilot, not a wacko," Nikki said, trying to soothe her friend.

"Are you saying airplane pilots can't be wackos?" Rox challenged.

"No, I'm not saying that. Look," Nikki said, exasperated. "Why don't you skip your e-mail for this afternoon and get some sleep? It'll still be here when you get up. Okay?"

When a yawn gave away her true fatigue level, Rox reluctantly agreed.

"You go on up. Slowly, and hold on to the railing. I'll power down the computer then come tuck you in, okay? Hell, I may even join you." As Rox turned and headed toward the stairs, Nikki watched the computer shut down and thought, *If you're messing with my friend, you're a dead man, Cass Conway.*

* * *

Cass powered up her computer the minute she got home. The shopping trip had taken much longer than she had anticipated, since Angie had stopped at a half-dozen stores and then insisted on getting lunch while they were out. The result was four miserable hours in the mall, and Cass was more than ready to leave when Angie finally declared herself finished.

Disappointment settled in the pit of her stomach when her inbox failed to yield any new messages from Rox. Sitting back in her chair, she sighed deeply and stared at the screen.

Staring at it won't make it happen, you know, Enforcer said.

What do you mean?

Staring at the screen won't make a note appear.

What do you think is wrong, E.?

Who says something's wrong? Maybe she's just busy. Maybe she's writing. Don't be so paranoid!

E., what if that bastard has beaten her up again and she can't *respond?*

I don't know, Cass. I just don't know. Look, you're not going to be happy until you fly out there and check things out for yourself. You know that, don't you?

I can't do that, E. What if I appear at her door and a healthy Rox answers it? I'd look pretty stupid for being so paranoid, don't you think?

Suit yourself, but don't complain when I say, "I told you so."

Maybe I should send her another note. No, that would seem desperate.

You are *desperate, aren't you? If not, you sure are acting like it. Why don't we go over to the gym and work off some of this nervous energy?*

I really don't want to go to the gym.

You're wound up as tight as a cuckoo clock. Either we go to the gym, or we go out and get laid. Your choice, although I prefer the latter.

Cass stopped pacing and looked over her shoulder again. "I'll change into my gym clothes," she said, heading for her bedroom.

* * *

Rox and Nikki curled up together to take a two-hour nap, their bodies cuddled against each other affectionately. Upon awakening, they lay on their sides facing each other, but not touching. For the next hour, they talked about everything imaginable—from Rox's books to Chris to philosophies of life. Rox loved spending quality time with Nikki; it was just like it had been when they were in college. While the other girls were out drinking, partying and getting laid, Rox and Nikki would talk. Sometimes lying in bed like they were now, sometimes curled up on the couch, sometimes sitting on the floor. Their body language always seemed to reflect the subject matter.

Rox spent the rest of the afternoon writing, while Nikki prepared dinner. After a leisurely dinner of pasta marinara, salad and garlic bread, Rox looked longingly at her computer before deciding to ignore her e-mail a while longer and take a relaxing walk along the shoreline with her best friend. Accordingly, Nikki and Rox stepped onto the sand off the back deck to take a stroll along the beach.

"Nikki, do you think I'm rushing things with Cass?"

Nikki appeared to ponder the wet sand that forced its way between her toes as she walked barefoot on the edge of the surf. "Maybe, Rox. You've only known him for, what, three weeks?"

"It feels like so much longer than that, like I've known him forever. There's something about him, but I can't put my finger on it. It's as if I've known him before. It all feels so familiar, like destiny. Know what I mean?"

Her friend walked along quietly, contemplating her own situation. She had known Jerri for only a short time before she wanted to commit her life to her. The difference was that she and Jerri met first and then fell in love, not the other way around. "Roxie, I *do* believe that people can fall in love quickly. Hell, I didn't know Jerri for much longer than you've known Cass before I was sure of my love for her."

"But?" Rox prompted.

"But we had the luxury of meeting face to face and getting to know each other that way before we acknowledged how we felt."

Rox was silent as she thought about Nikki's comment.

Nikki looked over at her friend. "Rox, what if the two of you meet and you're not compatible? What if you don't appeal to each other physically? What then?" She continued without giving Rox a chance to reply. "You'll end up getting hurt, that's what. Honey, you give your heart too freely. Look at Chris. You gave your heart freely there too, and look where it's ending."

They walked quietly along the beach for a while before Rox replied. "Cass is different. I can feel it." She gave her friend a mournful look before adding, "Of course, it's all for naught if the woman on the phone earlier today is his girlfriend."

"You don't know that," Nikki protested.

"You're right, I don't. Maybe I should ask him."

"Maybe you should."

Rox stopped walking and looked into Nikki's eyes. Smiling, she leaned in and kissed her affectionately on the lips. "Thank you, my friend. You know I love you with all my heart, don't you?"

Nikki nodded and smiled as they locked arms and resumed their walk.

The solitary figure by the tool shed watched the affectionate scene between the two women. *You bitch. You will pay for this, for the lies and the humiliation. You will pay.*

* * *

Cass stood under the shower spray. The trip to the gym had helped alleviate her frustrated anxiety, but enough remained to make her edgy. *I wonder if Rox answered my last message yet.*

Resolving not to make herself crazy waiting, she stepped out of the shower and toweled off. She hung the towel back on the rack and stood naked in front of the full-length bathroom mirror, looking at herself. Turning this way and that, she noted that the large bruise from the crash landing was starting to fade. Facing the mirror again, she sighed, then glanced at the clock, trying to decide between going out to dinner and ordering in. It was nearly five p.m.

I need to get a life, she thought. *I hate eating alone... I hate living alone... I hate being alone.* She grabbed some clothes and got dressed. *Angie, I hope you're not too busy tonight, 'cause I plan on hanging around till closing time.* She ran a comb quickly through her hair and exited the bathroom.

Cass stopped and took a long hard look at her computer as she headed for the front door, almost giving in to the urge to log on and check e-mail. Finally, she forced herself to put one foot in front of the other and headed out to dinner.

"What can I get you, sweetie?" Angie asked, sitting down across from Cass.

Cass looked up and smiled. "How about the beef stew and salad?" she said. "Oh, and coffee, please."

"Good choice." Angie wrote the order on her pad. Before leaving to place the order, she looked at her adopted daughter carefully. "Are you all right, honey?"

Cass looked puzzled. "Sure, why do you ask?"

"I don't know. You look preoccupied or something," Angie said hesitantly. "Let me go place your order, then I'll grab us both some coffee. Looks like you need to talk." She rose to her feet and walked away.

It amazed Cass how Angie always knew when something was bothering her, and she smiled to herself. *She's a real gem... a true friend.*

Angie came back with the coffee and sat down again. She pushed one of the cups over to the younger woman and gave her a direct look. "Okay, spill it. What's bothering you?"

"I don't know, Ang. I guess I'm being impatient. I can't get Rox out of my mind."

"Ah, Rox. I should have known. Have you heard back from her yet?"

"Not today. It kind of worries me. I told you that she lives in an abusive situation, and it turns out that the person she's living with has beaten her several times. In fact, the last beating was just a few days ago. I'm really afraid for her, Angie."

"Is she alone?"

"No, a couple of friends are staying with her. I feel better about that, but… I don't know. Damn, I wish I could be there with her."

"Why aren't you? Why don't you fly to Maine and check things out? At least you'd have peace of mind."

"That's what E. said," Cass replied absently.

"E.?"

Damn! "Uh… uh… E… Elizabeth—a friend of mine at the gym," Cass said haltingly.

Angie looked at her through narrowed eyes. *What are you hiding, Cassidy Conway?* Pushing the thought aside for a moment, she continued. "If it'll make you feel better, Cass, go to her."

"I'll give it a few more days. If things still don't feel right, maybe I'll do just that. In any case, I have a two-day flight to Durango scheduled for Monday and Tuesday, so I can't do anything until at least Wednesday."

"Order up, Ang!" came the call from the kitchen.

Angie patted Cass's hand. "That'll be yours. After dinner, we'll talk some more."

Cass nodded and waited for Angie to return with her meal.

Chapter 23

Rox stared at the blank screen and wondered what she should write. She had argued with Nikki about climbing the stairs to the third story, but her friend had finally relented and helped her up to her office. Rox had strict orders to call her when she was ready to come downstairs.

How do I ask him? She considered some possibilities. *Cass, do you have a girlfriend? Cass, are you playing cybersex games with me? Cass, do you really care about me, or are you just messing with my head?* Her heart beat rapidly at the thought of Cass not being honest with her. *Why do I care so much? Could it be that I...*

Rox rose from her chair and started pacing, eyeing her computer as though it were an enemy about to attack. *Do I love him?* She shook her head. *I do, don't I? How can that be? I've only known him for three weeks. Damn!* She started pacing again. *Oh, God, what if he's playing games with my head? What if he's one of these kooks who pretend to be something they aren't so they can lure innocent women into dangerous situations? All right, calm down, Rox. Think. You know he's legitimately a pilot—his name was all over the newspaper earlier this week—but what about the woman in his apartment?*

Rox was still pacing when Nikki climbed the stairs to the attic.

"Hey, girl, can I interest you in a glass of iced tea?" she asked, handing over the extra glass she was carrying.

Rox accepted the tea, avoiding Nikki's eyes. "Thanks."

Nikki noticed this immediately, and placed a hand on Rox's arm. "Whoa, what's wrong?"

"Wrong? What could be wrong? Here I am, covered in black and blue marks, a cast on my arm, madly in love with a man I've never met. A man who's probably cheating on me this very moment! What could possibly be wrong?"

Taking the iced tea from Rox, Nikki put both glasses down on the desk and faced her friend. She took her by the forearms and turned her so that they were looking directly at one another, then lifted Rox's chin. "Did you say you're in love with him?"

Rox's eyes immediately filled with tears. Nodding slightly, she fell into Nikki's embrace and began to cry. "What am I going to do? I love him. I can't help it, I do. I know I haven't known him for very long, but... but... Damn it, Nikki, what am I going to do?"

"Roxie, Roxie, baby, shh. It's okay. Honey, please don't cry," Nikki said, trying to soothe her distraught friend.

After long moments, the tears subsided and Rox stood in the circle of Nikki's arms trying to compose herself. "Are you all right?" Nikki asked, pulling back to look at her.

Rox nodded, still avoiding Nikki's eyes for fear she would break down again. "What am I going to do, Nik?" she whispered.

Nikki hugged her again, then led her over to the desk and sat her down in the office chair. "Well, for starters, you're going to write to Cass and ask about the woman in his apartment."

"I don't know what to say to him," Rox protested.

"Don't worry. I'll help you think of something."

Rox clicked on the "New Mail" icon and started to compose a note to Cass.

"Okay, how's this?" she asked, after a few moments of typing.

> Dear Cass,
> Thank you so much for your concern. I'm also afraid that Chris may return and cause more damage, personal or otherwise. Let me assure you that I am never alone. Nikki or Jerri, sometimes both, are with me at all times. I don't believe I'm in any grave danger.
> I really do appreciate you giving me your phone number—

"Rox," Nikki said, turning away from the screen for a moment, "Do you think you should give him *your* phone number?"

"No, not unless he asks for it. I want to make sure this will work out before I start giving out information like that."

Nikki nodded, and they put their heads together again as she read the rest of the text.

> I really do appreciate you giving me your phone number. Actually, I called earlier today and a woman

answered. Maybe a housekeeper? In any case, you weren't home.

I need to be blunt here for a moment. I need to know what your intentions are toward me. Cass, I am falling in love with you. If that love cannot be reciprocated honestly, then we must end this e-mail relationship. I can't bear the thought of continuing with a pretense if there is no chance that you will ever truly love me. Please don't be angry with me over this inquiry. I have lived in hell for the past six months, and it's about time I moved on to a brighter future. I know you've told Nikki that you love me, but are you in love with me?

Again, forgive my bluntness, but I need an answer to that question before we can go on.

I love you, Cass, but I cannot allow you to hurt me. I have lived in pain for much too long already.

Please let me know where your heart lies.

Rox

"You weren't kidding when you said you needed to be blunt, were you?" Nikki observed.

Worried, Rox re-read the last few paragraphs. "Do you think it'll scare him off?"

"Well, it'll either scare him off or reel him in for life. It all depends on how he feels about commitment."

"Nik, I can't let him hurt me. Chris has done enough of that to last a lifetime."

Nikki hugged her fiercely. "I know, sweetheart, I know. Okay, send it."

In seconds, the note was on its way to Cass. The two friends watched, each absorbed in her own thoughts.

It will kill me if he answers "No," Rox mused.

I will kill him if he answers "No," Nikki vowed.

* * *

Cass left the diner at closing time. She had stayed, ostensibly to keep Angie company, for nearly three hours after she'd finished her supper. In truth, she dreaded the thought of returning to her empty home. She dragged herself through the door, then eased her tall frame down onto the couch and reached for the remote control. Channel-surfing failed to produce anything that held her interest, so she turned off the TV and tossed the remote onto the coffee table. She tipped her head back and sighed deeply.

Go ahead, Enforcer urged.

Cass ignored the voice.

I know you can hear me. It won't do you any good to ignore me, you know.

Aw, come on, E., back off, will you?

No, I don't think so. You know you want to.

E.!

Cass, you don't exactly have a Super Bowl party going on here. I'm bored. Now get off your ass and do it!

God damn it! You aren't going to leave me alone until I do, are you?

You got it, girlfriend.

Cass rose to her feet and headed to the office, then waited nervously for the computer to boot up. After a few moments, she threw up her hands in exasperation. "Why the hell can't multi-million-dollar semiconductor manufacturers make a computer that's ready the instant you switch it on?" She started the even lengthier logon into e-mail. After what seemed like an eternity, the server delivered new mail to her inbox. Her heart skipped a beat as she saw Rox's address.

Opening the message, she quickly perused its contents.

Dear Cass,

Thank you so much for your concern. I'm also afraid that Chris may return and cause more damage, personal or otherwise. Let me assure you that I am never alone. Nikki or Jerri, sometimes both, are with me at all times. I don't believe I'm in any grave danger.

I really do appreciate you giving me your phone number. Actually, I called earlier today and a woman answered. Maybe a housekeeper? In any case, you weren't home.

I need to be blunt here for a moment. I need to know what your intentions are toward me. Cass, I am falling in love with you. If that love cannot be reciprocated honestly, then we must end this e-mail relationship. I can't bear the thought of continuing with a pretense if there is no chance that you will ever truly love me. Please don't be angry with me over this inquiry. I have lived in hell for the past six months, and it's about time I moved on to a brighter future. I know you've told Nikki that you love me, but are you in love with me?

Again, forgive my bluntness, but I need an answer to that question before we can go on.

I love you, Cass, but I cannot allow you to hurt me. I have lived in pain for much too long already.

Please let me know where your heart lies.

Rox

Whoa! Break out the cold ones! Cass, old buddy, looks like you scored big-time, Enforcer said.

"A woman answered my phone?" *E., she said a woman answered my phone. I wonder who that was.*

Fuck the woman, Cass. Well, not literally. Oh, hell, you know what I mean. Look, she said she's falling in love with you.

"Cass, I am falling in love with you," she read again. Suddenly, she jumped to her feet and pointed to the monitor. *"E.! She said she's falling in love with me!"*

No shit, Sherlock! E. replied. *Hello? Is anybody home?*

Cass started pacing again, hugging herself in agitation. *Oh, shit! Now what do I do?*

You sit that butt of yours right down there and answer this e-mail. Don't get cold feet now, Cass. This is what you wanted, remember?

Nodding, Cass sat down in front of the keyboard and composed a response.

My dearest Rox,

Reading your note evoked such a sense of love and longing, I could hardly contain myself. Never did I think that you'd return my love so quickly. Rox, I have been in love with you almost from the beginning.

Sweetheart, I know you've just come from a very brutal relationship, and I understand your need to be blunt. Let me assure you, my love, that your heart is safe with me. I will never hurt you, Rox. That is a promise, and I do not make promises lightly.

How could I be angry with you for wanting to know my heart? In my last letter, I asked that you share your soul with me. I can't expect you to do anything I'm not willing to do myself, so by all means, ask me anything you'd like. My heart belongs to you.

You asked what my intentions are. Rox, I have never felt such intensity of love for another in my entire life. Thoughts of you fill every waking moment. What are my intentions? My intentions are to meet you one day soon, sweep you off your feet, and carry you away into the sunset. My intentions are to make you happier than you have ever been, for the rest of your life. My intentions are to love you, cherish you, hold you near, make love to you long into the nights and to carry your scent on my skin through the days. My intentions are to grow old with you, and to hold you in my arms as I take my dying breath. These are my intentions, Rox.

I love you with all my heart. I need to be with you. Just say the word and I will be on the next plane.

You are my heart, Rox. Come fly away and be my love.
Cass

"What do you think?"
Go for it, Cass. It's a great note, Enforcer replied.

* * *

Nikki slept soundly in the guest room, with her arms and legs wrapped around the spare pillow. She often slept that way when Jerri worked late. She was a light sleeper, so she was partially awakened by the sounds of someone rummaging around in her room.

"Jer? Honey, stop making so much noise and come to bed," she said into the darkness, never lifting her head off the pillow.

Several seconds of silence followed as Nikki waited for her wife to join her. When it became apparent that Jerri wasn't coming to bed, Nikki sat up and looked into deep brown eyes. Her eyes flew open wide as a club made contact with her skull, then blackness enveloped her.

"Nikki! Nikki!" Jerri cried, calling her wife back into consciousness.

Nikki's eyes opened slowly, and the light from the bedside lamp blinded her with pain. She flung her arm up to cover her eyes.

"Oh, my God," Nikki moaned as her hand found the lump on her head. "What happened?" She looked around and suddenly sat up, which caused a wave of dizziness and nausea. She fell back onto the bed, then grabbed Jerri's arm. "Jerri, where's Rox?"

Jerri gently pressed her down. "Settle down, love. The ambulance crew is with her."

Nikki forced her way back into a sitting position. "What? Jerri, I need to see her." She threw her legs over the side of the bed and attempted to get up.

"Stay down, Nik. You'll see her soon enough. In fact, you'll be sharing an ambulance ride to the hospital with her. Please lie down." Jerri's voice cracked with emotion.

Nikki started to cry. "Jerri, it was Chris. I saw the brown eyes and blonde hair just before I lost consciousness. How bad is Roxie?" she asked faintly.

"Bad enough to be checked out in the emergency room, love, but it could have been worse. I think I interrupted the attack when I came home."

That news made Nikki cry harder. Sitting up again, she wrapped herself around her wife and buried her face in the taller woman's chest. "You could have been hurt, too."

Jerri rubbed Nikki's back as she soothed her fears. "Yeah, but I wasn't, so don't fret over it, okay?" She held her wife close.

"Jerri, we're ready to go. Does Nikki need a stretcher?" asked a voice from the doorway.

Jerri looked back over her shoulder. "No, Dan, I don't think so. I'll walk her down to the ambulance. We'll be right there." She turned back to Nikki. "Can you make it with my help or do you want me to carry you?"

Nikki reached up and cupped the side of Jerri's face, noticing for the first time that there were tears in the dark-haired woman's eyes. Smiling slightly, she said, "No, I'll lean on you, love, just like I always do."

Jerri kissed the smaller woman tenderly before smiling at her and extending her hand. "All right, let's go." She helped Nikki to her feet and led her out of the room.

Nikki held Rox's hand all the way to the hospital as she sat leaning against Jerri. Rox was a mess. Blood liberally coated the front of her nightshirt, face, neck and arms.

Jerri was thankful that Rox was unconscious, since that saved her from having to deal with both her wife and her best friend being injured at the same time. She reached up and brushed blonde tendrils away from Nikki's forehead, making the smaller woman smile. "Are you all right?" Jerri asked.

Nikki sniffed back a tear then nodded. "It's just a bump, Jer," she said, feeling around for the lump on her head. "Poor Roxie, on the other hand... " The sentence trailed off as she looked at her friend lying unconscious on the stretcher.

"Honey, it looks worse than it is," Jerri said as she reached over and touched the side of Rox's face. "As far as I could tell, she has a head wound, which accounts for most of the blood, and she's been struck repeatedly about the face and neck. Her vitals are stable. She's going to be very sore, and maybe a little self-conscious about her appearance for a while, but I think she'll be fine."

Nikki looked at her wife and wondered how on earth she could maintain such a clinical attitude when it was their best friend lying there, in serious trouble. She knew it took a special kind of person to work on an E-crew, someone who could detach themselves emotionally when necessary. But she sometimes found it hard to understand.

Looking down at Rox, Nikki brushed a bloody strand of hair from the bruised face. A solitary tear fell, and she closed her eyes and sniffed back the deluge that was sure to follow if her resolve wavered. "Jerri, what are we going to do?" she asked. "Some protector I was, huh? I didn't even hear Chris come into the house."

Jerri wrapped her arms tighter around Nikki. "Don't blame yourself for this, sweetheart. If Chris is determined to get to her, it will happen, one way or another. We can't protect her 24 hours a day. Besides, I'm not sure how much you could have done against him, anyway. He's a lot bigger than you are."

Nikki nodded as she brushed the tear from her face. After a few moments, she looked at her wife. "I know you don't like to hear this, but she really needs a man around the house. Someone who can protect her against the likes of Chris."

"She doesn't need a man. What she needs is Chris to be caught and put behind bars," Jerri replied adamantly.

"I still think she'd be safer with a man in the house." Nikki gave her wife a sheepish look, knowing how she felt about women taking care of themselves.

Jerri was about to argue the point further when the ambulance pulled up to the emergency room bay.

Several hours later, in the wee hours of the morning, Nikki and Jerri left the hospital. As she climbed into a taxi, Jerri looked over at a very sullen Nikki and took her hand. "Nik, she's going to be all right. They just want to keep her overnight for observation. We'll be able to take her home tomorrow morning."

Nikki wasn't in the mood to be coddled. She pulled her hand away and dropped her chin to her chest. "I'm tired. I just want to go to bed," she said softly.

Jerri nodded, then pulled Nikki's head in and placed a kiss on her forehead. "How's your head?"

"Hurts like hell," Nikki replied. "I'm going to take some drugs, then hit the sheets."

"Good plan," Jerri answered, releasing her and sitting back for the ride to Rox's house. "Do you want to go home for the rest of the night, instead?"

Nikki shook her head. "Our cars are at Rox's. We might just as well stay there tonight."

"What if Chris comes back? I'm not a man; I might not be able to protect us."

A bit touchy, are we? Nikki shook her head ruefully, choosing not to respond to the sarcasm in Jerri's voice. *I'm sorry, love. I didn't mean to offend you, but Rox really does need someone in her life to protect her.*

Nikki sat up. "Of course!"

Jerri raised an eyebrow. "'Of course' what?"

"We need to get to Rox's right away. I have an e-mail to send."

Chapter 24

Nikki was out of the taxi as soon as it pulled into Rox's driveway. She ran into the house, powered up the computer and logged on to the Internet using Rox's user ID and password.

Jerri walked up behind her as she patiently waited for the process to complete. "What are you doing?"

"I'm taking care of Rox's security problems," Nikki replied.

Jerri raised her eyebrows.

Nikki looked back at her wife. "What?"

"How do you propose to do that?"

"I'm sending a note to Cass. He's said twice now that he'd jump on the first plane east if Rox needed him. I'd say she needs him now, wouldn't you?"

Jerri narrowed her eyes. "Nik, aren't you overreacting a bit? I mean, yes, Chris did manage to get into the house undetected last night, but now that the police have been alerted, they're watching the place. It won't happen again."

"We don't know that. And what if Chris stalks Rox and catches her away from the house?" Nikki asked, accessing Rox's e-mail program.

"Honey, what makes you think Cass will just drop everything and fly here? He does have a job, you know."

"Well, he said he would." Nikki turned in her seat and looked up at her wife. "Jerri, why are you so against this? What are you afraid of?"

Jerri leaned down and spun the chair around so that Nikki was facing her. She grasped the arms of the chair on either side and looked Nikki in the face. "I'm afraid Rox will get hurt. I'm afraid this guy won't be for real. I'm afraid he won't live up to his word. Sweetheart, Rox doesn't need to be disappointed right now. She doesn't need to deal with the pain of rejection on top of everything else."

"I don't think that will happen. I've read all the notes this guy sent her, and either he really loves her or he's the world's greatest con artist."

"That's what I'm afraid of. That's exactly what I'm afraid of."

Nikki maintained eye contact with her wife and spoke adamantly. "Jerri, I have to do this… for Rox's sake."

Jerri narrowed her eyes and stepped back. "Rox won't be thrilled about this, you know," she warned.

"I won't tell her," Nikki's tone was matter of fact. "And I'll delete the message from the 'Sent' file as soon as it transmits." Jerri shook her head in disgust and Nikki continued, "Don't look at me like that! She needs protection. Obviously, you and I can't provide it. I don't know what else to do." There were tears in her eyes as she admitted her inability to help her friend.

Jerri hated to see Nikki cry. Throwing up her hands, she conceded. "All right. Do what you think you have to, and let's cross our fingers that Rox doesn't get hurt."

Nikki nodded. She turned back to the keyboard, typed the word "HELP!!" in the subject line, and then wrote the message.

> Hi, Cass,
>
> This is Nikki. As you can see, I'm using Rox's e-mail account to send this note.
>
> Rox is in serious trouble. Now, before you panic, let me say that at this moment, she's safe. In fact, she's in the hospital again, at least for the night. Chris managed to break into the house around midnight last night. Rox and I were the only ones home, since Jerri was working. He knocked me out cold and then attacked Rox while she slept. Jerri interrupted the attack when she came home, but Chris managed to escape. The police have issued an APB, but so far, no luck finding the bastard.
>
> Rox is a mess. She's not critically injured, but she has a concussion and her face is so black and blue that even I barely recognized her. She looks so pathetic that it makes me cry to see her.
>
> You said in your last note that you'd jump on the next plane east if she needed you. Well, I would say that she needs you desperately right now. Last night's attack, while I was in the house with her, is evidence that she needs more protection than I can give her. Jerri is with her during the

day, but even an idiot like Chris wouldn't be stupid enough to attack in broad daylight. Jerri works mostly at night, so that leaves me here to protect her alone. Obviously, I am not capable of doing the job, at least not by myself.

She needs you, Cass. Please, if it's at all possible, find a way to come to her, to be here with her, at least until Chris is caught and put behind bars. She lives in Rockland, Maine, at 1163 Oceanview Terrace. Any taxi at the airport can bring you here. Please hurry. There's no telling when he might strike again.

We'll stay here with her and protect her to the best of our ability, but she needs more than we can give her. Please hurry.

Nikki

Nikki let the pointer of the mouse hover over the "Send" button for a moment or two before clicking and sending the note on its way. She released a deep sigh of relief and closed her eyes, confident that Cass would come through.

From her position behind her wife, Jerri watched the scene. As much as it galled her to rely on outside help, she knew that she wouldn't be able to get Nikki to leave Rox home alone. And as long as Nikki was going to insist on staying with Rox, Jerri had to admit that having another person in the house was a good idea. She took a step closer to her wife and started massaging Nikki's shoulders.

Nikki nestled her head back against Jerri's abdomen and gave a satisfied moan at the pleasure being administered to her shoulders.

After a moment or two, Jerri leaned in close to Nikki's ear. "Sweetheart, you need to go to bed. It's nearly three a.m."

Nikki nodded in reply.

"All right, then. Why don't you head upstairs? I'll grab a couple of pain relievers and some water and be right behind you, okay?" Jerri kissed her wife's cheek.

With another nod, Nikki rose to her feet and faced Jerri. She saw love and concern in the taller woman's eyes. She smiled and folded herself into Jerri's arms, then wrapped hers around her wife's waist and buried her face against her chest. "I love you," she whispered, placing a kiss between Jerri's breasts.

"I love you too, sweet one." Jerri kissed the blonde head resting just below her chin. Pulling back, she held Nikki at arm's length and said, "Okay, you head upstairs. I'll be up in a bit."

Nikki tilted her head back and accepted another kiss before turning to go. "Don't be long, love."

* * *

Cass couldn't believe it was almost eleven p.m. by the time she sent the note to Rox. *Why does it take me so long to write a note to her? I can't seem to do it in less than two hours.*

Her flight to Durango was scheduled to take off an hour earlier than usual the next morning, and Cass knew she should get some sleep. She decided to shower before bed, and stepped into the bathroom where she stood for long moments thinking of Rox. Finally, she stripped off her clothes, starting with her shorts and panties.

Closing her eyes then, she pulled her t-shirt over her head and held it close to her breasts as her mind filled again with thoughts of Rox. Suddenly, she felt warm hands touching her naked hips. She gasped for breath and dropped the t-shirt to the floor, but held her eyes tightly closed for fear the sensory illusion would fade. Standing perfectly still, she waited for the specter's next move.

Cass felt the hands move slowly upward, kneading the supple skin gently. The palms went flat against her skin, moved very slowly past her hips and rested lightly on the skin on either side of her navel. Then the hands pulled her backward ever so slightly and Cass felt her bare butt come in contact with soft, warm curves. She wanted to open her eyes, but feared that reality would take the place of the wonderful fantasy she was feeling. Instead, she leaned forward and rested her forehead on the mirror as the hands on her abdomen started a slow circular movement, massaging her taut muscles.

Slowly, they moved upward until they cupped her breasts, and then pinched erect nipples between thumbs and forefingers. Cass turned around and leaned her back against the mirror as she moaned in pleasure. Her neck arched and sent a cascade of long, dark hair down her back. The hands kneaded her breasts, each pinch and caress sending bolts of desire crashing into Cass's core. By the time they moved on, Cass was writhing in agony born of desire.

Before she could catch her breath from the attack on her breasts, the ghost hands started moving again, tracing a circular path down the length of her body and stopping at the top of her pubis. Cass's hips began to rock forward, urging the hands to continue.

After a brief hesitation, they did. One hand slipped between dark curls, while the other circled behind and firmly cupped Cass's butt.

Cass moaned loudly as fingers slipped in and out of her slick folds, gently teasing as they passed over her swollen nub. Deeper and deeper they explored, with two, then three fingers thrusting deep inside her. Cass's knees were so shaky that she was barely able to hold herself up as she felt herself climbing closer and closer to orgasm. Faster and faster the hand worked, until a guttural moan escaped from deep in Cass's throat and she screamed the name of her deliverer. "Rox!" she cried as she plunged over the precipice, leaning heavily against the mirror to keep herself from falling.

As the tremors began to subside, Cass turned toward the mirror and opened her eyes, only to glimpse a wisp of red-gold hair over her shoulder.

Looking behind her, she confirmed that she was alone. She turned back to the mirror and studied herself carefully as she removed her hand from between her legs and thought again of the beautiful woman who had pushed her to the act of self gratification.

The incessant ringing was really getting on Cass's nerves. She picked up the alarm clock and read the time, then replaced the clock and burrowed down under the covers. Seconds later, she jumped up again.

"My flight's an hour early this morning. I almost forgot!"

She hopped out of bed and hurried to get dressed. "God damn it! I should have set the clock for an hour earlier," she said, and mentally thanked God that she had showered the night before.

I hate mornings, she sputtered to herself. *Especially when I oversleep. Damn it! I won't have time to look at my e-mail before I go. Why did I ever agree to do these overnight flights, anyway?*

You signed on for them to take your mind off Patti, remember? the ever-present Enforcer piped in.

E., you're not going to lecture me about oversleeping again, are you?

Oh, no, never. You actually got to bed at a decent hour last night. You did, however, tire us out pretty "handily" before jumping in the shower. But you won't hear me complain! No way, not me, oh, no. I quite enjoyed that little trip to the moon, Cass, old buddy. We should do that more often, don't you think?

I don't have time to discuss this right now; I'm running late. Have you seen my shoes?

Under the coffee table in the living room, right where we kicked them off last night. You're a pig, you know. If you'd pick up after us, you wouldn't be wasting time looking for shoes.

The scolding was not appreciated. *Give me a break, E. I'm really in a hurry here.* Cass found her shoes and slipped them on. After dragging a brush through her hair and applying a little blush and mascara, she was out the door for her two-day trip to Durango.

* * *

Nikki woke abruptly at around nine the next morning. She looked at the clock and moaned, then dropped her head into her hands. *I can't believe I slept so late!* she thought, before remembering what had happened. She frowned as she reached up and carefully felt the sore spot where she had been struck the night before. *If I hurt this badly, I can only imagine how Rox feels.*

Nikki decided to go and pick up Rox without waking Jerri, who had worked until midnight the night before and then come home in the middle of Chris's attack. She would have to return to work at noon, after less than five hours of sleep.

An hour later, Nikki was showered and ready to go. She leaned over Jerri's sleeping form, gently kissed her cheek and whispered endearments in her ear.

Jerri shifted in her sleep and reached up, capturing Nikki with one arm and pulling her down to the bed.

It was all Nikki could do not to squeal and wake her partner. Several moments later, she managed to wriggle out of the embrace and climb out of bed. A moment in the bathroom to comb her hair again, and Nikki was on her way to the hospital to get Rox.

Rox paced back and forth in the hospital room, waiting for Jerri and Nikki to pick her up. The horrific events of the night before played over and over in her mind. One minute she was sleeping soundly; the next she felt a sharp pain at the back of her neck as her head was cuffed from side to side by sharp blows to the sides of her face. Her assailant sat astride her waist, raining blows on her face with both fists. Mercifully, she lost consciousness and did not wake again until hours later, in the emergency room at the hospital. Nikki's and Jerri's worried faces were looking down at her. *It's becoming a habit. A habit I surely need to break.*

"Hey, girlfriend, are you ready to go home?"

The breezy question interrupted Rox's recollections, and she turned to see Nikki standing at the entrance to her room, a teary-eyed smile on her face. Smiling back, she took two quick steps toward her friend and fell into her warm embrace. They clung to each other in quiet desperation as all the hurt and anxiety Rox had been feeling for the past several months bubbled to the surface and spilled out across her face and down her cheeks.

"It's okay, love. Cry it out. That's it, let it all go, sweetheart," Nikki held the injured woman in her arms and stroked her back. "Come on, let's go home." She led Rox to the door.

When they were in the car heading home, Nikki reached over and grasped Rox's hand. "Are you okay?"

Rox nodded slowly, her head low.

"Hey," Nikki said, reaching over to lift her friend's head. "Things will get better for you, Rox. I promise."

Rox looked at her friend intently. Brow furrowed, she shook her head slightly. "How can you say that? How can you be so sure?"

Nikki was tempted to tell her about the e-mail to Cass, but until he responded, she didn't want to get her friend's hopes up. So, she just sighed. "Please, don't give up, Rox. Things will get better. Believe me, honey, they will."

It was Rox's turn to sigh. She gave an unconvinced nod as she stared down at her hands, clasped in her lap.

They pulled into Rox's driveway and she saw her neighbors going about their typical, everyday chores—cutting the grass, weeding the garden, cleaning up flower beds. She averted her head self-consciously and shielded her bruised face with her hand as she climbed out of the car. Several curious glances were directed her way as she started toward the house.

"Mind your own business!" Nikki shouted at the most shameless members of the group, who stared openly. Resting her hand on Rox's back, she ushered her into the privacy of her home and away from the prying eyes of her insensitive neighbors. "Christ, that pisses me off," Nikki griped, once they were inside.

"They're just curious, that's all. It's human nature."

"They weren't curious enough to come and see what was happening when Chris was beating the shit out of you for the last six months. Don't tell me it wasn't obvious to them that something was wrong. I didn't see any of them rushing to your aid then, so they can keep their nosy eyeballs to themselves now!"

"What's up?" said a sleepy voice from the top of the stairs.

Nikki and Rox looked up to see Jerri coming down the stairs.

"Hi, baby," Nikki replied, approaching her wife to kiss her lips as she reached the bottom stair. "I was just commenting on how helpful Rox's neighbors are."

"Helpful, my ass," replied Jerri as she checked out Rox's bruises with a professional eye. "They'd stand by and let Chris kill her as long as it didn't interfere with their own lives."

"All right, enough about my neighbors. I need to get to work. I still have a deadline, bruised or not." Rox brushed Jerri's hands away and headed for the stairs.

"Rox, I'm going to throw together some lunch and bring it up to you, along with an icepack for your jaw, okay?" Nikki said.

"I'm fine. Really, I just need to get to work."

"Damn it, Roxanne Ward. Why does everything have to be a battle with you? Just accept the help and get over it. I'm not going away, so get that through your stubborn head."

Nikki pointed toward the stairway. "Now, you can trot your little ass up those stairs and start writing if you want, but I'm still bringing you lunch and an icepack, got it?"

Rox and Jerri looked at each other with identical miniscule grins.

"Ah, Rox, I'd do what I was told if I were you. I've learned not to mess with her when she's PMSing," Jerri murmured.

"*I am not PMSing!*" Nikki shouted after them as they retreated up the stairs, soft chuckles trailing in their wake.

Chapter 25

Jerri settled Rox in front of her computer and returned to the kitchen to help Nikki put together a simple lunch of veggie wraps, fruit salad, and iced tea. Their conversation centered on Cass.

"Do you think he replied yet?" Nikki asked.

"I don't know. If he has, Rox hasn't read it yet," Jerri said. "She definitely would have said something. When she finds out, you're dead meat. You know that, don't you?"

Nikki winced. Rox was fiercely independent. In fact, she had never even given them permission to stay with her. They simply hadn't given her any choice. That was why Nikki had sent the note to Cass without telling Rox—she wouldn't have allowed it.

"As independent as Rox is, she sure didn't use it against Chris very often," Nikki observed.

"It's amazing what you'll do for love. I mean, look at me. I used to be independent too, and now… well, now I'm quite PW'd," Jerri said, intentionally baiting her wife.

"PW'd?" Nikki looked at her questioningly. "What the hell is that?"

Jerri tried not to smile. "You know—pussy-whipped."

Nikki's jaw nearly hit the floor. "Pussy-whipped? Pussy-whipped! Jeraldine Lockwood, you are *not* pussy-whipped!"

Jerri winced at the use of her given name. "Jesus Christ, Nikki, don't *ever* use that name. Please! And by the way, I am so pussy-whipped. I do things for you and because of you that I would never do for anyone else."

Nikki thought about it, and realized that maybe she was right. Jerri had changed a lot since they'd met, and she knew that her influence played a big part in it. The changes were largely positive, but Nikki could see where some of them had resulted in a seeming loss of independence for the taller woman.

"Jerri, do you ever regret changing for me? I mean, you have made a lot of concessions, sometimes at the expense of your own wishes. Do you ever regret it?"

Jerri rinsed fruit juice off her fingers and wiped her hands. She walked over to Nikki with one end of the towel in each hand and smoothly looped it around the back of the smaller woman's neck. Tugging lightly, she pulled Nikki's face close to hers. After a long, tender kiss, she drew back and looked her wife directly in the eyes.

"Nik, I love you with all my heart, but I would not compromise my values for anyone, including you. The changes I made, I made willingly; I made them because I needed to. The fact that they were changes you wanted me to make was purely coincidental."

Seeing the doubtful expression on her wife's face, she continued. "Sweetheart, I don't consider those changes to be a loss of independence, I see them as a concession to making the woman I love happy. If I'd had to struggle with them, I wouldn't have made them. Truth is, I'm happier now than I've ever been before. I owe that to you."

Nikki smiled and gave her a long, passionate kiss, then buried her face between Jerri's breasts and sighed deeply. "I love you, Jerri," she whispered. "I hope Rox can find this kind of happiness some day."

"Well, Little Miss Busybody, your e-mail may have started the ball rolling in that direction. Let's just hope he catches it and rolls it back."

"If he's smart, he will."

Jerri nodded and lowered her mouth for another kiss. "We'd better take Rox her lunch before she wonders what we're *really* doing down here." She winked suggestively.

"Well, we *could* tell her that you were being pussy-whipped."

"Literally?"

"Oh, yeah!" Nikki molded her body against Jerri's.

"Care to give me a little demonstration?"

"It will be my pleasure, dear heart." Nikki slid her hand between Jerri's legs and squeezed lightly.

"My God, Nik!" Jerri nearly doubled over as a bolt of desire shot through her. "Do you think Rox can wait a little while for lunch?" she asked, bending Nikki over the table.

"Hey, I thought you two were making lunch. What are you really doing down there, making love on my kitchen table?" came a shout from the third floor.

Jerri rested her face against Nikki's shoulder and chuckled. "So now she has X-ray vision too. Sheesh."

"Time to feed the beast, my love. I'll save the whipping for tonight," Nikki promised, giving Jerri an evil look.

"I'm counting on it." Jerri helped Nikki up from the table and then grabbed the tray of food.

The three women sat around the coffee table in Rox's office, enjoying their lunches and chatting. Nikki was eager to know whether or not Cass had replied to her e-mail message, but couldn't think of a way to ask without making Rox suspicious. She decided to wing it.

"So, have you heard from Cass lately?" Her voice was as innocent as she could make it.

Rox narrowed her eyes. "Nikki, are you up to something?"

Nikki nearly choked on her tea. "N—no. Why do you ask?" she managed to say.

"Because you get this odd look on your face whenever you're trying to hide something from me. I can always tell when you're up to no good. Spill it!"

Jerri threw a knowing smile in her wife's direction.

"I'm not up to anything, really. I was just wondering if Cass had written lately," Nikki said defensively.

"Actually, I'm not sure," Rox confessed. "I haven't even logged on yet. I'm so far behind on the book that I went directly to work without checking my e-mail."

Nikki stared at her best friend as if she had grown a third eye in the middle of her forehead. "Rox, how on earth can you *not* check your e-mail? After that last note you sent him, I'd think you'd be checking it hourly. Geesh, woman, you must have nerves of steel."

Rox looked startled. "I was so caught up in the book that I forgot all about that. You're right though—I'd better get on line and check it out." She got slowly to her feet and shuffled to the computer.

Nikki and Jerri exchanged nervous glances as Rox sat down in front of the monitor.

"Okay, let's see," Rox said as her inbox opened. "Three new e-mails: publisher, publisher, Cass. Here is it," she said, double-clicking on the third message.

Nikki and Jerri looked over her shoulder as she read the note. Nikki held her breath, wondering if it was a response to the one she'd sent to Cass the previous evening.

My dearest Rox,

Reading your note evoked such a sense of love and longing, I could hardly contain myself. Never did I think that you'd return my love so quickly. Rox, I have been in love with you almost from the beginning.

Sweetheart, I know you've just come from a very brutal relationship, and I understand your need to be blunt. Let me assure you, my love, that your heart is safe with me. I will never hurt you, Rox. That is a promise, and I do not make promises lightly.

How could I be angry with you for wanting to know my heart? In my last letter, I asked that you share your soul with me. I can't expect you to do anything I'm not willing to do myself, so by all means, ask me anything you'd like. My heart belongs to you.

You asked what my intentions are. Rox, I have never felt such intensity of love for another in my entire life. Thoughts of you fill every waking moment. What are my intentions? My intentions are to meet you one day soon, sweep you off your feet, and carry you away into the sunset. My intentions are to make you happier than you have ever been, for the rest of your life. My intentions are to love you, cherish you, hold you near, make love to you long into the nights and to carry your scent on my skin through the days. My intentions are to grow old with you, and to hold you in my arms as I take my dying breath. These are my intentions, Rox.

I love you with all my heart. I need to be with you. Just say the word and I will be on the next plane.

You are my heart, Rox. Come fly away and be my love.
Cass

Rox swallowed hard as she finished reading the note, and tears filled her eyes as she re-read the tender words. "I've never read anything so beautiful in my life." She covered her mouth to stifle a sob.

"Wow, looks like this guy has fallen for you big-time. How do you feel about him?" Jerri asked.

"I love him. Don't ask me how or why. I know we've only known each other a few weeks, but I really do love him. I can't believe he loves me, too."

"Oh, it's more than that. This man is infatuated with you. Head over heels, wouldn't you say, Nik?"

Nikki covered her disappointment at not seeing a reply to her call for help. "What? Oh... yeah, I agree. Looks like you didn't scare him away after all, Rox."

Jerri glanced at Nikki, then turned her attention back to Rox. "What's next? More chat, more e-mail, maybe another phone call?"

"For starters, I should probably respond to this message," Rox replied. "After that, who knows?" Moving her hands to the keyboard, she began to write. Her two friends watched over her shoulder.

My dearest Cass,

Your words bring such joy to my heart I can hardly contain it. I'm in love with you, too. I don't know how it could have happened so quickly; we haven't even met, at least in the physical sense. Still, I find that you've become a vital piece of my life. I very much want to meet you in person. To touch you, to feel your heart beating beneath my fingertips.

I do feel safe with you, Cass. I trust that you will never hurt me. I really need that in a relationship right now. I look forward to knowing your heart and soul. I promise to treat them tenderly and to never hurt you.

So, it seems our intentions are the same, my love. When I read the moving letter you sent -- words of love and commitment, promises of happiness and cherished moments -- it sends my heart soaring. I want to make love with you all night and carry your memory with me through the day. Like you, I wish to walk by your side through many years of life and love, only to lie in your arms as I take my dying breath. I am content in the knowledge that our love will endure the separation of life and death, and that we will meet again on the other side, where we will truly be together for all eternity.

I need you, Cass. I love you. Come to me, my love, and be happy in my arms.

Rox

As the three women watched the message disappear into the cyber-recesses of the Internet, Jerri whispered into Nikki's ear, "If your note doesn't get him here, that one certainly will."

Nikki nodded her agreement as she leaned forward and wrapped her arms around Rox.

The urge was strong and insistent; Nikki fought to ignore it. Eventually, nature triumphed over will and she threw the covers off and got up to answer the call of nature. Still half asleep, she dragged her feet as she shuffled through the darkened hallway back toward the guest bedroom. Near the door, she realized that something wasn't right. *Was that a light I saw at the top of the stairs?* Nikki looked at her watch; the illuminated face read *12:46.* Wide awake now, she headed back toward the stairway. "Damn you, Rox," she muttered.

"Okay, Gerald, how does this sound?" Rox was saying, just as the door to her office swung open.

"Roxanne Ward, are you out of your mind? It's after midnight!"

Rox looked back over her shoulder and barely managed to hold back a grin as she saw her friend's disheveled appearance.

"Well? Do you have anything to say for yourself?" an exasperated Nikki demanded.

Rox turned her eyes back to the computer monitor. "At my age, I didn't think I needed permission from my mommy to stay up late," she said, deadpan.

Nikki crossed her arms and adopted a stern pose. "Hello? Do the words 'you need your rest to recover from the latest beating that asshole boyfriend of yours bestowed upon you' strike a familiar chord?"

Rox stopped typing and swiveled her chair to face Nikki. "I'm already late for my deadline. I need to do whatever I can to make up for lost time, even if it means putting off sleep. I'll rest when the book is finished."

"You might be dead before the book is finished, at this rate."

Rox couldn't resist teasing Nikki when she was being melodramatic. "Well, you know what they say—a truly good artist becomes more popular after their death than while they're alive. Maybe if I kill myself writing it, the new novel will become an immediate best seller."

"You are incorrigible," Nikki growled, charging out of the room and down the stairs.

Just home from work, Jerri was unwinding by playing with her Legos when Nikki stomped down the stairs. She looked up from the Lego hospital she was building, and said, "She's being stubborn, isn't she?"

"You know, I always thought you were the most stubborn person I knew, but Rox has you beat by a mile," Nikki answered. "That woman makes my blood boil sometimes."

Jerri chuckled and resumed her construction. "I don't know, Nik. I'd say you run a pretty close second."

"What? Jerri, I am not stubborn."

Jerri looked at her wife and raised an eyebrow. Her expression spoke for her.

"Don't look at me like that. I am not stubborn," the blonde repeated.

"Yes, you are," Jerri replied.

"No, I'm not!" Nikki retorted.

"Are too."

"Am not."

"Are too!"

"Am not!"

"Persistent, too." Jerri grinned, loving every minute of Nikki's protestations.

"I am not. Jerri, how can you say that? I try very hard to be patient and kind and understanding. I make a point of compromising whenever possible. I'm not stubborn. I'm not!"

"Persistent, too," Jerri repeated.

"You—! You did that on purpose, didn't you?" Nikki demanded, finally catching on to Jerri's baiting.

Jerri just gave her a smugly guilty grin.

"Why, you little shit!" Nikki kicked Jerri's hospital and demolished it. "You left out 'vindictive'," she added, and stomped off to bed.

Tuesday's dawn found Rox still awake. She had spent the entire night working on her book. She ran into Nikki in the second-story hallway, both of them on their way to the bathroom.

"'Morning," Nikki said sleepily. "Did you sleep well, Rox?"

Rox gave her a guilty look, then slipped into the bathroom without answering.

Nikki stared at the closed door and narrowed her eyes as she realized what had just happened. Pounding on the door, she shouted at her friend, "Roxanne, don't you dare tell me you were up all night!"

"All right, I won't," Rox called through the door.

"Damn it, Rox. Damn it all to hell!" Nikki stood with her hands on her hips as Rox opened the door. "Chris beat the living shit out of you two days ago, remember? Christ, woman, you've got to let your body recuperate. Staying up all night is just plain stupid. What part of that don't you understand?"

"What I don't understand is what gives you the right to dictate my life for me, Nikki."

"What gives me the right? The fact that I love you, that's what gives me the right, Rox."

Rox made no reply to that. She just dropped her head and reached up to rub her forehead, left hand poised on her hip. Looking up into her friend's face, she allowed a slight smile to breach her frown. "You're right, Nik. I'm sorry, I was on a roll and I simply couldn't stop."

In the face of her friend's apology, Nikki's anger dissipated. Dropping her own defiant posture, she reached out and hugged Rox. "I'm sorry too," she said. "But you really do need to get your sleep, Roxie."

"I will. In fact, I'm on my way to bed right now. I'm beat."

"Literally," Nikki added, which made the two women chuckle.

"Wake me up around noon, will you?"

"Noon; got it. Now, listen to your nurse and get your butt to bed."

"Yes, ma'am." Rox saluted Nikki and marched off to her room.

Nikki shook her head like an indulgent parent, took care of her own bathroom chores and then headed back to bed to snuggle with her wife.

"What was the big argument about?" Jerri asked as she wrapped Nikki in her arms.

"I'm sorry, love. Did we wake you?

"Nature was calling anyway. So what was the argument about?" Jerri repeated as she pushed herself into a sitting position.

"She was up all night, and she's just now going to bed."

"Rox is a big girl, you know. She really is capable of taking care of herself."

"I know, and under normal circumstances I'd agree with you. I'm sure there have been countless nights where Rox has worked straight through, but she was healthy then. Christ, Jerri, she was beaten up just the other day! Don't you think that she needs to give her body a chance to recover before she pushes it?"

Jerri rose and turned to look down at her wife on the bed. "I won't argue with that logic, Nik, but sometimes you tend to push the boundaries of your friendship. Know what I mean?"

Nikki's brow furrowed. "No, what *do* you mean?"

Jerri leaned over the bed and rested her hands on either side of her wife. "I know you love Rox very much, but you tend to be a little overprotective around her... and... and..."

"And what?" Nikki demanded.

"And maybe a little bossy," the dark-haired woman finished tentatively.

Nikki's eyes widened. "Really?" Her eyes started to tear. "I didn't realize."

"I know you didn't, love. It's just that you've got such a big heart and you want so desperately for Rox to be happy. You've got to realize that she's responsible for her own happiness, and no matter how much you do to protect her, she needs to make her own decisions." Jerri continued, hoping that she wasn't about to dig a hole for herself. "You're a wonderful friend, but friends are supposed to lend support and guidance, not provide step-by-step instructions. See what I mean?"

Nikki turned her head and stared at the wall.

After a long silence, Jerri kissed her on the cheek. "Nature calls. I'll be right back, love."

Nikki looked inward. *Is she right? Am I bossy? Have I tried to control Rox's life? I only want what's best for her. I wouldn't ever do anything to hurt her. What if Jerri is right? I need to talk to Rox when she wakes up this afternoon, and I need to tell her about the e-mail I sent to Cass. It was wrong of me to send it without Rox's knowledge. I am such an idiot sometimes!* Feeling better now that she had resolved to set things right, Nikki rolled over and drifted off to sleep.

Jerri returned to find Nikki curled up in a ball on the far side of the bed. Knowing she had hurt her wife's feelings, she climbed into bed and spooned herself tightly behind the smaller woman, pulling her in close. *I love you, little one. I'm sorry I hurt you, but sometimes you push the Good Samaritan thing a little too far. I'd hate to see your friendship with Rox suffer because you care too much.*

Her wife seemed to meld instinctively into Jerri's longer frame, allowing herself to be cuddled as both women slept.

Nikki reached over and shut off the alarm. *Ten o'clock? It feels like I just went to bed.* She rolled over and reached out to shake Jerri awake. "Honey, it's ten o'clock, time to get up."

"But I don't wanna go to school," Jerri mumbled.

Nikki chuckled as she leaned over the tall woman to kiss her gently on the cheek. "Come on, sweetheart. Wakey-wakey."

Jerri opened one eye and saw blue-green eyes looking back at her. Smiling, she said, "Good morning, Munchkin," before pulling Nikki's head down for another kiss. She opened the other eye and said, "Coffee."

Nikki laughed and climbed out of bed. "I'll go put a pot on. Get your buns out of bed, okay?"

Twenty minutes later, a freshly-showered Jerri wrapped herself around Nikki and nuzzled her neck as the smaller woman stood at the kitchen counter pouring two cups of coffee.

"You smell good." Nikki tilted her head to the side to allow better access to her neck.

"Good enough to eat?" teased Jerri.

"That depends on whether you want to be late for work," Nikki replied, reaching back to pull her closer.

Jerri read the signs and pushed forward, trapping Nikki against the counter. She grasped the smaller woman's breasts and ground her hips into Nikki's butt.

"Oh, God, Jerri, if you keep that up, you will definitely be late for work." She pressed the back of her head against Jerri's shoulder.

"Mmm," Jerri murmured.

Collecting herself, Nikki turned around in Jerri's embrace and reached up to cup her wife's face. "Sweetheart, you've got to go to work in a few minutes. Let me fix you some breakfast and we'll continue this discussion tonight, okay?"

Jerri leaned forward and kissed Nikki soundly. "No, you sit and let me make you some breakfast. How does a veggie omelet sound?"

"Wonderful. I'll make the toast."

Half an hour later, Jerri was ready to leave for work. She kissed her wife soundly. "Hold that thought. I promise that tonight will be a night to remember."

Closing the door behind her departing wife, Nikki sighed and looked around the living room. *Rox won't be up for another hour yet. What to do, what to do?*

Nikki hated being bored. After tidying up the kitchen, she searched through Rox's bookshelves looking for something interesting to read, but nothing caught her eye. Her mind wandered to the one place she had been avoiding—Rox's e-mail. She was anxious to know whether Cass had responded to her plea for help. Without further hesitation, Nikki bounded up the stairs and logged onto the Internet. Disappointed when there was no reply from Cass, she started having doubts about his sincerity.

"Where the hell is he?" *Damn him! If he's playing with her heart, I'll kill the bastard.*

According to the clock on the desk, it was nearly noon. *I guess I'd better wake Rox.* Nikki rose from the chair and went downstairs.

Late in the afternoon, Nikki put down a glass of iced tea beside Rox, who was working away on her book. She kissed her on the head and leaned over her shoulder to read the latest material. "I can't wait to beta this thing for you."

"Looks like it'll be ready in a week or two," Rox replied absently. Suddenly, she stopped typing and swiveled her chair around to face Nikki. "Have I told you lately how much I love you? You've been such a wonderful friend. I don't know what I would do without you and Jerri," she said. Nikki blushed at the praise. "You know," Rox continued, "looking back on how we met, I realize now that my life would be very different if you hadn't beaten the shit out of that idiot who was trying to rape me. I owe you so much, Nikki. Thank you for being my friend."

Nikki leaned down and hugged Rox fiercely, making her wince at the pressure. "Oops, sorry." Nikki released her hold. "How about a walk on the beach? You really need to get some fresh air."

"Sounds good." Rox shut down the computer. "Afterwards, I'll give you a hand with dinner, or maybe we can just order takeout."

"Cool. Come on." Nikki reached for Rox's hand.

Soon the two friends were walking arm in arm along the beach, enjoying the setting sun, the light sea breeze, and some pleasant conversation. Their heads dipped together on occasion, and smiles were on both their faces as they kicked up the surf and squished wet sand between their toes.

The stalker watched as the two friends enjoyed their walk, angry thoughts of revenge churning in his irrational mind. *Soon, Roxanne, soon. You won't escape me this time.* Chris watched the retreating silhouettes fade into the sunset.

Chapter 26

"Man, what a rough couple of days," Cass whined, kicking off her shoes and dropping onto her couch. She leaned her head against the back, rested her feet on the coffee table and sighed. "How can you get so tired just from sitting?"

Cass, you really need a housemate. All this talking to yourself is really getting me worried, Enforcer piped up.

Cass's stomach growled loudly.

Time to visit Angie, Enforcer suggested. *Airline food sucks, and after two days of eating that swill, I'm looking forward to some good cooking. Get your ass in the shower so we can go to dinner.*

Cass did as she was told, thoroughly enjoying the warm spray of the shower massage against her skin. She was sore and stiff from long hours in the cockpit and sleeping on hard hotel-room beds. *I need to find another job,* she thought. *One that doesn't put me in the cockpit for such extended periods of time.*

While towel-drying her hair, Cass sauntered into the office to power up the computer.

What the hell are you doing? I thought we were going to dinner.

E., I haven't checked my e-mail for three days. I need to see if Rox responded to my last note. We can get some dinner afterwards.

E-mail can't wait for a couple of hours? Geesh, you're pussy-whipped already.

I am not! I'm just concerned that she'll think I'm unresponsive, that's all.

Bull! Enforcer exclaimed. *You can't fool me, Cass. You're madly in love and you'll do anything to make her happy.*

The beleaguered woman threw her hands up in the air. *So what if I am? Yes, I'll do whatever it takes. Happy now?*

Whatever it takes, huh?

Whatever it takes.

The server delivered three pieces of new mail into Cass's account, but Cass had eyes for only one—the one that read "HELP!!" in the subject line.

"Oh, my God!" She opened the message and began to read.

> Hi, Cass,
> This is Nikki. As you can see, I'm using Rox's e-mail account to send this note.
> Rox is in serious trouble. Now, before you panic, let me say that at this moment, she's safe. In fact, she's in the hospital again, at least for the night. Chris managed to break into the house around midnight last night. Rox and I were the only ones home, since Jerri was working. He knocked me out cold and then attacked Rox while she slept. Jerri interrupted the attack when she came home, but Chris managed to escape. The police have issued an APB, but so far, no luck finding the bastard.
> Rox is a mess. She's not critically injured, but she has a concussion and her face is so black and blue that even I barely recognized her. She looks so pathetic that it makes me cry to see her.
> You said in your last note that you'd jump on the next plane east if she needed you. Well, I would say that she needs you desperately right now. Last night's attack, while I was in the house with her, is evidence that she needs more protection than I can give her. Jerri is with her during the day, but even an idiot like Chris wouldn't be stupid enough to attack in broad daylight. Jerri works mostly at night, so that leaves me here to protect her alone. Obviously, I am not capable of doing the job, at least not by myself.
> She needs you, Cass. Please, if it's at all possible, find a way to come to her, to be here with her, at least until Chris is caught and put behind bars. She lives in Rockland, Maine, at 1163 Oceanview Terrace. Any taxi at the airport can bring you here. Please hurry. There's no telling when he might strike again.
> We'll stay here with her and protect her to the best of our ability, but she needs more than we can give her. Please hurry.
> Nikki

In shock, Cass stared at the screen until Enforcer broke her reverie.

Cass... Cass! God damn it, girl, snap out of it. Your woman is in danger. Get your ass in gear and do something about it!

"Rox." Her voice was a hoarse whisper. "Hold on, sweetheart, I'm on my way." She sprang to her feet and ran through the condo, grabbing her car keys as she headed for the door.

Wait, did you get the address?

Cass stopped in her tracks, one hand on the door handle. "Damn it! No, I didn't." She ran back to the office and sent the message to her printer, waiting impatiently as the machine worked. "Come on, come on," she urged, grabbing the piece of paper as it was ejected.

Aren't you going to shut the computer down? Enforcer asked.

"Fuck it! I don't have time." Cass sprinted out the door.

"I don't care what it costs, book me on the next flight to Maine, damn it!" Cass leaned menacingly toward the ticket clerk.

The nervous clerk typed the destination into the computer and then waited for the program to bring up flight information, chancing a furtive glance at the tall, anxious woman. As she had thought, there were no flights available for that evening, a fact she reluctantly relayed to her would-be passenger.

"What?" Cass shouted. "There has to be something. Here, let me have the phone," she demanded.

Cass dialed a number and waited impatiently, drumming her fingers on the counter top. Finally, the connection was made. "Jimmy? Jimmy, this is Cass. I need to book a flight to Maine for this evening. It's vital that I get on a plane tonight. Someone I love very much may be in danger... I need to get on a plane tonight!" she insisted. "No! I don't want to hear about special favors for pilots; I need a flight out *tonight*!" she yelled. "For Christ's sake, then rent me a charter jet; I'll fly it there myself." She listened a moment, then responded, "Yes, I'm fucking serious... Good... All right... When will it be ready? Two hours? Fine... Okay. I'll be on Runway Three in half that time. You'll need to find a replacement for my Thursday flight into Mexico; I don't think I'll be back by then... All right. And Jimmy—thanks. I owe you one. Goodbye." She hung up the phone, thanked the reservations clerk, and went home to collect her flight bag.

I wish real life was more like one of your science fiction novels, Rox, so I could just teleport myself to you instantly instead of flying for eight hours across the country. Damn it! I wish there was a way to get to you faster. It was nearly midnight, and Cass's flight still hadn't been cleared. *I'm not going to reach you until ten or eleven a.m. your time. I hope I'm not too late.*

Flight clearance was finally granted, and Cass taxied the jet onto the runway. Minutes later, she was gaining altitude and on her way to the East Coast.

You really should have gotten some sleep before taking off. You flew for six hours earlier today. How are you going to stay awake long enough to fly eight more?

Don't worry about me, E., I'll stay awake. I have to; Rox needs me.

I certainly hope so. You won't be much good to her dead, Enforcer pointed out.

Seven hours and thirty-eight minutes later, Cass landed in Augusta, Maine, thirty-five miles northwest of Rockland. She touched down at 10:32 a.m. EDT, thoroughly exhausted. The next twenty minutes were spent in the airport ladies' room, splashing cold water on her face to revive her tired body. After that, she hired a taxi to take her to Rockland.

* * *

Well, Nikki, I've decided that you have to die too, seeing as you never leave her side, Chris thought, watching the pair of prospective victims.

It was eleven o'clock on a beautiful Maine morning, and Nikki and Rox were drinking their coffee outside as they discussed ideas for the next section of Rox's book. Jerri had worked the night before and was still sleeping.

As they talked, Nikki's mind wandered back to her conversation with Jerri the night before, about Cass's lack of response to Nikki's message. *I don't think he's being sincere in his declaration of love. I want so desperately for this guy to be the one for Rox, but another part of me doesn't trust his intentions. Maybe I should tell Rox about the note.* Jerri had been willing to give Cass the benefit of the doubt, but had left the decision to Nikki.

* * *

Jerri rolled over and looked at the clock. *11:17.* Sometimes she hated working the night shift. It always seemed as if half the day was gone before she rolled out of bed. She sat up and rubbed the sleep from her eyes, then got up and tugged on a t-shirt and boxers. She went straight to the bathroom, then downstairs for a cup of coffee. She filled her cup, peeked onto the back deck to say good morning to Nikki and Rox, then started for the shower. On her way to the stairs, she heard a knock at the front door. She pulled it open and saw a tall, dark-haired woman. She looked vaguely familiar.

"Hi," Jerri said. "May I help you?"

"I'm looking for Roxanne Ward."

"She's on the back deck. May I ask who's calling on her?"

"Cass Con—"

"You're shitting me!" Jerri interrupted, taking a step backward. "You're Cass? Holy Mother of God! Rox is going to... Jesus, I don't know what she'll do!"

"When was the last time you heard from Cass?" Nikki asked as she sipped her coffee.

"Let me think... a few days ago, I guess. Why?"

"Well—" Nikki was interrupted by a yell from the living room. It was Jerri's voice.

"Rox, there's someone here to see you."

At the door, Jerri was still staring at Cass.

"May I come in?" Cass asked uncertainly, still standing on the front porch holding the screen door open.

Jerri stepped back to let her enter. "Sure, sure; come in. Sorry about that."

"Well, you know who I am... And you are?"

Jerri shook herself. "Oh, I'm Jerri Lockwood, Rox's friend. Nice to meet you." She offered her hand, grinning widely. *Man, Rox is gonna have a cow,* she thought. *Wow, Cass is even better looking than her picture.*

At the sound of approaching footsteps, both women looked toward the door to the kitchen.

On the back deck, Nikki gave Rox a quizzical look. "Are you expecting any visitors?"

"Looking like this?" Rox indicated her colorful bruises. "No way! I wonder who it is."

"Well, there's only one way to find out," Nikki replied, hoping that it was Cass. She rose to her feet and held her hand out to Rox. "Come on."

"Nik, will you go find out for me? I really don't want to be seen like this."

"No, Rox. Come on, don't be such a chicken. Let's go."

Rox gave in and allowed Nikki to help her to her feet. They went through the kitchen and toward the living room.

The door between the kitchen and the living room swung open, and Rox and Nikki walked through. Rox stopped dead as she came face to face with a beautiful, dark-haired woman who towered over her by at least eight inches.

Nikki looked questioningly at Jerri, who just grinned.

"Oh, my God, Rox!" The stranger's voice was anguished. She stepped forward, reaching out for Rox.

Rox narrowed her eyes. *Why does she look so familiar?* "Do I know you?"

The woman seemed taken aback by Rox's reaction. "Rox, it's me, Cass," she replied, hand still extended.

Rox and Nikki gasped at the same time. "You can't be. Cass is… is… " Rox stammered, eyes darting side to side as if she were looking for an escape route. "This can't be happening. It can't be." She began to panic. *Cass is a woman? A woman. It can't be!*

As Cass's palm touched her cheek, Rox brushed it off and backed away. "No! Don't touch me!" she yelled, cringing. "Oh, my God; oh, my God." She turned and ran back into the kitchen.

Puzzled and alarmed, Cass looked at Jerri and Nikki.

Jerri pointed to the door. "It leads to the beach. If you love her, go after her."

Cass headed for the door as Nikki looked at her wife. "But but… but… Jer?" She started after Cass and Rox.

Jerri held on to her arm "No, let them be. This is a huge shock for Rox. Give them time alone. If they truly love each other, it won't matter."

Rox felt a desperate sense of panic as she ran across the sand toward the surf. *Oh, my God; oh, my God.* Her head swam with confusion as she peered over her shoulder to see if Cass had followed her. Before she could look back, her flight came to an abrupt halt as she hit a solid figure that appeared in front of her. She felt as if she'd run straight into a brick wall. "Chris!"

"Hello, Roxanne. My, you have such lovely color in your face today," he taunted, and grabbed her by the throat.

"Chris," she repeated, scrabbling at his wrists as he lifted her by the neck. "Pl... please... don't."

"You've humiliated me, Roxanne. You *and* your girlfriends. They're going to die too, right after I'm finished with you."

"No, Chris... please." She tried desperately to take the pressure off her neck as her toes left the sand.

"Shut up, bitch!" he screamed. "Don't tell me you didn't fuck them! I saw you kissing them! How could you?" His hands tightened around her throat.

"Rox! Rox!" a voice cried, from several yards down the beach.

Chris looked over Rox's shoulder at the tall, dark-haired woman running toward them, then raised his eyebrows and looked back at Rox. "A new prospect, Rox? What's the matter, two aren't enough for you?"

Choking, Rox fought to pull air into her lungs. She was barely conscious.

Seeing her precarious position, Cass stopped short. *This must be Chris.* "Chris, put her down," she warned. "Put her down and walk away from her. I don't want to have to hurt you."

Chris looked at the woman and laughed. "You don't scare me, bitch. I don't know who the hell you are, but if you know what's good for you, you'll walk away and forget what you saw here."

Nikki was standing on the back deck to watch the drama unfold when she realized that Chris had appeared and had attacked Rox. While Cass had him distracted, she ran onto the beach and circled around behind him. "You son of a bitch!" she screamed, as she jumped on his back and began pummeling his head with her fists.

Chris dropped Rox and grabbed Nikki by the hair. He flipped her over his back and slammed her onto the sand near Rox, then pulled back his foot and kicked her solidly in the ribs.

Jerri was not far behind. Fueled with anger as she watched Chris fling Nikki to the sand like a rag doll, she launched herself at him in a full body tackle and brought him to the ground. By the time Chris shook her off and got back to his feet, Cass was facing him in a classic Tae Kwon Do stance.

Chris laughed. "Am I supposed to be afraid of you, little girl?"

"Last time I looked, I wasn't exactly little," Cass said, and kicked him in the jaw with the heel of her foot. He went crashing into the surf.

Jerri pounced on him then and started smashing her fists into his face. When Cass finally pulled her off, Chris lay in a heap at their feet.

"Damn, but that felt good!" Jerri's fists were still clenched. "I've wanted to do that for months."

Cass glanced over to where Rox and Nikki still lay on the sand. "Jerri, he's out cold. Please check on those two while I find something to tie up this bastard with until the police come."

Chris sat securely handcuffed in the back of a police cruiser. While Cass gave her statement to the police, Jerri settled Nikki in the passenger seat of their car. Rox moved to get into the back seat, and Jerri put a gentle hand on her arm. "Rox, you should stay here with Cass while I take Nikki to the emergency room. She needs to have her ribs checked out."

"Jerri." Rox's tone was pleading. She didn't want to be left alone with Cass.

"Honey, I know this is uncomfortable, but you have to deal with it. Just listen to your heart, okay?" She kissed Rox on the cheek and then got into the car.

Rox poked her head through the open window on the passenger side and kissed Nikki lightly on the head. "I'm sorry," she whispered.

Nikki's ribs were aching, but she managed a smile. "I'll be okay. I'll call you as soon as I get home."

Rox nodded, then waved as her two friends left for the hospital. The police cruiser drove off shortly afterward, leaving her standing awkwardly in the driveway with Cass. She watched the police cruiser until it was out of sight, then jumped when she felt a hand on her arm.

Cass immediately pulled it away. "I'm sorry, I didn't mean to startle you."

Rox wrapped her arms around herself and nodded. "It's okay," she said. "Maybe we should go inside."

The tension was palpable as the pair moved into the house. Rox kept as much distance between them as she could, wishing she were anywhere but alone with Cass. Once inside, however, her upbringing asserted itself. "Can I get you anything—coffee, iced tea?" she offered as they entered the foyer.

This woman is Little Suzie Homemaker! Would you like some tea, kind sir? Enforcer mocked. *Maybe this was a mistake.*

No, E. There's something else going on here. I don't know what it is, but I intend to find out. Cass reached out and took Rox by the shoulders.

"Rox—"

Rox shook off Cass's hands, waving her own arms in the air. "No! No, please, don't touch me!" She crossed to the other side of the room, wrapping her arms around herself.

Cass was thoroughly confused. This was not the woman with whom she had shared loving and intimate e-mails. "Rox, honey, talk to me. What's wrong?" Her hands were spread and her voice was pleading.

Rox looked Cass in the face for the first time and was captured by her brilliant blue eyes. Their gazes held for several moments Threads of attraction spanned the physical distance between them, scaring the hell out of Rox.

"Rox?"

"You're a woman!" Rox blurted.

Cass's brow furrowed, and she stood to her full height.

No shit, Sherlock! How the hell could she possibly think you were anything but *a woman? Even a blind man could tell that. This woman is a head case; run while you still can!*

Cass shook off the offending thoughts and took two steps toward Rox, who immediately backed up the same distance. Cass stopped and stared at her. "Rox, I don't understand. You know I'm a woman. I sent you a picture," she stammered.

When Cass mentioned the picture, Rox's head snapped up. *Of course! She's the woman in the picture, and I thought she was the man! Oh, my God, Roxanne, you really fucked up this time!*

"Cass," Rox said softly, "I assumed the man in the picture was you. I'm sorry." Her eyes filled with tears. "I'm so sorry."

Cass put one hand on her hip and massaged her forehead with the other. Sighing deeply, she tried to think back to what she had written about the picture. *I'm attaching a scanned photo of me and my co-pilot so you can see for yourself.* Her eyes closed and her head dropped as she mentally kicked herself. She hadn't said which person was which. *I'm such a screwup. No wonder she was confused.* She shook her head. *God, how can I fix this?*

"Rox." Cass started toward the smaller woman again, but Rox put up a hand to stop her. Her breath caught in her throat as she tried to control the emotion in her voice. "Rox, please let me touch you... let me hold you," she pleaded. "I promise not to hurt you."

Looking into Cass's eyes was Rox's undoing. What she saw there went straight to her heart and filled her body with such a rush of heat that she thought she was going to faint. Confusion filled her and she nodded slightly, giving the taller woman permission to envelop her in a loving embrace.

Cass slowly pulled Rox into her arms, then held her close and caressed her back soothingly. *She feels so good in my arms.* As she felt the woman begin to relax, she buried her face in the fair hair.

Hello? Enforcer interjected. *Earth to Cass! Don't you get it? She's not into chicks.*

The words crashed in on Cass with such force that she felt like someone had punched her in the stomach. Slowly, she relaxed her hold. Tears clouded her vision as she took a step backward, trembling hands dropping to her sides.

Rox was amazed by the sense of loss she felt when Cass released her. Part of her wanted to reach out and cling desperately to this woman. She had felt so safe, so loved. The other part of her wanted to run away, as far as possible. *This isn't supposed to be happening,* she thought. *As close as Nikki and I are, I've never even considered this type of relationship. Why do I feel this way? Why does it hurt so much?*

Rox stifled her sobs and hugged herself tightly to reduce their impact on her injured body.

"Rox, I'm sorry. I... I... " Cass stammered through her own tears. She'd never felt such pain in her life, and she knew that her heart was breaking. Her breath came in short pants; her eyes darted around wildly for some sign that this wasn't really happening. Never before had she felt such despair, even when Patti had died. "Rox, I love you," she managed to say. "I thought you knew. I..."

Rox moved forward and reached up to touch the side of Cass's face. "Cass," Rox whispered through her tears, "I care about you too. The fact that you're a woman doesn't change that. It does, however, change the way I view what I feel."

Cass grasped Rox's hand and pulled it close to her chest. "What do you mean?"

Rox dropped her chin for a moment, then looked up into captivating pools of blue. "Cass, I've never been attracted to women. I don't know if I can. I just don't know," she whispered, shaking her head.

Cass rested her forehead against Rox's and closed her eyes, allowing tears to flow freely down her cheeks. Swallowing hard, she resigned herself to the inevitable. "I understand, Rox. It breaks my heart, but I do understand."

Rox drew back and took Cass's face between her hands. Looking directly into her eyes, she allowed her own tears to fall as she sought words to comfort Cass and allay her own fears. "No, Cass, you don't understand. I *do* care for you, but these feelings terrify me. I've never felt this way about a woman. I don't know if I can do it. I need time," she pleaded.

Cass stepped back. She wiped the tears from her cheeks with the back of her hand and forced a smile. Nodding, she said, "Uh... maybe I should go. I'm sorry, Rox... sorry that I messed things up so badly." She turned and walked toward the door.

Rox beat her there. She slammed the door and blocked it with her body. "No, Cass. You're not going anywhere. You look like you're dead on your feet. When was the last time you slept?"

"Rox, please." Cass reached for the door handle.

"I said, *no*," Rox said forcefully. "Now answer my question. When was the last time you slept?"

Cass put her hands on her hips and wondered if she should physically move Rox out of the way. "Rox... "

"Damn it, Cass Conway, I said you aren't going anywhere," Rox declared, still blocking the door.

Cass threw her hands up in defeat. "All right, then. I haven't slept since Monday night."

"Monday *night? Cass, that was two days ago, for Christ's sake," Rox scolded. "The only place you're going is to bed." She took Cass's arm and pulled her toward the stairs.

Cass resisted. "This isn't necessary, really."

"Oh, yes, it is," Rox insisted. She turned Cass around and pushed her toward the stairs. When it was obvious she was getting nowhere, she pleaded, "You flew all the way across the continent to protect me from Chris. Please let me do this for you."

Cass saw the forlorn look in Rox's eyes and knew she was powerless to resist. "All right. I'll stay, but just for a short while. I'll take a nap and then be on my way."

Rox didn't know what to say. Part of her wanted to hang on to Cass for dear life, but fear of facing the truth overruled her heart and demanded she let go.

"A nap it is, then."

Chapter 27

Rox had been up for half an hour and was pouring her first cup of coffee when the phone rang. "Hello?"

"Hi, Rox. How are you feeling this morning?" a grumpy voice asked.

"Nikki!" Rox exclaimed. "I'm pretty sore and quite a sight to look at, but otherwise, I'm okay. How are your ribs?"

"Bruised and tender, but not broken."

"Well, you'll need to take it easy for the next several days. Ribs take forever to heal. Take it from me, I've had a lot of experience with that particular injury lately," Rox quipped, trying to bring a bit of humor into a humorless situation. "I'm really sorry you ended up in the middle of this mess."

"I'm not. At least that bastard is in jail where he belongs."

"Yeah. Maybe now I'll have some peace."

"Rox, how about dinner tonight at our place? You can bring your taco salad... and Cass, of course," Nikki added hastily.

"Dinner sounds good to me, but I can't commit for Cass."

"Speaking of Cass, how did things go last night?"

Rox giggled. "None too subtle, are we?"

"Look, Rox, my ribs hurt, my head is pounding, and I've got my period. Don't mess with me this morning, okay? Just answer the question."

"You got your period, huh? Well, that explains the frustration in your voice," Rox teased.

"Roxanne Ward!" Nikki yelled into the phone.

"Okay, all right. Chill, will you? She went to bed after you left."

"Alone?"

"Of course, alone! Sheesh, Nikki, what do you think I am?"

"Right now, I'd say you're lucky. Six feet of gorgeous in your bed? Yep, I'd say you're damned lucky."

"She's not in my bed, she's in the guest room."

"Technically, that's your bed too."

"Aarrgghh! Nikki, don't you have anything better to do with your time than harass me?"

"No."

"Anyway," Rox continued, "she went to bed shortly after you and Jerri left yesterday, and she's been sleeping ever since."

"Rox, that was, let's see… eighteen or nineteen hours ago. She's *still* sleeping?" Nikki asked incredulously.

"Well, she hadn't slept for about thirty-six hours before she got here. She was exhausted." Rox was starting to feel a little uneasy now. She decided she'd check on Cass as soon as she hung up.

"So, what happened?" Nikki asked.

"What do you mean?"

"You know, after we left. Things were pretty tense. I hated to leave you like that."

"Well, we talked for a bit." Rox sighed deeply. "I just don't know what to do. Damn it, I have feelings for her, but they scare the shit out of me. Help me out, here; this isn't exactly my area of expertise."

"And you think it's mine?"

"Come on, Nik. You're attracted to women, so tell me—how am I supposed to feel? How am I supposed to act? What am I supposed to do now?" Rox was visibly flustered, her free hand flying around in the air punctuating her questions.

"Honey, calm down. What do you mean, how do you act? Just be yourself, for crying out loud. Do you think we use a manual with step-by-step instructions?"

"I don't know. Cut me some slack," Rox whined.

"Okay. Look, there are no rules, no expected behaviors. You just need to follow your heart." Nikki paused to collect her thoughts. "Rox, this isn't about being gay, it's about being in love. So you're in love with a woman. Yes, that changes things, but it's still love. Don't you see?"

Rox was silent as she considered Nikki's words.

"Roxie?"

"I'm here," she said. "I have so much to think about. Listen, I'm going to run upstairs and check on Cass. I'll call you later this afternoon, all right?"

"All right. Just call me if you need to talk. Promise?"

"I promise. I'll talk to you later, Nik. Love you."

"Love you too, sweetie."

Still holding the receiver, Rox stared into space until the buzzing from the open telephone line broke her reverie. She snapped out of her trance and hung up the phone, then took a deep breath and headed for the stairs.

Rox climbed the stairs to the second story, nervously anticipating the coming conversation. She was beside herself with anxiety and thoroughly confused about what she was feeling. *Calm down. Nikki's right, this is about love. Just for a moment, forget that she's a woman. You'd know exactly what to do if she were a man. Think. Take it slowly.*

Still agonizing over the matter, she stood outside the bedroom door and knocked softly. "Cass?" She waited a moment. "Cass?"

After several moments, she was still waiting for a response. At last, she pushed the door open and peered inside.

The room was empty, the bed made.

"Cass?" Rox entered the room and looked around frantically. She turned and ran out into the hall to check the bathroom. The door was open, the room vacant.

"Cass?" she called again, her voice more anxious.

Maybe she went exploring. Navigating the stairs to the attic office as quickly as her injuries would allow, she reached the top and looked around the empty room. She even investigated the widow's walk, walking completely around it. Nothing.

"Where is she?" She stepped back into the office, and suddenly wondered if Cass had gone for an early morning walk on the beach. Back out on the widow's walk, she looked up and down the shoreline. Cass was nowhere to be seen. In fact, the beach looked totally deserted. Rox was frowning as she went back into the office.

Thoroughly mystified, she returned to the guest room Cass had occupied, and immediately saw something she hadn't noticed earlier—a piece of folded paper lying on top of the pillow. She looked down at the paper for long moments before hesitantly reaching for it. It was a note. She unfolded it and looked at the strong, bold hand it was written in, and her mind acknowledged the appropriateness of the style even as she began to read.

> *My dearest Rox,*
> *I know this is taking the coward's way out, but I couldn't bear to say goodbye to you this morning. I have lost my heart to you, dear love. I lost it the day I looked into*

emerald green eyes staring up at me from the back of your book cover. No one has ever affected me this way before.

As I looked into your face yesterday, my heart and soul completely surrendered to you... they no longer belong to me. I saw something in your face as well—confusion, fear, anxiety. I didn't know at the time what caused those negative emotions. I didn't know until later, when I realized you'd confused Brian's identity with mine.

I have so much to be grateful for in my life, the best of which was the opportunity to love you. I'm sorry that I hurt you. That's the last thing I ever wanted to do. I'll never forgive myself for deceiving you, dear love, even though it wasn't my intention to do so.

I'm afraid, Rox. I'm afraid that I'll never again find the kind of love I felt for you. I'm afraid that I'll never again feel the way I feel when I'm with you. When I lost Patti three years ago, I never expected to fall in love again, but it happened, and I've fallen so deeply that I allowed that love to blind me to the possibility that you would not reciprocate. I have been a fool.

I'm sorry -- for deceiving you, for hurting you, for leaving the way I am... but most of all, for not being what you want and need.

For the record, the offer still stands. I will be here whenever you need me. Please don't hesitate to contact me by phone or e-mail. I will always be there for you, Rox. All you have to do is call.

I love you, Rox. I always will.

Cass

A tear fell onto the page as Rox blinked. *Damn you, Cass.*

Sitting down heavily on the edge of the bed, she let the note fall to the floor as she buried her face in her hands and started to cry. When her tears ran dry, she threw herself back on the bed and stared at the ceiling. *Why does this hurt so much? I barely know her. She's a woman, for God's sake. I know I feel strongly for her, but... she's a woman!*

For the next half hour, she vacillated between anger and regret, with anger winning out in the end. She rose from the bed, retrieved Cass's note from the floor, and climbed the stairs to the attic.

By the time the computer had finished booting up, Rox was incensed. She opened a new message and poised her hands over the keyboard, ready to vent. She began to type.

> *Cass,*
>
> *When I saw that you were gone this morning, my first instinct was panic, quickly followed by regret, and finally by anger. You are right -- you took the coward's way out. Damn you, why did you run? You waltzed into my life, announced that you were in love with me, then poof! You disappeared.*
>
> *How the hell am I supposed to react to that? Do you always drop bombshells on people and then run before they explode? You had no right to do that to me.*
>
> *It's true, I mistook your identity. How could I do otherwise? I've never been attracted to women, not before you came into my life. I won't deny that this terrifies me. In fact, it scares the shit out of me. And by the looks of your abdication, it scares you too.*
>
> *I don't appreciate you leaving the way you did. I would have liked for us to spend some time talking this over, but you've made that more than a little difficult by putting 3,000 miles between us. Christ, I could just shake you!*
>
> *All right, I'm going to end this note before I say something I'll really regret. Know that I still care deeply for you, and I really do want to continue our friendship. Please don't pull away from me now. I need your help to understand what I'm feeling for you.*
>
> *I'll talk to you later,*
> *Rox*

Rox sent the note and watched her anger scorch its way into cyberspace. Settling back in her chair, she felt her anger and anxiety ease as she logged off the Net and opened her word processor to continue working on her book.

Later, Rox stood on her back deck, leaning against the railing and sipping a cup of strong black coffee as she looked out over the ocean. She had been pacing back and forth in front of the computer all morning, visions of long dark hair and blue eyes invading her thoughts and making it impossible for her to concentrate on writing.

She kept checking her e-mail, hoping that Cass would respond to her last message. Having read over the copy in her "Sent" file at least a dozen times, Rox again chastised herself for being so harsh. *After all, I was the one who turned and ran away from her when we first met. I can only imagine how that must have made her feel. She obviously had no idea that I thought she was a man.*

I wonder if I should call her? Rox looked out over the water again. *No, she probably wouldn't talk to me anyway.* Sighing deeply, she drank the last of her coffee and went back into the house.

The phone rang as she headed for the stairs and she detoured to pick it up. "Hello?"

"Hey, Rox. What's up?"

"Hi, Nik. Nothing much, just taking a coffee break."

"What time are you coming over tonight?"

"Tonight?" Rox was obviously confused.

"Dinner, remember? You're supposed to bring your taco salad. Hello, anybody home?"

"Shit, I forgot all about it. Yeah, all right. Um, how about sixish?" Rox sputtered, embarrassed that she'd forgotten their dinner date.

Nikki picked up on the hesitant tone in her friend's voice. "Hey, are you all right?"

"I'm fine, Nikki. Just a little preoccupied."

"You *are* bringing Cass along, right?" No answer. "Rox?"

"No. She's gone," Rox admitted, snapping out of her funk.

"What do you mean, 'she's gone'?" Nikki demanded.

"She's gone. I checked on her after we talked. She left a note apologizing for leaving."

"Well, that bites."

"Maybe it's better this way, you know? I mean, she's a woman, right?"

"And your point is?"

"Aw, come on, Nik, you know what I mean. Man, I hate this love shit."

"Feel like talking about it?"

"Maybe tonight at dinner, okay? Six sharp, taco salad. I'll be there." Rox's tone was determinedly cheerful.

Nikki was not convinced. "All right, we'll see you at six. But we're *not* done talking about this, you got that?"

"Got it," Rox replied. "I'll see you tonight then."

"Tonight. Love you, toots."

"Right back at you, Nik," Rox chuckled. "See you later. Bye."
She hung up the phone and went back up to try working again.

Chapter 28

"Cass!" a voice shouted. "Cass, open the goddamned door!"

Cass lifted her head off the pillow and looked around, not quite sure where she was. At last, she realized that she was in her own bed and that someone was pounding on her front door. According to her clock, it was 9:08.

"Cassidy Conway, you open this door right now or I'll bust it down!" said the voice. "Do you hear me?"

Cass struggled to her feet, then half-walked, half-staggered across the living room to the front door.

"All right, I warned you!"

Cass opened the door just as Angie launched herself toward it, and the older woman came flying through it and landed face down on the floor. Cass stood over the prone figure with her hands on her hips. "You sure know how to make an entrance, Ang," she said dryly.

Angie reached up. "Don't just stand there, help me up!" After Cass helped her to her feet, she turned on the tall woman. "Where the hell have you been? I've been worried sick!" She paused for breath. "You haven't answered your phone, you weren't at work, you didn't come to the diner for your meals… Christ, woman, are you *trying* to make me gray?"

"I was out of town."

"For three days? Where did you go, Europe?"

Cass walked wearily to the couch and sank down on it. She dropped her face into her hands and rubbed it vigorously, then ran her fingers through her hair. Suddenly, she looked up at her friend. "Did you say three days?" she asked. "What day is it?"

Angie sat on the coffee table in front of Cass and reached forward to feel her forehead. "Are you all right?" she asked. "You don't seem to be running a fever."

Cass endured the affectionate attention. "Ang, what day is it?"

"It's Friday, and you've been gone since Tuesday. The airline told me that your Mexico run arrived on time Tuesday night, but they hadn't seen you since. Where were you?"

"Friday? Wow! I just slept for nineteen hours."

Angie took Cass's face in her hands and looked directly into her blue eyes. "Talk to me, sweetie. I've been worried sick about you. Where have you been?"

Cass frowned, thinking of her hurried trek across the country on Tuesday night, the tumultuous meeting with Chris on the beach, and her heartbreaking encounter with Rox later that afternoon. Her eyes filled with tears and she closed them tightly, hoping Angie hadn't seen the torment in their depths.

"Cass, I can see the pain in your eyes."

Damn.

"Talk to me, love."

Cass opened her eyes and tears trickled down her cheeks.

The sight of the strong, competent woman in this state was more than Angie could take. She moved to the couch and opened her arms. Cass immediately fell into them, sobbing like an infant. Her heart-wrenching cries tore through her friend, who shed tears right along with her.

Eventually, Cass managed to compose herself.

"Now, Cass, please tell me—why are we *both* crying?" Angie wiped her eyes with the back of her hand.

Cass sniffed loudly, then spoke. "Maine. I was in Maine."

"You went to her? Cass, she isn't… "

"No! No, Angie, she's not dead. She's very much alive. Banged up, but alive."

"Thank God." Angie was relieved, but puzzled. "So, tell me about it. Why are you so upset?"

Cass rose to her feet and started pacing. Angie's head followed her like a spectator's at a slow-motion tennis match. She was just about to lose patience when Cass stopped pacing and looked at her.

"Angie, Rox isn't gay."

Now Angie was very confused. "Cass," she said haltingly. "What do you mean, 'she isn't gay'?"

"She isn't gay, Angie. The bastard that's been beating her up is a man. She's spent the past two years in a relationship with a man. Don't you get it? She's straight."

"But Cass, you sent her a picture. It was after she saw the picture that she said she was falling in love with you."

Cass dropped her head and sighed deeply. Very softly, she said, "I sent her a picture of Brian and me. She thought Brian was me."

Angie looked stunned. "I'm so sorry," she managed. "That must have been so difficult for you. How did Rox take it?"

Dropping to the floor where she stood, Cass sat cross-legged and looked up at Angie. In an anguished voice, she said, "At first, she wouldn't even let me touch her. In fact, she ran away from me when she realized who I was. It broke my heart, Ang."

"You went after her, I hope?" Angie asked hesitantly.

"Yeah, I did. I chased her right into the arms of the son of a bitch who's been beating her. We had a nice little encounter on the beach. Let's just say he won't be eating solid foods for a while."

"Serves him right. Is Rox okay? I mean, did he hurt her again?" Concern tinged Angie's voice.

"A few more bruises on her neck, but nothing permanent. She was fine later that afternoon when the police took the bastard away."

"What happened then?"

Stretching her legs out in front of her and crossing them at the ankles, Cass leaned back on her hands. "Her two friends left us there together—it was really awkward—and we talked. She confessed to having been confused about my gender... and confused about what she was feeling for me."

"Just what *is* she feeling for you, Cass?"

"She says she cares deeply about me." Cass leaned forward. "She's confused, Angie. She's never been attracted to women before, so she's scared."

"And you're heartbroken," Angie observed. "Cass—"

"No, don't say it." Cass held up her palm for emphasis. "I don't want to hear how she's breaking my heart. I set myself up for this. I never mentioned my gender in any of my messages. I assumed she knew, and you know what they say about people who assume. Well, you're looking at the world's biggest ass."

"You said you'd slept for the past nineteen hours, so that means you got home Thursday afternoon. Has she tried to contact you?"

Cass tilted her head to the side. "Well, I didn't hear the phone ring... "

"What about this wonderful e-mail you're always talking about?"

"I haven't checked. I've been asleep the whole time."

Angie threw up her hands. "Well?"

Cass nodded. She unfolded her long legs and rose to her feet, stamping them to shake off the uncomfortable prickling that had already set in.

Soon, Cass and Angie were sitting in front of the computer waiting for the server to deliver new mail to her inbox.

"I thought modern technology was faster than this," Angie commented.

Cass resisted the urge to smack the monitor. "Don't even go there," she warned as her inbox chimed its signal for new mail. There were two e-mails from Rox.

Noting that the first one had arrived just after she'd left for Maine on Tuesday, Cass was reluctant to open it and read the loving words she was sure it contained. She hesitated, then moved the mouse pointer over the "Delete" icon and prepared to erase the note.

Angie grabbed the mouse away from her. "What are you doing? You haven't read it yet."

"I don't want to read it. She sent that one before I flew out there on Tuesday. Everything's changed now. What's in that e-mail doesn't matter any more."

"Are you saying she's a liar?"

Cass looked at her incredulously. "Are you baiting me intentionally?"

"Well?" and before Cass could say anything else, "Then what have you got to lose? Open it." She slid the mouse back to Cass.

Steeling herself, Cass clicked on the first new message and watched its text appear on the screen.

My dearest Cass,

Your words bring such joy to my heart I can hardly contain it. I'm in love with you, too. I don't know how it could have happened so quickly; we haven't even met, at least in the physical sense. Still, I find that you've become a vital piece of my life. I very much want to meet you in person. To touch you, to feel your heart beating beneath my fingertips.

I do feel safe with you, Cass. I trust that you will never hurt me. I really need that in a relationship right now. I look forward to knowing your heart and soul. I promise to treat them tenderly and to never hurt you.

So, it seems our intentions are the same, my love. When I read the moving letter you sent -- words of love and

*commitment, promises of happiness and cherished moments
-- it sends my heart soaring. I want to make love with you
all night and carry your memory with me through the day.
Like you, I wish to walk by your side through many years of
life and love, only to lie in your arms as I take my dying
breath. I am content in the knowledge that our love will
endure the separation of life and death, and that we will
meet again on the other side, where we will truly be
together for all eternity.*

*I need you, Cass. I love you. Come to me, my love, and
be happy in my arms.*

Rox

Cass could hardly see the screen through the blur of her tears. As
she struggled for control, Angie wrapped warm arms around her
quaking shoulders.

She kissed the top of her head and whispered, "Sweetie, I can't
believe such beautiful words could be written without the author
meaning them. I can almost feel the love radiating from the screen.
Give her a chance, Cass. She's confused, and she needs time."

Cass sat back in her chair and tried to calm her strained nerves,
avoiding looking at the computer screen lest she start crying again.
"That's what she said—she needed time." She forced a weak smile.

"So let's have a look at the other one," Angie suggested.

Cass sat still for a few seconds, looking nervously at the icon on
the screen.

"Well? Open it!" Angie demanded, smacking Cass on the arm
with the back of her hand.

Cass displayed the message on the screen for them both to read.

Cass,

*When I saw that you were gone this morning, my first
instinct was panic, quickly followed by regret, and finally
by anger. You are right -- you took the coward's way out.
Damn you, why did you run? You waltzed into my life,
announced that you were in love with me, then poof! You
disappeared.*

*How the hell am I supposed to react to that? Do you
always drop bombshells on people and then run before they
explode? You had no right to do that to me.*

*It's true, I mistook your identity. How could I do
otherwise? I've never been attracted to women, not before*

you came into my life. I won't deny that this terrifies me. In fact, it scares the shit out of me. And by the looks of your abdication, it scares you too.

I don't appreciate you leaving the way you did. I would have liked for us to spend some time talking this over, but you've made that more than a little difficult by putting 3,000 miles between us. Christ, I could just shake you!

All right, I'm going to end this note before I say something I'll really regret. Know that I still care deeply for you, and I really do want to continue our friendship. Please don't pull away from me now. I need your help to understand what I'm feeling for you.

I'll talk to you later,
Rox

Angie leaned down over Cass's shoulder and digested the words in front of her. Then she straightened up and swatted Cass on the back of the head.

"Ow! What was that for?" Cass rubbed her head resentfully.

"You ran?" Angie's voice was filled with disbelief. "You *ran*? I can't believe it, Cass. Of all the stupid things to do!"

Cass swung her chair around. "Stupid? Did you say stupid?" she challenged. "Don't you get it? She's straight. She doesn't play with girls. I don't have the right equipment."

Angie took Cass by the shoulders and swung her back to face the terminal. "Go back to the first message and read it carefully. Then look at the second one again. Read the last sentence," she instructed, her hands still on Cass's shoulders.

Cass did as she had been told, and got to the last sentence.

Please don't pull away from me now. I need your help to understand what I'm feeling for you.

"Cass, what's she's feeling for you is as plain as day... in both letters."

The words finally sank in, and Cass gasped. She reached back and covered Angie's hands with her own. "There's hope, Ang. There's hope!"

Cass was pacing again. Her arms were wrapped tightly around her waist and she was chewing on her bottom lip.

"Damn it, Cass, stop wearing a path in the rug like that. Will you sit down and answer the woman?"

"I don't know what to say, Angie. I feel like such a fool, running out on her like that."

"You can start with an apology." Angie saw doubt in Cass's face. "If you do nothing, you'll always wonder. Are you willing to live with regret for the rest of your life?"

Listen to her, Enforcer urged. *She couldn't possibly have gotten that old without learning a thing or two.*

E., why do you have to be so rude? Cass stared at the computer screen, silently contemplating Angie's words.

Oh, for Christ's sake, woman! Sit your ass down in the chair and write the goddamned e-mail, Enforcer demanded.

"Cass?" Angie prompted, a little worried by her friend's trance-like state.

Angie's voice snapped Cass out of her considerations. "Oh... sorry, I guess I zoned out for a minute." She ran a trembling hand through her hair and gave her friend a panic-stricken look. "I don't know what to say to her. I've been such a fool; I never even gave her a chance. I don't blame her for being angry with me."

"Well, from the sound of that last message, she's a little more than angry," Angie deadpanned.

Yeah. You'll never get laid now.

"Jesus Christ, will you butt out, E.?" Cass said aloud, before she could stop herself.

Angie looked at her friend with concern. "Cass, maybe you should go back to bed for a while."

Brushing off her slip-up, Cass sat down at the computer. "No. No, I think I need to write this note."

"Want some help?"

"Would you mind?" Cass asked hopefully.

Angie pulled up a chair. "Not at all, sweetie, not at all."

Dear Rox,

I don't know where to start except with an apology for running off like that. It was a stupid and cowardly thing to do, and I'm sorry. I hope you can find it in your heart to forgive me. You're obviously very angry with me, and I wouldn't blame you if you never spoke to me again.

I don't know what came over me. Given our e-mail and chat exchanges, I guess the prospect that you couldn't return my love had never crossed my mind. You've made me see how arrogant I've been. I'm sorry.

Please believe that I never intended to deceive you. I assumed you knew I was a woman. I was totally oblivious to the possibility of mistaken identity. I was a fool to have sent that picture of Brian and me. I certainly understand how you assumed that I was Brian. I should have been clearer.

Where do we go from here? You said in your last message that you need me to help you understand your feelings. I'm not sure I can do that without first understanding them myself. How do you feel, Rox? You said once that you were starting to fall in love with me. Does my being a woman change that? Should I walk out of your life right now and never bother you again? I'm willing to do that if it's what you really want. It would break my heart, but I would do it for you.

I still love you with all my heart. I'm afraid that I'll never love anyone else the way I love you. I want you to know that you can depend on me for anything. Just call, and I'll find a way to be at your side.

I will never forgive myself for the pain and confusion I have caused, but if you can find it in your heart, please forgive me.

I love you,
Cass

"How does that sound?" Cass asked as Angie scanned the note.
It sounds like you're pussy-whipped—BIG-TIME!
Cass ignored Enforcer.

"It's a start, sweetie. Send it and let's see what happens."

Cass clicked and watched the note disappear from the screen. Sighing again, she logged off and shut down the computer. She glanced at Angie and asked, "Shouldn't you be at the diner helping with the lunch crowd?"

"Damn." Angie looked at her watch. "Roger's going to kill me, and it's all your fault. Just for that, you get your butt dressed and come help me," she demanded.

Cass raised an eyebrow. "You don't really expect *me* to cook, do you?"

"Are you kidding? I'd like to keep my customers coming back, thank you very much. No, I don't expect you to cook, but you can sure as hell wait tables."

"That I can do," Cass replied. "I'll be ready in a second." She dashed into her bedroom to change, happy to have a distraction from thoughts of green eyes and red-gold hair.

Chapter 29

Rox was on a roll. She had managed put thoughts of Cass out of her mind long enough to start making good progress on her writing when a deep rumbling from her stomach disrupted her train of thought. The burning sensation that accompanied the sound was too uncomfortable to ignore. She glanced at the clock and was startled to see that it was nearly three, and it occurred to her that she hadn't yet made the taco salad for Nikki's dinner. "Damn."

She logged on and checked out her inbox, deeply disappointed when it was still empty. The burning feeling in her stomach turned into a sea of nervous nausea as a rush of regret washed over her. She logged off, saved her work from that morning and shut down the computer.

It wasn't enough that she was running late. When she went to the kitchen, Rox found she had only half of the ingredients for the salad and that quick trip to the supermarket was necessary. Trying to conceal the worst of her bruises, she donned jeans and a long-sleeved shirt, a baseball hat, and an oversized pair of sunglasses.

A glance at the clock told Rox she was back on track; it was only a little after three. She rushed down the stairs and out the front door. At 3:06 p.m., the exact moment that Rox locked the door behind her, Cass's message arrived in her inbox.

"Where do you want me to put it?" Rox asked, holding a cookie sheet heaped with taco salad.

"There should be some room in the fridge," Nikki answered as she waved her friend into the house and closed the door behind them.

After a struggle, Rox managed to open the refrigerator door and slide the salad inside without dropping the bag of chips she was also holding. She nudged the door shut with her foot, set the chips on the kitchen table and shrugged out of her jacket. "What's for dinner?"

"Steak, baked potatoes and succotash." Nikki was at the sink scrubbing three large baking potatoes. "Jerri's on the back deck turning the steaks right now."

Rox put her arms around her friend and rested her head between the blonde's shoulders. They stood that way for a minute or so, savoring the feeling of love and friendship.

"Thanks for the invite, Nik," Rox said as she released her grasp. "What can I do to help?"

"We're going to eat out on the deck. Why don't you set the table?"

"Consider it done." She collected plates, silverware, iced tea glasses and napkins, and took them out onto the deck.

"Hey, girl," Jerri called.

Rox unloaded the dishes on the table and walked over to the grill to collect an affectionate hug from her friend.

"Hi, Jer," she said, her reply muffled as the taller woman pulled her into a tight embrace.

Jerri nodded toward the load of dinnerware on the table. "I see she's put you to work already."

Rox chuckled. "Oh, yeah. That's just like Nikki. She invites me over and then expects me to do all the work."

"She used to do that to me when we were dating, until one day she put me to work cooking. That was the first and last time she ever did that. Making sure the steaks don't burn is about as far as my cooking talents go." Jerri grinned.

"Sounds like Chris—" An uncomfortable silence descended. "Damn."

Jerri rubbed Rox's back. "It's okay, hon. After a while, that won't happen any more."

Rox nodded, and excused herself to set the table. As she completed her chore in silence, Jerri watched her covertly from the grill.

"Nik, how did you know?" Rox scooped taco salad onto a chip and stuffed it into her mouth. It was nearly midnight, and the three friends were sprawled on pillows in front of the fireplace with the taco salad and chips at the center of their tableau. A small fire cast a warm glow over them as the evening wound down.

"How did I know I was gay?" Nikki replied. "Rox, we've talked about this at least a dozen times."

"I know, but humor me. Obviously, I have a whole new reason for asking this time. What was the defining moment for you?"

Nikki wiped her hands on a paper towel. "I've always known I was different. When I was a teenager, all the other girls were fawning over Leif Garrett and Parker Stevenson. I just didn't get what they saw in those guys. I mean, I hung posters on my bedroom walls just like all the other girls, mostly to fit in, but I just didn't get it. On the other hand, I thought Linda Carter and Nancy McKeon were absolutely to die for. I really didn't understand what I was feeling at the time, Rox." She took a long drink from the straw in her soda can. "I remember having a huge crush on my camp counselor and on a couple of the girls at school, but at the time I didn't associate those feelings with being gay. Hell, I dated guys in high school."

"So when *did* you know?"

Nikki grinned at the dark-haired woman sitting across from her. "That's easy—when I met Jerri." She saw Jerri smile at her in response. "I knew the minute I laid eyes on her that what I was feeling was more than a crush. It was mind-boggling; it completely devoured me. All at once, those feelings from my childhood made sense."

Rox needed more. "And how did you feel about that? Were you scared?"

"Terrified. I was raised with the traditional male/female view of romantic love, and my parents were active members in a very intolerant church. All my friends were straight. I felt like an outcast. But none of that mattered, compared to how I felt when my body reacted so strongly to Jer's presence. God, she could turn me on with a smile. And the first time she kissed me... well, let's just say thank God for panty liners." Nikki laughed and shook her head.

"I'd never felt that way before, especially not with the boys I'd dated. They made me feel dirty and used, even though I hardly let them touch me. Look, my point is this—when I met Jerri, my true nature was awakened. I could have tried to ignore it or fight it. I could have done what was expected of me and married a nice young man, but I didn't. I couldn't. I had to accept what I was feeling as my truth, and learn to live with it. I was lucky to have Jerri. She was so gentle and patient with me." She reached out to cup her wife's face.

Touched by the depth of her friend's emotions, Rox took a deep breath. She turned to Jerri. "What about you, Jer? When did you know?"

"I think I've always known," replied Jerri. "When I was a teenager, I fell in love with my best friend. I didn't tell her for fear of rejection, but I knew. I knew exactly what it was. I was obsessed with pleasing her. I couldn't do enough; I couldn't spend enough time with her. If she knew, she never let on. I agonized over her for months, and eventually I migrated toward several other girls who were either gay or bisexual and joined their crowd. Unfortunately, they weren't the nicest girls in town, and soon I was smoking and drinking and running wild. They initiated me into lesbian sex, and they weren't very gentle about it. The wild behavior pretty much followed me into college, and it amazes me that I managed to graduate. Anyway, I didn't actually settle down until I met Nikki." That drew a smile from her wife.

"It was love at first sight. She melted my insides right on the spot. I couldn't breathe, and my heart was pounding so fast I thought it would explode. All I had learned about sex and love flew out the window. I couldn't imagine making love to Nikki as I had been taught. It seemed so rough, so primitive. Our first time was very awkward for me. There I was, the experienced one, fumbling around because I didn't know how to treat her gently. She was very patient with me, and together we learned how to please each other. It was the most wonderful feeling in the world." Jerri directed her words to Rox, but maintained eye contact with Nikki.

Rox looked her two friends. It was clear that she needed to excuse herself and bring the evening to a close. "Oh, wow, look at the time," she said brightly. She climbed to her feet as her friends continued to look into each other's eyes. "I'll... just... let myself out."

She left the room quietly, retrieved her jacket from the back of a kitchen chair, and then headed for the door. As she was pulling out of the driveway, she paused and looked back at the house. One by one, the lights went out on the lower level, leaving a single light illuminating the second-story bedroom. An intense pang of envy shot through her like a bolt of lightning, making her gasp and clutch the steering wheel, and her mind filled with images of Cass. Rox pressed down on the accelerator and headed for home.

* * *

"That's the last of them," Angie said, and locked the diner door behind the departing customer. Not wanting to be alone, Cass had decided to stay on and help with the dinner crowd, as well. She wasn't accustomed to being on her feet all day, and she was exhausted. Groaning, she dropped into one of the booths and rested her head on her crossed arms.

"Angie, I don't know how you do this every day. I'm wiped out."

"You get used to it."

Cass gave another tired moan.

"All right, get out of here. Go home and go to bed. I'll see you for breakfast in the morning, okay?" Angie went over and kissed Cass on the head.

Nodding, Cass dragged her tired body out of the booth and gave her a hug. "Good night. See you tomorrow, if I can get myself out of bed." She heard Angie's chuckle just before the door closed behind her.

As she entered her condo, she chastised herself for being so out of shape. *Jesus, I need to spend more time at the gym. I can't believe a woman almost old enough to be my mother ran me into the ground.* She slowly shed her clothes and then stepped into the shower.

Several minutes later, Cass was clean and dressed in lace-trimmed panties and an oversized t-shirt. She towel-dried her hair as she sat in front of her computer waiting for it to boot up.

Finished, she threw the towel on the floor and ran her fingertips through the unruly locks until she managed to assemble them into a more orderly state of disarray. Her hair was going to look like she'd spent the past hours making mad, passionate love with someone, but she didn't care. She was home, she had the weekend off and she wasn't planning on going anywhere. *Who the hell cares what my hair looks like?* By the time she had finished with her finger-combing, she was ready to log on to the Internet. She was quite proud of herself for waiting patiently this time. *Either I've learned patience, or I'm just too damned tired to care.*

Her patience was not rewarded, however, since her inbox was empty. She stared at the blank page for long moments before she logged off and dragged herself to bed. As she sat on the edge of the bed, Cass dropped her chin to her chest and sighed deeply. *I guess my apology wasn't accepted, E.*

Well, running off was a pretty shitty thing to do to her, Cass. I don't blame her for being angry.

"I know," Cass whispered as she climbed into bed.

* * *

Rox made herself a cup of hot chocolate as soon as she got home, and switched on the computer while her drink was heating. When it was ready, she opened her inbox. The server delivered three messages: one piece of junk mail, one from her literary agent, and one from CConway@Flyboy.com. Her breath caught in her throat as she reached shakily for the mouse.

> *Dear Rox,*
> *I don't know where to start except with an apology for running off like that. It was a stupid and cowardly thing to do, and I'm sorry. I hope you can find it in your heart to forgive me. You're obviously very angry with me, and I wouldn't blame you if you never spoke to me again.*

"Oh, Cass, I would never do that to you. God, I can feel the pain in your words. I'm so sorry," she whispered, feeling guilty for having chastised Cass the way she had.

> *I don't know what came over me. Given our e-mail and chat exchanges, I guess the prospect that you couldn't return my love had never crossed my mind. You've made me see how arrogant I've been. I'm sorry.*

"Cass, honey, it's not about your arrogance; it's about me misreading your notes and misinterpreting your picture."

> *Please believe that I never intended to deceive you. I assumed you knew I was a woman. I was totally oblivious to the possibility of mistaken identity. I was a fool to have sent that picture of Brian and me. I certainly understand how you assumed that I was Brian. I should have been clearer.*

Rox could feel Cass's pain. "I know you didn't intend to hurt me. Oh, I wish we could start over."

> *Where do we go from here? You said in your last message that you need me to help you understand your feelings. I'm not sure I can do that without first*

understanding them myself. How do you feel, Rox? You said once that you were starting to fall in love with me. Does my being a woman change that? Should I walk out of your life right now and never bother you again? I'm willing to do that if it's what you really want. It would break my heart, but I would do it for you.

"How do I feel? I wish I was sure," she replied softly. "Please don't walk out of my life, Cass. If you leave me, how will I ever be sure about my feelings, or know where my heart truly lies?"

I still love you with all my heart. I'm afraid that I'll never love anyone else the way I love you. I want you to know that you can depend on me for anything. Just call, and I'll find a way to be at your side.

"No. I won't hurt you like that again. You came to me once and I broke your heart. I won't allow myself to do that again," Rox choked out between her tears.

I will never forgive myself for the pain and confusion I have caused, but if you can find it in your heart, please forgive me.

"I do, Cass. I do. But can you forgive me?"

I love you,
Cass

After reading the note, Rox sat back in her chair and stared at the screen for several minutes before she composed a reply.

Dear Cass,
I've been regretting my note to you since the moment I sent it. I am so sorry for its harsh tone. I'm afraid that common sense yields to hurtful indignation when I'm angry. Please forgive me.
I am so confused. I'm feeling things now that are totally new and alien to me. I'm scared, and I don't know how I'm supposed to feel. Nikki says that this isn't about being gay, it's about being in love. I'm sorry, Cass, but I just can't ignore the gay aspect of this. Christ, this is hard!

Plain and simple -- I've never been attracted to women before, and what I feel for you scares the hell out of me. I don't understand it; I can't imagine it. I'm totally ignorant about lesbian love. Jerri says it's the most wonderful feeling in the world, but how do I know if it's right for me? Damn it, I'm so confused!

Tonight, I had a long discussion about gay relationships with Nikki and Jerri, and we talked about what to expect. They described their own experiences. So much of what they told me is terrifying, and just as much is exciting and enthralling. I've always considered myself a diverse, objective person, but it's way easier to remain that way when I am not directly involved.

Cass, help me. Help me understand what I'm feeling. I don't want to discount our relationship without exploring the way I really feel. I don't want to be on my deathbed 60 years from now wishing I had given us a chance.

Talk to me, please, Cass. I can't do this on my own. I need you.

Until later,

Rox

Rox read the note over one more time before sending it out. Glancing at the clock, she saw it was nearly two a.m. Yawning loudly, she rose from her chair and made her way downstairs to her room, where she disrobed and slipped a baseball jersey over her head. She crawled between the sheets, pulled the blankets up under her chin and laced her fingers behind her head. For the next half hour, she stared at the ceiling, unable to sleep.

What do I really feel for Cass? She certainly is beautiful... and intelligent... and capable. Do I love her? I don't know. Is this what love feels like? She shook her head impatiently. *Christ, I have got to get my life together. Maybe it's too soon to have a relationship. Maybe I need to give myself some time to recover from the Chris disaster.*

Rox rolled over onto her side and pulled her knees to her chest, which did nothing to calm her mind's churning. *Nikki and Jerri seem so sure of their love. Will I ever have that kind of security in a relationship? Could I have that with Cass? Do I want that with Cass?* She sighed. *I really do need to figure out my feelings, and I need to understand what this all means. More than that, I need to understand the consequences of entering into this kind of relationship.*

She sat up as a disturbing thought entered her mind. *Oh, God! What about Mom and Dad? What would they think? How would I tell them? "Uh, by the way, Mom, Dad, I'm a lesbian." Holy shit! How would they take it? Would they disown me? Can I send my father to his grave with that on his mind? God, I hate this!*

Too restless to sleep, Rox brought her knees up to her chest and wrapped her arms around then. Resting her chin on them, she cleared her mind of the disturbing thoughts. Soon, her eyes started to close and she nearly lost her balance and toppled onto her side. She caught herself, then lay down and pulled the blankets up again. Within minutes, she was fast asleep.

Chapter 30

Cass woke up at five thirty a.m. on Saturday, and due to her early night was unable to get back to sleep. By seven, she was up and dressed and had finished her morning run. After a leisurely breakfast with Angie, she ran home and showered, and by nine o'clock was comfortably curled up on the couch doing the newspaper crossword puzzle.

"Let's see," she murmured. "A five-letter word for non-postal telecommunication."

E-mail, Enforcer supplied.

"E-mail… yes, that fits. Thanks, E." Cass looked wistfully toward the office. *Do you think she's written, E.?*

Hell, you're a sucker for punishment. Go check.

Cass crossed the room in three strides and pushed open the door to the den. Soon she was sitting in front of the computer with her foot tapping nervously as she made threatening gestures toward the machine. Just as her patience had been stretched to the limit, the boot-up completed and she was able to log in. Knowing she would surely throw the computer out the window if she was forced to sit through a second process, she retreated to the kitchen and made a cup of coffee. When she returned to the office, the server had delivered one piece of new mail to her inbox. It was from Rox.

"She replied, E.!" Cass exclaimed, opening the note.

Whoop-tee-do, Cass. Do you want me to cheer or do cartwheels?

Ignoring her own caustic thoughts, Cass read the note three times, her heart lifting higher each time. Clicking the "Reply" button, she entered her response.

> *Dearest Rox,*
> *Please don't apologize for your harsh tone. I surely deserved it. I'm not generally a coward, but I couldn't bear the thought of your rejection. I've never been so heartbroken in my life.*

I know you're scared. I was terrified when I realized I was gay. It was all so new to me, and it wasn't very well accepted by my family or by the community I was living in at the time. I know it's hard to separate the emotions from the gender, but Nikki is right -- this is about love, and I love you with all my heart.

Rox, you are the only one who can decide if this love, my love, is right for you. I know how confused you are. The only way you'll know for sure is if you explore the possibility... at your own pace. Please let me be the one you explore it with. I promise to be patient; I promise not to push you into something you're not ready for. I know that in the end, you may decide lesbian love is not for you. That's a chance I'm willing to take.

Nikki and Jerri seem like wonderful friends and I think you can learn from their experience. Jerri's right -- it is the most wonderful feeling in the world to be connected to another human being on such an emotionally intimate level. Rox, the physical side of lesbian love is such a small part of what it's all about. It is a blending of two souls, two hearts, two minds. The physical expression only adds to the beauty. I so long to share my soul, heart and mind with you, my love.

I love you; I want to be with you. I want to help you understand these feelings. I want to be there to hold you when you open your eyes each morning. I want to make love to you each night. I want to hold you when you cry and take care of you when you're ill. I want to envelop you in a cocoon of love and protect you from the less pleasurable side of life. I want to dedicate the rest of my life to making you happy and whole. Talk to me, Rox.

I love you with everything that I am,
Cass

Sure that Rox would feel the love she had written into her words, Cass clicked eagerly on "Send" and held her breath as the message disappeared from her screen.

* * *

Rox woke up at nine, feeling refreshed, and her thoughts turned to her plans for the day. *I really need to get to work on this book. My publisher's going to kill me if I push the deadline back again.* An hour later, she was on the Internet collecting information about distant galaxies for her next chapter. When the phone rang, its sudden peal made Rox jump. *Jesus! Give me a heart attack, why don't you?*

"Hello?"

"Hey, Rox, can I interest you in some lunch?" Nikki asked.

"I'm kind of in the middle of research, Nik."

"Well, you've got to eat. I'll be there in an hour." Nikki hung up before Rox could object.

She hung up the phone and brought up her word-processing program, minimizing her inbox. Deeply absorbed in her writing, she was unaware of Nikki's arrival until her friend poked her head into the office.

"I'm taking orders, got any requests?"

Rox looked up and gave her best friend a brilliant smile. "Good morning, Nik. I didn't hear you come in."

"One of these days, Rox, leaving your door unlocked while you're squirreled away in this attic is going to get you ripped off," Nikki warned. "You're lucky I wasn't a burglar, or worse."

Rox shrugged and turned her attention back to the screen in front of her.

"Well?"

"Well, what?" Rox replied.

"Lunch?"

"Oh." Rox flushed, embarrassed by her distracted behavior. "Hold on, I'll give you a hand. I need a break anyway." She pushed herself away from the desk and followed her friend down the stairs. Just as she walked out of the room, an exclamation mark appeared next to the envelope icon on the bottom right corner of her screen. She had new mail.

"So, have you heard from Cass?" Nikki spooned some soup into her mouth.

"No, I haven't. I sent an apology last night for being so harsh in my previous note, but she hasn't replied yet." Disappointment was clear in Rox's voice.

"Maybe she's angry with you. You know, it was pretty rude of you to run away from her like that."

Rox placed her spoon on the table and wiped her mouth. She looked at her friend with sad eyes. "I know. I can't believe I did that.

It's just that I didn't know how to react. She's a woman, and that scared the shit out of me."

"How *do* you feel about her, Roxie?"

Rox's brow furrowed and she shook her head. "I don't know, Nik. I just don't know. I definitely feel something stronger than friendship, but I don't know that I'd call it love. It's all so confusing. Until Cass, it never crossed my mind that I could be gay. Christ, this really sucks! I just want to crawl into bed and wake up with everything resolved. I really don't want to deal with it."

Nikki nodded her understanding. "What's the next move?"

"I guess I'll wait to see if she responds. What else *can* I do?"

"What do you *want* to do?"

Rox's head dropped back and she closed her eyes, then opened them and stared at the ceiling for a moment or two before looking back at her friend. "I want this to be over. I want life to be good again."

Nikki gave her a wry smile. "I didn't hear you say you wanted her out of your life."

"No, you didn't. I just don't know." She finished her coffee. "Look, I've got to get back upstairs. I've got a book to write." She rose to her feet.

"Mind if I keep you company for a while? Jerri's working till midnight and it's lonely around the house when I'm all by myself."

"Sure, come on," Rox replied with a smile.

"Let me clean up here first. You go on, and I'll be there in a few minutes."

Once in the office, Rox fixed herself a cup of tea and took it out to the widow's walk to enjoy the ocean view while she drank it. As she leaned against the railing, she quietly contemplated her feelings.

Cass, why have you invaded my every thought? How can you walk into my life and turn it completely upside down? I've been forced to rethink my entire philosophy, reconsider all the beliefs that I've built my life around. Why am I allowing you to do this to me?

She took another sip of tea. *The dreams... what do they mean? Are we destined to be together? Have we known each other in a past life? What about the dream with the man and the horse—did I want him to be a woman? Is that why his gender changed partway into the dream? Am I subconsciously attracted to women? So many questions and so few answers. God, I'm so confused.*

Sighing deeply, she returned to her computer and brought it out of sleep mode. Her current file was waiting for her, but just as she began to write, she noticed the new mail icon at the bottom of the screen. Heart pounding, she opened her inbox.

Tears filled Rox's eyes as she marveled at the fact that Cass was still so loving, despite the harsh treatment she had received.

"Cass, why do you love me? After the way I treated you, I'm surprised you want anything to do with me."

She looked at her watch and agonized over taking more time away from her writing. *To hell with it. The book can wait; right now my heart needs attention.* She began to write.

> *Dear Cass,*
>
> *If anyone is a coward, sweetheart, it's me. When I first laid eyes on you and realized that "Cass" was a woman, I was terrified. I didn't know how to deal with it, so I ran. I am so sorry. When I put myself in your shoes, I realize how devastated you must have felt. I'm not in the habit of hurting people, and I'm ashamed of my behavior and my cowardice.*
>
> *Cass, how did you know you were gay? How did you deal with it? I have a queasy stomach just thinking about it. I've seen the relationship Nikki and Jerri have, and often wished I had one that was as loving and close. It wasn't possible with Chris. Is that because he's a man, or was he just not right for me? It's all so confusing.*
>
> *I don't know how my family would react. My father is dying. If he knew, would I send him to his grave with a broken heart? I can't do that to him, not even for my own happiness. Christ, this is so frustrating!*
>
> *You suggest that I explore the possibility before rejecting it out of hand. Part of me wants to vehemently deny that I'm gay, while another part is curious. That part of me wants to explore. That part of me wants to be with you, to learn from you. I know you'd be patient, Cass. If I close my eyes and imagine, I can see you holding me close, kissing me, making love to me. My only real exposure to love between women is from Nikki and Jerri, and it seems like every time I call them, I'm interrupting something. LOL! But to be honest, I don't know if I'm ready for this, and I'm so afraid of hurting you more if I agree to try and then fail.*
>
> *I so desperately want the emotional connection you speak of -- the blending of souls -- but I'm so afraid of*

hurting you and myself in the process. You can see who the real coward is.

Cass, what you offer is so tempting. I do long to wake up each morning in loving arms. Heaven knows, I didn't have that with Chris. To be surrounded by love and tenderness is more than I can imagine. I have never known that type of relationship. Damn it! Why is this so hard? Why can't I just say, "Yes, Cass. Come to me, love me, and let me love you?" Why? I have so much to think about... so much to deal with. I am so sorry to put you through this, Cass. It must hurt you terribly.

Well, I really have to get to work on my book, so I guess I'll sign off for now. My agent is becoming very impatient with me. You've given me a lot to think about. I know I owe you an answer. I will search my heart, and hope that soon I will be able to tell you how I feel. Thank you so much for being patient with me.

I'll talk to you later,
Love,
Rox

Rox sat for long moments staring at the screen after she sent the note, unaware that her best friend was standing in the doorway watching her.

Cass, please don't play with her heart. She's been through so much. She doesn't need more heartache. Sighing deeply, Nikki entered the room and settled on the couch to read while her friend typed furiously on her keyboard.

* * *

Cass paced the floor after sending her note to Rox, hoping that she would get an immediate reply. After half an hour, it was apparent that a timely reply would not be forthcoming.

Woman, you are pathetic, E. scolded. *Look at you. Ever hear the saying, "a watched pot never boils?"*

E., it's been a half hour. Maybe she's read my note and blown me off. Heaven knows she has a right to be angry.

Maybe she's busy. She's writing a book, isn't she?

Yeah, but...

But what? Cass, you really need to get a life. You're playing with fire here, you know. Rox digs men. You're setting yourself up for heartache, Enforcer warned.

I don't know that yet. She said that she has feelings for me. What if those feelings are love, or what if they could develop into love? If I walk away, I'll never know. She sighed deeply. *I don't want to be alone some day in the future, lying on my deathbed and regretting my cowardice. I have to find out if she can love me. I have to.*

Well, I guess we have some work to do then. I'll help you write the next message when she finally replies to your last one.

I don't know, E. You tend to get a little raw sometimes. You might scare her away.

Look, if this does *work out with Rox, all three of us are going to be living together, so she'd better get used to me now,* Enforcer reasoned.

Cass groaned.

What was that for? I'm not such a bad person; I've kept you on the straight and narrow for years.

Straight and narrow? You're kidding me, right? What about that time you had us skinny-dipping in the neighbor's pool in the middle of the night? Cass asked.

Yeah, but it was hot, and... and you were only 10 years old at the time, so who cares?

Oh? What about when you talked us into sneaking into the drive-in theater in Cathy's trunk, huh? I was stuck in there for six hours after she broke the key off in the lock. Some adventure that was!

It seemed like a good idea at the time. How was I supposed to know you were claustrophobic?

Cass continued. *And what about the time—*

All right, all right, you've made your point. So maybe my advice hasn't always been good, but we've had some fun haven't we?

Yeah, I guess. But we really need to be careful here, E. I don't want to lose her before I even have her.

Don't worry, I'll behave. In the meantime, you need to take your mind off the computer. Why don't you clean up this pigsty? Enforcer scolded. *You weren't raised in a barn. If your mom could see this place...*

"All right, already, I'll clean up!" Cass threw her hands in the air and got to her feet. For the first time in several weeks, she looked long and hard at the room. She saw used coffee cups on the desk, an overflowing wastebasket, newspapers and magazines stacked on the bookcase, and dust bunnies hanging from the ceiling and in the corners of the room. "It really *is* a pigsty. Christ, no wonder E. gets on my case." Determined to rectify the situation, she began to clean in earnest, e-mail temporarily forgotten.

Hungry and covered with dust, Cass stood in the center of the room, proud of what she had accomplished. Glancing over at the clock on the desk, she was shocked to realize it had taken her two hours. Though she was sorely tempted to check her e-mail, Cass decided to give Rox a little more time to respond by cleaning herself up and ordering a pizza for lunch. Forty-five minutes and a quick shower later, she was sitting in front of the monitor with a small pepperoni, mushroom and sausage pizza beside her as she waited for the computer to boot up.

At last, the server delivered a note from Rox@Starship.com into her inbox. She opened the note and read its contents. Twice.

Wow, Cass. She's really confused. That woman doesn't know if she's coming or going.

You're right, E. I have to be careful not to push her too hard. I don't want to scare her away. Damn, I hate this dating thing.

Yeah, especially with chicks who dig men.

She could be bisexual, you know. Give me a break, will you? Cass clicked on "reply." *Now, what to write back?* After a brief pause, she began to compose.

> *My dearest love,*
> *I should have made it clear that I was a woman right from the start. I understand why you were confused. "Cass" is certainly not a gender-specific name.*
> *At this point, I think a little background on me might be helpful. My full name is Cassidy Marie Conway. I'm 29 years old (soon to be 30), and as you know, I live in San Jose, California. I'm the older of two children. My brother Jeff died a few years ago in a car accident. Unfortunately, I've been estranged from my parents for the past several years. You see, they don't appreciate having a gay daughter.*
> *You asked how I knew I was gay. Well, I guess at some level, I've known since I was a teenager. I knew there was something different about me -- I just didn't have a name for it at the time. While my girlfriends were playing with dolls and fussing with their hair, I was busy playing*

baseball with the neighborhood boys. In high school, I wasn't interested in women's gymnastics or in making out behind the bleachers with the captain of the football team; I was interested in being on the football team (It's too bad they wouldn't let me.) I didn't put a label on my feelings until I met Patti. She captured me -- heart and soul. I only wish I'd known about her dark side before I fell in love with her.

I can't tell you why things between you and Chris didn't work out the way you would have liked; however, if Chris was always as much of a macho asshole as he was on the beach, that may shed some light on the situation.

Honey, I have met women who act like Chris. There are lesbian relationships that end up just like yours. Occasionally, one partner dominates the other to the extreme that it becomes a stereotypical "husband/wife" scenario. My relationship with Patti was headed in that direction when she overdosed. As much as I hate to admit it, I allowed her to manipulate and abuse me. I allowed her to treat me the way Chris treated you, right down to the physical abuse. The good news is that there are just as many loving, equal relationships out there as there are unequal ones. I'm offering you just such a relationship, should you choose to explore it. I want someone to share my life and love with on a totally equal basis.

As far as how your family would react to the possibility that you're gay, it's always best if you have their support. However, it's your life and your happiness we're talking about. If the good Lord is willing, you'll be around long after your parents are gone. You can't live your life for them, or you'll wake up one morning after they're gone and regret that you didn't follow your heart. If they truly love you, they will at least accept you as you are, even if they don't agree with your lifestyle. Obviously, I don't know your parents, so I'm not in a position to judge. As for your father dying, don't you think he'd rather die knowing you're happy? Think about that.

Honey, if there's even a small part of you that's curious, or that has felt something more than just sisterly affection for another woman, you owe it to yourself to explore your feelings. The loving relationship that is possible between two women just can't be described in words; it has to be experienced to be understood. It is so intense and personal, so loving and caring.

Rox, I love you. I desperately want to show you what my words can't convey. Please don't worry about hurting me. I am going into this with my eyes wide open. I know there's a risk; you may find that this type of love is not right for you. I understand that, and I'm willing to take the chance. You are worth any risk.

Let me come to you. Let me love you, and please allow yourself to love me. I'm not denying that it's a hard decision, but I hope you won't make it without first experiencing what I'm offering. Let me help you. I promise to leave you alone forever if this is not for you. Please, think about it.

I will wait for you forever, Rox. I know how scary this is. Just know that I love you, and I will never hurt you.

Good luck with your book.

With all my love,

Cass

Cass watched her note start its cyber-journey to Maine as she reached for the last slice of pizza. She grimaced when she realized it was cold.

"Damn." She looked at the clock. "Shit! It's after three o'clock. Why on earth does it take me so long to write to her?"

Because you're not as smooth and direct as I am. It's all that beating around the bush, Enforcer answered.

What do you mean by that?

Well, think about it. Damn, woman, you wrote her a book.

All right, smartass, what would you have written?

Me? I would have said: Bedroom, be there, Enforcer replied.

Oh, that's real smooth, E. She'd have been gone in a heartbeat.

Hey, if she can't take the heat, she should stay out of the kitchen.

Cass just shook her head as she took the cold pizza to the microwave.

* * *

"Dinner's ready," Nikki called up the stairs. There was no response, so she yelled again. "Rox!" Finally, she went in search of her friend. When she entered the office, she saw that she was still working away at the keyboard.

"Rox, honey, dinner's ready." When there was still no response, she said loudly, "Earth to Rox!"

Rox jumped. "Jesus Christ, Nikki, you scared me."

"Well, you weren't answering me. Do you always get this tuned out when you're writing?"

"When I'm on a roll, yes, I do," Rox replied. "Sorry."

"That's okay. Dinner's ready. Are you hungry?"

"Yeah, I guess I could eat. Let me check my e-mail first and then I'll be right down."

Nikki gave Rox her best "I'm in command" attitude. "I don't think so. Dinner's getting cold, and besides, you've been sitting at that thing all afternoon. You need to get up and move around. Come on, e-mail can wait while you eat."

Rox looked at her friend's indignant stance and challenging expression, and couldn't keep from laughing. "Oh, Nik, you are such a big wuss."

Nikki gave up her tough broad imitation and batted her eyelashes at Rox. "Well, I do declare, I am not a wuss," she said in her best Southern accent.

"Nikki Wuss Davenport. Yep, it fits. Has a nice ring to it too, don't you think?"

Nikki grabbed a cushion from the couch and threw it at Rox, clocking her on the side of the head with it.

"Ow!" Rox picked up the pillow and advanced menacingly on her friend, who was matching each of Rox's forward steps with a backward step of her own.

"Oh, no. Come on, Rox, I was just kidding. Really!" Nikki raised her hands to ward off the imminent attack.

Rox advanced until she had backed Nikki up against the couch. She put the index finger of her good hand on Nikki's shoulder and gave her a gentle push, then watched as she teetered against the back of the couch. Then Rox took the pillow and whacked Nikki on the shoulder, sending her sprawling over the back of the couch and onto the cushions below, where she landed on her back with her feet in the air. She lay there like a stranded turtle.

Rox laughed at her friend's absurd position. "God, it's a good thing Jerri isn't here, or I'd have to leave the room. There'd be no stopping her if she saw you like that."

"Damn you, Roxanne Ward," Nikki sputtered, rolling off the couch onto the floor.

Getting to her knees, she gave Rox a severe look, which made her friend turn tail and run for the stairs. Luckily, Nikki had tangled herself in the afghan that was thrown over the back of the couch, which gave Rox a substantial head start.

By the time Nikki reached the kitchen, Rox had poured two glasses of wine and was holding one of them out in front of her as a peace offering. She was smiling disarmingly. "Truce?"

Nikki tried to stay angry, but couldn't manage it. She gave Rox a lopsided grin and took the wine.

"To friendship."

"To friendship."

"To the sisterhood," Rox added.

"Abso-fuckin'-lutely!" Nikki responded, and they burst out laughing.

It was late in the evening when Nikki was ready to go home. She gave Rox a goodbye kiss on the cheek. Rox took Nikki's face in her hands and placed a gentle kiss on her lips.

"Good night, Nik. Kiss Jer for me, okay?" she said, then shooed her friend out the door. "Drive carefully!" She closed the door, returned to the kitchen, and made a cup of tea before going back up to work.

Looking at the stuffed giraffe beside her computer, she said, "What do you think of all this, Gerald? I have no problem being affectionate with Nikki. In fact, it feels pretty good. Does that mean I'm gay? And what about Cass? She sure is beautiful, isn't she?" Rox marveled at the ease with which she was able to talk about the issue. *Of course, I'm only talking to a stuffed animal, but it's a start.*

Suddenly, Rox realized that she did indeed feel good about the prospect of a relationship with Cass. She closed her eyes and imagined Cass's hands running up and down her arms and across her back. A sudden flash of desire ran through her and she shot out of her chair, eyes wide as she was gripped by an anxiety attack.

"Oh, God!" she exclaimed, clutching at her chest. Taking a deep breath, she tried to calm herself. "All right, Rox, you can do this. Calm down; calm down."

When her breathing eased, she sat back down in front of the computer. Placing her hands on either side of the keyboard, she took another deep breath and then reached for the mouse. Clicking on her e-mail icon, she watched as the server delivered new mail to her inbox. Among the messages was a note from Cass.

Rox's heart skipped a beat as she opened it. After avidly reading it several times, she composed a reply.

My Loving Friend,

Please don't apologize. I don't know why I assumed you were a man, except that I was guilty of gender bias. You see, when I looked at your e-mail addy and saw Flyboy.com, I correctly assumed that you were a pilot, but automatically thought "man." I'm the one who should be sorry. I was an advocate of women's rights in college; I should have known better than to be guilty of stereotyping.

I love your name. Cassidy... it's wonderful! You are very close to my age. I'm 27, and an only child. I'm sorry to hear that your parents don't accept your lifestyle. Honestly, I don't know how my parents would react. I don't know what it would do to my father if I had to tell him that I'm gay. We've never talked about gay relationships, except for Nikki and Jerri, of course. They accept them without issue, so I hope they would accept me as well, but I don't know if I can take the chance of breaking my father's heart. I know I can't live my life for them, but even the thought of telling them something like that... I just can't imagine it!

I'm so confused. I don't know what I'm feeling; I don't know what to think. Damn, I wish this wasn't so hard. I wish I knew for sure the desires of my heart.

Cass, you talk of an equal and loving relationship. I would accept nothing less, nor would I want less than that for you. I've had more than my share of abuse. I will never stay in that type of relationship again, and I'm sorry to hear that you had such a rough time with Patti. It sounds like we could both use a change.

I'm definitely curious about what a relationship with you would be like. I feel things for you that I have never felt before, for a man or a woman. I know what you're talking about when you speak of the loving relationship that's possible between two women. I see it every day between Nikki and Jerri.

Cass, I feel so close to you, but I don't know if it's love. Hell, I'm not sure I even know what love is. I thought I loved Chris, but I realize now that what I felt was dependence and fear. I do trust you, though. I trust that you won't intentionally hurt me, and that you would walk away if I asked you to. I don't know if I want that.

I have so much to think about. I'm curious, but I'm also afraid. I'm afraid of hurting you; I'm afraid of hurting myself. I'm afraid of making a decision I might regret. Please give me some time to work through this. Your love and patience mean so much to me. I will give you an answer soon, I promise.

You're in my thoughts,
Rox

Rox sent the message, sat back in her chair and dropped her chin to her chest. She sighed deeply. *Cass, why do you enchant me so? Why am I so clear about other things, but indecisive and weak when it comes to you?*

Too distracted to do any more writing, she yawned and shut down the computer, then slowly made her way down the stairs to her bedroom. Dressed in her oversized Mickey Mouse t-shirt, Rox climbed between the sheets and lay on her back, staring at the ceiling. Visions of azure eyes and flowing black hair filled her mind. Closing her eyes, she thought back to when she'd allowed Cass to hold her in her arms. Suddenly, her body was fully alert as a heated wave of desire rushed through her. Her back arched and her breath caught in her throat as her body throbbed with need.

Rox tried to get herself under control, but without her conscious decision, her hands started to roam over her body. Each touch heightened her awareness of the carnal pleasure she was sure she would experience at the hands of a certain tall, dark-haired lover.

Reaching under the hem of her shirt, she slipped one hand inside the waistband of her panties and slid it downward to her wet center. The other caressed her suddenly sensitive nipples. Eyes closed, she licked her lips and tilted her head back, a moan of desire escaping her throat as her fingers moved between slick folds.

"Oh, Cass," Rox plunged her fingers deep inside of herself. "I need you." She shuddered, arching her hips upward to meet each thrust. Soon she was writhing out of control, her mind nearly convincing her that Cass was actually there with her, pleasuring her with every stroke.

The muscles of her neck strained as her head tipped back as far as it would go. Her knees were bent and wide apart; her fingers worked furiously across her swollen bud. Her injured hand pinched her nipples firmly as her hips moved in time with her delving hand. A heartbeat later, her hips stilled, suspended above the bed as the first climactic wave ripped through her body. "Cass! God, I need you!" Rox's hips dropped onto the bed then rose again, suspended once more before settling again.

Rox lay on her side, hand still between her legs and desire rippling through her. Sweat drenched her body. Thoughts of a dark-haired lover flitted through her subconscious mind until she drifted off to sleep.

* * *

Cass had decided to work off her nervous energy at the gym. After a vigorous workout, she was on her way out the door when she ran into Jason.

"Hey, Cass," he said cheerfully. "Looks like I'm about to put my life in your hands."

Cass looked at him with a puzzled frown.

Kick him in the balls, Enforcer encouraged, making Cass smile slightly. Before she could reply, Jason continued.

"I'm booked on your flight to Durango this Monday. I've got some business in Mexico… a little schmoozing with my investors, if you know what I mean. Got to keep the customers happy, you know."

Self-important ass. Cass gave him a wry smile and nodded. "That's nice, Jason. Look, I've got a dinner date," she lied. "See you later." Giving him a disinterested wave, she left him standing at the entrance as she made her way to her car and drove away.

She had a leisurely dinner and some warm conversation with Angie, then drove home and went straight to her computer.

Cass glanced at the clock. *Nine o'clock, so it's midnight for Rox.* "Wow, I didn't realize it was getting so late. Time sure does fly when you're having fun."

"Come on, Rox, be there," she said hopefully as the server searched for new mail. Finally, she saw Rox's message appear. "Yes!" She grabbed the mouse.

Cass read the note carefully, intense feelings of familiarity and longing causing her stomach to clench. *Rox, why do I feel like I know you… like I've known you forever?*

Selecting "Reply" at the top of her screen, she wrote a response.

My Heart,

As I read your note, I felt familiar pangs of desire, longing and need. I don't know how to say this, but I think we're destined to be together. I feel this driving need to know you... to be with you... to love you. I feel like we've been together over many lifetimes. I know this sounds all New Age and stuff, but I really mean it. I've never felt this kind of connection with anyone in my life.

I've had dreams of you, Rox. We're together in a field of flowers, each blossom representing a lifetime together, past and future. The dreams end as I lean in to kiss you.

You once said that you believed in Kismet, and that our souls were bonded in some way. How else could the circumstances of our meeting have been arranged? We're 3,000 miles apart, and yet we found each other. That can't be a coincidence. Wouldn't we be denying our destiny by denying our attraction? I long to show you the wonder and beauty our relationship could have. Please don't let fear close your mind to the possibilities. I will show you how good our love can feel.

I don't know what to tell you about your family, considering I didn't have a very good experience with my own. All I can say is that if they love you, they'll want you to be happy. I believe I can bring you the happiness you deserve, my love.

I know you're afraid of the unknown, and afraid this is not really where your heart lies. Rox, please take the chance. Allow yourself to explore, to really feel, perhaps for the first time in your life. How can something that feels this right be wrong?

I know you need time to think about this, and I'll wait as patiently as I can. When you're ready to seek your true heart, let me guide you. The path may seem long and dark, but I know the way. Let my heart be a beacon to guide you, and I will envelop you in my love. Take all the time you need, lovely lady. I'll be here when you're ready.

I love you with everything that I am, Rox. Come home to me.

Cass

She read her note over carefully before sending it. *I love you, baby. Please accept my heart. It's my most precious possession and it wants to belong to you. Good night, my love.* With a full heart, Cass shut down the computer and went to bed.

Chapter 31

Rox rose early the next morning and decided to take a brisk walk along the beach before starting work. She dressed in spandex shorts, a sports bra, ankle socks, and running shoes. Tucking a hand towel into the waistband of her shorts, she filled her water bottle and headed out. An hour later, drenched in sweat but feeling remarkably good, she ran up the steps of the back deck and stopped in the kitchen to set up the coffeepot on her way to the bathroom. In the shower, she stood under the massaging spray and allowed the needle-like darts of water to pummel her skin until it was a healthy pink. She grabbed the soap and washcloth and spread thick, fragrant lather across her arms, chest, back, thighs and shins, then finally slipped the cloth between her legs.

"Oh!" She was distinctly tender. "I wonder... " A deep flush rose up her neck and into her face as she remembered the night before—how thoughts of a dark-haired woman had sent her into the throes of desire and led ultimately to self-fulfillment.

"God, if you can do that to me from three thousand miles away..." she mumbled, and leaned against the shower wall until the strength returned to her legs.

The rest of the shower was uneventful. Rox dragged a comb through her hair, slipped on a pair of panties and an oversized t-shirt, and headed to the kitchen for a cup of coffee.

She settled into her comfortable office chair and sipped coffee as the computer booted up. Soon, her eyes glazed as her mind turned to thoughts of Cass. *Cassidy Marie Conway. I really like that name. Sexy name, sexy woman.* She shook her head. *I can't believe I'm sitting here having these kinds of thoughts about a woman. But she* is *gorgeous; no denying that. And those eyes... God, this is so frustrating! I've never felt this way before.* Then the system finally came up, and moments later she was online collecting her e-mail.

Rox opened Cass's message and began to read. After the first paragraph, her heart was racing. "Oh, God... that dream! I've had it, too."

As she read, Rox became more and more emotional. *This is the most beautiful declaration of love I have ever read. I'm supposed to be the writer here, and yet you have voiced your feelings so eloquently, so beautifully. Thank you for this glimpse into your heart.* She finished, barely able to see through her tears.

She sat back and thought about what to write in reply, but words eluded her. She was a writer, supposedly skilled in prose and able to churn out a love story in record time, yet she was speechless when it came to her own life. Rox became more agitated with each passing minute. She had already shared her mind and her heart in her previous notes, and couldn't think what more there was to write. Finally, after staring at the screen long enough that the screen saver appeared, she abandoned the task and turned off the computer. She rose and paced back and forth across the office until she came to a decision. She was going to call Cass.

* * *

The alarm clock pealed. Cass jumped out of bed and stood in the middle of the floor, very disoriented. She started to panic when she saw the illuminated 7:00 displayed on the clock.

"Shit! My flight's in an hour, I'll never make it!" She was racing around assembling a clean uniform when the phone rang. Agitated by the interruption, Cass snatched up the receiver and spoke gruffly. "Yeah?"

"Well, a happy Sunday morning to you too, grump," said the voice on the other end.

Cass pulled the receiver away from her ear and stared at it, confused. *Sunday? It's Sunday?* She put the receiver back to her ear. "Who is this, and why are you calling so early?"

Early? Rox looked at the clock and realized her error. "Oh, Cass, I'm so sorry. The time difference is so easy to forget. Please forgive me for waking you up. Go back to bed; I'll call back later."

"Whoa, whoa! Wait a minute. Rox?" Cass asked incredulously. "Rox, is that you?"

"Yes, it is. But I've woken you up. Cass. I'll call back later."

"No! No. I mean, I'm usually up by this time anyway. Please, don't hang up." Cass sat down on the edge of the bed.

"Are you sure?"

"Positive! So, to what do I owe this pleasure?" Cass asked as cheerfully as the morning hour would allow.

"Your e-mail," Rox replied. "I have never read anything so touching in my life, Cass. I've never written anything that brought me to tears like your note did."

Cass frowned. "It wasn't supposed to make you cry."

"You touched my heart, in a good way. It was beautiful, and I had to tell you directly. E-mail sometimes feels too... impersonal."

"I know what you mean. Sometimes the written word just can't replace the sound of a voice."

"I really meant it when I said it brought me to tears. Do you really think we were destined to be together? I mean, could there really be something or someone out there controlling everyone's fate?"

Cass considered for a moment before answering. "I don't really know what brought us together, but I don't think it was coincidence. I mean, we live three thousand miles apart. It's unlikely that we would have met by accident. No, something's behind this... something familiar. I can feel it."

"You mentioned a dream," Rox began. "I've had a dream that sounds like the same one. I'm in a field of flowers—millions of them—picking a large bouquet, when I see a figure approach. It turns out to be you. You explain to me that all the flowers in the field are our lifetimes together, and that the ones in my arms are—"

"The lives we have already lived," Cass finished. "Don't you see? We belong together. We're connected on some spiritual plane."

"Cass, this is scaring me. If that's true, then it means we don't have the control over our lives that we think we have. I don't like the sound of that," Rox confessed. "If it's true, then someone or something out there planned for me to be with Chris... planned for me to be abused for six months... planned for you to be abused by Patti. Why?"

"Rox, I'm not saying this is the answer. All I'm saying is that I don't think it is purely coincidental that we met. I think there is some other force behind it. Call it Fate, call it Kismet, I don't know, but I don't think it's happenstance. I think it was meant to be." Several moments of silence ensued. "Rox, are you still there?"

"Yes, I'm here."

"You got quiet on me. Honey, talk to me. What are you thinking?"

"I don't know, Cass. It's just that... Well, it's hard to comprehend. I mean, the dream suggests that we knew each other in a past lifetime... several of them, in fact."

"Well, I don't know how you feel about me, but there's something very familiar about you, as if I've known you for a long, long time. I felt that in the dream and I felt it when we met in Maine. I can't explain it, but it's true."

"I know it's true. I've felt it too," Rox admitted. "Damn, but I wish I had the answers. This is very confusing and more than a little intimidating."

"I intimidate you?" Cass asked, surprise coloring her voice.

"No, I didn't mean *you* intimidate me, Cass. I meant the situation does."

"Rox... how do you feel about me?" The question was simple, but Cass knew her future happiness depended on the answer.

There was a long pause. "Part of me is terrified. Part of me is intrigued, and that part wants to explore this further. My mind is a jumble and so are my emotions. I'm having a very hard time sorting everything out. You've sparked a desire that scares me senseless."

Very gently, Cass asked her question again. "You've explained how you feel inside, but how do you feel about me?" After a long silence, she heard sniffling from the other end of the line. "Are you all right?" she asked softly.

"I'm sorry," Rox said, sniffling again. "I'm such a baby sometimes."

"Sweetheart, why are you crying?" Cass's voice was tender and she desperately wanted to be in Maine, holding Rox in her arms.

"I don't know. Maybe because I don't want to hurt you... maybe because I'm so confused. Cass, I don't have an answer to your question. I know I care deeply for you, but my heart is in such a confused state right now that I just don't know." Tears were evident in her voice.

"God, I wish I could be there right now, holding you in my arms and chasing away your tears. I'm so sorry for pushing you. You need time to realize your true heart. I'm sorry," Cass said. "Please forgive me?"

"There's nothing to forgive, really," Rox replied. "Uh... I need to get back to my book. I just wanted to hear your voice. I'm sorry I woke you up."

"That's all right. I'm so glad you called, Rox. Would you give me your phone number so I can call you later? I'd really like to speak to you again."

"Sure. It's 207-555-7231. There's an answering machine on the line, so if I'm not home or I'm too tied up to answer, leave a message, okay?"

"Great. Thanks for trusting me with the number. I can't tell you how much it means to me."

"You're welcome. Well, I guess I'll talk to you later, then," Rox said softly.

"Okay. Oh, and Rox... I love you."

"Bye, Cass." Rox hung up the phone. She took a deep breath and leaned back, resting her head against the chair. Slowly exhaling, she wrapped her arms around herself. *Why does life have to be so complicated?* Running her hands through her hair, she did her best to set aside the feelings and turn her attention to her writing.

Three thousand miles away, Cass hung up the phone and threw herself back across the bed. She rubbed her face vigorously and then lay still, her mind occupied with the woman of her dreams.

Rox, I love you with all my heart. I hope that some day soon, you'll be able to return that love. We are fated to be together, my love. I just know we are.

She closed her eyes and allowed visions of Rox to fill her mind, and drifted off to sleep as fantasies of two women in love—one fair and one dark—played out in her dreams.

You're a chickenshit.

What did you say?

I said you're a chickenshit! You asked her for her phone number so you could call her back, and now you're afraid to use it.

You don't know what you're talking about. I just don't want to interrupt her writing. And besides, I talked to her once already today.

You talked to her, what? Twelve hours ago? You said you'd call her later. This is later.

I don't know, E. What if she's busy? She has a deadline to meet, you know.

You'll never get her in the sack if you don't talk to her, came the pointed response.

Christ, is that all you think about?

Yes. Someone's got to look out for our needs!

This relationship isn't about sex. It's about fate, destiny, love. The physical expression of that love should be an afterthought.

Okay, time out! So you're telling me that you don't want to do the nasty with this chick? Enforcer was incredulous.

Not exactly. I just meant that it isn't the most important part of the relationship.

What relationship? There won't be *a relationship if you don't make contact. Now call her.*

Okay, okay. You're such a bitch sometimes, Cass shot back.

You'll pay for that later on. For now, get your ass in gear and call her!

Cass did as she was told. She was about to hang up when Rox finally answered.

"Hello?"

"Hi, Rox. This is Cass."

"Cass? Wow! I was just thinking about you." Rox said. "You've been in my mind since we talked this morning."

"Really?" Cass asked hopefully. "Look, I know it's after ten on the East Coast, but I wanted to call and wish you pleasant dreams before you turned in."

"It's early yet, Cass. I won't turn in for at least another three hours, and I'm so glad you called. It gives us time to talk before either of us needs to hit the sheets. You have to work tomorrow, don't you?"

"Yeah, I've got a two-day flight to Durango, Mexico. I'm starting to dread these overnight trips. I think I'll talk to my supervisor about a schedule change this week."

"Two days, huh? I'll miss you." Rox's voice was soft, and she twirled her chair around like a young girl, a sense of daring brewing in her chest at her tentative flirtation.

Cass was pacing, the portable phone pressed against her ear. She stopped in her tracks at Rox's words. "You're going to miss me? Do you mean it, Rox?"

"Of course I do." Changing the subject abruptly, she added, "So, what did you do with yourself today?"

Cass was caught off-guard, but came up with a quick answer. "Besides thinking of you all day? Let's see... I took my morning run, did some laundry, cleaned house, ironed my uniform for tomorrow... You know—boring stuff. How was your day?"

"I made a lot of progress on the book," Rox replied. "I'm beginning to make up for some of the delay caused by my broken wrist. My editor still isn't thrilled, but heck, sometimes real life gets in the way of the fun stuff, you know what I mean?"

"Yeah, I do," Cass replied, unsure of what to say next. After a few moments of awkward silence, she said hesitantly, "Rox, I don't want to push you, and I don't expect a response right now, but I want you to know that you mean everything to me. You are my heart, and I've never been so sure of anything in my life. When I described my day to you earlier, I left something out. I'm not much of a poet, but I wrote a poem for you. I'll e-mail it to you after we hang up."

Rox stifled a sob. *Cass, how do you touch me so?* She closed her eyes and a tear rolled down her cheek. "Could you read it to me now?"

Cass was a little embarrassed by the request. "Wouldn't you rather read it in private?" she asked hopefully.

"I will, later when you send it. Right now, I'd like to hear you read it to me. Please?" she asked in a small voice.

That was Cass's undoing. "All right. But I warn you, I'm not much of a poet."

Rox waited patiently while Cass retrieved the poem.

"Ahem." Cass cleared her throat before starting.

Rescue My Soul

In the wellspring of my soul,
I see the flames of desire
Burning brightly
In that oft-darkened place.
It is a new eventuality,
This warmly felt passion.
Foreign to my heart,
Alien to my being.
This fervor has a face,
With mane of gold
And orbs of green,
And beauty like no other.
I drown consentingly
In pools of emerald,
And cast away the lifeline
For I revel in my fate.
I find myself drawn
To the Temptress's charms,
Needing her goodness
Needing her love.
I want to fill her body
With my soul
And become one

With her heart.
I wander, incomplete
Through the deserts of life
Desperately wanting her
By my side.
She quenches my thirst
My longing and ache
As she fills me with her love
And rescues my soul.

Cass fell silent, profoundly embarrassed.

Rox fell silent too, but for a very different reason. Tears were streaming down her cheeks and she was too choked up to speak.

Misinterpreting her silence, Cass began to apologize. "I told you it wasn't very good," she began.

"Stop it," Rox demanded, speaking through her tears. "Please," she added softly. "I loved it. Your words have a way of touching me like no one's ever have." She sniffed loudly. "Your poem is filled with such emotion, I... I don't know what to say. I've never received such a wonderful gift. I'll cherish it forever."

"You really like it?"

"I love it. Thank you."

Cass had a wide smile on her face. "You're welcome. I mean every word, Rox."

"I know you do," Rox answered, and then surprised herself by yawning.

"Honey, you're tired. I'm going to let you go to bed. I'll be out of town tomorrow, but I'll get back on Tuesday afternoon. May I call you then?"

"I'd really like that, Cass."

"Okay, until Tuesday, then. I love you, Rox. Sleep well."

"I will. You, too. Have a nice flight, and I'll talk to you on Tuesday."

"Good night."

The call was disconnected, and both women retreated into their own private thoughts.

Get a grip. You really need to decide what it is you're feeling for this woman. Your entire future depends on it.

Rox yawned again as she powered down her computer and rose from her chair. A cat-like stretch brought a painful reminder that she was not yet healed from her injuries, and she decided to take a hot shower to chase away some of the soreness.

As she looked at herself in the bathroom mirror, Rox imagined Cass standing behind her, wrapping strong arms around her waist and pulling her tightly against her chest. Green eyes flickered closed at the image and pangs of desire spread through her body. Grabbing the edge of the sink for support, Rox took a deep breath to compose herself. When she'd regained her equilibrium, she stripped off her clothes and showered, then climbed naked into bed. Within minutes, she drifted off to dreams of dark hair and blue eyes.

* * *

Cass's mood skyrocketed. She was elated that Rox had liked her poem. It was only eight o'clock and she was nowhere near ready to sleep, so she decided to surf the Net for an hour or so before calling it a night.

If anyone had asked which sites she had visited, she would not have been able to tell them. She was so distracted by thoughts of red-gold hair and green eyes that she was merely going through the motions. Losing interest, she decided to send Rox a short note along with the poem she had been cajoled into reading over the phone.

What started out as a brief two or three lines turned into a full-blown letter.

Hi, my love,

How can one person change the life of another as thoroughly as you've changed mine?

Rox, I can't imagine my life without you. You've become part of me -- as vital as my heart and the air I breathe, a requirement to help me make it through the day. Your voice makes my heart flutter. My hands remember the feel of your skin. The memory of you sustains me in our separation, keeps me sane. I hold this memory close to my heart as I lie alone in bed each night, wishing with everything I am that you were here beside me.

It's my hope that the day is drawing near when we will be together, not as two halves of a whole, but as two entities merged into one. I have visions of the future:

visions of joy, love and family. I have visions of you saying "I do" as I slip a golden symbol of our love on your finger. I see nights spent wrapped in each other's arms, and days spent at work, daydreaming of green eyes and a smile so endearing it takes my breath away.

You complete me. There is a place in my heart that has never been touched by anyone but you, and never will be. My heart is yours to command. I'm powerless to resist. I don't want to.

I hope the day will come soon when my dream is fulfilled. Until then, keep me close to your heart and I will keep you close to mine.

I love you, baby.
Cass

Attachment: RESCUE MY SOUL

Cass read the letter several times before sending it on its way. It was late now, and she needed to get to bed if she was going to be sharp for her flight in the morning.

She logged off the Internet. When the wallpaper containing Rox's photo appeared, she kissed the end of her index finger and reached forward to trace the pictured lips.

"Good night, my love," she whispered, then shut down the computer and went to bed.

Chapter 32

At 7:20 Monday morning, Cass made her absent-minded way through security and boarded the plane for her flight to Durango. In the cockpit, she stared at the control panel as she let her mind wander to where she really wanted to be on that sunny morning—the coast of Maine, walking hand in hand along the shoreline with a beautiful woman. Sounds of the flight attendants moving around in the cabin broke her reverie, and she mentally shook herself and started her safety check of the flight instruments prior to takeoff. Ten minutes into the routine, the passengers started loading for the eight a.m. flight.

A familiar voice sounded from the entrance to the cockpit. "Hey, Cass!"

Cass lifted her head and saw Jason brushing off the insistent flight attendant, who was urging him toward the aisle of the plane.

"It's all right, Ginny," Cass said when she saw who was causing the commotion. "I'll take care of it."

Ginny nodded, then released Jason's arm and turned her attention to the other passengers.

Cass climbed out of the bucket seat, walked out into the companionway and stood to her full height. "How are you, Jason? It's good to have you aboard. Now, I'll have to ask you to be seated. We'll be ready for takeoff in a few minutes, and you'll be able to move about the cabin after we reach cruising altitude." She motioned for him to leave the cockpit area and find his seat.

"How about a personal tour of the cockpit later?" he asked suggestively.

Cass wanted to rip his throat out, but Enforcer wanted to do worse. *Why don't we wait until we reach cruising altitude, then push him out of the plane without a parachute?*

Instead, Cass crossed her arms and raised an eyebrow. "I'm afraid that's not possible, Jason. FAA regulations prohibit passengers from visiting the cockpit area, especially while the plane is in flight."

"Even first-class passengers? After all, it's customers like me who pay your salary," he said. There was a smug smile on his face.

Forget that last suggestion. Let's throw him into one of the turbine engines instead! Enforcer urged, fueling Cass's already short temper.

Smiling smugly herself, she turned her back on him and returned to the cockpit, throwing the words, "Sorry, no exceptions," over her shoulder. She could almost feel his look of displeasure at the curt dismissal boring into her back. Shrugging it off, she strapped into her seat and helped Brian finish the safety check.

"Ladies and gentlemen, this is your captain speaking," Cass said into the microphone. "We have been cleared for takeoff. Please be sure that your seatbelts are fastened securely and that the trays in the seatback in front of you are in the upright and locked position. Be advised that this airline recommends that your seatbelt remain fastened throughout the flight, or at the very least, while the seatbelt sign above your heads is illuminated. A flight attendant will review safety and evacuation procedures with you for the unlikely event of an emergency. As always, thank you for flying Southern Lights Airline and have a nice flight."

She clicked off the microphone and made a face at Brian. "I'm getting sick of making that speech. It's your turn next."

"Nope, not me. With rank comes privilege. Sorry." His ear-to-ear grin belied his words.

"Traitor," Cass mumbled, preparing the plane for takeoff.

After a ten minute wait on the runway, they were finally in the air and gaining altitude. When they reached cruising altitude, Brian put the plane on autopilot while Cass reached up and turned the seatbelt sign off, indicating to the passengers that they were free to move about the cabin.

"What's the weather look like between here and Durango? I really don't need a repeat of that joyride we took during the last storm," Brian said.

Cass chuckled as she checked the weather service reports. "Don't worry. Looks like clear sailing the entire way. Should be a pretty uneventful flight."

Brian sighed and relaxed in his seat as the cockpit door opened. Cass looked up to see Ginny standing in the doorway, a worried look on her face.

What now? Cass thought. "Yes, Ginny?"

Ginny fidgeted. "Ah, Captain Conway, we seem to have a problem."

Brian quickly turned in his seat. "Don't tell me we've been hit by lightning. It isn't even raining."

"What is it, Ginny?" Cass said, as patiently as she could.

"Uh… uh… "

"Oh, get out of my way," demanded a gruff voice from behind the nervous flight attendant.

"Jason," Cass said sharply. "I thought I told you—"

"I don't give a fuck what you told me, bitch! I'm in control here now." He pulled a gun with a silencer on it out of his jacket.

"Oh, shit!" Brian put his hands up and Ginny fainted.

"Jason, just what do you think you're doing?" Cass demanded, more annoyed than frightened.

"What does it look like I'm doing? This is a gun, you're a pilot, and we're in a plane. This is a fucking skyjacking, what else?"

"A skyjacking? Why, Jason?"

"Cass, you'd better be careful how you talk to him," Brian warned, speaking under his breath.

Cass threw him an impatient look while she waited for Jason's answer. "Well?"

"I have a little business deal you're going to help me with."

"Bullshit! I'm not helping you with anything," Cass said calmly.

Jason aimed the gun at Brian's left thigh and fired.

Brian clutched his bleeding leg. "Fuck, he shot me!" He groaned in pain as he tried to staunch the flow of blood.

Cass's eyes widened and her stomach lurched.

There was an evil look in Jason's eyes. "Now, I think you should cooperate. Don't you agree?"

Cass nodded, her eyes not leaving Brian's wounded leg. "He needs a doctor."

"He'll get one, just as soon as you land the plane in San Diego," Jason said.

Cass looked at him in confusion. "San Diego? You could have easily driven to San Diego. Why skyjack a plane?"

"San Diego is just our first stop," Jason clarified. "We'll fly to our final destination after we get rid of the dead wood. Now, we can either unload the plane on the ground in San Diego, or we can throw the passengers out one by one while we're still in the air. It's your choice, but either way, they're getting off the plane. I don't need complications on board during this flight. Do you understand?"

"Damn it, Cass, do as he asks." Brian removed his necktie and wrapped it around his leg as a makeshift bandage.

Cass's eyes narrowed as she turned to stare back at Jason. "All right. I'll do as you say, but if you harm another person aboard this flight, all bets are off. You got that?"

Jason backhanded Cass across the face. Her head snapped to the right, and blood from her split lip spattered the cockpit door. He grabbed a handful of her hair and jerked her head back toward him, then hissed into her face, "Get this straight, bitch. You don't give the orders here, I do. Understand?"

He shoved her away and took a step back. "Now, get on the radio and tell them you're making an emergency landing in San Diego. Call it engine failure, call it anything you want, but if you tip off the authorities and keep us from getting back in the air, you're a dead woman."

Cass wiped her mouth on the sleeve of her jacket, then radioed San Diego air traffic control.

"San Diego, this is Flight 7231 from San Jose, en route to Durango, Mexico, requesting an unscheduled landing."

"Flight 7231, this is San Diego. Is this an emergency? State the purpose of your request."

"No emergency, San Diego, just a slight malfunction of the panel instruments. Request transfer of passengers to another plane and a maintenance crew to look at the problem. ETA, one hour," she said calmly.

"Unscheduled landing approved, Flight 7231. Estimated time of arrival, one hour."

Cass shot a venomous look at Jason as she clicked off the microphone and replaced it in its cradle.

He just grinned at her. "Good girl," he said condescendingly. "Cooperate like that and everything will be fine." He sat down in the navigator's seat behind Brian and kept the gun trained on Cass as she turned her attention back to the controls.

Keeping her eyes forward, she started to ask questions. "Tell me, Jason, how did you get the gun on board?"

Jason puffed out his chest in pride. "That was the easy part. I smuggled it on board in with the food supplies. I have connections with the company that caters for your airline." The smug smile was back.

"I assume you're doing this for money. Being a used-car salesman certainly isn't lucrative enough to pay for the lavish way you're living."

"Bingo!" he said loudly. "Give that girl a prize. Oh, yeah, it's definitely for the money. Lots of money, and you're going to help me make it. If you're a good girl, you might even get a cut. If not, well, let's just say that one less lesbian bitch in the world won't make a difference."

Brian's jaw dropped at this revelation. Realization was written all over his face, and clearly he was recalling his repeated failures to seduce her.

Cass shot him a look that told him to keep his mouth shut, or else.

Snapping his mouth closed, Brian turned his attention back to his throbbing leg.

"Okay," Cass continued, her back still to Jason. "So what do I have to do to earn this cut?"

Jason became animated. "Now you're talking. First, we get rid of wimp-boy here," he said, indicating Brian, "and all the passengers. Then we go meet my contacts, pocket the cash, load the shipment and airdrop it just over the border, where people will be waiting to pick it up. When we land back in San Diego, you get your cut of the take and we go our separate ways."

Cass glanced back. "It's that simple, huh?" she asked. "How much do I get?"

Jason looked at her suspiciously and thought hard before answering. *Shit! I really need her to fly the plane. Damn it, I'll have to give her a decent cut to get her to cooperate.* "How about twenty-five percent of the take?" he offered.

Cass raised an eyebrow. "Twenty-five percent? You expect me to take all the risks and you're only offering twenty-five percent?"

What the hell are you doing? Enforcer asked. *You can't seriously be thinking about going along with this doofus!*

Shit! Shit! The greedy bitch! Damn! "Okay, thirty percent, and that's final."

Cass turned around in her seat and looked him straight in the eye. "No deal," she said. "Forty percent or nothing. It should be fifty percent, but you *did* mastermind this whole thing, so you deserve a little extra."

Jason's chest swelled when she acknowledged his crafty planning. He pretended to contemplate the counter-offer for a few seconds, then reached forward and shook her hand. "Deal."

Cass, you traitorous... Goddamn it, woman, what are you doing? Enforcer yelled.

E., calm down. Don't you see what an idiot this guy is? He thinks we're in on this now. Trust me. I know what I'm doing.

I knew we should have pushed him into the turbines. I knew it, Enforcer grumbled.

Cass turned back to the controls, sparing Brian a momentary look. His head was leaning against the headrest, his face pale. She reached over and touched his knee, drawing his attention to her. She gave him a slight smile and a conspiratorial wink, then turned to Jason. He held the gun, but the balance of power was teetering precariously between them.

"We'll be landing in San Diego in about twenty-five minutes. You'll need to revive Ginny so she can prepare the passengers for the landing."

Jason did as he was told and shook Ginny awake, trying not to startle her into unconsciousness again.

Ginny's eyes opened wide as she looked up into his face.

"Get up," he ordered harshly. "You have a job to do."

Cass looked over her shoulder to where Ginny was still lying on the floor. "Ginny, just cooperate and everything will be okay. You need to act as though nothing is amiss. Do you understand?"

Too scared to speak, Ginny managed a slight nod.

"Okay. I need you to inform the passengers that we're landing in San Diego due to a mechanical failure. Tell them they'll be transferred to another plane." Cass paused to be sure Ginny understood. "Once the passengers are off the plane, you'll be allowed to go. Brian will get off the plane as well, but I'll stay on board."

Ginny glanced at Brian and for the first time realized that he had been shot. "Oh, my God!" Her eyes flew to the gun in Jason's hand. "You shot him?"

"Yeah. And if you don't play your cards right, you'll be next. You got that?" The harsh words caused Ginny to shrink away from him.

Cass rolled her eyes. "Back off, Jason. She needs to be convincing in front of the passengers. Your plan won't work if you scare the shit out her." Glancing at the still-prone Ginny, she said, "It's all right, Ginny. Just hold it together and no one will get hurt."

"It's kind of late for that, isn't it?" Brian asked sarcastically.

Jason sneered. "One more word out of you, pretty-boy, and you'll be bleeding from both legs."

"That's enough," Cass reprimanded. "Let's get this show on the road. We'll be landing soon and we don't have time to waste."

Ginny scrambled to her feet and straightened her skirt. Her eyes met Cass's as she reached for the door handle, and the reassuring look she received seemed to steady her.

Once Ginny was gone, Cass turned to Jason and smiled slightly in an attempt to gain more of his confidence. "Almost there," she informed him. "You'd better buckle in for the landing." She indicated the navigator's seat behind Brian. Again, Jason did as he was told, and within moments they were on their final approach into Lindbergh Field.

As soon as the plane came to a halt, shuttle buses arrived to transport the passengers to another aircraft. Jason held Ginny and Brian in the cockpit until the passengers had deplaned. As the last one left, he grabbed Ginny and pressed the gun to her head.

"That isn't necessary, Jason," said Cass.

"Let's just say it's a bit of insurance, Cass. A reason for you to get back on the plane after getting rid of dork-boy."

Cass frowned deeply at the unexpected turn of events. She had planned on not returning to the plane, thus stranding Jason and foiling his plan, but she couldn't abandon Ginny. Reluctantly, she took Brian's arm and helped him to the entrance.

As the two of them emerged from the plane, Cass instructed the ground crew to back the luggage cart up to the stairway. They gave her questioning looks, but did as they were told as she helped Brian to the stairs. When the crew saw that he was injured, they rushed forward to help Cass carry him down the stairs and settle him in the front seat of the cart. She then turned calmly to the crew chief and pointed back up the stairs.

"We're being skyjacked," she said. "Unless you want someone to end up dead, you'll take this man and head back to the terminal right now. If you resist or make a scene before the plane is back in the air, he will kill me. He's already shot Brian, so he's not afraid to use the gun. Do you understand?"

She could see fear in the workmen's eyes as they struggled with the dilemma of leaving her on the plane with the skyjacker.

"Please, don't try to be heroes, or one of us will wind up dead," she whispered. "Please, just go."

After a tense moment, the men retreated with their injured cargo and Cass re-boarded the plane.

"Let her go, Jason," Cass demanded as she entered the cockpit and began preparations for takeoff.

Jason shoved Ginny forward and watched as the terrified woman scurried off the plane.

Proud of his planning abilities as well as his ability to talk Cass into abetting his cause, Jason settled himself in the co-pilot's seat while Cass communicated with the control tower.

"This is Flight 7231, requesting permission for takeoff," she said into the microphone.

"Flight 7231, you have been grounded for faulty controls. Please abort takeoff procedures," the tower responded.

"I repeat. This is Flight 7231, demanding permission for takeoff. We are being skyjacked. I need immediate clearance. Is that understood?"

A brief silence followed her words. Finally, the radio crackled to life again.

"Flight 7231, abort your takeoff procedure. The authorities have been notified and are on their way. I repeat: abort your takeoff procedure."

"No can do, control tower. I am taxiing into position. Clearance for takeoff required immediately."

"Abort takeoff procedures, Flight 7231. Clearance denied!"

Enough was enough. "Look, you officious asshole, I have a gunman here about to blow my brains out if I don't get this bird into the air. Can I make myself any clearer than that? Clearance is required, *now*," Cass demanded.

There was another silence before the tower responded, "Clearance granted, Flight 7231. Do not break communication. The crisis team has just arrived. What is your destination?"

Now Jason lost patience. Grabbing the microphone, he shouted, "Our destination is none of your business, fuckhead! You'll have us on radar once we're airborne, so what's the problem?"

"This is John Everett of the crisis control team. No need to become upset, sir. What are your demands?"

"My demands are that you leave us the fuck alone and let my partner here fly the plane. Do you understand?" Jason replied sarcastically.

Cass cringed at the word "partner."

Christ, now the entire world will think you're in on this. Damn it, woman! What a mess. What's Rox going to think of all this? You are blowing it big time, Enforcer scolded.

Cass's eyes flew open wide and she whispered, "Rox," as she opened the jet engines to full throttle and the airplane sped down the runway. Soon they were airborne again.

Once the plane reached cruising altitude, Cass looked over at Jason and forced a grin. "Well, we're on our way," she said, raising her hand for a high-five.

Jason slapped his palm against hers. "You were great, Cass!" He shook his head. "Wow, talk about a narrow escape. Our names will go down in the history books, right next to Bonnie and Clyde."

Cass groaned at the thought of being immortalized in print next to Jason.

"You know," he continued, "We might want to consider skipping the country after we complete the shipment. I mean, we'll be branded as criminals, so it might not be safe to re-enter the U.S."

Cass pretended to contemplate the suggestion. "You might be right, Jay. We should give it some serious thought. By the way, what exactly is in that shipment we're supposed to pick up?"

Jason looked around as though there was someone else on board who might hear him. In hushed tones, he said, "Cocaine. About a thousand kilos."

Holy shit! The man wants to put a ton of illegal drugs on this plane! Cassidy Conway, you turn this plane around right now, Enforcer demanded. *I will* not *be involved in any drug deals.*

"That's what I thought," Cass said with forced calm. "So, I assume we're flying into...?"

"Bogotá," Jason supplied and Cass nodded.

Enforcer made one last attempt at convincing Cass to abandon her course of action. *Cass, you and I both know we're already in big trouble for stealing this plane. I really hope that sexy writer in Maine is going to want you with a criminal record. Do you think she'll wait while you do time for drug trafficking?*

Cass felt a pang of sadness at this reminder of what she had to lose. If things didn't work out the way she was planning, she would definitely lose Rox, and possibly her life. Of that, she was very sure. But she was also determined not to let Jason or the Colombian drug lords succeed in exporting their poison.

Chapter 33

Early Monday morning, Rox awakened with just enough time to shower and get to her eight o'clock appointment with her editor to review the progress on her manuscript. She cajoled and coddled the unhappy man for two hours, assuring him that she would work overtime to make the planned publication date.

It was nearly ten-thirty by the time Rox got home and she was starving. She went straight to the kitchen and whipped up a fluffy vegetable and cheese omelet, toasted an English muffin and brewed a cup of rich butter-rum flavored coffee. She carried her gourmet fare to her office and set it on the desk while she powered up the computer, intent on working diligently on her book for the rest of the day. Her hope was to make enough progress that she could take a break the next afternoon and talk to Cass for a while when she returned from her flight to Mexico.

Rox was unable to resist checking her e-mail before she got down to work. As she expected, there was a note from Cass.

> *Hi, my love,*
>
> *How can one person change the life of another as thoroughly as you've changed mine?*
>
> *Rox, I can't imagine my life without you. You've become part of me -- as vital as my heart and the air I breathe, a requirement to help me make it through the day. Your voice makes my heart flutter. My hands remember the feel of your skin. The memory of you sustains me in our separation, keeps me sane. I hold this memory close to my heart as I lie alone in bed each night, wishing with all I am that you were here beside me.*
>
> *It's my hope that the day is drawing near when we will be together, not as two halves of a whole, but as two entities merged into one. I have visions of the future: visions of joy, love and family. I have visions of you saying*

"I do" as I slip a golden symbol of our love on your finger. I see nights spent wrapped in each other's arms, and days spent at work, daydreaming of green eyes and a smile so endearing it takes my breath away.

You complete me. There is a place in my heart that has never been touched by anyone but you, and never will be. My heart is yours to command. I'm powerless to resist. I don't want to.

I hope the day will come soon when my dream is fulfilled. Until then, keep me close to your heart and I will keep you close to mine.

I love you, baby.
Cass

Attachment: RESCUE MY SOUL

Rox's heart was fairly bursting as she opened the attachment and read the love poem. Settling back in her chair, she decided to look inward and really analyze how she felt about the dark-haired beauty. She closed her eyes and tried very hard to imagine what her future would be like both with and without Cass. She quickly came to the realization that she simply saw no future without Cass; every imaginable scenario included the tall pilot. Trying to think of a future without her caused only heartache.

Rox opened her eyes and stared at the computer screen. "Oh, my God, I'm in love with her. I love her!" Feeling giddy, she dialed Nikki's number.

"Hi. No, this isn't Nikki, this is a machine. Don't you hate that? Jerri and I are probably gone or asleep. Leave a message after the beep, and we'll get back to you. If it's an emergency, page me at 555-351-7100. Ta-ta for now."

"Nikki, I love her, I love her! I can't believe it, but I'm in love with her! Call me!"

Moments later, the phone rang. It was Jerri, returning Rox's call.

Rox was still sitting in her office, lost in thought. "Hello?"

"Hey, Rox, I just listened to your message. Congratulations, girlfriend. It's about time you realized where your heart's been for the past while. I'm really happy for you," Jerri said enthusiastically.

"Jer?" Rox asked. "I'm sorry. Did the phone wake you?"

"No, I was just getting out of the shower. I'm scheduled to work the noon-to-midnight shift, so I was up already. So, what's the next step?"

Rox was still a little dazed. "The next step?"

"Yeah, you know—Cass, I love you, I want to spend the rest of my life with you... That kind of thing."

Rox's head snapped up, her eyes wide. "God, I haven't thought that far ahead yet. Help me out here, what *do* I do next?"

Jerri held the receiver in one hand and towel-dried her dark hair with the other. "You could start by calling her and telling her," she suggested. "I'm sure she'll be thrilled with the news,"

"Oh, my God, how do I do that? Do I just blurt it out?"

"Just call her. Call her right now. No sense in waiting."

"I can't. She's on a flight to Mexico until tomorrow."

"Then you've got an entire day and a half to think of an approach," Jerri said. "Why don't you run it by Nikki? She'll be home by five."

"Good idea, I'll do that. Thanks, Jer."

Rox hung up the phone and stared at the monitor. After some time, she realized that her story was no further along than it had been when she'd turned the computer on nearly an hour earlier. Shaking off her preoccupation, she logged off the Internet and began to write.

Several hours later, Rox was startled by the jangling of the telephone beside her. She had been so absorbed in her manuscript that she'd tuned out the world, but the sharp ring of the telephone refused to be ignored.

"Hello?"

"Rox!" The voice at the other end of the line was excited. "I just heard the news!"

"Nikki?" Rox was surprised until Nikki's statement registered, then she chuckled. "I see you've been talking to Jerri. Got any advice for me?"

"Yeah. Dump her, *now*."

"What?" Rox was thoroughly confused. "Nikki, how can you say that? I've just realized I'm in love with her."

"Roxanne Ward, you don't need this kind of complication in your life. You can't be in love with her. She's no good for you."

"Nikki—"

"No, Rox. Do you want to spend the rest of your life running from the police? You can't do this." There was no reply. "Rox, are you there?"

"Nikki, what the hell are you talking about?" It was Nikki's turn to be silent. "Talk to me," Rox demanded.

"You don't know, do you?"

"Know what? That I'm getting really pissed? Damn it, talk to me!"

"I was watching the TV in the nurse's lounge and there was a news flash about a plane being skyjacked. Rox, it was Cass's plane, and according to the report, she's in on the skyjacking."

Rox dropped the phone into her lap, her eyes widening in disbelief.

Nikki's voice came from the receiver. "Roxanne, pick up the goddamned phone!"

Rox held the receiver to her ear. "It can't be true. Cass wouldn't—"

"Wouldn't she? How much do you really know about her? You were the one who was worried that she was an Internet wacko. Maybe you were right."

"No. No, I don't believe it. I'm calling the airline. What channel were you watching?"

"Channel Three. It was a news flash, and they've been giving updates every half hour or so. I'm leaving work early today and coming straight to your house, okay? I don't want you to be alone. Jerri won't be home until about one o'clock in the morning, so I'd be going home to an empty house anyway. I should be there in about an hour. Don't leave."

"All right, I'll be here. And Nik... thanks."

"Honey, you know I only want you to be happy. Maybe we can work through this mess together, okay? I'll be there soon. Bye."

"Bye, Nik." They disconnected and Rox placed the receiver back in the cradle. Looking at the work she had just completed, she realized that nothing she accomplished would mean anything if she lost Cass. *Oh, my God, I may never get the chance to tell her I love her.* At that thought, she dropped her face into her hands and began to cry.

When Nikki walked in an hour later, Rox was sitting on edge of the living room couch, her eyes glued to the television. Her body was stiff with tension, and she clutched a handkerchief that was wrinkled with worry and damp with tears. Nikki immediately enveloped her in a hug, allowing Rox to release some of the tension and to lean on her for support as they watched the latest update together.

"And now, a late-breaking bulletin on this morning's skyjacking of Flight 7231 from San Jose, California to Durango, Mexico. When the news first broke, it was believed that pilot Cassidy Conway was a key participant. Captain Conway was recently hailed as a hero for safely landing her plane after it was struck by lightning. Authorities apparently know the identity of the second perpetrator, but have not released it at this time. New sources tell us that he is Jason Hayer, an acquaintance of the pilot.

"According to reports, the skyjacking took place shortly after the plane's departure from San Jose International Airport. Citing faulty controls, the plane made an emergency landing in San Diego, California, just after nine-thirty this morning. Passengers were immediately unloaded. Before takeoff, Co-pilot Brian Anderson, who had been shot in the leg, was assisted from the plane by Captain Conway and turned over to the ground crew. Moments later, flight attendant Ginny Caswell exited the plane unharmed. The plane then received clearance to take off again with Captain Conway at the controls. Suspicion was cast on Captain Conway when the second skyjacker referred to her as his 'partner' in a transmission to the radio tower."

"Nikki, this can't be happening. Cass wouldn't *do* that." Rox's indignant outburst subsided as the news report continued.

"Since our earlier report, new information has come to light from an interview with co-pilot Brian Anderson. During the interview, Mr. Anderson indicated that Captain Conway was not a willing participant, that she was blackmailed into cooperating with the gunman in order to save the lives of the passengers and crew."

Rox pounded Nikki on the arm, pointing to the TV with her other hand. "See, see? I told you she wouldn't do that!"

"Hush," Nikki replied, trying to listen to the rest of the report.

"The FAA is still viewing Captain Conway's participation in this event as potentially suspect, though significant doubts have been raised about the nature of her involvement. The destination of the aircraft is unknown at this time, but radar tracking indicates that it's heading toward Colombia. An ongoing investigation into Mr. Hayer's recent activities has uncovered contacts with Colombian drug lord Carlos Santonio. More on this story as it becomes available. For Channel Three News, I'm Meaghan Adams. We now return you to your regularly scheduled program."

Nikki clicked off TV and tossed the remote onto the coffee table. She looked at Rox with concern. "Well, what do you think?"

"I don't think she's in on it. Brian was there, he should know." Rox rose and started pacing.

Nikki stood and stopped her in mid-stride. She wrapped her arms around Rox and pulled her close, trying to comfort her. "I sure hope you're right. I guess we need to give her the benefit of the doubt for now."

"Christ, Nik, she's stuck on a plane with an armed lunatic! What are we going to do?" Rox asked frantically.

"Right now, we're going to wait and see what develops. What else *can* we do? We don't even know for sure where they're heading."

Rox nodded and fell back onto the couch. She turned the television back on and began channel-surfing for late-breaking news.

Nikki watched, her heart breaking for her friend and her mind hoping Cass was innocent—and safe.

Chapter 34

The rest of the flight to Colombia went smoothly. Jason spent most of the time outlining his plans to Cass, including telling her the names of his contacts and when he was to meet them, while Cass pointedly ignored the constant radio calls that were an attempt to pinpoint their exact location. As they approached the Bogotá airport, Jason gave her new course coordinates.

"What are these?" she asked.

"The coordinates for the landing strip we're going to use for the pickup."

"Landing strip? Jason, where exactly *is* this landing strip?" Cass asked, concerned.

"Well, in the middle of the jungle. But don't worry, it's been cleared real good," he assured her.

"Cleared? Damn it, Jason, just how small is this landing strip? This is a large plane, and we need lots of runway to land and take off."

"I don't know—fifteen hundred, two thousand feet? How am I supposed to know?"

"Look, asshole," she said, grabbing the front of his shirt, "I'm in no mood to crash-land another plane, you got that? If the *landing strip* isn't long enough, I'm heading back to the public airport."

Jason pushed her back, pulled out his gun and held it to her head. "You'll land this plane where I tell you to land it, understand? If we damage it too badly to fly it out, we'll buy another one. We'll have enough money to buy whatever we want."

"And if I refuse?"

"Then I put a bullet in that pretty head of yours as soon as we're on the ground," Jason replied.

Cass sneered, but reset the plane's course. For about the fiftieth time, she regretted her decision to become involved in this mess. *Don't even say it, E.!*

285

What, "I told you so?" Nope, not me. I'd never *say that, even though you surely deserve it,* Enforcer replied. The plane began its descent toward the jungle terrain.

Within minutes, the landing strip came into view. "You expect me to land the plane on *that*?" Cass pointed at the roughly cleared strip of dirt. It looked just barely long enough, but unless she was very lucky, its bumpy surface was sure to damage the landing gear.

Jason looked through the windshield and admitted to himself that Cass was right—it wasn't the ideal place to land a plane, but it was too late to argue about it now. Swallowing his anxiety, he tightened his seatbelt and smiled reassuringly at Cass. "You can do it, Cass. You're a great pilot. After all, you crash-landed that plane in San Diego without losing even one passenger." He holstered his gun and grabbed the nearest object that looked secure.

"That was on a paved runway," she said tersely as she lowered the landing gear and prepared for a rough landing.

Then the wheels touched down on the rough surface and the plane began shuddering down the strip. Cass reversed engine thrust, trying to slow the aircraft before they ran out of space. Jason sat in terrified silence, his head bobbing with every bump and divot the wheels rolled over. A scant one hundred feet short of the trees, the plane finally rolled to a stop. Jason crossed himself, thankful for the rough, but safe landing, and turned to Cass.

"I *knew* you could do it!" he exclaimed happily, reaching out to shake Cass's hand. "I knew you'd be the perfect choice for this job."

Cass looked at him through narrowed eyes. "Just how long have you known you were going to do this, Jason?"

"For a while, now. I chose you because you seemed like an easy in, and because you seemed so calm and composed all the time. I figured you'd do well under pressure. Then, when you crash-landed that plane... well, that sealed it for me."

Cass shook her head, irked that she had been such an easy target. "What now?" she asked, unfastening her seatbelt.

"Our ride should be waiting for us over by the trees. We'll meet with them, they'll take us to the compound and we'll transact the deal. As soon as the shipment arrives, we'll load it onto the plane, refuel, and head out."

"As soon as the shipment arrives? Do you mean we could be here for a few days?" Cass asked. "What if they spot the plane from the air?"

"Got it covered. My business associates hired some locals to camouflage it with foliage as soon as we deplane. Later, they'll turn it around for us." He ushered her ahead of him out of the cockpit.

As they opened the door, a group of laborers pushed up a crude ramp so they could descend from the plane. Several other men were dragging large branches and vines toward the plane, presumably to begin the camouflage.

Cass glanced over her shoulder to ask Jason where they would be staying. Before she could speak, she felt a hard object come down on the back of her head and her consciousness faded.

"You, my dear, will be staying in secure quarters," Jason gloated as he stood over her unconscious form.

* * *

"Rox, come eat something," Nikki called from the kitchen.

Tense with worry, Rox had spent the entire afternoon perched on the sofa, channel-surfing for news of the skyjacking.

"Rox," Nikki called again, this time planting herself on the couch next to the distracted woman. "You've been sitting here all afternoon. You've got to eat. Starving yourself won't help the authorities find her any faster."

The signs of heartbreak were so apparent in Rox's features that it made Nikki teary-eyed to look at her. She took Rox's hand and held it close to her heart. "Honey, I know the waiting is hard," she said softly. "Look, why don't I bring a tray in here and we'll eat something together while we watch for updates. Okay?"

Rox nodded. "Thanks, Nik. I appreciate it."

Nikki returned carrying a tray laden with soup and salad, which she set down on the coffee table in front of them. "There, now eat up," she ordered.

Rox reached for her soup spoon just as a news update flashed across the screen. She immediately dropped the spoon and turned up the volume.

"Early this morning, a Southern Lights airliner was skyjacked shortly after takeoff from the San Diego airport. The plane, which was originally bound for Durango, Mexico, has only Captain Cassidy Conway and passenger Jason Hayer on board. It is believed that Hayer is the skyjacker, but Captain Conway's involvement is under investigation at this time. The plane was last located near Bogotá,

Colombia, and has since disappeared from radar. It is believed to have either landed or crashed in the dense jungle of the Bogotá region."

Rox was stricken. "Oh, my God, no!"

"At this time, authorities are conducting an air search and have yet to find evidence of crash-site debris," the reporter continued.

Even though she was struggling with her own doubts, Nikki sought to encourage her friend. "Rox, calm down. They haven't found any evidence of a crash. I'm sure she's all right."

"Authorities are speculating about the motive behind the skyjacking. It is believed that Jason Hayer has connections with known drug lord Carlos Santonio, and may be involved with the increased influx of drugs into Southern California over the past several months. As for Captain Conway's role in the skyjacking, the airline is convinced of her innocence and is standing by her. More on this story on Channel Three News at six."

Rox stayed in front of the television for the rest of the evening, but by midnight, she had learned nothing new. The authorities had found no trace of the plane or of a landing strip in the thick jungle. The lack of news caused mixed feelings in the emotionally fragile woman. No news was good news as far as a crash landing was concerned, but she was increasingly worried that she would never see Cass again.

These and similar thoughts raced through Rox's mind as she lay in bed that night, staring at the ceiling and wishing with everything she was that she had told Cass that she loved her. For all she knew, Cass was lying dead or dying amidst crash debris, deep in an unfriendly jungle. Her pillow was damp with tears when she finally managed to fall sleep.

Some time later, Rox was startled by a loud, clanging noise. Then someone grabbed her, dragged her kicking and screaming through the darkness, and threw her into a damp, dingy cell. The air reeked of mustiness, and she could make out only indistinct shapes through the darkness.

Her landing raised a cloud of dust that made her sneeze uncontrollably. When she could breathe again, she sat up, wondering where she was. Suddenly, she heard a faint moaning. Kneeling perfectly still, she listened until she heard it again. It sounded like someone nearby was in great pain.

"Hello?" she called. "Is anyone there?" There was no reply, just another soft, pained moan.

Realizing she wasn't going to receive a coherent answer, Rox crawled toward the source of the sound until she encountered a body. Recoiling, she sat back on her heels and tried to get her frightened heartbeat under control. *Whoever it is surely can't harm me,* she thought. *They need my help.* Having convinced herself, she leaned forward once more and felt her way around.

As her eyes became accustomed to the darkness, Rox could see shapes more clearly, and strained to make out the form in front of her. Locating the person mostly by touch, she soon realized it was a woman, who moaned as Rox touched her.

"Shh… it's okay. I won't hurt you," she crooned to the injured woman.

With some difficulty, she managed to maneuver the woman into her lap. They were close to a wall, and she leaned against it, cradling the woman's head and brushing sweaty bangs out of her eyes. Rox studied the woman's face in the muted light and realized it was Cass. "Cass! What have they done to you, my love? I'm here for you, honey. I won't leave you." For what seemed like a long time Rox sat murmuring words of encouragement, promising not to leave, all the while fearing for her own safety and that of her injured companion. Several times, she asked Cass where they were, but the other woman was unable to respond with anything more than grunts and moans.

As the sky lightened toward dawn, the blue eyes filled with tears and the injured woman reached up to touch the side of her face. "Rox," Cass rasped.

"I love you, Cass," Rox said as she looked down at the bruised face.

Cass tried to smile, and gently squeezed Rox's hand as she closed her eyes and slid back into unconsciousness.

"No!" Rox screamed, sitting up and throwing off the covers. She scrambled out of bed and paced back and forth across her bedroom, her eyes wide with terror and her heart pounding.

"Oh, my God, oh, my God!" she chanted. As she paced, she ran her hand over her face and through her hair, trying desperately to make sense of the dream. "Cass, where are you?" she whispered into the night. "I've got to find you."

Picking up the phone, she dialed Nikki's number.

"Hello?" said a groggy voice at the other end of the line.

"Nikki, she's in trouble!" Rox exclaimed.

"Rox? What the hell? Do you know what time it is?" Nikki asked irritably.

"I'm sorry, but Cass is in trouble. I just had a dream, or maybe a premonition. She's in trouble and I've got to find her."

"You saw her in a dream? Rox, go back to bed. There's nothing you can do from here."

"I know. That's why I have to go find her."

"What? Roxanne, are you sleepwalking? Damn it, woman, you can't be serious."

"I have to, Nik. I just have to. I can't bear to sit here any longer doing nothing."

"If you're serious about this, I'm coming with you."

"No, I have to do this by myself. If the dream comes true, I don't want you anywhere near where I'm going," Rox said. "I'll talk to you when I get back."

"Rox, don't do this. If you think you know where she is, call the authorities," Nikki urged.

"That's just it. I don't know for sure. I'll contact the authorities when I have more information." Rox was getting frantic. "I have to go, don't you see?"

"There's no talking you out of this, is there?" Nikki asked, her voice filled with resignation.

"No, there isn't. I have to do this, Nik. Please try to understand."

"All right, but please be careful. And if there's anything I can do, please, *please* contact me. Promise me, Rox."

"Okay, I promise. Thank you, Nikki. I love you."

"I love you too, Rox. Be careful. Call me the moment you find out anything, okay?"

"I will, Nik. I'll talk to you later. Bye."

Rox powered up her computer and logged onto the Internet.

"Okay... Bogotá, Colombia." Rox selected the "Travel" icon on the search engine. Ten minutes later, she was booked on the first available flight to Bogotá, scheduled to leave Maine at ten the next morning.

* * *

"Oh, my God," Cass moaned as she tried to move. Her head hurt like hell and she was covered in sweat and grime. She was lying on a dirt floor, complete darkness surrounding her except for a sliver of moon dimly visible through a barred window. *Where the hell am I?*

Just then a door opened, the light from beyond it momentarily blinding her. Then it was dark again and she lay still, listening to the noises that were coming from the direction of the door. It sounded like someone feeling their way around in the darkness. She tried to sit up, but fell back to the dirt as waves of pain spread through her head, causing her to moan again.

"Hello?" a woman's voice called softly. "Is anyone there?"

There's someone in here with me, Cass thought as she failed for the third time to bring herself into a sitting position. Again a soft, painful moan erupted from her throat.

Before she knew what was happening, Cass felt something touch her face, causing her to jump and cry out.

"Shh… it's okay. I won't hurt you," a voice said softly.

After a few moments of painful maneuvering, Cass's cellmate managed to lift her head and place it on her lap. She brushed the bangs out of Cass's eyes and seemed to be looking down at her. Through the haze, Cass realized the woman was Rox. *Rox!* she thought, unable to find her voice through the pain. For a long time, Rox held her, speaking words of encouragement and promising not to leave her.

"What have they done to you, my love?" she heard Rox say.

Cass tried to reply, but her throat was constricted with dryness.

"I love you," Rox said.

A feeling of euphoria washed over Cass as she slipped away into the darkness once more.

"No!" Cass screamed, bolting upright and grabbing her head in an attempt to stem the nausea caused by her sudden movement. *Was Rox really here, or was it just a dream?*

"Oh, God, I'm going to be sick." Cass crawled into a corner and emptied the meager contents of her stomach onto the dirt floor. Dizzy and weak, she crawled back to where she had been lying and leaned against the wall. Dropping her head into her hands, she thought about the dream. *Rox, why do I keep seeing you in my dreams?*

Her attention then turned to her surroundings, and she realized she was in some sort of cell. "I am in deep shit."

No kidding, Dick Tracy, Enforcer replied sarcastically.

No comments from the peanut gallery, if you don't mind.

Bullshit! E. exclaimed. *You get some notion in your head to save the world from drug lords, then we're knocked out and confined to these wonderful guest accommodations, and* then *you leave a lovely pile of puke in the corner to stink up the place even worse than it already smells! We'll probably die in this hellhole, and you want me to shut up? I don't think so!*

I'll figure out how to get us out of this. Her hopes faltered as she looked around. *Don't ask me how, but I will.*

Before Enforcer could reply, the cell door banged open and slammed into the wall behind it. Jason strutted into the room like a bantam rooster into a chicken coop.

"Well, well, well," he said, walking around Cass, his thumbs hooked into the suspenders holding up his pants. "You've finally decided to rejoin the land of the living. Sorry for the bump on the head, but I had to keep this location secret. What better way to do that than for you to be unconscious while you made the trip?" Jason laughed at his own humor. "No hard feelings?" He squatted down in front of Cass and extended his hand.

Don't do it, Cass, Enforcer warned.

Cass looked at Jason's hand and looked away.

Jason rose to his full height and sighed. "Have it your way, then. I see our little liaison is over. That's a major mistake on your part, Cass. It would have been so much easier on you if you had continued to cooperate." He stepped back. "Now I'm afraid we'll have to make sure you understand that I'm in charge and there's nothing you can do about it." He nodded to the armed man who had come into the room behind him.

The man handed his machine gun to Jason and grabbed Cass's shirt. He hauled her to her feet, slammed her against the wall and punched her in the stomach. He then proceeded to beat her senseless. When he dropped her, Cass lay once more in a boneless heap on the floor, blood trickling from her mouth and nose.

After the thug retrieved his machine gun and went back to the door, Jason squatted down in front of Cass. "There's more where that came from if you won't go along with us, Cass. We need you to fly the drugs out. Be a good girl and do what you're told and you just might make it out of this little adventure alive. Pleasant dreams." He stood and left the room.

Cass, I hope you invested in a cemetery plot, 'cause I think we're going to need it.

Eat shit and die, E., Cass replied, and then passed out.

Chapter 35

Rox set her alarm for six, but got up about an hour before it went off. She hadn't been able to get back to sleep after her terrible dream. After a quick shower, she dressed in cargo shorts, t-shirt, ankle socks and sturdy hiking boots. The next half hour was spent packing for her trip to South America. Since she had no coherent idea of what situations she might encounter, she just grabbed a duffel bag and threw in a few light tops and shorts, several changes of underclothes and her passport—by the grace of God, current from her trip abroad to promote her last book.

With about an hour to spare before she had to leave for the airport, Rox fired up her computer. She wanted a copy of Cass's picture, which she would show to the local citizens in hopes that someone would recognize her. "Now, where did I store that file?" Rox searched through the picture folder on her hard drive. "Ah, there it is!" she said as the photograph of Cass and Brian was displayed on the screen. "Thank God I didn't delete it." She printed the picture, tucked it inside a book to protect it, and added that to the contents of her bag.

Just after ten a.m., Rox was chewing nervously on a fingernail as she looked through the small porthole window at the ground crew directing the plane out of the gate and toward the runway. *At least we're on time.* She tugged on her seatbelt and pressed her head back against the cushion. She felt as through someone had punched her in the stomach. Folding her arms across her midsection, Rox took a deep breath and sighed. *It's going to be a long flight.*

* * *

Cass slowly got to her knees, trying not to jar her head and start another round of dry heaves. She had tried to stand just an hour earlier and ended up on her face, retching uncontrollably. Her head was pounding, her vision was blurred, and every muscle in her body ached from the beating she'd received a few hours earlier.

At last, she managed to prop herself up against the wall and take stock of the damage. She knew that her swollen nose, undoubtedly blackened eyes and split lip must make her look like a boxer on the losing end of a fight. A shaky hand determined that her hair was in a state of wild disarray and peppered with bits of straw, but there were no new lumps on her skull. Moving carefully, she checked her arms, legs and hands. *No broken bones.* She grimaced as she touched her face. *Except maybe my nose.* She could already feel a bruise forming on her midsection, where the machine-gun-toting gorilla had first struck her.

How the hell am I going to get out of this?

The door swung open and a petite young girl slipped quietly into the cell, carrying a tray. She looked no older than fifteen or sixteen. She had large, dark eyes and skin the color of coffee with cream. Her face was framed by a mane of long, curly black locks. She approached Cass cautiously and placed the tray on the floor. It held a bowl of soup and a roll.

As she started to leave, Cass tried to detain her. "Wait!"

The young girl stopped, but kept her back to Cass, apparently afraid of repercussions if she were caught talking to the prisoner.

"Please, come back," Cass asked, reaching one hand toward the girl. "I won't hurt you, I promise."

When the girl looked back at Cass, her face reflected her confusion. Cass restated her plea in Spanish. *"Por favor, vuelve aquí. No voy a hacerte daño... te lo prometo."*

The girl turned and slowly walked back into the room, her eyes shifting between Cass and the door. When she reached Cass, she bent down next to the tray and started fussing with the food as if to make the guard believe she had a reason to stay.

Cass caught on immediately, and began speaking in a low tone. *"¿Por favor, dónde estoy? Necesito irme de aquí y encontrar mi avión. ¿Me puedes ayudar?"* she pleaded. ("Please, where am I? I need to get out of here, and I need to find my plane. Can you help me?")

The young girl raised her eyes to meet Cass's gaze. There was fear in the girl's eyes, but Cass thought she was not afraid of her, but of the situation. She also realized the girl was struggling with the question of whether or not to help her escape. Cass held her gaze as she waited for an answer, but none was forthcoming.

A voice called from the other side of the door and a frightened look flashed across the girl's face. She straightened up and darted out of the room, giving Cass a sympathetic look as she went.

The cell door was slammed shut after the girl with a loud clang. The unkempt guard on the other side spat tobacco on the floor and grinned through the opening in the door, exposing stained, decaying teeth.

"Comes, gringa. Nada más hasta la cena," he said, chuckling as he walked away. ("Eat, woman. No more until dinner.")

Cass looked at the soup and roll that had been left for her and pushed them away, not wanting to risk trying to keep the food down on a queasy stomach.

Cass paced back and forth across her cell, trying to come up with an escape plan. She had inspected every square inch of the room, looking for weak spots—a loose bar on the window, a loose brick in the outside wall, anything to give her hope. Several hours of exploration later, she came to the conclusion that the only way out was through the door, which was guarded.

She'd had no contact with anyone since the girl had left that morning. The guard was ignoring her, though she kept asking him where she was. Jason hadn't shown up, either. *Shit! How long is he going to keep me in this hellhole?*

As if in answer, the key clinked in the lock and the door swung open. Jason entered the cell and gestured to the guard to lock the door behind him. He carried a gun into the cell with him, which he kept trained on her.

"Well, Cass, have you had enough time to think over your predicament? I'd rather not force you to fly the plane out, but if necessary, I will. It's for your own good, you know. If you were smart, you'd change your mind and do whatever you could to see that the goods are delivered quickly and safely."

Cass looked at the man with disgust. "And just where will these drugs end up, Jason, in some schoolyard?" she asked pointedly as she crossed her arms over her chest.

"What happens to the drugs after I deliver them is no concern of mine," he said. "Once I make the drop, I wash my hands of the whole mess."

"You make me sick," Cass sneered. She walked to the far corner of the cell and looked out the barred window, her back turned to the armed man.

"What am I going to do with you?" Jason asked, shaking his head. "You *will* fly the plane out, you know. One way or another, you'll fly it out. It's up to you how uncomfortable you want to be while you're doing it."

Still looking out the window, she replied, "I won't help you destroy innocent lives, especially the lives of children."

"Then I guess it'll be your life that's lost." He cracked her across the back of the head with the pistol and she fell to the floor of the cell, unconscious.

* * *

By the time the plane landed in Bogotá, eight hours after she had left Maine, Rox was exhausted. The one-hour layover in Miami hadn't eased her foul mood, nor had the noisy little brat who'd been in the seat in front of her during her connecting flight to Bogotá. She was ready to spit nails by the time she finally collected her bag and headed for the exit.

The blazing sun outside was a stark contrast to the weather she had left behind in Maine, and Rox sweated her way through finding a taxi and then a hotel. A short time later, light-headed from the altitude, she was sitting on the bed considering a plan to find Cass.

"I guess I should start with the local police." She left the hotel and hailed a white taxicab. When the driver hopped out to open her door, she asked, "Do you speak English?"

"*Sí, Señorita.* Good English."

Rox smiled. "Take me to the police station, please."

"You have trouble?"

"I'm looking for a friend."

"Okay, *sí,* right away."

It was a short drive. Rox paid the driver and entered the squat stone building. She approached the reception desk and waited until the clerk looked up. "I'd like to speak with the Chief of Police, please." The officers at the front desk gave her disinterested glances, so she assumed that he didn't know much English. Frustrated, Rox paced back and forth, wracking her brain to figure out how to make them understand.

Finally, she had an idea. She went to the desk and said two words: "Carlos Santonio." Within seconds, the desk officer and another nearby drew their guns, backed her up against the wall and frisked her for weapons. Then they escorted her unceremoniously to a holding cell, threw her inside and locked the door behind her.

"Hey, let me out of here!" she yelled through the bars as the police officers walked away. "Damn it! I said let me out of here!"

Furious at being treated like a criminal, Rox paced for several minutes until an officious looking man in a business suit approached her cell. "Good afternoon, *Señorita.* I am Chief of Police Juan Peña."

"Thank God!" Rox exclaimed. "There's been some kind of mistake. I haven't done anything wrong. Your men threw me in here for no reason."

"Not entirely without reason, *Señorita,* " the police chief replied. "It appears that you wish to claim connections to the drug lord, Carlos Santonio, no?"

"Yes... I mean, no! I mean, yes, I mentioned him to your officers, but that doesn't mean I'm involved with him. Señor Peña, I've done nothing wrong. I'm here looking for information—"

"Just what kind of information, may I ask?"

"Information about a plane that was hijacked in San Diego yesterday. I need—"

"So, you are connected to the hijacking? Are you the contact, the middle man, so to speak? Being involved in drugs is a serious crime, Miss...?"

"Ward. My name is Roxanne Ward, and no, I'm not connected to the hijacking. And I've never done drugs." Rox was frustrated that she couldn't get her point across. "Damn it! I had nothing to do with the hijacking. I'm looking for Cassidy Conway. She was piloting the plane."

Police Chief Peña's eyes narrowed. *"Señorita* Conway? That is very interesting." He started to pace, then he stopped and looked at Rox. "You know your government believes she is in on the hijacking, don't you?"

"I know they think it is a possibility," Rox corrected. "But it's not true."

"I see," said Peña, resuming his pacing. At length, he stopped directly in front of her. "Well, Miss Ward, we will have to investigate your story before we can release you. It is very important that we cooperate with the U.S. government in anything to do with drug dealers."

"I'm *not* a drug dealer!" Rox exclaimed, hands on her hips.

"We shall see, Miss Ward. In the meantime, please make yourself comfortable. It will take a while to check out your story." He walked away from the cell.

Rox was beside herself. "I... I..." she stammered, unable to voice her frustration. "May I at least make a phone call while I wait?" she called after him.

Peña stopped and looked back. "One call." He motioned to a uniformed officer, who came and unlocked the door. "This way."

Rox followed Chief Peña down the hall to a small room containing a table, two chairs, and a telephone. The door was left ajar and a guard posted while she made her call.

"Nikki, please be there," she said muttered as she charged the call to her home number.

After several rings, the phone was answered with a groggy, "Hello?"

"Jerri, is that you? Jerri, is Nikki home?" Rox asked.

"Rox? What time is it?" Jerri asked sleepily.

Rox glanced at her watch, "It's almost nine-thirty your time. Jerri, I'm in trouble. Is Nikki home?"

When the words registered, Jerri sat bolt upright in bed. "No. She's gone to the movies with her mother and sister. What do you mean you're in trouble, Rox? Talk to me."

"I'm in Bogotá, Jer—"

"Whoa, whoa, whoa! Wait a minute, Bogotá? As in Colombia?" asked the dazed paramedic.

"Yes. Look, I'm in jail and I really need—"

"Jail! Roxanne, what the fuck are you doing in jail?"

"Damn it, stop interrupting and listen to me! I came here looking for Cass. I mentioned a drug lord's name and was immediately arrested. Now they think I'm involved in the skyjacking and drug dealing. It's such a mess!"

"Okay, okay, calm down," Jerri said, running her hand through her hair. "What do you need me to do?"

"Call my lawyer for me. I don't have her number or I'd have made the call myself. Her name is Jeanette Campbell, and she's in the book. She needs to call the Chief of Police here in Bogotá. His name is Juan Peña. He's got to understand that I'm *not* a drug dealer," Rox said, desperation creeping into her voice.

"All right, I'll take care of it. Honey, please be careful. I want you to come straight home as soon as they release you, okay?"

"No, Jer. I came here to find Cass. I know she's here somewhere, and I'm not leaving until I find her. Didn't Nikki tell you where I was?"

"To tell you the truth, Nik and I haven't spent a waking moment together since I went to work yesterday morning," Jerri said. "This damned schedule keeps us apart too much. But never mind about that. Rox, please be careful."

"I will. Thanks so much for making the call, Jerri. I'll call again later to let you know how things are going," she said. "Kiss Nikki for me, okay?"

"Okay, Rox. I'll call your lawyer right away, and I'll talk to you soon."

As soon as she hung up, Rox was escorted back to her cell.

* * *

Cass woke to feel her head resting in someone's lap, and thought she was dreaming about Rox again. "Rox?" she whispered as she opened her eyes, but then saw the slender, brown-eyed girl who had brought her food earlier that day.

Cass smiled, trying to put the girl at ease. *"Hola."* ("Hi.")

The girl smiled back and ran a cool, damp cloth over Cass's forehead.

"Gracias. ¿Cómo te llamas?" ("Thank you. What is your name?")

"Ana."

"Gracias, Ana," Cass said again. *"¿Pero, dónde estamos?"* ("Thank you, Ana. But, where are we?")

The girl leaned in close. *"No permiten decir. Me golpearían si supieran que he hablado,"* she said fearfully. ("I am not allowed to say. They would beat me if they knew I told you.")

Cass nodded, still hopeful that she would be able to win the girl's trust.

A gruff voice came from the doorway. *"¡Ana! Bastante. Esa es una prisionera, no es una huésped mimada. Salga de ahí ahora mismo."* ("Ana! Enough. She is a prisoner, not a pampered guest. Come out of there at once.")

Ana scurried to her feet. Looking back at Cass, she said, *"Te he traido algo para cenar. Es buena comida. Lo prepare yo misma."* ("I have brought you some dinner. It is good food. I made it myself.") Then she was gone.

Cass watched the girl leave and then dug into the food hungrily. She hadn't eaten her soup and roll earlier, so she was famished. It was indeed good food, and she ate every bit of it. With her stomach satisfied, she settled herself back against the wall. Her head was pounding, so she closed her eyes and tried to will the pain away.

"Have you changed your mind about cooperating?" said Jason, standing behind the safety of the barred door.

Cass could see his silhouette through the bars. "I need something for this headache," she said. "And I need to use the bathroom." She closed her eyes again.

The heavy door creaked open and there was a moment's silence before she heard an object drop to the floor and then the door closing again.

"There's your bathroom." Jason chuckled, pointing at the bucket he'd just thrown into the room. "As for the headache, live with it. It's your own fault. All you had to do was cooperate, Cass. Expect to be in pain until you do." With that, he was gone.

* * *

Midnight found Rox still pacing back and forth in her cell. *What's taking my lawyer so long? Cass, please be all right. I need you. I love you. If anyone is listening up there, please keep her safe.* Somewhere around two in the morning, Rox gave up and lay down on the thin mattress on the floor in the corner of the room. Exhausted, she was soon fast asleep.

* * *

Cass's eyes drifted closed, then her chin dropped to her chest, snapping her awake. Shaking her head, she repositioned herself against the wall, willing herself to stay awake. Since she couldn't do anything about her immediate predicament, she turned her thoughts to a more pleasant subject. *Rox, I love you. I will make it through this hell. I have to; I need to see you again. I need to touch you.*

She struggled to her feet and began to pace, fatigue and pain making her stumble in the dim light. Judging by the position of the moon, she guessed that it was after midnight. When it occurred to her tired brain that she might find refuge in sleep, Cass curled up on the straw mattress in the corner of the room and slept.

Chapter 36

Early the next morning, Rox was awakened by the sound of a key turning in the lock on her cell door.

"Good morning, *Señorita,*" Chief Peña said cheerfully. "You are being released."

"I am?" asked Rox, still groggy from sleep.

"Yes. You should have told me last night that you were here doing research on your next book. I am a big fan of yours, *Señorita.* I have read all about your aliens. Miss Campbell called me early this morning and let me in on your secret research. Tell me, *Señorita* Ward, will there be a police chief in your next book?"

It took a moment, but Rox finally caught on to what he was saying. *Thank you, Jeanette!* "Er... as a matter of fact, yes. You see, my next book will be about aliens landing in South America, and..."

Rox spent the next few minutes sketching the plot of her "new" book—a heroic South American police chief saves the world from invading aliens. By the time she left the police station, she had been fully exonerated and had received a personal dinner invitation from the chief.

* * *

When Cass awoke the next morning, her headache was back in full force. She sat up on the straw bed, dropped her head into her hands and moaned.

You know, the last time you woke up with a headache like this, you got drunk the night before, Enforcer pointed out.

Who *got drunk the night before?*

Well, okay, it was me. Are you happy now?

What I wouldn't give if this truly *was a hangover,* Cass replied.

Amen to that. What are we going to do?

I don't know, E. This place is just too well guarded. We need some help. If I could only get that little peasant girl—

301

Don't you think she's a little young for you, Cass?

Oh, for Christ's sake, E. I wasn't talking about getting her into bed. All I want is some help. Sheesh.

All right, all right. I'm sorry. I'm under a lot of stress here. Give me a break, Enforcer said defensively.

Okay, where do you want it—your neck, your leg?

Before Enforcer could respond, the door to the cell opened to admit Ana, who was carrying a breakfast tray.

"Buenos días, Señorita," she said, placing the tray on the bed next to Cass. ("Good Morning, Miss.")

Cass smiled. *"Por favor, quédate conmigo un rato,"* she asked, patting the mattress beside her. ("Please, sit with me a while.")

Ana looked nervously toward the door, then reluctantly sat on the edge of Cass's bed while she ate.

"Tienes ojos muy hermosos," Ana murmured. *"Están tan azúles."* ("You have beautiful eyes. They are so blue.")

Cass smiled again, trying to make the girl comfortable. *"Gracias,"* she said. Then she looked Ana directly in the eyes. *"Ana, necesíto tu ayuda. Me estan forzando a volar drogas muy hermosos país. Necesíto escaparme de aquí."* ("Ana, I need your help. I am being forced to fly drugs out of this country. I need to escape.")

Ana knotted her hands in her lap. Tears filled her eyes as she replied, *"Me matarán y mi familia si te ayudo. No se que hacer."* ("They will kill me and my family if I help you. I don't know what to do.")

Cass reached over and put her larger hand on top of the girl's. *"Entiendo, Ana. Tienes que proteger a tu familia. Gracias de todas maneras."* ("I understand, Ana. You must protect your family. Thank you anyway.")

"Ana, apurate, muchacha. El jefe quiere que vallas al mercado," the guard's voice boomed from the doorway, startling both women. ("Ana, be quick in there, girl. The boss wants you to go to the market.")

Ana rose to her feet and looked at Cass, sadness and regret filling her eyes. *"Lo siento,"* she whispered. ("I am sorry.")

* * *

Her freedom regained, Rox wasted no more time. She went directly back to her hotel, showered, changed her clothes and then hit the streets armed with Cass's picture. It was all too clear that she would get no help from the police department, so she would have to find Cass by herself. For the next four hours, Rox walked the streets of Bogotá showing the picture to hundreds of people. At least half of them seemed to have no idea of what she was talking about. The heat was unrelenting, and she was getting a headache from the thin air.

She entered the public marketplace thoroughly frustrated by her lack of success, but determined to persevere, and began showing the picture around again. Time after time, she received confused looks or negative responses. On the verge of giving up in exhaustion, she stopped a beautiful young girl with large brown eyes and curly black hair who was choosing fresh produce at a vegetable vendor's stall.

"Excuse me, miss, but have you seen this woman?" Rox asked, handing the picture of Cass to the girl.

The girl looked questioningly at Rox, obviously not understanding what the woman was saying. Then she glanced at the picture and promptly dropped her market basket, scattering its contents on the ground.

Rox knew she had hit pay dirt. "Here, let me help you," she said, gathering some of the spilled merchandise.

The girl was trembling as she accepted the basket back from Rox. *"Gracias, gracias,"* she said nervously, and turned to flee.

Rox grabbed her arm before she could escape. "Please wait. You have seen her, haven't you? You know where she is."

A spate of emotions flitted across the girl's face as her eyes locked with Rox's.

"Please, I love her," Rox pleaded, placing her hands over her heart in a gesture that she hoped would transcend language. "I need to find her."

Even though the girl didn't seem to comprehend Rox's words, she must have understood the love and hope in her eyes. She handed back the picture and raised her eyes to meet Rox's tear-filled ones. She nodded, then took Rox's hand and led her through a network of alleys. They arrived at a residence that was little more than a hovel, and entered. After placing her basket on the table, the girl turned to Rox and took the picture of Cass out of her hand. She looked at it closely, then turned to stare deeply into Rox's eyes. Rox held her gaze, her own eyes filled with desperation and determination.

The girl motioned for Rox to wait while she went into an adjacent room, from which she returned a few minutes later with a frail old man whom she settled in the chair opposite Rox.

"Abuelo, esta mujer necesita nuestra ayuda. Tiene a su amiga detenida en ese el complejo. La estan forzándo a transportar drogas fuera del país," the girl said to the old man as he listened intently. ("Grandfather, this woman needs our help. Her friend is being held in the compound. She is being forced to transport drugs out of the country.")

The old man nodded, a solemn look on his face.

"Al fin, podremos vengar la muerte de Pedro si ayudamos a su amiga. Por favor, habla por mi." ("We can finally avenge Pedro's death if we help her friend. Please talk for me.")

The old man looked intently at Rox, then spoke. "I will help. I will avenge Pedro's death."

Rox was thrilled that the man spoke English. Finally, she was getting somewhere! *"Señor,* please, my name is Roxanne Ward. I need to find my friend. I fear she is being held against her will. I must find her."

The old man turned to the girl and translated Rox's words. The girl responded, *"La mujer de quien ella habla es prisionera de Carlos Santonio. La llevare allí, pero será peligroso."* ("The woman she speaks of is a prisoner of Carlos Santonio. I will take her there, but it will be dangerous.")

"Señorita Ward, my granddaughter, Ana, says she knows where your friend is, and that she will take you there. It will be dangerous. These are evil men. They murdered my ten-year-old grandson, Pedro, when he wandered onto their property on his way home from school. He was an innocent child. We will have our revenge and you will have your friend," he said, tears welling in his eyes.

Rox reached forward and grasped the man's hands. "Thank you," she said, her own tears flowing as freely as the old man's. "When do we leave?"

The old man turned to Ana and translated Rox's question.

"Al anochecer," said the girl. *"Entonces será menos peligroso."*

"My granddaughter says you must leave after dark. It will be safer then," the old man repeated. "It gets dark very early this time of year, so we don't have much time. Please, you must join us for a meal while we wait and plan."

* * *

Cass felt like crawling out of her skin. She hated being confined, especially in small places. After Ana left that morning, she spent most of the day exercising and going through Tae Kwon Do drills. There was no telling when an opportunity for escape might present itself, and she wanted to be ready. She was hampered slightly by her injuries, but the discipline and concentration techniques learned as a part of the martial art helped her overcome the pain and work through her routines. It was nearly dinnertime when she finished, and she was desperately in need of a shower.

"Very impressive," said Jason, standing at the cell door.

Cass had been so absorbed in her drill that she hadn't been aware of her audience. She turned sharply toward the door, her body glistening with sweat, her heart beating rapidly, her hands clenched into fists at her side. She glared at Jason, her hatred apparent.

Jason took a step backward, then recalled that the cell door stood between him and the dangerous-looking woman. His cocky air returned and he stepped up to the bars.

When he had locked her in the cell, he had been sure he could break her spirit and gain her cooperation. Now he wasn't so sure. So far, she had resisted all his efforts—threats and beatings. *If I just had something I could hold over her.*

They were loading the plane that evening. He could leave that night, but not without a pilot. *I need her help, but the bitch would rather die than fly that plane.* He decided he had nothing to lose by running a bluff.

"Hey," he called from the door, "you might like to know that the plane is being loaded. We'll fly out later tonight."

"You mean, *you'll* fly out tonight. I'm not going, Jason."

"No, you're going to fly it out. There aren't any other pilots around here. Well, none that are experienced enough to fly a large jet and can be bought."

"I will not help you break the law."

"Don't be so sure of that," he said. "I didn't want it to come to this, but I've got something of yours that you'll never see again if you don't cooperate tomorrow."

Cass gasped, and her head snapped around toward the door. "Roxanne?"

Yes! What a stroke of luck. Jason, you're a genius. With calm he wasn't feeling, he grinned. "Yes, Roxanne. And if you don't fly that plane out of here tomorrow morning, she's a dead woman. Do you understand me?"

Cass gave him a venomous look. "If you hurt her, I'll kill you!"

Jason laughed and walked away, calling over his shoulder, "See you in the morning, Cass. Get some sleep; it'll be a long flight."

She dropped heavily onto the straw mattress, let her shoulders slump forward, and cradled her head in her hands. He had her, and they both knew it.

* * *

After dinner, the three of them discussed rescue strategies. Through her grandfather, Ana explained the layout of the compound and described the main residence as well as the outbuilding where Cass was being held. Rox insisted that under no circumstances were the girl and old man to put themselves in danger. Not any more than they already were, at least. Darkness fell, and it was time to leave.

Keeping to the back roads and shadows, Ana led Rox through the countryside until they came to the heavily-guarded, fenced compound. Ana knew each guard's position, so she and Rox were able to slip by undetected. Inside, they made their way to a cluster of buildings at the end of the long driveway. As they approached the main building, Ana went ahead. She walked up the main steps and into the house just as she had done countless times before.

Once Ana was inside, Rox crossed the lawn and approached the outbuilding. It was too heavily guarded. She would never be able to slip by unnoticed. So, she did the next best thing: she walked right up to a guard and tapped him on the shoulder. "Excuse me, but I seem to be lost."

The guard whipped around and leveled his machine gun at her chest. He yelled something, and other guards rushed up to secure the intruder. A few uncomfortable minutes later, Rox was face to face with a man who introduced himself as Carlos Santonio.

"So, my dear, would you mind telling me who you are, and what you are doing on my property?" He poured brandy into a snifter.

"I'm here to do some research on a book. I'm Roxanne Ward, and I write—"

"Science fiction. Yes, I've read your books. Very charming." Santonio sipped his drink. "But what has that got to do with me?"

Rox went into writer mode, wringing her hands and looking around nervously. "The basis for the book is a group of futuristic teenagers who find a stash of drugs that were hidden by a well-known drug lord in the twenty-first century. The story line centers on the chaos caused by their discovery."

"Let me guess," Santonio said. "I get the honor of being the famous drug lord."

"Why, yes," Rox confirmed. "You're a very smart man," she added sweetly.

"And you are a very stupid woman," returned the drug lord. "Do you really think I will let you live, now that you know the location of my home?"

Rox hadn't anticipated this outcome, and it occurred to her that she should have at least called Nikki and told her where she was going.

"Throw her in with the other American," Santonio told the guards. "We'll get rid of them both at the same time."

* * *

Cass was in a state of despair. *I've got no choice. For Rox's sake, I have to fly the plane out.*

You know they're going to kill her anyway. Along with us, I might add, Enforcer said.

Always the optimist, aren't you, E.? Damn it, there's got to be a way to stop this.

"*Bien, grilla. Mete el culo aqui dentro.*" said a gruff voice from the doorway. ("All right, bitch. Get your ass in there.")

Cass looked up as the door opened and a person came sprawling through onto the floor. The door slammed shut again, leaving them in silence.

"Cass?" asked a small voice.

"Rox? Rox!" Cass jumped up from the mattress and bolted to the figure on the floor. "Rox, baby, is that really you?" She fell to her knees and took the smaller woman into her arms.

"Cass! Oh, my God, Cass, are you all right?" Rox hugged Cass back as tightly as she could.

For a few minutes, the two women just held each other close. Tears flowed freely as each made certain the other was whole and relatively unharmed.

Sitting back on her heels, Cass took Rox's face in her hands. "Honey, what are you doing here?" She tried to see Rox more clearly in the semi-darkness.

"I came to find you. I had a dream. You were injured, and we were in a cell, just like this one. It was horrible," Rox rambled.

"Shh. It's okay. I had the same dream, sweetheart. What does it mean, do you think?"

"It means we belong together. It means we're destined to spend many lifetimes together. Cass, it means I love you." Rox looked at Cass through tear-filled eyes. "I love you with all my heart and soul. I love you with everything that I am. I'm sorry it took me so long to see it."

In that moment, Cass's world changed forever. Nothing else mattered except the beautiful woman she held in her arms. Letting her forehead rest against Rox's, she whispered, "You are my life. I will devote the rest of my days to loving you and making you as happy as you've made me today." She lowered her mouth and captured Rox's lips in a tender kiss.

Rox was breathless, unable to fill her lungs as intense waves of emotion and desire overwhelmed her. She had never felt so much from a mere kiss. Convinced then that what she was feeling for Cass was wonderful and good, she knew that she wanted to spend the rest of her life loving this woman.

Cass rose and led Rox to the straw mattress in the corner of the room. "Not exactly what I'd imagined for the first time I'd lie beside you, but at least we're together."

Bodies entwined, they lay whispering endearments and talking about the wonderful future they would share. Neither spoke of the very real possibility that they wouldn't have a future. Here and now, they had each other. For the moment, that was enough.

A short time later, they heard voices coming from the hallway. Cass propped herself on her elbow and motioned for Rox to listen.

"*¿A que debo este convite?*" one of the guards asked. ("To what do we owe this treat?")

"*El Señor Santonio quiere darte gracias por sus esfuerzos con los prisioneros,*" a familiar voice replied. ("Señor Santonio wishes to extend his thanks for your efforts with the prisoners.")

"That's Ana," Cass whispered.

"I know."

"What do you mean, you know? How do you know Ana?" Cass was amazed.

"It's a long story, my love, and I'll explain it on the way home. Right now, Ana is carrying out phase two of our plan." Even in the dim light, Rox could see Cass's confused expression, and she placed a gentle kiss on her lips. "I'll tell you everything later, sweetheart. She's giving them wine laced with sleeping pills."

Cass's eyebrows rose. "Sleeping pills? Phase two? Rox, what have you been up to?"

"Later, my love. Right now, we have to get ready to get out of here. Are you all packed?" she asked, joking.

Cass felt around, taking an inventory of her body parts. "Yep, everything I need is right here and ready to go."

"Good. It's only a matter of time, now." She pulled Cass back down onto the mattress and snuggled up close to her.

Cass was all too happy to accommodate this request, and she put her arms around Rox and held her tight.

Half an hour later, they heard two dull thumps. The guards had fallen onto the floor.

"Vengan, señoritas. Tenemos muy poco tiempo. ¡Tenemos que apurarnos!" Ana said through the door. ("Come, ladies. We have very little time. We must hurry!")

The sound of jingling keys was followed by the creak of the door as the portal to freedom swung open. Holding Rox's hand, Cass followed Ana through the hallways and into the open courtyard. Keeping to the perimeter, Ana led the two women into the woods beyond the compound and down a well-traveled path through the trees. As soon as they were out of sight of the buildings, Cass stopped.

"¿El avión está a fines de este sendero?" she asked. ("The plane is at the end of this path?")

When the girl nodded, Cass took her hand. *"Ana, quieres venir con nosotros? Si Santonio se entera de tu traición, el te mandará a matar."* ("Ana, do you want to come with us? If Santonio learns of your betrayal, he will have you killed.")

"No puedo. No puedo dejar mi abuelo. Estaremos bien, no se preocupen. Tenemos familia en el interior. Solamente sigan esta senda. El avión se encuentra sobre una milla en esta misma dirección." ("I cannot. I cannot leave grandfather. We will be all right, don't worry. We have family in the interior. Just follow this path. The plane is about a mile ahead.")

"Entiendo, y buena suerte a los dos. Yo nunca podré recompensarte por tu ayuda, pero gracias por..." she gestured to Rox and then toward the plane *"... todo. Debemos nuestras vidas a ti."* ("I understand, and good luck to you both. I can never repay you for your help, but thank you for everything. We owe you our lives.")

Rox gave Ana a hug and kissed her cheek. *"Gracias, Ana."*

Ana hugged her back. *"Es por Pedro..."* she said, then dipped her head shyly. *"Y por el amor."* ("For Pedro. And for love.")

Cass and Rox watched Ana slip into the safety of the trees, then continued down the path. They had just caught sight of the plane, about a hundred yards ahead of them, when they heard a burst of noise from the compound.

"I guess they know we're gone," Cass said with a wry grin. "Nice of them to announce it, though. Come on, we'd better run."

The camouflage had been removed from the plane, probably when it had been loaded earlier in the evening, and the engines were idling in preparation for takeoff. Unfortunately, it was also being guarded by two men armed with machine guns.

"Shit! How are we supposed to get past them?" Rox asked.

"You leave that to me," Cass replied, and she moved closer to the edge of the clearing.

Rox grabbed her arm. "Are you crazy? They have guns!" she hissed.

"Don't worry, I can do this." After a parting kiss, Cass circled around the clearing for a better line of approach. Sneaking up behind the first guard, she cleared her throat to get his attention, and then punched him as he turned around. Before he could aim his machine gun, her right foot struck him on the side of the head. He went down hard and lay motionless at her feet.

The other guard came running, only to be tripped by a tree branch Rox swung at his shins. He fell to his knees and she whacked him several times, much the same way Nikki had done to her college attacker years earlier. She didn't stop until he, too, lay motionless on the ground. Catching Cass's eye, Rox grinned.

Suddenly, a horde of armed thugs spilled into the clearing. Cass grabbed Rox's hand and pulled her up the makeshift ramp and into the plane. She kicked the ramp away and closed the door just as the *guerrillas* opened fire.

Cass threw herself into the pilot's seat and started flipping switches. "Rox!" she yelled. "Strap yourself into the seat beside me and hang on! We're in for a rough takeoff, and I just hope we have enough runway." She ducked reflexively as a burst of gunfire peppered the plane.

Rox screamed as the small window next to Cass was shattered by the spray of bullets.

"Hold on, Rox!" Cass engaged full throttle and the plane shuddered violently as it rolled over the rough terrain toward the trees at the edge of the clearing.

"We're going into the trees!" Rox shouted.

"Grab that wheel and pull!" Cass yelled, motioning Rox to pull back on the elevator control in front of her.

At the last moment, the plane rose from the ground, veering sharply into the sky and skimming the top of the trees. Once they were airborne and the plane had leveled out, Rox pried her fingers off the controls. With a huge smile on her face, she looked over at Cass and her exhilaration vanished. Cass was slumped in her seat. Her hair was flying in the wind coming through the shattered window, obscuring Rox's view.

Frantically, Rox unhooked her seatbelt and climbed out of the co-pilot's seat. She gathered the hair away from Cass's face, and her heart jumped when she saw the red stain on her shirt. She turned the pilot's face toward her and noted the pallor of her skin.

"Cass, talk to me. You're hurt. Tell me what to do," she pleaded.

"I've been hit... in the shoulder. You've got to stop the bleeding," Cass said weakly.

Willing herself not to panic, Rox went in search of bandages. After pawing around for a few minutes, she grabbed several white towels from the flight attendant's station. On her return to the cockpit, she found Cass struggling to reach the autopilot computer.

"What is it?" Rox knelt on the floor next to the injured woman.

"We need to set the autopilot for Miami. That's the shortest flight path to the U.S."

"Okay, talk me through this."

Rox followed instructions precisely as she programmed the autopilot for Florida. Immediately after that, she concentrated her efforts on staunching the flow of blood from Cass's shoulder. She packed the wound with the towels, then wrapped her belt around the improvised bandage and cinched it tightly, cringing with each moan that escaped Cass's lips during the process. "I'm sorry, my love," she kept repeating as she ministered to the wound. With the wound dressed, she brought washcloths from the bathroom and cleaned as much blood as she could from Cass's face, neck and arm.

Rox had never been so frightened in her life. She was thousands of feet in the air, in a plane full of illegal drugs, alone with an injured pilot with whom she was madly in love. If it wasn't for the fact that at any minute Cass might pass out and leave her to fly the plane by herself, she would have laughed.

She did her best to keep Cass lucid during the three-hour flight to Miami, but the pilot kept fading in and out of consciousness. About an hour into the flight, they radioed ahead to Miami to request emergency landing clearance and an ambulance. Miami Air Traffic Control stayed in constant touch with them throughout the flight, offering flight and weather information and medical advice.

Rox changed the bandages twice. The pile of bloodied towels was growing at an alarming rate. There was a serious possibility that Cass would die from loss of blood before they reached Miami. As they drew near, she could stay conscious for only a few minutes at a time.

Rox was scared to death. *There's no way in hell I can land this thing myself, and Cass is in no condition to do it, either.* As the airport came into view, she began to panic. She climbed out of her seat, grabbed Cass by the front of her shirt and shook her.

"Cass! Cass, honey, if you don't wake up, we're both going to die. Do you understand me? I can't land this plane! Cass, please wake up!"

Cass blinked up at her, head lolling as she struggled to remain conscious.

"Cass!" Rox shook her again, hard. "When I said I wanted to spend the rest of my life with you, I didn't mean the afterlife! Now, please wake up." No response. "I need you, Cass!" Rox shouted, directly into her face.

Blue eyes flew open, and Cass struggled into a sitting position and grasped the flight controls. "Buckle up. Might be... rough landing." She managed a half grin.

Rox smiled back as she strapped herself into her seat again. "You're good at this crash-landing thing, right?"

"Right," Cass replied, fighting to keep her eyes open. "Need you with me, Rox. Don't have the strength to do it alone." Her eyes were fixed on the runway.

"Just tell me what to do."

The atmosphere was tense as the plane drew nearer to the runway. Cass summarized landing procedures for Rox, including when to decelerate and when to reverse engine thrust to slow the plane once the wheels were on the ground.

Rox prayed that she wouldn't have to try and carry out the procedures alone.

As they began their final approach, Cass looked over at Rox. "We can do this. We have the rest of our lives together ahead of us."

"Together, Cass. I love you."

They hovered briefly above the blacktop before the wheels touched down. The plane jarred sharply and then fishtailed as the rubber hit the pavement. Cass was struggling not only with the controls, but with staying conscious through the landing. She was rapidly losing both battles.

"Reverse thrust," she said weakly, and Rox reached over and put the engines into reverse. Both women were thrown forward in their seats as the engines whined their protest at the sudden change in direction. The plane fishtailed again, nearly out of control.

"Oh, shit, oh, shit!" Rox yelled as she saw they were running out of pavement. "We're going to crash!"

"More reverse thrust," Cass directed.

Again, inertia threw them forward in their seats as the whole plane shuddered and slowed. They were losing momentum quickly, and so far, safely on the ground. Rox looked over at Cass for reassurance and found her crumpled over the controls, blood oozing from a wound in her forehead. Horrified, Rox realized she had hit her head on the control panel during their last maneuver.

Unable to tend to the injured woman until the plane had come to a complete stop, Rox was forced to look on helplessly. Finally, the plane came to rest, dangerously close to the end of the runway.

Rox leapt out of her seat and to Cass's side. When she pulled her upright, Cass's head slumped over onto her right shoulder. No amount of talking or coaxing would bring her around. Searching frantically for a pulse, Rox found none.

Chapter 37

Rox groped for Cass's wrist, becoming frantic when she was unable to find a pulse there, either. "You can't be dead, you just can't be," she sobbed, clinging to Cass and shaking her violently in a futile attempt to rouse her.

Seconds later, the door crashed open and an armed DEA agent burst into the cockpit. He trained his gun on Rox, who looked up at him and clung even more tightly to Cass. The agent looked at the uniformed pilot lying motionless in the arms of the fair-haired woman. "Is that Captain Conway?"

Rox nodded, then screamed at him as he reached out to touch Cass. "No! Don't touch her!"

A second agent entered the cockpit. "Lieutenant, we've checked the plane thoroughly. No sign of other passengers, sir."

The lieutenant's nod both acknowledged and dismissed the other man, and he turned his attention back to the two women. He reached for the microphone clipped to his shoulder. "This is Agent Parmer. Two occupants in the cockpit; request an ambulance immediately." Lieutenant Parmer then addressed Rox. "What is your name?"

Rox didn't answer. She held Cass's blood-streaked head in her lap and rocked the limp woman back and forth. "Come on, baby. Please wake up. I love you, Cass. I need you. Please wake up."

She heard sirens. Moments later, two white-coated paramedics came into the cockpit. Rox looked up at them. "Help her, please," she begged, and watched their faces carefully as they checked Cass's vital signs. The grave glances that passed between the two men gave Rox a sinking feeling of dread. *Cass, please don't leave me. I need you. Please come back to me.*

As one paramedic left the cockpit, the other spoke calmly to the distraught Rox. "My partner has gone to get the backboard. We need to evacuate Captain Conway from the plane. Do you understand?"

Rox tightened her grip on Cass. Tearful agony filled her voice. "Don't take her from me. I need her."

"What's your name?"

"Roxanne Ward."

The paramedic touched Rox lightly on the shoulder. "Roxanne, we need to take her to the hospital. You're not doing her any good by hindering us."

The second paramedic appeared in the doorway, the backboard in his hands.

Rox looked at the medic in the doorway, then threw herself over Cass. "No! I can't let her go."

The first paramedic stood and grasped Rox by the shoulders, pushing her backward as the second paramedic pried her hands away from Cass.

"No! No, don't touch her!" Rox screamed as she fought the two men. Lieutenant Parmer stepped forward to restrain her, and very soon the paramedics had strapped an unresponsive Cass to the backboard and carried her out to the waiting ambulance. Rox sat helplessly in the cockpit as she watched her soul being carried away.

Agent Parmer spoke to her. "You'll need to come with us, Miss Ward."

Rox's eyes were blank and unseeing, the pain of losing her love chasing all other thoughts from her mind.

He reached down and took Rox gently by the arm. "Come on. It's time to go."

She allowed the agent to lead her from the plane. As she stepped out, she saw that the aircraft was surrounded by police and FBI agents. She looked frantically for the ambulance, but it was already gone.

"Where have they taken the..." Rox bit her lip. "Where have they taken Cass?"

"Jackson Memorial Hospital."

Dazed, she shook her head. "I have to... I have to..." She began to cry.

"There's nothing you can do for her now," Parmer said. "But you might be able to help us. Will you come with me to police headquarters?"

Rox nodded. She accompanied Parmer to an unmarked black sedan and was whisked away to police headquarters in Miami, to be interrogated about the drug activity they had uncovered in Bogotá. For hours, the DEA grilled her for information, and she gave them all the details she could remember about Carlos Santonio and the location of his compound. She answered their questions in a dull monotone, the pain in her heart aching with unrelenting persistence. She was determined to clear Cass's name by providing the DEA with as much information as possible, so they could apprehend and punish the bastards who had taken from her the person she loved more than life itself.

After the debriefing, Agent Parmer approached Rox and put a hand on her shoulder. "Would you like a ride to the hospital? We're going to try to ask Captain Conway a few questions, and we'd be happy to give you a lift."

Confused, Rox looked at them. They were out of their minds. How could they interrogate a dead woman? "But... how? She's gone."

"The captain couldn't have gone anywhere, she was too badly..." Realizing what Rox had meant, Agent Parmer dropped to one knee in front of her and took her hand. "Miss Ward, I thought you knew—Captain Conway isn't dead. We just received word that she's out of surgery and has been moved to Intensive Care. She lost a lot of blood, and it was touch and go for a while, but she's very much alive."

"Alive?" Rox stared up at his face, afraid to believe, afraid it was just a cruel joke. "She's not...?" As he shook his head, joy flooded through her entire being. "Can we go now, right now? Lights and sirens?"

Agent Parmer smiled in understanding. "Absolutely."

Once at the hospital, Rox refused to leave Cass's side until the injured woman awoke. As she gradually regained consciousness, Cass looked at her through cerulean eyes filled with such love that it turned Rox's insides to mush.

"Hi," Cass whispered hoarsely.

Rox's tears fell onto Cass's cheeks as she leaned forward to place a delicate kiss on the dark-haired woman's lips.

"Welcome back, my love," Rox choked out. "Don't you ever do this to me again, do you understand?"

"Or else what?" Cass teased.

"Or else I might have to hurt you," Rox replied, smiling broadly through her tears and leaning in for another kiss.

* * *

It had been nearly two weeks since their dramatic escape from Bogotá. Cass had just checked out of Miami's Jackson Memorial Hospital, and now she and Rox were at the airport waiting to board flights that would take them to opposite ends of the country.

"I don't want to leave you," Rox whispered, and she wound her arms tightly around Cass's waist. Cass's good arm held her close, while the injured arm hung helplessly in a sling around her neck.

She touched the side of Rox's face and turned it upward until their eyes met. "Sweetheart, we've talked about this. I'm going to be tied up for a while. The rehab alone will take weeks, and the DEA is by no means through with me yet. And then there's the trial. Heaven knows how long that will take. You need to go home and finish your book. I'm sure your publisher is frantic."

"I don't care about the book, Cass. I need to be with you."

Cass's heart soared, but it was obvious that firmer measures were required. "I need to be with you, too. Believe me, love, I want nothing more than to be with you every minute of every day, but we both have loose ends to tie up before we can be together. I don't want anything hanging over our heads when we finally commit our lives to each other. Please, Rox, don't fight me on this."

Rox closed her eyes, letting a tear escape.

Cass saw the tear and kissed it away. "Please don't make this harder than it already is," she whispered. Rox nodded her compliance and rested her head over Cass's heart. Cass sighed deeply and closed her eyes, savoring the closeness.

Their loving embrace was broken by the sound of the P.A. system. "Now boarding, Flight 235 to Rockland, Maine."

Rox looked up and fear showed in her eyes. "Come back to me, Cass. Please."

Cass's eyes filled with tears. "I promise." She joined their lips for a tender kiss, then put her forehead against Rox's and whispered, "Now go, before I lose my resolve."

Rox nodded, then kissed Cass once more. "I love you, Cass."

"I love you too, Rox."

As she watched Rox disappear into the jetway, her heart broke.

* * *

On the flight back to Maine, Rox agonized over how to break the news of her newfound sexuality to her parents. Being in love with a woman required a whole new mindset. She had never realized how difficult it was to be "different." Never in her previous relationships had she had to think about her partner's gender before mentioning him to anyone. Never before had she had to worry about what people would think of her because she was with him. Falling in love with Cass gave her new respect for those who dared to follow their hearts, regardless of what others might think.

Cass, I love you with all my heart, and I've so longed for the kind of loving relationship Nikki and Jerri have, but I never guessed it would be this hard. I thought I'd find that love with a man. I was overwhelmed and terrified when I realized my "man" was a six-foot, dark-haired woman with drop-dead gorgeous blue eyes. Will I ever feel comfortable enough with our relationship for it to become second nature? Will I ever stop worrying what others will think?

Rox tortured herself, imagining all sorts of rejection from her family, friends and community. The only people she knew she could count on for support were Nikki and Jerri. She worried herself sick over what her parents would say, and spent the rest of the flight agonizing about her father dying with disappointment in his heart over his daughter's new lifestyle.

When she exited the plane in Rockland, Nikki was waiting for her. Rox flew into her friend's arms and cried uncontrollably as Nikki did her best to console her.

"Shh, it's okay. Everything will be all right." Nikki led a distraught Rox to the lounge and ordered coffee for them. While they waited, she put a hand over Rox's and waited patiently as she composed herself. "Feel like talking about it?"

"Nik, I'm scared. I love her so much. It totally destroyed me to get on that plane and leave her in Miami. I want so desperately for us to be together."

"But?" Nikki knew there had to be more behind Rox's emotional outburst.

A lapse in the conversation ensued as the waitress delivered their coffee.

Rox blew her nose. "Loving Cass is so complicated. How am I going to tell my parents? What will my publisher think? I'm so confused."

Nikki sighed as she saw the emotional pain in her friend's eyes. Clasping their fingers together, she squeezed them tightly. "Rox, what do *you* think? What do *you* want? This isn't about pleasing your parents or your publisher. This isn't about pleasing Jerri or me. It's about living your life to the fullest. It's about sharing your life with someone you love. It's about following your heart and knowing you are doing what is right for *you*. Honey, your parents love you. Trust them."

Rox inhaled deeply and tried her best to smile. "I'll try."

"Do you want me to go with you when you tell them?" Nikki offered.

Rox looked down into the dark liquid before her, as if the answer might lie in her cup. "As much as I would like to take you up on that, Nik, I'm afraid I need to deal with this one on my own. I'm not sure how they'll react, and I really don't want to make you—or them—any more uncomfortable than necessary. I love you dearly for offering, though."

"Just know that I'm here for you, Rox. You know you can call me any time and I'll be there in an instant, right?"

Rox stood at the foot of her parents' driveway and watched Nikki drive away. They had come here directly from the airport. She wanted to talk to her parents immediately, before she lost her nerve.

Before she even got to the door, her mother opened it and came to meet her on the landing with open arms. "Thank God you made it home safely! Come in, come in." She released Rox from the hug and linked arms with her. "I hope you thanked Nikki for us, too. I don't know what we would have thought if we'd only heard the news the way the media was telling it."

Rox nodded, and was enveloped in another tight embrace and then held at arm's length as her mother looked her over from head to toe.

"My baby, are you all right?"

Rox was overwhelmed with emotion. All she could do was cry and cling to the woman she had always depended on to fix scraped knees and broken hearts.

Her mother took her suitcase and directed her into the house. "Come, let's sit. We have a lot to talk about." She led the way to the couch, where they sat side by side.

Rox laid her head in her mother's lap, just as she had done when she was a child and needed consolation. Maternal fingers ran soothingly through her hair, brushing it back from her forehead as she cried out her sorrow. The sobbing subsided as Rox regained control of her tender emotions.

Dot Ward broke the silence. "Are you ready to tell me about it, sweetling?"

Rox almost began to cry again as her mother used one of the pet names from her childhood. *Will I always be your sweetling, Mama? No matter what?* She sat up and looked directly at her mother. "Mama, I have so much to tell you, there's so much you don't know, but I'm terrified of hurting you and Daddy."

"Don't you worry about your daddy," a deep voice said from behind her.

Rox turned around and saw her father standing in the doorway between the living room and the kitchen.

"Daddy!" She jumped up and ran to her frail father, who stood as tall and strong as his condition would allow.

Alden Ward brushed her fussing aside, then wrapped his arms around his daughter and hugged her. "Dumpling, there is nothing you could tell us that would change how much we love you."

I sure hope that's true, Daddy.

Rox helped her father to the couch, then began pacing the floor. Her parents waited quietly until she was ready to speak. She glanced at them nervously. "Mama, Daddy, there's much about my life with Chris that you don't know about, so much I've kept from you. Chris wasn't the kind of person you thought he was."

Rox paused, trying to decide how to describe the horror that her life had been. "There were times when he was abusive—both physically and emotionally. So many of the cancelled dinners, so many of the excuses for not coming to see you were to allow time for the bruises to fade."

"I knew it, Dot!" Alden said in a sudden burst of anger. "I knew something was behind that strange behavior. If I get my hands on that son of a bitch, I'll break his neck!" The excitement caused the elderly man to break into a fit of coughing.

"Daddy! Daddy, please calm down. Mama, please get him a glass of water." Rox sat beside her father and rubbed his back as he regained control of his breathing.

Alden looked into his daughter's face and tears filled his eyes. "Kitten, my one wish for you before I go is to see you happy. Nothing is more important to me now. Please tell me you're no longer with him."

Dot returned with the glass of water and handed it to Rox, then sat on the couch beside her husband and held his hand. "Thanks, Mama. Chris is out of my life now, Daddy. Here, drink this." Rox held the water to her father's lips. After a moment or two, he calmed down. She handed the glass to her mother and knelt on the floor in front of them.

For several moments, Rox sat back on her heels and contemplated her hands, folded in her lap, then took a deep breath and looked at her parents. "Mama, Daddy, you know I love you both very much and I would never intentionally do anything to hurt you, but I have something to tell you that I am so afraid will break your hearts."

Dot reached out to touch her daughter's cheek. "What is it, dear? You know you can tell us anything."

Rox met her mother's eyes and her brow furrowed as she struggled with the words she feared to speak. "I've met someone, and I've fallen deeply in love."

"And?" Dot noted the spark in her daughter's eyes.

Rox covered her face with both hands. "God! This is so hard!"

"Kitten, just say it. You've met someone new; so tell us all about it," Alden urged. "Please, just tell me this new person will treat you better than Chris did."

Rox looked at her father. "Daddy, I have never felt such intense, romantic love in my life."

He looked confused. "Then what's the problem?"

Rox shifted nervously. "Well, it's kind of an unconventional relationship, and I'm not sure you'll find it acceptable."

Dot Ward smiled at her husband and then leaned toward Rox. "Roxanne, honey, look at me." When she had her daughter's full attention, she said, "Sweetheart, do you love her?"

Rox's eyes flew open in shock. "How... how did you know?" How had her mother guessed she was in love with a woman?

"Well, I've heard you refer to Nikki and Jerri's relationship as 'unconventional.' I just assumed that's what you meant. So, do you love her?" Dot repeated.

"More important, does she love you?" added Alden.

Rox's eyes misted as she looked at her parents. "What I feel for her goes beyond love. She's all I can think about. She's my first thought when I awake and she fills my dreams at night. I've never felt so loved and so safe in my entire adult life. It's such an incredible feeling! Do I love her, Mama? Yes. I love her with everything that I am. Does she love me? Daddy, she loves me enough to have flown three thousand miles in one night just to save me from Chris. She's one reason Chris is now in jail on assault charges. She's prepared to change her entire life for me. We complete each other, Daddy. I've never been so sure of anything as I am of our love."

"Are you happy with her, Kitten?"

"Happier than I've ever been in my life, Daddy. I can't see a future without her."

Dot Ward rose and reached for her daughter's hands. She helped her to her feet, then enveloped her in a warm embrace. "Roxanne, you know all we want is your happiness. If this woman makes you happy, then you have our full support. It may not be the lifestyle we would have chosen for you, but you are your own woman and you need to live your life as you see fit. Just please don't stay in this relationship if things don't work out. Please don't let this develop into the same horror you must have lived through with Chris."

"Cass would never hurt me, Mama. I'm certain of it. She's the most wonderful, loving person I know—well, besides you and Daddy, that is," Rox chuckled.

"Cass? That's an unusual name."

"It's short for Cassidy, Mama. She's the airline pilot who was with me in Colombia."

"Well then, when do we get to meet this young woman who's made our daughter so happy?" Alden asked cheerily.

"Right after the DEA and the FBI are finished with her... and after she finishes the rehabilitation for the bullet wound in her shoulder." Rox cringed at the shocked expressions on her parents' faces.

"Time out!" her father exclaimed. "Maybe you should start from the beginning."

* * *

Cass sat in Angie's diner, pushing her food around her plate. Angie approached the table to refill her still-full coffee cup and took advantage of the opportunity to scold her favorite customer and surrogate daughter.

"Cass, why don't you just move to Maine and get it over with?"

"I can't do that just yet. There are too many roadblocks. The Feds told me to stay put until they've got what they need to nail Santonio and Jason Hayer, I've got to give my notice at the airline and sell my condo, and my physical therapy schedule goes well into next month. Damn it! This is driving me crazy."

Angie sat down. "Hon, I'm worried about you. You've been back for two weeks now and I haven't seen one smile on your face. You're not eating, and considering those dark circles under your eyes,

I'd guess you're not sleeping, either. Follow your heart, Cass. Go to her and be happy."

Cass looked into Angie's eyes and tried to hold back her tears. "I want to, Ang. I want to so badly it hurts, but I can't." She looked down at the table while tears trickled down her cheeks.

Angie reached across the table and took her by the chin. "Cassidy Conway, I'm only going to say this one more time—get your ass on a plane and go to her. Let the Feds know where you are. They can contact you just as easily in Maine as they can in California. As far as your job is concerned, you're on medical leave. Use that as your two weeks' notice. You can do your physical therapy in Maine; I'm sure they have fine doctors there. Oh, and don't worry about your condo. I'll sell it for you. There, the roadblocks are all gone. Now go to her."

A glimmer of hope appeared in Cass's eyes. "You make it all sound so easy."

"It *is* easy, honey. Just do it. Go to her, Cass. You belong together. Apart, you're dying."

* * *

Rox sat in front of her computer and tried to write an epilogue for her book. Given the circumstances, her publisher had been remarkably patient with her, but that patience was wearing thin. She was frustratingly close to completing the job. All she needed was an ending that tied the story together and provided closure for the main characters. Try as she might to concentrate on her work, her mind kept wandering to long, dark hair and cerulean eyes that took her breath away. The ache in her heart was impossible to ignore. *Cass, where are you now? What are you doing? I long to be with you. Please tell me it will be soon.*

Rox glanced at the clock and realized it was nearly five. *Damn. I've been sitting here for most of the day and all I have to show for it is half a page of notes. Aarrgghh!* Unable to focus on her work, Rox rose from her chair and carried her cup of tea out to the widow's walk. She stood at the railing and looked out over the ocean, comparing the color of the water to Cass's eyes. *Yeah, I've got it bad. Everything I see reminds me of her.*

Cass gazed out the window as the plane entered its final approach to the Rockland airport. The sight of the Atlantic spread out before her made her realize why Rox loved her home state so much.

From quaint little villages to historical lighthouses, there was a sense of history and serenity about the place that contrasted sharply with the hustle and bustle of San Jose. *I'm so looking forward to settling down here with you, Rox. Living our lives quietly and unobtrusively, being free to love and live at our own pace, and spending the rest of my life making you happy.*

Half an hour later, Cass was in the back seat of a taxi, on her way to 1163 Oceanview Terrace. Less than two miles from Rox's house, the taxi came to a complete stop. A long line of traffic stretched ahead of them.

Cass frowned. "What's the holdup?"

The taxi driver glanced into the back seat. "Construction. They're repaving all the roads between the airport and the ocean. Tourist traffic has caused a lot of problems with potholes." The taxi driver looked at his watch. "And it's also rush hour. Yep. Rush hour combined with construction—a taxi driver's nightmare."

"Any idea how long we'll be stuck here?"

"Hard to tell."

Cass tried to be patient. After fifteen minutes and about a hundred yards, she couldn't take it any longer. She handed the fare, along with a very generous tip, to the driver. "What's the fastest way to Oceanview Terrace?"

"Must be something special there for you to be in such a hurry," the man remarked.

I'm on my way home. "You have no idea. So, what's the fastest route by foot?"

"By foot, the fastest way to get there is along the beach." He pointed to the end of the side street where they were stalled. "The beach is at the end of this street. It's just a few blocks away. Take a left when you reach the sand and start walking. You should be there in no time."

"Do me a favor and deliver my bags to that address, okay? Just leave them on the front porch." Cass thanked the driver, then swung the door open and climbed out of the car.

She hadn't taken more than five steps in the sand before she realized she'd have to remove her shoes, otherwise the sand accumulating inside them would wear the skin right off her feet. She sat on a nearby log and removed her shoes and socks, then rolled up the legs of her jeans. She also took off her light denim jacket and tied it around her waist, then massaged the stiffness in her left shoulder.

Shortly afterward, she was once more moving in the direction of Rox's house.

* * *

Rox tilted her head back and savored the last bit of tea in her cup. She leaned against the railing of the window's walk and closed her eyes, enjoying the breeze blowing off the ocean. The smell of salt water and seaweed, which she'd always loved, hung heavily in the air. It was the first thing she noticed each time she stepped outside her door, and the first signal that she was home when she stepped off a plane after a book tour. It was also connected with the sense of familiarity and comfort she had known in her childhood. *I wish you were here, my love. In no time, you'll come to love our home as much as I do.*

Rox sighed and opened her eyes as she turned to go into the house, then stopped as something caught her eye. Still some distance down the beach, a figure was walking in her direction. Time stood still as her gaze remained fixed on the approaching figure. *Can it be?* She moved slowly down the length of the walk, closer to the beach. As the figure approached, Rox realized it was a tall woman with long, flowing dark hair and a lean build. The woman was barefoot, with the legs of her jeans rolled up to her knees and a shirt or jacket tied around her waist. "Oh, my God! *Cass?*"

The closer the figure came, the more certain Rox became. She could barely contain her excitement. "Cass! Cass!"

Cass halted as she heard someone calling her. Looking in the direction of the voice, she spotted Rox standing on the widow's walk surrounding the third story of her home. She was waving her arms wildly and shouting Cass's name. Cass could barely find her own voice. She whispered, "Rox." Then, with more volume and excitement, she returned Rox's call with equal zeal. She broke into a run as she realized she was just moments away from holding the woman she loved.

Rox tore through her office and threw herself down two flights of stairs to the first floor. She dashed through the house onto the back deck that led to the beach, cleared the stairs in one jump and landed on her hands and knees in the sand. Then she got to her feet and ran as fast as she could toward Cass.

Both women were moving as quickly as the loose sand would allow, but it seemed like an eternity before they were in each other's arms. Both were crying, and neither could speak. Intense emotion robbed them of their voices. Finally, Cass lowered them both to the sand and gently pulled Rox on top of her long frame, taking care not to place too much weight on her injured shoulder. Their eyes locked and then their lips met in a searing kiss that left them both gasping.

Rox found her voice first. "Cass, you came home. My God, I love you so much. Please say you'll stay forever."

"Forever, my love. I'll never leave you again, Rox. I can't bear to be away from you."

Rox reached down and tucked stray locks of Cass's hair behind her ears. Their eyes met again. "Each day that passed without you made me realize that what I feel for you is real. I've never been more miserable in my life than I was without you. You sent me home to finish my book, Cass, but I haven't been able to concentrate enough to make much progress. My thoughts kept turning back to you. In fact, I was on the widow's walk thinking about you just before I saw you walking down the beach."

Cass kissed her again. "Now you know how I felt all those weeks before you were sure you loved me. The uncertainty was so hard. Then you appeared in my jail cell and my whole life changed. We were sitting in a dingy, filthy, bug-infested jail, and I was happier than I'd ever been in my life. I never want to leave you again, Rox. There are still loose ends that need to be resolved, though. The DEA isn't finished with me, and I've got at least a month of physical therapy to go, but I couldn't wait any longer."

Concern filled Rox's eyes. "Oh, my God, I forgot about your shoulder!" She rubbed her hand gently across the injury. "How does it feel?"

"It's getting better. I just need to be careful not to do too much too soon. I'll need to find a physical therapist in Rockland."

"I'll ask my dad's doctors to recommend one." Rox studied Cass's face. "Cass, when I thought you had died on that plane, it tore my heart to shreds. I had just found you, and all at once, I thought you were gone. I've never been so heartbroken in my life, except maybe when you sent me home alone."

Cass nodded solemnly. "I know. It was the hardest thing I've ever had to do. I never want to send you away from me again, Rox. I couldn't bear it."

Rox just nodded, and traced the side of Cass's cheek with her fingertip. Her eyes followed the path of her finger, then looked directly into the blue eyes gazing back at her. Her voice was raspy as sparks of emotion passed between them. "Make love to me, Cass."

They walked hand in hand down the beach toward Rox's Victorian home. By the time they reached the back deck, Rox was a nervous wreck. Part of her was desperate to make love to Cass, to share the ultimate expression of love with the beautiful woman, but the rest of her was terrified. *I love her with all my heart, but what if I find the physical expression of that love is not for me? I have so much to learn. What if I'm woefully inadequate and I disappoint her?*

A shower was in order, since they were covered with sand from their romp on the beach. Rox trembled with fear and desire as they stood face to face in the bathroom.

"You're trembling," Cass said. "Please don't be afraid, Rox. I promise not to hurt you. If I do something unpleasant or hurtful, just tell me to stop and I will."

"I'm not afraid of you hurting me, Cass. How could you possibly do that? I'm concerned about disappointing you, my love. I don't know what to do."

Cass lowered her head and dropped butterfly kisses across Rox's shoulder, making the shorter woman shiver. "You could never disappoint me. Please don't be afraid." Cass eased Rox's t-shirt over her head and dropped it to the floor, then ran gentle fingertips across her shoulders. "You are so beautiful." An intense, consuming wave of desire ran through her body.

Enforcer made a sudden appearance. *Don't move too fast, Cass. Remember, she's new at this.*

I know, E., I know. I just want her so badly. I love her with all my heart and I want to show her just how beautiful our love can be.

Just be patient, Cass. Be patient.

I will.

Rox barely made eye contact with Cass as the catch on her bra was released, freeing her breasts. She looked away as Cass stroked their fullness. Her legs were trembling and threatening to fold beneath her—from both the heated desire in her abdomen and the excitement growing in the pit of her stomach.

Cass noticed Rox's diverted eyes and lifted her chin. "Sweetheart, look at me."

Rox looked into smoky blue eyes. The bold desire she saw in their depths was unlike anything she'd even seen before.

"Rox, you are the most beautiful woman I have ever seen. You are perfect in every way. Thank you so much for giving your heart to me. I will cherish it and protect it for the rest of my life."

Overwhelming desire and love filled Rox's being, and her chin quivered with emotion. "I love you with all my heart, Cass."

Cass smiled. She took one of Rox's hands, kissed the palm, then placed it on her own chest. "Feel my heart beating, Rox. This belongs to you. Please keep it and protect it forever."

In an act of boldness, Rox lifted Cass's shirt over her head and added it to the pile of clothing on the floor, then placed a gentle kiss between Cass's breasts. "I promise to protect it always."

"Thank you, love." Cass unbuttoned Rox's denim shorts and pushed them off her hips to the floor.

Rox stepped out of them and kicked them aside. Boldness born of desire consumed Rox as she did the same for Cass, crouching before the tall woman to push the jeans down the length of her long, slim legs. She offered her shoulder for support while she freed Cass's feet from the tangled mass of denim around her ankles.

As Rox rose to her full height, she took a step back and looked at the tall beauty before her, who was clad only in high-cut bikini briefs and a bra. She realized that she was extremely excited by the vision before her. *Is it because I love you, or have I been subconsciously attracted to women all along?* She knew in her heart that it didn't matter. She was going to spend the rest of her life with Cass.

Rox stepped forward and entered the circle of Cass's arms. She traced her fingertips along the lacy edge of Cass's bra before she reached behind the tall woman and unclasped the obstructing garment. Her breath came in rapid pants as her eyes explored the perfect roundness of Cass's breasts. "They're perfect," Rox whispered as she leaned forward and took an erect nipple into her mouth.

"Oh, my God, Rox!" Cass nearly doubled over as a bolt of desire shot directly to her groin.

Alarmed, Rox jerked her head back. "Did I hurt you?"

Cass closed the distance between them. "No! God, no! Rox, your touch is like liquid fire. I want you so much, my love. Let me love you."

Rox looked into Cass's eyes and nodded, then reached out to push Cass's panties from her hips. Her own panties soon joined them on the floor.

Cass turned on the shower. When the water had warmed, they stood beneath the spray in each other's arms, mouths locked in a deep, probing kiss.

Rox suddenly broke the embrace and leaned back against the shower wall.

"What is it, Rox? Do you want to stop?"

Rox raised heavy-lidded eyes and smiled slightly. "That's the last thing I want to do, my love, but if we don't get this shower over with soon, I won't last long enough to enjoy what I'm sure lies ahead."

Cass grinned and stepped back, then handed the soap to Rox.

They cleaned sweat and sand from their bodies without further contact. When the shower was over, they toweled each other dry, hints of flirting and teasing punctuating the process. By the time they were finished, the sexual tension between them was almost unbearable.

Cass took Rox's towel and threw it over the edge of the tub, then brought her hands to her lips. She held Rox's eyes as she kissed each palm and then brought them close to her heart. "I want you so much right now I can hardly contain myself, but I need to be sure you want this as much as I do. I don't want to rush you into anything you're not ready for, my love."

Rox kissed the hollow at the base of Cass's throat. "I've been waiting for this moment since I realized I loved you. I can't imagine any better way to express how much I love you than to give myself to you completely. Sweetheart, I *do* want this, more than you know."

She led Cass across the hall to her bedroom and encouraged her to sit on the bed, then knelt before her. She looked up into blue eyes. "I don't know what to do," she confessed. "Teach me, please."

Cass took Rox's face between her hands. She covered her mouth with her own and thrust her tongue deep into the moistness of Rox's mouth.

Desire exploded through Rox as she fought to breathe without breaking the deliciously satisfying kiss. She rose to her feet and pressed Cass back onto the bed and climbed on top of her. Straddling her abdomen, she effectively pinned the taller woman to the bed. Her mouth hovered just a hair's breadth away as the tip of her tongue flicked across Cass's lips.

"Rox, please—I need more."

Rox could barely breathe. Desire dominated her actions. She moved her lips from Cass's mouth to her ear. "I'm on fire. Please tell me what to do. Tell me how to please you."

"Touch me, Rox. Touch me everywhere. Don't be afraid to explore. Nothing you could do would displease me."

Rox explored her lover's body gently, and gained an immediate appreciation for her soft, supple curves. She savored the feel, taste and texture of her taut skin. Soon, she learned which caresses drove Cass to distraction, as beautiful blue eyes betrayed her reaction to each touch.

As bold as she was trying to be, Rox was still uncertain how to bring Cass to orgasm. She fumbled nervously until Cass took her face between her hands and kissed her.

Her eyes locked on Rox's. "Relax, sweetheart. Do what comes naturally, what feels right. Touch me the way you like to be touched. It will be okay, I promise."

Concern etched Rox's forehead as she once again began to caress Cass. She suckled tenderly at Cass's breasts and ran her hands over Cass's abdomen.

Cass begged silently for more. *Come on, baby. Take me.*

Damn it, Cass. Haven't you been listening? She's been asking for help for the last half hour. Show her what we like; what turns our stomach to mush. Give the poor woman a break. This is all new to her.

Cass realized E. was right—she would have to show Rox how to make love to her. She took Rox by her shoulders, locked her legs around hers and flipped her over.

Rox looked up at Cass with a startled expression on her face.

Cass let all the frustration and desire she was feeling show in her eyes. In a low growl, she said, "I want you, Rox. I want to fill you. I want to make you scream my name when you come."

Rox didn't know whether to be defiant or submissive, so she decided to be a little of both. *You asked her to show you, now hang on for the ride... but make her feel the bumps and turns as well.* She looked into Cass's eyes. "Try to make me scream."

The challenge drove Cass over the edge and she plunged into Rox's neck, nipping and sucking and leaving marks that would surely show the next day. "God, Rox," she groaned, "I've wanted this for so long." She moved lower, leaving a trail of gentle bites and kisses along Rox's shoulder and breast.

Rox threw her head back and cried out as desire consumed her. "Oh... my... God! More... please!"

Cass drew one of Rox's erect nipples into her mouth and bit down gently.

Rox nearly rose off the bed as both pain and desire shot directly to her core. "Aaahh! God... Cass!" She grabbed Cass's hair and pulled her closer.

Cass continued her assault on the other nipple, and Rox writhed helplessly with desire as her lover began to move further south. She still had no idea how Cass planned to fulfill her, but by the time the dark-haired woman reached her triangle, Rox was drenched and eager for release of any kind. Frustration and need drove her to tears as she pushed Cass to take her. "Cass, baby, please—I need you. I want you so badly. Please, I can't take any more of this. Cass..."

Rox's pleas sparked such a strong emotional response in Cass that she stopped her descent and gathered Rox into her arms.

Rox was sobbing as she wrapped her arms around Cass's neck.

"Honey, talk to me. Tell me what you need, love."

"I need you to love me, Cass. Please, I can't wait any longer."

Rox's plea for release nearly pushed Cass over the edge. She laid a gentle kiss on Rox's lips, then slowly moved downward, not stopping until she reached the wet softness between her legs. She pushed the trembling limbs apart so she could feast on the essence of the woman she loved.

As soon as the questing tongue made contact, Rox stiffened and screamed.

"Cass!"

Sensing her lover had already begun to climax, Cass inserted two fingers into Rox's wet center and thrust forward firmly. She felt Rox ripple around her fingers, and the sheer sexuality of her release caused Cass to climax herself.

Wave after wave of orgasm tore through both women until Rox begged Cass to stop. "Ca— Cass, please. Please stop. Oh, my God, Cass. Hold me, baby, please."

Cass gently withdrew her fingers and gathered the sobbing Rox into her arms. "It's okay, I've got you. Let it go, sweetheart. I love you so much, Rox. Thank you for letting me love you."

Rox was unable to respond, and she drifted off to sleep.

Chapter 38

Rox awoke early the next morning and found Cass sleeping beside her. A rush of love filled her heart and tears filled her eyes as she remembered the previous evening, and the way Cass had so tenderly initiated their lovemaking. Twinges of desire began to build within her as she recalled the sensual intensity they had shared. The depth of her need both exhilarated and terrified Rox. Never before had she felt so out of control. The experience had left her changed, and she realized that she had made the right choice in acknowledging her new sexuality. *But as I recall, last night was fairly one-sided. I can't believe I fell asleep so quickly.*

Rox rolled onto her side and watched her lover sleep, noticing many little things that made the twinges grow into a blaze. Cass lay on her back, one arm thrown above her head and her face turned toward Rox. Her injured arm was tucked safely by her side. Her long hair partially obscured her face, and her chest rose and fell as she slept. *She looks so cute like that!* Unable to stop herself, she leaned down and placed a gentle kiss on Cass's cheek.

Cass's hand flew up to brush away the annoyance. "Umm."

Rox giggled quietly, then laid a second kiss on the sleeping woman's cheek. Again, the hand flew up. The third time she leaned in, Rox found herself flat on her back with mischievous blue eyes looking down at her.

"And just what do you think you're doing, my love?"

"Uh... well... you looked so cute lying there, I just couldn't resist."

Cass raised an eyebrow. "'Cute?' Is that the best you could come up with?"

Rox decided to confess. She reached up and touched the side of Cass's face. "Actually, I was thinking about last night." She averted her eyes, blushing a deep shade of crimson.

"Hey... Hey, sweetheart, look at me. Last night was beautiful. *You* are beautiful, Rox. Last night was the most perfect, loving experience I have ever had. Thank you for allowing me to share it with you."

Tears began to well in green eyes. "But you *didn't* share it with me, Cass. Last night was all about me. I was totally inconsiderate. Christ, I couldn't even stay awake long enough to make love to you. I'm so sorry." Rox closed her eyes and the tears fell.

Cass rolled onto her back and pulled Rox into her arms. She held her, gently kissing her head from time to time, until the tears stopped. "Are you all right, my love?"

Rox nodded, but remained silent.

"Okay, let's talk about last night. Rox, the pleasure I was able to bring to you was one of the most fulfilling experience of my life."

"But—"

"And before you say another word, you *did* take care of me last night."

"I did? How?"

Cass rolled onto her side and propped herself up on her elbow. "Sweetheart, I won't lie to you and tell you Patti was the only other woman I've been with. There have been several, which I'm not proud of. But I will tell you that I've never been with anyone who affects me the way you do. The difference is that I'm in love with you, Rox. Wait, that isn't entirely true. What I feel for you goes way beyond love—I am in *need* of you. You're part of me, Rox; I feel what you feel. Last night when you climaxed, I couldn't help but go along for the ride."

"But it's not the same, Cass."

"Sweetheart, last night was just one of many nights we'll share. I'm honored that I was your first, and I fully intend to be your last and your every one in between. You'll have ample opportunity to make love to me, and I intend to take full advantage of every one."

Rox grinned. "Well, there's no time like the present, huh?"

* * *

For the third time, Nikki rang Rox's doorbell and then shook the doorknob, trying to open the locked door. Jerri sat on the porch railing with her arms crossed, watching as her wife began pacing back and forth in frustration. She wondered who owned the suitcase left sitting on the porch.

"Nik, she's probably not home."

"She's got to be home. Her car is in the driveway."

"Maybe she's gone for a walk."

"Jerri, something doesn't feel right about this. She hasn't answered the phone since last night, and now she's not answering the door. And then there's that suitcase over there. I'm worried about her."

"Why don't you just use the spare key?"

"You're right, I'd forgotten about that!" Nikki reached under the doormat and grabbed the key, then unlocked the door. The two women stepped inside. "Rox? Rox, are you home?"

No answer.

"She's probably not home."

"No, she's got to be here. She could be sick or something. I'm going to search the house."

Jerri rolled her eyes, but followed her wife as she searched the first story. "Maybe she's on the back deck, writing. She could easily miss the phone from out there."

"Good thought," Nikki replied, returning moments later shaking her head. "Second floor."

"For the last time, she's probably not home."

Jerri's voice fell on deaf ears. Nikki was already on her way upstairs. Jerri's long legs allowed her to catch up with her shorter wife by taking the stairs two at a time, and she reached Nikki's side just as she opened Rox's bedroom door.

"Rox? Aaah! Oh, my God!"

Rox and Cass scrambled up, clutching at the sheets. "Aaah!" they screamed.

Nikki ran back into the hallway while Jerri stepped into the bedroom and grabbed the door handle. "Sorry about that," she said. "Just... go back to whatever it was you were doing." She closed the door and turned to Nikki, who was sitting on the floor with her back propped up against the wall and her face in her hands. "Well, that's a fine kettle of fish."

Nikki looked up. "Oh, my God, did you see that?"

"Yeah. Pretty cool, huh?"

Just then, the door swung open and a bathrobed Rox stormed out. "Nicole Davenport! Where the hell are you?"

Cass, wearing an oversized t-shirt and a pair of Rox's boxers, joined Jerri. They watched Rox pull Nikki to her feet and pin her against the wall.

Jerri glanced at Cass. "Congratulations."

Cass grinned.

Both women crossed their arms and watched the scene unfolding in the hallway.

Rox was livid. "What the hell did you think you were doing, barging into my bedroom like that?"

Nikki launched a counter attack. "Well, if you'd answer your phone, I might not have to come all the way over here to check on you!"

Rox's anger evaporated. "That was you?"

"You're damned right that was me! If you'd answer your phone once in a while, I wouldn't have to worry about you so much. And what's with locking the door, all of a sudden? Did you know there's a suitcase sitting on your front porch?"

"That's mine," Cass offered.

Nikki turned and walked toward Cass.

"Oh-oh, you're in trouble now," Jerri whispered to a still-grinning Cass.

"And you! When did you arrive in town?" Nikki turned back to Rox. "Why didn't you tell us she was coming? It would be nice to know these things, you know!" And back to Cass, "Considering the little surprise I just walked in on, I assume you're here to stay?"

Cass's spoke directly to Rox. "Forever, if she'll have me."

"Good. It's about time she had someone to love and protect her. Less work for me!"

Cass put an arm around Nikki. "Me being here won't affect how much Rox needs and loves you, Nik. Hell, from what I've seen, protecting her is a full time job! Maybe you, Jerri and I will find a way to manage it. What do you say?"

Rox and Nikki worked together to load four plates with ham and cheese omelets and generous servings of home fries. Then, each woman carried two plates to the table and placed one in front of her mate.

"Here you go, sweetheart." Rox kissed Cass on the head and joined the others at the breakfast table.

Cass dug into the fluffy omelet. "This is great, Rox. A girl could get used to this."

Jerri chuckled. "Let me guess—you can't cook, right?"

"Hell, no! I can't even boil water."

"Neither can I, but unfortunately that means we get to do the dishes afterward. They cook, we clean."

Cass grimaced as Nikki interrupted her exchange with Jerri. "So, Cass, tell us about the trial."

"There's not much to tell, at least not yet. Rox and I were able to give the DEA enough information that there was a raid on Santonio's estate. Jer, would you toss the catsup over here, please? Thanks."

Rox wrinkled her nose at what Cass was doing to her omelet. "Ew! You're ruining it with all that catsup."

Cass stuck her tongue out at Rox and continued to squeeze the bottle.

"If you're going to stick your tongue out, you'd better be ready to use it, love."

Cass grinned broadly. "It's a date!"

Nikki smiled at Jerri and ran her foot up and down her wife's leg as she enjoyed the interaction between their friend and her new lover.

Cass continued with her story. "Anyway, both Santonio and Jason Hayer were captured in the raid and are now awaiting trial. It hasn't actually started yet, but I'll be called to testify when it does. Rox probably will be, too."

"Whether I'm called or not, I'm going with you. Now that I've got you, I'm not letting you out of my sight."

Cass leaned over and kissed her. "I'm a willing captive, love. I might even volunteer to be handcuffed, later on."

Rox blushed to the roots of her hair. "Cass!" She gave her a light punch on the shoulder.

"Ow! That's my bad arm, woman!"

"Oh, my God, I forgot. I'm sorry, sweetie. Here, let me kiss it better for you."

Jerri's interest was piqued. "That's right, you were shot. How's the shoulder healing?"

"The wound is pretty much healed, but the muscle damage needs therapy. In fact, I need to find a new therapist in the next day or two."

Nikki spoke up. "I'll find one for you, Cass. Let me ask around at the hospital."

"That would be great, Nikki. I'd really appreciate it."

"So, Cass, I assume you're planning to move here from San Jose?" Jerri continued, as if her wife had not interrupted.

"As far as I'm concerned, I've already moved here. I still need to pack up my belongings and sell my condo, but I've given my notice at the airline. My friend Angie and her husband are taking care of most of the details for me, so I don't have to go back until I'm ready to sign the papers and pack up."

"Are you going to apply at the airlines here?" Nikki asked.

"That, or start my own charter business. I've accumulated a nice little nest egg over the past few years, and I can use that to get it off the ground."

Rox looked around the table at her partner and two best friends and the camaraderie that was evident among them warmed her heart. *How did I get so lucky? I couldn't possibly ask for more in my life. I have my health, a beautiful home, a generous income, wonderfully supportive parents, two close friends who I love dearly, and now a partner who completes me in every possible way. If it weren't for Daddy's health, life would be perfect.*

Jerri looked at her watch. "Well, kiddies, I hate to eat and run, but it's already eleven and I'm working the noon-to-midnight shift today."

"I'd better hit the road, too. My mom is expecting me to take her shopping," Nikki added.

Cass and Rox walked their friends to the front door. "Why don't you two come to dinner over here, for a change?" Rox asked. When her friends agreed, she said, "Seven okay for you?"

"If you're up by then," Nikki teased.

Rox frowned at them with mock severity. "Go on, get out of here. You don't want Jerri to be late."

After they left, Cass followed Rox back to the kitchen and stopped her as she began to clear away the breakfast dishes. She took the dirty dishes from Rox's hands and put them back on the table. "Whoa, there, what are you doing? I'll take care of this. You need to go work on your book."

"Are you sure, Cass? I really do need to finish it. My publisher is awfully unhappy about all the delays."

"I'm positive. Now, scoot." She smacked Rox lightly on the butt to shoo her away.

* * *

Rox worked diligently on her book while Cass occupied herself exploring the beach and searching the classified ads for small charter planes. It was nearly five o'clock when Rox typed "The End" and sent the final draft of the manuscript to her editor. "Finished, at last!" She rose from her chair and stretched her arms high above her head, bending and twisting to work out the stiffness in her back from sitting still for so long. Then she made a cup of hot chocolate and carried it out to the widow's walk. Leaning against the railing, she looked out at the ocean.

There's a storm coming in, and it's going to be a violent one. Rox shivered in anticipation. She took a sip of her cocoa and drew the salty air deep into her lungs. A small smile tugged at the corner of her mouth as she thought about a stormy night several months earlier... the first night she had talked to Cass in chat. She sighed again, lost in remembrance until she felt a strong pair of arms encircle her from behind.

"I love you."

Rox folded herself into the embrace of the tall, dark-haired woman who stood behind her. Turning to face her, she leaned back against the railing and wrapped her own arms around her lover's waist. "I love you too, Cass, with all my heart." She tilted her face up to accept the searing kiss she knew was coming.

Several breathtaking moments later, the kiss ended. Cass pulled Rox closer and held her as she rested her head on the spot just above Cass's breasts. They stood together as the storm approached, the gusting winds blowing their hair around.

Safe in the embrace of the woman she loved, Rox recalled how desperately lost she had felt when she thought Cass was dead. A slight shudder ran through her body in response to the traumatic memories. *So much has happened since that day, my love,* she thought, pondering the last several weeks and the life they had started to build together. *Thank you so much for joining me here, for moving three thousand miles across the country to be with me. You'll never regret it, I promise.* A shiver of desire trembled through her.

"Come inside, Rox," a seductive voice purred in her ear. "You're shivering, and it's going to rain soon." Even as Cass spoke, the first raindrop fell on the decking.

Rox looked up at Cass just as a bolt of lightning lit up the sky, followed by a crack of thunder. She caught her breath, the barely restrained violence of the impending storm filling her with excitement. She was filled with intense emotion, and with passion she could scarcely contain. "No, Cass. Stay out here with me. Make love to me, here... now."

Cass smiled broadly, realizing she had mistaken the cause of the shivering. Anticipating the effect of the storm on her lover's libido, she cupped Rox's chin and captured her lips in a kiss. Her tongue danced in and out of Rox's mouth, eliciting moans of pleasure. She felt a deep sense of love and fulfillment that she had never felt with anyone else. *I would happily give up flying and commit myself to being your love slave, if that was what you wanted.*

After thoroughly tasting her lover's mouth, she worked her way along the edge of Rox's jaw and neck, where she left several love marks, suckling greedily while Rox pulled her closer.

"God, Cass!" A flood of moisture bathed the apex of Rox's thighs.

Cass was nearly out of control herself as her hands roamed appreciatively over Rox's body.

Rox entwined her fingers in Cass's hair and directed her lover's probing mouth. Arching her head back as Cass pressed her against the railing, Rox offered complete access to her throat, which Cass quickly accepted.

"Rox, Rox, I need you, need to make love to you." Cass tugged Rox's shirt out of the waistband of her shorts and slipped her hands under her shirt and over the bare skin beneath.

Rox trembled with uncontrolled passion at the contact as the rain pelted down on them. Cass sparked a need deep within her, and Rox thought she would burst if she didn't get relief soon. "Cass, take me, please!" she begged.

Cass surprised the smaller woman by wrapping her good arm around her waist and lifting her off the deck. She swung her around, then gently placed her down again with her back against the wall of the house. Pressing the entire length of her body against Rox, Cass took her hands and raised them over her head, pinning them gently against the building. She looked deep into her eyes. "Tell me what you want, love. Tell me what you need."

Rox thrilled to the undiluted passion in her partner's eyes. "I want you to make love to me. I need you inside me," she said breathlessly.

Thunder rumbled nearby and palpable sound waves rolled over them, making them both shudder in anticipation of what was to come.

Rox tried to lean far enough forward to reach Cass's neck with her mouth. When her effort proved futile, she growled, "Cass..." and pulled her hands from the taller woman's grasp. She was on fire. Unable to resist any longer, she grabbed the front of Cass's shirt and tore it open, sending buttons flying. Next, she reached behind the taller woman and unfastened her bra, allowing her lover's generous breasts to spill free. Rox's mouth thoroughly explored every inch of the enticing flesh, taking special pleasure in suckling the erect nipples.

Rox's passionate assault fueled Cass's need. "God, Rox! Please, baby, I need you now... please!" She writhed against Rox, pressing her harder against the wall of the house.

As if in harmony with their rising passion, the rain fell harder and a flash of lightning lit up the sky.

With strength she didn't know she possessed, Rox reversed their positions and pushed Cass up against the wall of the house. She fell to her knees, then reached up and jerked loose Cass's belt and the snap at her waistband, so she could pull her shorts down to her ankles.

Cass closed her eyes as Rox started her exploration. It took all her willpower to remain standing while Rox's tongue trailed along her inner thigh.

Rox slipped her tongue between the folds of Cass's sex and she pressed her legs further apart to give herself better access. Placing three fingers in her own mouth, Rox wet them thoroughly before poising them at the entrance to her lover's core.

Urgent with desire, Cass captured Rox's gaze and held it as she bent her knees and pushed herself down onto Rox's hand as the smaller woman thrust upward. The sensation was incredible.

Soon, Rox was pumping furiously into Cass, barely able to control her own desire as the taller woman thrust downward, her head thrashing from side to side.

Cass lost control as her orgasm began to flood through her. "Rox, Rox! I love you, baby," she screamed into the wind and rain raging around them.

"God, I love to watch you like this. Come for me, baby," Rox gasped, intensifying her lover's pleasure.

When the spasms subsided, Cass couldn't stand up any longer, and she slid down the wall to the deck. Rox guided her fall, lay down with her and held the trembling woman.

When her breathing returned to normal, Cass rolled them over so the smaller woman lay on top of her. Wrapping her arms around Rox's shoulders, she kissed her passionately. "I love you," she said. "That was absolutely wonderful, Rox. Now it's my turn to do the same for you." She spared a moment to send a quick "thank you" heavenward, then slid her hands up and down bare skin.

Rox's hips gyrated in response, and her eyes begged her tall lover for more. Seeing the urgency in her face, Cass reached up to place a gentle kiss on her mouth. "Be patient, my love," she whispered. "I would never leave you wanting."

Rox closed her eyes and drew in a sharp breath as the promise shot a bolt of desire directly to her groin. "Please hurry!"

Cass flipped them over. With Rox lying on her back, a naked Cass straddled her thighs and slid her hands under Rox's t-shirt. The rain had increased to the point that Rox's shirt was plastered to her skin. With little effort, Cass tugged it over Rox's rain-soaked hair and threw it against the wall of the house, where it stuck for a moment before falling to the deck.

As she looked down at the woman lying beneath her, Cass found her heart filled with a sense of awe that this wonderful woman loved her and wanted to spend the rest of her life making her happy. Tears mixed with rain and ran onto Rox's breasts. Cass leaned down and trailed her tongue around the perfectly formed mounds. She made circles on her lover's skin, avoiding the painfully erect nipples.

In agony from the tender torture, Rox arched her back and pushed her chest into the air as she demanded the satisfaction she craved. "Cass, please!"

Cass accepted the invitation eagerly and suckled each of Rox's nipples in turn, biting and nipping unmercifully as Rox writhed beneath her. Lightning lit up the stormy sky, sending shadows dancing across Rox's face. Her hips began to buck and Cass realized she was pushing her to the point of no return. Climbing off, Cass knelt beside Rox and removed her shorts and the lace panties beneath them. Soon Rox was totally naked, lying on the deck with the rain pummeling her and her sensuous form exposed for her lover to sample.

Rox moaned loudly as she reached out and pulled Cass closer. "Cass... God, Cass... please, I can't wait any longer." She was teetering on the edge of orgasm.

Cass placed two fingers near her lover's entrance and pushed them deep inside.

Rox's lower body bucked in response. "More, Cass. Please, I need more!"

Cass immediately complied, adding a third finger and setting up a steady, thrusting rhythm. Rox's body stiffened. Feeling the beginnings of her orgasm, Cass added her little finger.

A jagged bolt of lightning and deafening crack of thunder shook the world as Rox fell over the edge. She screamed her ecstasy as her body spun out of control.

The two women lay entwined in each other's arms, the gentle rain cleansing the evidence of their lovemaking from their skin. They talked of love and commitment, and of spending the rest of their lives together.

Rox traced Cass's right eyebrow with her thumb, and her hand came to rest on the side of her face. "Thank you for flying into my heart, Cass," she said, smiling.

Cass smiled back, and leaned in for a gentle kiss. "You're welcome," she replied. "It wasn't easy, but we survived. On a wing and a prayer."

Rox nodded. "Yes, my love—on a wing and a prayer."

Cass rolled over so she lay on top of Rox. She looked directly into her eyes, and an aura of seriousness came over her. "Um, Rox, there's one more thing you need to know about me."

Rox narrowed her eyes as sudden fear filled her heart. "And what would that be?" she asked, worried that Cass had some dark secret that would keep them apart.

"Well, you see, I have this friend named Enforcer..."

Photo credit: Wendy Ellis, © 2004

About the Author

Karen D. Badger, better know to her online fans as "kd bard," was born in Vermont at the end of the Hippie era. She is the second of five children and was raised by a divorced mother, who to this day remains one of her best friends. Karen graduated from college in 1978 with a B.A. in Drama. Later, she returned to school and in 1994 earned a B.S. in Mathematics. She currently works as an Engineer in the semiconductor field, and fills her spare time with writing, family and friends.

Married right after college, Karen worked full time while raising two sons who are now grown. A few years ago, writing became an escape when she underwent a much needed lifestyle change, in the process reinventing herself as an independent woman. In April of 2005, a beautiful baby boy came into her life when her first grandchild was born. Kyren is the apple of his Nona's eye. Karen never looks back: "If you look back, you'll trip over what's in front of you and fall flat on your face!" She looks forward to many fulfilling years of writing and watching her family grow.

Blue Feather Books is proud to offer this excerpt from Val Brown and MJ Walker's popular novel,

Connecting Hearts

Available now, only from

Bluefeatherbooks
L I M I T E D

www. bluefeatherbooks.com

Denise could never have imagined just how the events of the past two months would change so rapidly. She had given up writing altogether, a higher purpose taking precedence over even the most cherished aspect of her life. Sara. Her aunt had declined at a rate much swifter then even the doctors had expected. During the first few weeks after Denise had widened the doorframe to Sara's bedroom the old woman had begun to lose all strength in her ability to walk. It wasn't long before the need for a wheelchair became a high priority.

It had been a hard transition to make; neither Denise nor her aunt were prepared for the loss of independence that it entailed. Not only had Sara's lower body strength departed, but her upper body's strength too. There were the occasional good days when Sara did manage to complete the odd task by herself, but for the most part it became impossible, and she declined a little more every day.

To say that Denise hadn't felt the strain would have been a lie. Even the poet would admit to herself that some nights when she had finally made her way to bed-if she hadn't fallen asleep on the sofa first-she would pass out as soon as her head hit the pillow. It wasn't just looking after Sara that took it out of Denise. There were many times while she would be dressing Sara or brushing her teeth that the old woman would just sit and cry. Not that Denise minded in the slightest; she was adamant about taking care of her aunt. She would do whatever she had to and whatever it took.

Denise had made many alterations to the house. She had converted the downstairs bathroom, installing a liftable seat into the shower to make it easier for Sara to still enjoy the luxury of taking a warm shower. She had constructed a higher frame for her bed to make lifting from the wheelchair to the bed and vice versa much more convenient.

Days alternated between good and bad. Between days when Sara would seem stable, to days when her emotions would overwhelm her, or her disease would advance further and she would lose a little more strength and independence. Denise did know that she needed somebody, and had gone through the motions of interviewing several nurses. But deep down inside something was missing. She felt none of these men or women would look after Sara the way she wanted. Denise also knew that as much as Sara had insisted that they hire a nurse, the old woman hated the idea of having a complete stranger look after her in ways that she was finding difficult enough allowing her niece to undertake some things.

Through it all Denise had managed to keep her resolve with the help of one person. Randa. Though thousands of miles away, the nurse had provided help and emotional support to Denise when she needed it most. The friendship had grown, and even Denise would acknowledge that. Never did she expect that she would be able to share aspects of her life with anybody the way she had done with this woman.

Sometimes when the day had been especially draining, Denise would retreat to her room and look at the picture of the woman who unknowingly gave Denise the emotional strength she needed to carry on when times were rough. Never had she felt the ability to be so open with another individual, and never had she thought she would come to care for somebody as much as she found herself doing with this woman. She enjoyed their correspondence, their contention on the superiority of British or American chocolate and their easy friendship.

As Christmas approached she had no doubt about the fact that she would send Randa a gift, and Sara had wanted to do so as well. Denise had told Sara about their constant chocolate debates, and so Sara had asked her niece to send the nurse a selection of her favourite chocolates. Denise, on the other hand, found the prospect of purchasing a gift slightly more difficult. She wanted to give Randa something that echoed her appreciation and sentiment towards the woman, but she found it hard to recognise exactly what that was. Fortunately, it didn't take long for her unconscious mind to make the decision; she just hoped Randa would remember exactly what this object was.

Denise had ventured into her bedroom and had crouched down under her bed to retrieve a small shoebox. Inside this box she kept the trinkets and memorabilia of her parents. Her father's silver hip flask, cuff links, and a single cigar that was a constant reminder of his aroma. Her mother's earrings, bottle of perfume that had long since spoiled, lace handkerchief embroidered with her initials and an antique bracelet.

It was the bracelet that Denise was looking for, a simple golden charm bracelet with one charm, a golden capsule that unscrewed to reveal a small scroll of paper. Upon this scroll, in very small print, was Shakespeare's "Sonnet Number 116." As a child, the charm and sonnet inside had fascinated Denise. She had explained to Randa that it was this poem that had sparked her desire for lyrical verse.

Hoping Randa would appreciate and comprehend the raison d'être behind the gift, Denise had placed it into a small red velvet-inlaid wooden box and had wrapped it in silver paper with a light-blue ribbon. She had mailed the package a day later.

Find this and other exciting Blue Feather Books
at

www. bluefeatherbooks.com

or ask for us at your local bookstore.

Blue Feather Books, Ltd.
P.O. Box 5867
Atlanta, GA 31107-5967

Tel: (678) 318-1426
Fax: (404) 378-8130

Printed in the United States
42392LVS00004B/67